ARGENTERRA

The Silverlands Book One

DONNA MAREE HANSON

First published by Aust Spec Fiction (Donna Maree Hanson) in 2016.

A CIP record for this book is available from the National Library of Australia.

ISBN: 9780975721742 (ebook)

Dewey Number: A823.4

Print on Demand format: 9780975721735

Edited by Kaaren Sutcliffe.

Cover design by Frauke, Croco Designs

Map by Russell Kirkpatrick

To report a typographical error, please email donnamareehanson@gmail.com

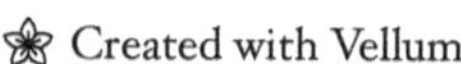 Created with Vellum

To my grandies, Madelyn, Yumi and Alexander. May you have many adventures and reach your full potential

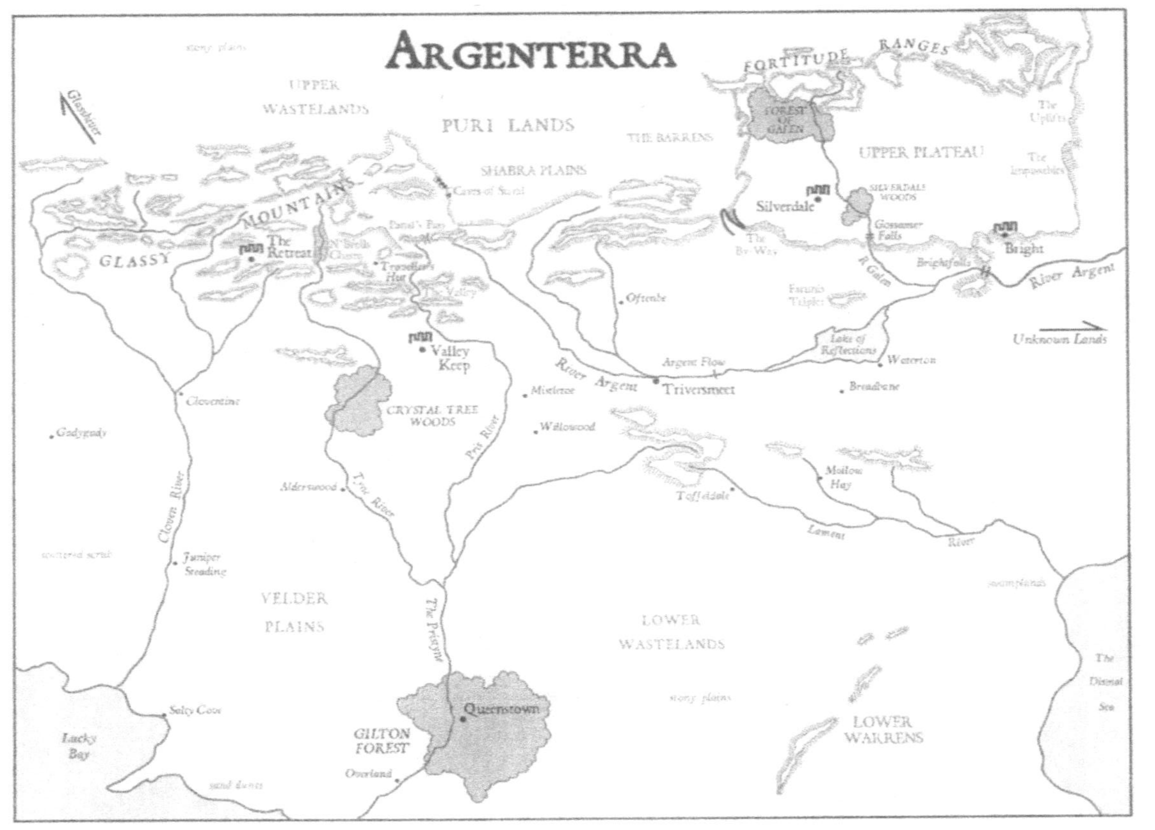

ARGENTERRA
Glassleer
stony plains
UPPER WASTELANDS
PURI LANDS
THE BARRENS
SHABRA PLAINS
FORTITUDE RANGES
FOREST OF GALEN
UPPER PLATEAU
The Uplift
The Impossibles
SILVERDALE WOODS
Silverdale
Gossamer Falls
Bright
Brightfalls
R Galen
River Argent
Caves of Surel
MOUNTAINS
Daniel's Pass
The Retreat
N'Deth Chasm
Traveller's Hut
The Valley
GLASSY
The By-Way
Oftenbe
Faeun's Triplets
Lake of Reflections
Unknown Lands
Valley Keep
River Argent
Argent Flow
Triversmeet
Watterton
Broadvane
Cloventine
Mistletoe
Willowood
CRYSTAL TREE WOODS
Gadygudy
Pris River
Mellow Hay
Aldersword
Toffddale
Tru River
Lament River
scrublands
scattered scrub
Juniper Steading
VELDER PLAINS
The Pristyne
LOWER WASTELANDS
Salty Cove
stony plains
LOWER WARRENS
The Dismal Sea
Lucky Bay
GILTON FOREST
Queenstown
Overland
sand dunes

❧ I ❧

LOST

THE LOW ROOF loomed over Sophy's head as she ducked to enter the next lot of tunnels beneath Castle Crioch. "God, it stinks in here."

"You're the one who wanted to go on a ghost tour. Stop complaining." Aria lifted her lantern and leant in closer to the stone wall, her nose wrinkling. "The quilts and flowers would have smelled nicer, but no, you had to do something more adventurous."

Sophy peered over Aria's shoulder to see what her best friend, now foster sister, was looking at. "You could've said no."

In the cracks between the stones, mortar had bubbled and oozed, leaving a rust-coloured trail of froth. Aria screwed up her face. "Gross. I can't believe I let you talk me into this. These old dungeons and tunnels are disgusting and creepy."

"I seem to recall that I have to suffer the quilts and flowers once we get out of here. That was the deal, right?" Sophy said.

"Yes, and you're not getting out of it." Aria sent her a piercing glance clearly discernible in the gloom. "You owe me. I haven't recovered from that awful story of murder and ghosts the guide told us."

Ahead, the guide in question's voice echoed off the walls and the rest of the tour group were lost in the shadows. "Don't stress, it's only a tour," Sophy said, waving her hand to dispel the dank stench. "It'll be over soon." She shrugged. "They just make up the stories anyway. Besides, I'm here to protect you if anything really monstrous comes clumping towards us."

Aria scoffed and resumed walking. "You'll have to. My phone doesn't have a signal down here. I can't even call for help."

The hair on the back of Sophy's neck rose and she swung around. Something was there—a man-like shape in the darkness, with red, glowing eyes. Sucking in a breath, she blinked instinctively, but when she looked again there was nothing. Unsettled, she said nothing to Aria who was already creeped out.

In a few minutes they had caught up with the stragglers from the tour group. Brady, their tour guide, had a broad Scottish accent, rolling his 'r' and mumbling half the rest. Light from lanterns flickered and jerked as people moved. Sophy listened a bit harder as the story Brady related took a nasty turn. "An' the Laird returned to find the heads of all his loved ones hanging from the walls..."

Her gut twisted. Betrayal, murder, ghosts lamenting. Were people really that nasty? As she listened a bit longer, she decided they could be.

"How much longer?" Aria asked. "Mum and Jeff will be waiting for us." The tour rounded a corner.

Sophy drew out her phone to check the clock display. "Another half an hour, I think. I'm sure Maralain and Jeff will figure out the tour is running late. Don't worry about it."

"I want to go back right now." Aria hissed the words in her ear with a decided edge of panic

"Now?" Sophy turned her astonished gaze to Aria. "But—"

Aria grabbed her upper arm and squeezed with fingers like claws. Aria's eyes were wide, her breaths coming in short pants. "I need to get out of here."

"Like now?"

The light from the lantern quavered in Aria's shaking hand. "Yes!" Aria's voice was hoarse and hard.

"I don't understand."

Aria's fingers dug harder into Sophy's bicep. "Oh god! I think I'm having a panic attack."

"What the? A panic attack?" Sophy gaped at Aria. "But the tour isn't that scary."

Aria covered her mouth, as if holding back a scream.

"I don't understand...why..." Sophy was cut off. The tour moved off again.

"Sophy, please, I'm being squeezed in half. I can't breathe." Aria sobbed. That hit Sophy right in the empathy spot.

"Okay. I'm sorry I didn't realise." Sophy cast around looking for an emergency exit. But this was an old Scottish castle and not an amusement park ride where they could hit an emergency stop button. The tour group had turned a corner. Sophy had a choice: race up there and get Brady to turn back, or they could reverse their steps and go back to the beginning. It would cause less embarrassment to Aria if they just found their own way back. She grabbed Aria's hand. "Come on, we'll head back to the start. We haven't come that far."

Aria kept a tight hold of Sophy's arm. "Thank you," she whimpered.

They turned the corner and walked for a few minutes. A deep groan enveloped them. Aria screamed, bending over and holding her stomach. The floor pitched and rolled. Sophy's heart thumped and her mind went white with terror. She barely kept on her feet. Dust rained down on them. "Quick! The doorway!"

Aria's breathing sounded like a bicycle pump but she didn't move. Sophy snatched at her jacket and dragged her over. "Come on. Hurry up!"

The tremor continued. Aria let out a scream and looked ready to bolt away. "No, wait. Don't run," Sophy said as she fought to keep Aria in the doorway. Weren't doorways the best place during an earthquake?

Aria screamed, panic taking hold. "Noooooo."

Sophy's heart sounded like a heavy disco beat: boom tish, boom tish. She peeled Aria's fingers off the lantern and placed it on the floor. Screams still fled Aria's mouth, creeping Sophy out. "Stop it." Aria didn't listen so Sophy gave her one across the cheek. Aria stopped mid-screech and then cried into Sophy's shoulder.

The earthquake ended, but the ground didn't seem to stop moving. It was as if the foundations of Castle Crioch were reorganising themselves and the dull thuds reverberating under her feet meant the building may not have survived intact. Could the towers have fallen? They had survived the quake but weren't out of trouble. She gulped: there was a big pile of stone above their heads between them and safety.

Sophy couldn't believe their luck. Was Scotland prone to earthquakes? Not that she'd heard. And if it was, why didn't someone say so before they came down here into the bowels of this place? Sure it'd stood for hundreds of years, but if she had known it was seismically unstable she would have thought twice about it. Maybe.

She listened for voices, hoping to hear others from the tour or the guide. It was eerily quiet except for the sound of grit hissing as it fell, timbers creaking overhead and her heart beat.

Aria stiffened, her finger nails pinching Sophy's shoulders. "What's that?" The absolute dread in her voice chilled Sophy. Peeling Aria's fingers from her shoulder, she turned.

"What the hell?"

Before them was a tunnel, one that oozed moisture and smelled weird, like freshly mown grass. Aria grabbed onto the waist of Sophy's jeans. "Don't."

"Don't what?" she replied stepping forward. "It wasn't there before."

"Sophy—"

A glove of cold air enveloped them, snatched them up and dragged them into the tunnel. Sophy screamed and flailed about, her stomach dropping to her toes. Aria's voice was in her ears so she seized onto her and drew her close. They were freefalling. Was it possible to die of fright? Eyes slammed tight, her ears popped with the change in air pressure. She struggled to come to terms with what was happening, yet even in the centre of her fear her brain worked. They were travelling somewhere: how or why she didn't know.

Sophy clung tightly to Aria as wind howled in her ears and snatched her breath away. Her long hair whipped about trying to suffocate and strangle her at the same time. When she dared to open her eyes, nothing but a blur of indecipherable colours surrounded them. The silvery tunnel sucked them down its gullet and become a nothing: a no space, a place of wind and noise and disorientation.

A sudden shift in direction and their bodies dropped, gravity returning abruptly. A force pulled Aria from her grip, her scream falling rapidly away.

No time for panic. A blazing light stunned Sophy just before she thumped to the ground, winded. For a long, uncomfortable moment she couldn't breathe. She tugged at the strap of her shoulder bag wrapped around her neck. Then the world went dark.

Sophy came to. She must have blacked out, but for how long? A second, a minute, an hour? Pushing herself up on her hands, she tried to orient herself, relieved she still had her bag and her precious phone. The light was dim, not dark like the tunnels beneath Castle Crioch.

Wind crashed through dark-leaved trees filling the space around her. An early sun dispelled the shadows cast by their trunks. How did she not get snagged in the branches when she fell? Glancing up, she wasn't sure she had fallen. A sudden pain pierced her forehead. What had happened? She couldn't quite recollect the last few minutes of her life. They were on a ghost tour. Except now she was here. And here wasn't there. "Ohh?" she moaned. Everything hurt—her head, her face, her ears. There wasn't a part of her that didn't feel twisted and bent out of shape.

A shrill scream sounded over the sound of the wind in the trees. Her head jerked up. "Aria?"

Sophy lurched to her feet and staggered at the pain in her head. Aria's next scream impelled her forward; she had to find Aria, had to protect her.

Aria's screams allowed Sophy to gain her bearings. Aria was close by. Sophy's fingers clung to the bark of the nearest tree, but creaking branches made her push away quickly. She didn't want to be squashed if one fell. Around her, light flickered. Dark patches came and went in her peripheral vision. She thought someone was there yet, when she turned, there was no one. Before she reached the shelter of the surrounding woods, a strange wind rocked her, and it felt as if bits of her were ripped away.

"I must have hit my head," she said to herself. "I'm imagining things."

Stepping under a large tree, Sophy called out. "Aria? Aria."

No answer. Sophy kept walking. How had they had become separated? Short shrill screams pierced the wind. Sophy sped up.

⚜

ARIA SCREAMED AGAIN. UNHURT, OPENING HER EYES PROVED TOO difficult. She was somewhere else. Felt it, knew it in her heart. It was in the air, in the ground and in the trees surrounding her. The taste of this place was on her tongue. She screamed again and then let her panic go.

As her heartbeat slowed, she drew in a breath of clear, sweet air. Instead of scrunching her eyes shut, she opened them. Living things around her exuded golden warmth. She saw life flowing through the trees; saw it in the water burbling in the stream beside her.

Calm, she told herself, be calm.

Crawling on hands and knees, she put her hands on the trunk of the nearest tree and felt the faint pulse of its life. Snatching her hand back, she curled herself into a ball and rocked back and forward. It couldn't be happening, it couldn't, she said like a litany to herself.

Sounds assaulted her ears, making her lift her head and hold her breath. Birds, insects, soft leaves fluttering on a light breeze, all made joyous, vibrant and overwhelming noise. She heard Sophy calling her name. What had happened? How had they ended up in this place, this beautiful place? She could barely remember what she was doing before finding herself here.

⚜

SOPHY DUCKED UNDER A LOW-LYING BRANCH AND PUSHED THROUGH some undergrowth. With her ginger curls covering part of her face, Aria sat on the ground, next to a pool fed by a small stream. Relief rushed over her: thank goodness.

Sophy knelt next to her. "Are you hurt?"

Aria didn't respond and kept staring wide-eyed at her surroundings. Sophy's head pulsed with pain and her stomach twisted in knots. She leaned over to vomit on the ground. All she wanted to do was lie down and sleep until the weakness faded, yet some instinct made her resist the urge.

"Sophy?" Aria spoke at last. Sophy brushed the hair out of Aria's face, and quickly assessed her for injury. Aria was unharmed, not even a graze on her arm or a smear of dirt on her jeans. Her eyes though were still wide and staring.

"I am here. We're okay."

Aria's green gaze met hers, focusing finally. "We are not...not..."

"No. No. We're okay. We're fine."

Aria shook her head. "This place is different. I can see it, feel it. And look, my phone screen is completely blank. Nothing at all."

Sophy's brows cinched together. "I know something weird happened—"

"We are someplace else. I can feel life here, see it in the trees."

Sophy's mouth fell open. Aria spoke with such conviction that she became uneasy. She cast a glance around her, but all appeared to be normal. "No, we haven't. We're in Scotland—"

"The castle is not there."

Sophy shifted her head, trying to pinpoint the castle, the road, the village and couldn't. She couldn't explain what happened. They were in the tunnel on a ghost tour...She shook her head. Nothing. She couldn't remember. "Well, maybe we're lost." She noticed Aria assessing her. "What?"

"Your eyes...your eyes..." The hint of panic in Aria's voice sent fear crawling up Sophy's spine.

"What?" Sophy pressed her fingers around her eye socket, thinking it quite likely that her landing had caused a black eye.

"The colour has changed from dark blue to...to well...black. And your skin...so pale..."

"Right, I'm calling Maralain. She'll know what to do." Sophy pulled her phone out of her shoulder bag. The display was dead.

"It's not working, is it?" Aria asked.

Sophy shoved the phone back into her bag, with a sigh of

resignation. "No. The battery must be dead, though it was fully charged before we went on the tour. Well, if somehow we...er...the castle is not there then there must be a road or a village or a police station around here."

"Do you really think so?" Aria's voice sounded calmer.

"Yes, of course I do." Even though Sophy was rattled by their experience, she needed to be strong for Aria. The sooner they found Maralain the better things would be.

"I doubt if you can walk anywhere," Aria commented her gaze fixed on Sophy's shaking hand and then pushed her hair behind her ears. "You're not well."

Dappled sunlight fell upon the nearby pond, revealing clear water and clean stones along the bottom.

"I think I'm okay. Some water might help." Sophy crawled over to the water's edge and splashed cold water over her face. Turning back to Aria, she asked, "Better?"

Her foster sister stood surveying the trees and the pond. Their gazes met and Aria nodded. Something in her expression led Sophy to believe that her looks had not improved.

✦

They walked for a few hours with no sound of traffic or signs of people. Aria had not renewed her unnerving chatter about 'feeling or seeing life' in her surroundings, which allowed Sophy to file it away under hysteria in a moment of crisis. She tried not to let the complete absence of technology or human habitation unnerve her.

They entered a glade. In the centre, Sophy saw a beautiful, silver-barked tree. Sunlight reflected off its prism-like leaves and the air shimmered with colour, shifting and fading as the wind tugged lightly at the branches. Sophy's heart lurched as she tried to get her brain to understand what it was that she was seeing.

Aria gasped. "Look at that!"

"Yes, odd," she agreed. Her gaze roamed about the clearing, trying to put a frame of reference on what they were seeing and experiencing. "Is it real?"

"Beautiful..." Aria said in an awed whisper.

The crystal-clear, almost-silver leaves were vaguely oval shaped with protrusions that made them appear like small, solid stars. They looked as if they could fit into the palm of her hand. Was it a construction of some kind? Was it safe?

Aria reached out and touched one of the leaves.

"Don't!"

Too late. The leaves began to play music. The sound reverberated around the clearing, like little bells tinkling. The melody amplified as it bounced off the forest, flowing back upon itself, deepening the song with multi-layers of notes.

"Listen to that," Aria's expression was full of rapture.

Sophy tried to block out the discordant sound. Even with her ears covered, the nerve-twisting feeling managed to snake up through her jaw into her eyes. Glancing upwards, Sophy spotted two silver leaves floating ever so slowly down. They mesmerised her, fluttering and skipping before her eyes. She couldn't dodge out of their way. One landed on her chest, right below her collarbone. Disappearing through her clothes, it seared her skin. Pulling at the neck of her t-shirt, she tried to get rid of it, but she couldn't see it, only feel it delving into her flesh.

She tried to warn Aria, but pain overwhelmed her and a strange sense of dislocation coursed within her body. Falling backwards into scattered leaf mulch, she heard Aria say, just before she lost consciousness, "Do you hear that? Feel that? Delightful...magic."

Next thing she knew, Aria was leaning over her and shaking her by the shoulder. Sophy's mouth opened, guppy-like, but no sound came out.

"Wake up! Did you faint?" Aria asked, cradling one of the crystal leaves in her hand.

"I'm okay," Sophy finally managed to say in a croaky voice.

"That's good. You know, Sophy, this tree, it's not normal. Now I'm certain that—"

Sophy sat up and saw movement at the edge clearing. "Sssh"

"What is it?" Aria asked. "Do you hurt somewhere?"

"There's someone there." She pointed to the woods behind Aria.

Two archers crept out of the woods behind a man, who slowly approached them. He was young looking, maybe twenty-something, and wore coffee-coloured hose and a brown and green leather jerkin. Sophy was hoping that they were caught up in some kind of medieval re-enactment. Her gaze flicked to the tree, and she quickly squashed that train of thought.

"Lord." Aria gasped and absent-mindedly dropped her leaf.

"Run! Get away," Sophy said, keeping the man in her line of sight.

"It's all right. He means us no harm."

"Are you nuts?" More archers, with arrows nocked, emerged from the cover of the trees. Their chance of escape evaporated.

Aria turned to her. "They glow with a golden light and mean us no harm."

"But they have arrows pointed at us." Sophy climbed to her feet and tried to position herself in front of Aria. Obviously, Aria was affected by their fall.

The stranger approached them, hands held out from his sides. He was tanned and well built. Sophy could also see his clothing in more detail. The collar of his white undershirt, embroidered and elegant, kissed the edge of his clean-shaven, squarish chin. At first he bowed from the waist, left hand sweeping before him and then he looked quizzically at them both. In a smooth and rich voice, he said, "Please move away from the Crystal Tree."

Aria gaped. "I'm not getting that." She turned to Sophy and raised her eyebrows.

Sophy had understood him and that made her frown. "He said to move away from the tree."

Holding on to Sophy's arm, Aria took a step in the direction the man indicated. Aria whispered, "How can you understand him?"

"Don't know, but perhaps we should do as he says before they decide to let those arrows fly." Sophy took another step away from the tree, bringing Aria with her. Angling her head over her shoulder, she checked the position of the archers. Arranged in a rough semi-circle, they had bland expressions, but there was no mistaking the tension in their hands as they held the arrows on the strings.

"What language is he speaking? It sounds familiar, but I can't seem to grasp it," Aria said.

Frowning, the young man kept his gaze on Aria's dropped leaf, glinting in the afternoon sun. He bent to pick it up, took a long step in their direction and placed it gently into Aria's hand. She didn't flinch or edge away and appeared quite comfortable with the stranger getting close to her. The men surrounding them shared looks and murmured. Sophy couldn't quite catch what they were saying.

"The Crystal Tree has gifted you with a leaf, my lady," he said, his gaze lingering on Aria.

"This?" Aria said, holding the delicate crystal leaf. "It's very beautiful." She smiled, then looked over her shoulder at Sophy. "I can understand him now." She lifted the leaf. "I was right. It's magical."

"Sure it is. Why are they pointing arrows at us?" Sophy glowered at the man. When his gaze met hers, his mouth tensed. She tried to fix her hair by hooking the loose strands behind her ears and refrained from scratching her neck. It didn't seem to help.

"Forgive me," he began, facing Aria. "My name is Dellbright. The Crystal Tree Woods are in my care, and the tree itself is sacred to us. It does not give gifts lightly."

"We didn't harm the tree," Aria said, smiling shyly. "I think it sang to us."

He nodded. "We heard. We do not often meet travellers in these woods. Have you travelled far?"

Aria smiled at him again. "Yes...er we don't know, actually."

Sophy moved forward to stand by Aria, ignoring as best she could the six archers with arrows clenched against their bowstrings.

"This is...Sophy and I'm called Aria... Where are we exactly?"

"You are near my home, Valley Keep," he said.

"Do you have a phone? We need to make a call," Sophy asked.

"A phone?" He shook his head. "No. I do not..." He chewed his lower lip, then as if remembering himself, he said, "Forgive me for being so discourteous, but I must ask you to accompany me."

Sophy heard one of the men behind her whisper. "There are two of them..."

When she swung round to look at who was talking, she met blank expressions. Turning back, she saw Dellbright take a gold chain from around his neck. "Please let me," he said, holding out his hand for Aria's leaf. He deftly attached the leaf to the chain. "May I?" he asked and, after Aria's nod, placed the chain around her neck.

"Thank you," Aria said.

His eyes, full of suspicion, moved to Sophy's face. He didn't ask if she had a leaf. Then again, she didn't want to say what happened to hers. She scarce believed it had happened and didn't expect anyone else would either.

"The archers are here because of the Puri raiders. Do not be alarmed."

"Raiders?" Sophy repeated, feeling dizzy. "What are they?"

"Nothing to worry about, I assure you," he said as they followed him out of the glade and into the forest. The archers disappeared into the surrounding trees. Sophy could only see one or two of them at any time, their presence enough to prevent escape.

The party continued walking, for perhaps an hour, when Dellbright stopped.

"Would you like to rest? You appear tired."

"Yes," Sophy said as she dropped to the grass.

"Can I get you some water to drink?" Dellbright asked.

"Thank you," Aria said breathily. "Water would be great, wouldn't it?"

Sophy nodded. Dellbright stared at the ground and took a few steps to the left. He knelt down and spoke.

Sophy's eyebrows shot up, and she looked over to Aria, who smiled as if the goings on around her were perfectly natural. Curious, Sophy climbed to her feet and followed Aria to stand near where Dellbright knelt. Water bubbled up from the ground like a playground tap. What the hell?

Dellbright glanced up, eyes crinkled with a smile. "Come closer and drink. The water is fresh and sweet."

Aria knelt, leaned over and drank deeply. "That's delicious. Thank you."

Sophy leaned over, her lips tracking the water as it slid back into the ground. She pulled up short of the grass and frowned. Dellbright's mouth hung open, and his cheeks grew pink. "I do not understand. I have never seen it act this way before. Please, I will call it again."

And he did, but as soon as she drew closer, it fell away. Her proximity to the water was driving her crazy. The suspicious look Dellbright gave her didn't help. After three more tries, and Dellbright's increasingly sour expression, Aria asked if she could look in Sophy's shoulder bag. Aria took the cap off a deodorant spray and rinsed it before filling it and handing it to her.

Sophy drank deeply, having the cap refilled many times before quenching her thirst. The water receded into the ground, with only a small damp patch of earth to evidence its existence. Fixing her eyes on Dellbright, she asked, "How did you do that?"

"I asked and it was *given*."

"*Given*? What is *given*?" Aria asked.

Dellbright turned toward Aria. "You do not know of the *given*?" His gaze shifted between their blank faces. "Argenterra is famous for its *given*, bounty and craft."

Aria said. "Won't you tell us about them?"

Sophy sat down on the ground and groaned with her head in her hands. Argenterra! A bloody nutter! This was taking the whole ghost tour thing way too far.

"Are you all right?" Aria asked, squatting beside her.

She threw her head back and glared at them both. "I'm fine. What is wrong with you?"

Aria leaned back and replied, "I feel perfectly well." Then turning her attention back to Dellbright, she said, "Please, tell us."

"Very well. The water was *given*. Bounty is for taking and Craft is what we make with our hands."

Aria drew her curls behind her ears. "I'm not sure what you mean, are your clothes *given*, bounty or craft?"

He looked aghast. "My clothes are craft, of course, but of the very basic craft, I assure you." Gesturing to the trees, he stood up. "Fruit on the trees is bounty. It can be plucked. However, if it is not the season for fruit, the *given* will ripen it. Such is the way of a traveller who finds himself without sustenance. If he asks, Argenterra will give it to him."

He stopped for a moment as if thinking of a better way to explain.

Then he walked to a bush that was full of green leaves and small closed buds. "The water was *given*, but it was there under the ground. I only asked it to come to the surface, thus not so difficult. This bush has the possibility of a flower." He spoke quietly to the bush and stroked it leaves. The bud grew and opened to a beautiful, green-petalled flower, which he handed to Aria.

When his eyes fell upon Sophy again, the smile in them died. "Let us continue on," he said blandly and marched ahead, stopping to make sure Aria was following.

Sophy kept opening and closing her mouth. The land? Bounty? Was everyone but her crazy? She raced after them. Two archers flanked her, giving each other hand signals.

"So, Dellbright, are you some kind of magician?"

He turned back to her. "All who live in this land may ask and it will be *given*. Wait, I think I know what you are asking. Do you mean am I an adept?"

Sophy nodded, she thought that's what she meant.

"No, alas, I am not an adept. The adepts are recluses who study the mysteries of the land. They have spent many hundreds of years studying them, including the *given*."

He continued walking, eyes constantly straying to Aria. Sophy chewed her lips and tugged on her hair. There was too much to process, too much to deal with. Her heart beat a little faster, and she tried to quiet her anxiety, until a couple of archers leapt out of the trees and startled her.

❧ 2 ☙

GIFTS OF THE CRYSTAL TREE

ARIA COULD SEE the edge of the forest and the smattering of sunshine as it gilded the edges of the leaves. A faint breeze shifted the branches. As they passed through the last of the trees, she saw green fields gently undulating, and the folds of darker hills beyond. Aria breathed in the clean, fresh air and the feeling of life that washed over her, filling her up. She marvelled at the thought she was in another world. The concept and the reality no longer frightened her. Argenterra felt like home. Now she was out in the open, she noticed the sunlight had a bluish hue, another hint they were somewhere else entirely.

Dellbright emerged from the forest behind her. There was something about his smile and the way he looked at her. Her breath caught when he grinned at her. The essence of him glowed like a beacon. Aria looked away in case he could read her thoughts in her expression. It was not right to feel that way about someone she hardly knew. Then came Sophy, a pale echo of herself. Aria could hardly account for the difference in Sophy, her beauty smudged as if by an ineffective attempt to erase it. Now with almost translucent skin, she appeared bloodless, particularly with her dark, straight hair emphasising her pallid complexion.

Aria could not take her gaze away as Sophy stumbled to a halt to take in the view

"Is your friend well?" Dellbright asked her quietly, leaning in close.

"I'm fine," replied Sophy as she stepped beside them. "Stop asking."

Dellbright stepped ahead of them allowing them some privacy.

"You have been acting a little...well, strange," Aria said.

"I'm not acting strange. I thought you were, acting all friendly with our captor."

"But he's nice. Can't you see that? Can you see any of the beauty around you, the colours, the freshness, the life?"

Sophy cast her gaze around. "It looks pretty enough, but nothing out of the ordinary. Do I need to remind you that we're prisoners? They're as likely to kill us as they are to smile at us. I don't trust this place, or him."

Sophy's comments were like a punch in the stomach. "I don't understand you. Are you experiencing something different from me?" Aria could sense things she hadn't before. Lowering her lashes, she looked at the archers and then at Dellbright. She could see that golden glow to them, a new ability to be sure, but Sophy was a faded version of her former self—and had no golden glow. Closing her eyes to shut out her view of them all, the sense of the other men was still there, although diminished in intensity.

"Please follow me," Dellbright said, interrupting her little experiment. "There is someone I would like you to meet."

"Aria? Do you have my bag?" Sophy asked.

Aria lifted her empty hands. "No. We must have left it behind when we stopped for a drink."

"But it has my phone in it as well as other things. We have to go back for it."

Aria considered her surroundings. This place did not have technology as far as she could see. The bows and arrows hinted at a society less advanced than their own. Dellbright's clothes were well made to the point of envy, but still hand crafted. Making an issue of going back for the phone would be pointless. There was no network to support it, and no electricity to recharge the batteries. She was about to say so to Sophy when Dellbright interrupted again. "I am sorry your possessions are missing. We do not have time to go back for them now. It will be dark soon. Is it important?"

"No. I do not think it is," Aria replied, adding when Sophy let out an inarticulate sound of protest, "I'll talk to her." While they followed Dellbright, Aria did her best to reassure Sophy that the phone was useless and not worth worrying over. Besides, she reminded Sophy that the ghost tour had been her idea, after all and that their current predicament was therefore her fault.

A camp came into view with rows of triangular tents, encircling two larger ones. The late evening sun caused the shadows to lengthen. The sound of men talking and horses neighing reached them. Sophy stopped complaining about the missing mobile phone and gaped at the scene unfolding before them.

৩৵৶

Sophy's trepidation grew. The leaf in her chest sat like a hard lump, and she ached to push at it, except that would draw attention. About twenty men lounged outside tents, dressed in similar clothing to Dellbright and his archers. Some pretended to be busy, but Sophy saw that they peered at them as they walked between the tents to a larger, green tent.

Aria's lecture about the lack of technology, while annoying, appeared to be true. What she was seeing had to be real. She really was somewhere else. There was a magic called the *given*, which she could not feel, but could see the results of, and there was a crystal leaf embedded in her chest.

Before she had any time to adjust to these profound happenings, two men lifted the flap of the large green tent, and Dellbright ushered them inside. Sophy tensed as she examined the shaded interior. Light from a brazier spilled over the patterned rugs, and there were big, colourful embroidered cushions scattered around the floor. On her left was a flat-topped chest, and in the gloom she could make out other items of furniture.

"Excellency?" Dellbright called.

A tall, broad man with long, almost white, blond hair bound in a queue, stood up from behind a desk and came forward. He was wearing a dark blue vest and beige trousers. At first he looked askance at them, then recovering quickly, he laughed softly. "Cousin, what strange game you have caught for dinner? Two ladies snared in Crystal Tree Woods. I am in awe of your skill."

Dellbright grimaced and flushed slightly. "Lady Aria and Lady Sophy, let me introduce you to his Excellency, Oakheart of the Silverbow, the high king's ambassador, among other things," Dellbright said politely. "He jests, of course."

Sophy couldn't restrain her eyebrow at Dellbright's honorific. She didn't think she'd ever been called a lady before, except when being scolded while in school.

"Pleased to meet you, excellency," Aria said as she curtsied elegantly, a smile lifting the corners of her mouth.

On the verge of being overwhelmed, Sophy stood there dumbly and it wasn't until Aria coughed purposefully, that she tried to curtsey. "Pleased to meet you, my lord, I mean...excellency." Then she cursed herself for being so awkward.

"Please call me Oakheart. Everyone else does." He smiled at Sophy, but she couldn't tell if it was a real smile. Although, he did not put on the charm for Aria in the way Dellbright did.

Pulling out a chair, he sat down and stared at them. "This is most unusual, cousin," he said to Dellbright, but his eyes never left them. Aria stood radiant, and Sophy could only feel dishevelled. They looked at her as if there was something terribly wrong. Did she have two heads?

Since the ambassador made free to study them, she decided to do likewise. Oakheart's skin was tanned but his features were bland, like a pile of sand. His green eyes were his most remarkable feature.

"How long were you in the woods before Dellbright found you?" Oakheart asked, suddenly all business.

"Not long," Aria said.

"'Tis said that the pathway that leads from other worlds to Crystal Tree Woods is transient. I am afraid you cannot return the way you came."

Sophy's head spun and her knees trembled. "We can't go back?"

"This is the first time such an event has occurred in my lifetime. We know the histories and the tales, but as far as I know none have been able to find that pathway again."

"So you were expecting us?" Sophy found that rather sinister, considering the welcome they had received.

Oakheart scratched his chin and shrugged. "There were signs that led us to believe a visitor was to arrive. It grows late. I think 'tis best that you rest here for the night so we can arrange to take you safely to Valley Keep in the morning. Dellbright might have mentioned we are wary of Puri raiders. They do not often venture this far south. But it pays to be careful at a time like this. Forgive me if I place guards around this pavilion. 'Tis for your protection. We will have a meal sent in." Oakheart glanced at Dellbright.

"Yes...and some hot water for bathing..." Dellbright added, his cheeks reddening.

Oakheart stood, smiled again, and tugged on the hem of his vest, which Sophy could see was actually a doublet. "Perhaps we will break our fast together at sunrise."

Aria smiled. "Thank you for your hospitality."

"But this is your tent, isn't it?" Sophy asked Oakheart.

Aria jumped in. "We aren't putting you out, are we?"

Oakheart frowned. "Nay, I will share with Dellbright. And as he does not snore...overloudly...I shall be comfortable. I thank you for your concern."

Dellbright lifted the tent flap, and Oakheart, a whole head and shoulders taller than him, crouched down to exit the tent.

"I don't like this..." Sophy said and went to peek out the tent flap. A guard wearing a blue tabard stood there. She stepped back and put her hands on her hips. "Dellbright was waiting for us and now we can't leave. I don't believe this crap about Puri raiders. What are they?"

Aria frowned. "Sophy, don't be difficult. Where would we go?"

Sophy plonked herself down on one of the cushions, grabbed a chunk of her hair and began twirling it around her fingers. "Why do they look at me strangely? Do I look that bad?"

Aria's expression grew serious. "I don't know how to tell you this, but you look different...like a faded you."

Sophy stopped twisting her hair and her chin dropped. "I do not."

"You do. If I can see it, maybe they can too." Aria arrayed herself gracefully on one of the cushions.

Sophy sat forward. "Really? What does that mean?"

"I don't know, but it could be why they are acting wary. We are strangers, after all."

Sophy climbed to her feet and paced on the carpet. "Pfft! They think I'm an evil apparition, do they?"

"I don't know...what they think. But I know we can trust them."

Sophy stopped her pacing and face Aria. "They like you, I can tell. Somehow you look beautiful here."

"What do you mean?" Aria's expression was puzzled yet slightly eager.

"Not that you didn't before, but it's more pronounced. Your skin shines. I can't explain it."

"Oh," Aria replied. There was a smile on her face as her gaze roamed over the interior of the pavilion.

There was a hail from outside the tent. The flaps opened and a couple of guards brought in two servings of roast vegetables and meat. Aria thanked the guard, who replied, "Water is being heated for your bath and will be brought to you shortly."

"Thanks," Sophy said to the men as they left. Turning to Aria she added, "Well, we don't have to worry about them being vegetarians." Sophy's stomach growled loudly.

"Oh, Sophy."

"What? I haven't eaten for ages...a day... maybe more."

With a nod from Aria, Sophy began wolfing down the food. Aria ate hungrily, too, but took a touch longer to chew. Sophy had already put down her plate when there was another hail from outside the tent. When Aria invited whoever it was in, four of the blue tabard wearing guards came in, followed by four green clad ones. Each group carried an oval bath tub, oozing steam, which they carefully placed on the matting.

As the guards filed out, a shy, young guard left a pile of fresh clothes on top of the chest by the opening, then bowed neatly and left. Sophy stepped over and did a quick inspection. There were two lightweight, pale lemon-coloured linen shifts, with fine, rose-scented soaps carved into the shape of rosebuds nestled within them. Several linen towels sat at the bottom of the pile.

Aria tied the flaps of the pavilion shut. "Okay," she said. "We've got some privacy so let's get busy. I feel like I've been rolling in muck." She started to peel off her t-shirt. "There's a fancy chamber pot over behind that screen."

Sophy headed to the corner to relieve herself and then wasted no time in stripping off her jeans and t-shirt and easing into one of the tubs.

"I never thought I'd feel such pleasure again," Aria said with a drawn out sigh as she lowered herself in the water and lathered the perfumed soap.

Sophy let the hot water ease her mind. "You think we can trust these people. Why?"

Aria rubbed soap across her left shoulder and met Sophy's eye. "I can see their essence shining out of them, at least, I think that is what it is. Sort of overwhelming at first, but I'm getting used to it. The Crystal Tree was something else altogether. When I touched it, I was reborn. What did you feel?"

Sophy splashed around in the bath, flicking suds. "Besides incredibly ill? Nothing. Everything is the same for me. I don't get it. Until I saw the Crystal Tree and Dellbright, I just thought we were lost." Sophy tentatively touched the spot where the leaf dwelt. That was too hard to talk about. "Dellbright's *given* was a tad interesting."

"You know, when he used the *given* I could feel it happening. This place..."

"Don't tell me about that. I couldn't feel anything, except my eyes bugging from my head. What about your parents? They must be beside themselves by now."

Aria let out breath slowly and lay her head back to stare at the roof of the tent. "They will be worried. But there's nothing we can do about it, is there?"

Sophy lathered some more soap on her skin. "I guess."

"I'm happy to be here."

"We don't have much choice, do we? There are guards outside. Perhaps you may have noticed them."

Aria smiled as she lazed in the tub. "I like here, guards and all."

"Especially Dellbright," Sophy muttered under her breath. She glanced over at Aria, but her friend had undone her braid and was diligently scrubbing her scalp. Sophy washed the soap from her own hair.

Sophy had only that moment slipped into her shift and was drying her hair when there was another hail from outside. Aria quickly wrapped a blanket around herself where she was lying down on some cushions. Sophy undid the tent flap and gazed out. Four men waited. She stepped back, and they walked in and removed the tubs. Too late, Sophy saw that one of them had gathered up their discarded jeans, t-shirts and underclothes.

"Hey, wait. Don't take those..." she said. Already, the tubs were through the flaps, if she didn't act quickly, there wouldn't be much she could do. Frustrated, she halted the last guard as he turned to bow. "May I have our clothes back?"

"Good rest, my lady," he said as if he hadn't heard. He bowed and departed.

Perplexed, Sophy redid the flaps. Sighing heavily, she went to the cushions she was to share with Aria. Why did they take their clothes? To wash them? That thought made Sophy uncomfortable. Leaning back, she huddled into her blankets to ponder their situation.

"Is everything all right?" Aria said sleepily from under the covers.

Sophy put out the lamp and a rich darkness filled the pavilion. "Yes, everything is fine. Go to sleep."

❧ 3 ☙

VALLEY KEEP

MORNING LIGHT PEEPED in through the gap in the tent flaps. Sophy tried to ignore it, but as Aria stirred from the covers, wrapped herself in a blanket and searched among the cushions, she had to wake up.

"What's the matter?" Sophy asked croakily.

"I can't find our clothes. Did you put them somewhere?" Aria asked as she shifted cushions and tossed them around.

Sophy groaned. "The guards took them when they came to empty the bath water."

"Why would they do that?"

Sophy threw off her covers and climbed to her feet. "I don't know. You're the Argenterran expert."

"Funny, ha ha. You could have said something." Aria plonked down on a cushion and stared into space.

"I didn't want to worry you, okay. We're already prisoners. Now we're next-to-naked prisoners."

Aria glared at her. "Sophy. Please stop. I'm telling you, things will be fine."

Sophy stood up, and ran her fingers through her tangled hair. "I wish you'd see reality. We can't go anywhere without our clothes."

A voice boomed outside the tent. "Good morn, my ladies?"

With one panicked look at Sophy, Aria raced over to undo the tent flap. A lone guard bowed and handed her a pile of folded clothing. Sophy squinted through the opening. The other guards were still in place.

"Thank you," Aria said quietly to the guard and dropped the tent flap behind her. Sophy retied it to give them privacy and went over to where Aria had placed the bundle.

"What's this?" Aria picked up a dress from the pile, unravelled it and examined it closely. It was a pale green gown made with fine cloth and laced with thin, silvery threads. It had a short bodice and a full gathered skirt.

Sophy had to blink once or twice. "Clothes? Beautiful clothes." Immediately, her eyes were riveted to the other gown. Fashioned in the same style, except the colour of the fabric was like dark blue sapphires. When she picked it up, two pairs of soft boots fell on the floor and there were two sets of longer trousers, with padding on the inner thigh.

"Ooh, it's lovely," Aria crooned as she fingered the green silky dress, lingering on the jewelled bodice. She held it up against her. "What do you think?"

Sophy felt some trepidation. "Nice. But the style is strange. Doesn't look historical. What about the ugly underwear?"

"We're in another world, not back in time. I'm sure the underwear has a purpose."

"But what about our things? I prefer my jeans," Sophy said, putting down the blue gown. "I'm not into pretty. You know that."

Aria glanced at her quickly, draping the green gown against her body. "I'll wear this one. You know the blue suits you best."

Sophy sighed. They had nothing else to put on so she guessed it wouldn't hurt to wear it—even though it did feel as if she was giving in too easily. It took a while to dress using the undergarments provided. After fixing their hair, Aria gave Sophy a once over, pursed her lips and shook her head.

Sophy groaned. "It doesn't matter. As you look absolutely perfect, I don't think how I look will have much bearing on anything."

OAKHEART FOLDED HIS BLANKET, HANDED IT TO THE YOUNG GUARD assisting him, and sat down on a stool to bind his boots with leather laces. The two strangers had been upmost on his mind and the reason he had not slept well. There were two young women from another world in his tent. The concept was both exciting and daunting. What surprised him most is that he had no trouble communicating with them. Aria seemed right at home. The other girl, Sophy, reacted as if her world had fallen down. Even though she was hard to make out, he found himself sympathising with her predicament. How would he react if he had been taken elsewhere? He loved Argenterra and would hate to leave it.

His cousin muttered for the tenth time that morning, which brought a smile to Oakheart's face. Dellbright shook his head in consternation and water flicked all over Oakheart. "What can this mean? I am completely baffled," Dellbright said, voice muffled by a towel.

"Yes, 'tis a puzzle, but I am sure the exercise of a little patience will reveal all."

Dellbright punched his arms through the sleeve of his leather jerkin. "'Tis easy for you to say. Your life is not affected by this. You told me it was time for the Gift of Crystal Tree Woods to arrive. Did not your study among the adepts give you any inkling that this situation would arise?"

Oakheart put his foot in his other boot, unperturbed by his cousin's angst. "No, I do not think I have heard aught of two women emerging from the woods at the same time. Think of it this way. You have choice. There are two Gifts of Crystal Tree Woods, others have not been so fortunate."

"Fortunate? How can you say that? What if I choose wrong?"

Oakheart looked up from tying his boot. "Wrong, Cousin?" Something in Dellbright's words struck him as odd.

Dellbright paused for a moment. "Oh...one is a vision and the other an apparition..."

With a shrug, Oakheart finished with his boots. He relaxed,

realising that Dellbright's perception was superficial. His cousin had not glimpsed something unseen in young Sophy. "Your choice seems clear, unless you wish to choose both." Oakheart stood up, foot resting on the stool, and stared at his cousin.

Dellbright creased his brow and frowned "Both? You cannot be serious."

Oakheart could not restrain himself any longer and chuckled. "'Tis rumoured that the Puri can word their marriage oaths to allow them to take more than one wife. You know the queen of the Gilton Forest has three husbands. 'Tis not impossible." Oakheart's grin was wide and his chest heaved as he held back a belly laugh.

"Indeed you are not." Dellbright kicked Oakheart's stool, nearly toppling his tormentor. "How can you laugh at my situation? I will complain to the high king about your behaviour."

With that, Oakheart broke out into roar of laughter that nearly toppled him back onto his bed. "He will laugh more than I," he managed, when he could gain a breath. "Dellbright captures the Gifts of Crystal Tree Woods and surrounds them with archers. Then he bemoans his fate because the mysterious woods have doubled his gift. It shall be written down as 'Dellbright's Dilemma.' Indeed, I should scribe it myself."

Dellbright's brows drew together in a dark line and his eyes glittered with anger.

"You will not dare such a thing. I did what I thought was best, considering the circumstances."

Oakheart saw a sulk coming on and wiped the tears of laughter from his eyes.

Ignoring his cousin's pouting, Oakheart asked, "Does this Sophy fill you with fear? Or is it just that she is not as pleasing to look upon as the beauteous Aria? I think it the latter, for you have not stopped talking about her." Indeed, Oakheart was a fair way falling for Aria himself. He reserved judgement on Sophy, though. She was a puzzle, hard to see, as if there was a shadow on her. Only close observation and, perhaps, time would reveal her mystery. He had yet to ascertain if her slightly sour demeanour was temporary, brought on by result of being in Argenterra, or a permanent fixture.

Dellbright threw a cushion at him and stepped outside their shared tent. "Let us eat before you become a ravenous snow bear."

Oakheart was glad to see that the bad mood threatening to overcome Dellbright had evaporated. Oakheart smiled as he, too, stepped out into the bright morning light. Underway were early preparations for their departure. The sounds of packing, of horse tack jingling and the murmur of voices floated around. He rubbed his stomach. "I am very hungry, Dell. All this mirth has taxed me somewhat. I hope you ordered extra food."

Dellbright's eyes rolled up and a smile quirked at the corner of his lips. "Oh, in the very least, cousin. My cooks double the portions when they know you are visiting. Come, the ladies await."

Oakheart briefly clasped Dellbright's shoulders as they headed for the pavilion. He could tell by Dellbright's pace that he was eager to see young Aria again.

SOPHY LOOKED UP WHEN SHE HEARD FOOTSTEPS OUTSIDE THEIR tent.

"May we enter?" said a rich voice from outside. There was no mistaking Dellbright's tone or the way Aria's eyes lit up.

"The mess, quick," Aria whispered, pointing to the array of blankets and bedclothes. While Sophy quickly hid most of their mess, Aria took her time undoing the tent flaps and checking that her dress was in order.

Slightly dazzled by the sunshine, it took a moment for Sophy to realise that breakfast had arrived along with Dellbright and Oakheart, who both bowed from the waist.

"We hope you slept well. May we join you to break our fast?" Oakheart asked smoothly, as if they were guests rather than captives. A couple of guards came in and set up a table and chairs, then laid platters of food, bread and baked vegetables and something grey in a large, steaming pot.

"My ladies, you do look most becoming in those gowns," Dellbright said, his eyes resting on Aria. Sophy's sense of unease grew. Dellbright was paying her sister too much attention and, to top it off, both of these Argenterran men seemed to have changed their manner.

Dellbright turned to her, his smile superficial. "The blue suits you, my lady," he said.

Sophy arched her eyebrow. "Thank you," she answered with forced politeness.

Aria said as she gracefully took her seat. "We are truly grateful for your kindness."

Dellbright sat beside her. Oakheart focussed on the food, scooping a large portion of grey porridge from the pot.

Sophy watched him and said, "I am not so easily grateful. You had our tent guarded all night. I think you're glad that we are finally clean and no longer smell like we've been rolling in a sewer."

"Really..." Dellbright spluttered, his face darkening with shame or anger.

Sophy batted her eyelids with over exaggerated innocence.

"Please, ignore her comments. Sophy likes to kid around," Aria said.

"I'm right though, aren't I?"

Oakheart, his look appraising, said, "'Tis true that you appear more comfortable than you were last eve."

Sophy scoffed. "See, I was right. He's too polite to say so to our faces."

Aria nudged her under the table and smiled at both of the men while scooping something that looked like a roast potato onto her plate. Sophy took the hint and changed the subject. "Where did these gowns come from?" She gestured outside. "I didn't see any women who could have lent them to us."

"Sophy, that's rude."

Sophy quirked a defiant eyebrow and moved her legs from Aria's reach. "It's a fair question."

Dellbright leaned forward to catch Aria's eye. "Indeed, Lady Aria, I am delighted to tell you that I sent for them. They arrived from my keep early this morning."

Aria smiled back at him. "That was very kind of you. We—"

"Why couldn't we have our own clothes back?"

Sophy saw Aria's face flush and knew that she would probably punch her at any moment.

"We burnt them. I am sorry. They were beyond repair." Dellbright looked away and then down at his plate.

Sophy's face heated and she chewed at her lip, wondering what she could do or say about the situation. Aria appeared calm about the demise of their clothing. Yet Sophy felt as if she had been cast away. They were her only link to her world, to her identity. It was as if Dellbright had single-handedly disconnected her from her life.

Oakheart's green-eyed gaze fell on her again. "I would like to eat. There is toffelporridge, my favourite. So, if you will forgive me..." He reached over, scooped another lump of grey, thick sludge into his bowl, and made inroads into devouring it.

Dellbright served some food to Aria. "All food is Oakheart's favourite," Dellbright explained as he helped her to some bread.

From that moment, everyone seemed intent on their food. Sophy played with the porridge, which was a little bland.

After a protracted silence, Oakheart tried to introduce some conversation. He spoke about the weather. He waxed long on the subject, today's weather, yesterday's weather and tomorrow's weather. He continued on about the bad weather last week, near the Argent Flow, the unseasonable weather last month in Silverdale atop the upper plateau and the freak storm in the Gilton Forest. Sophy repressed a shudder and the desire to roll her eyes. Was he a weather man? She had never heard anyone stretch out such a banal topic. She ground her teeth.

Aria ate and talked quietly to Dellbright. Sophy could barely swallow the food and turned her attention to Oakheart, examining his well-formed, large, long-fingered hands. There were calluses, from his sword, perhaps, and some minor scars from nicks and cuts. She thought furiously. He is a warrior. But they said he was an ambassador. Did that mean that it was dangerous here or was everyone a practiced swordsman? Maybe these Puri raiders they spoke about were real.

During conversation, Sophy noted that Aria was able to extract some information from Oakheart. His last name 'Silverbow' related to an archery competition he had won at the age of sixteen in his hometown of Silverdale. The prize had been bow etched in silver designs. Since then the name had stuck. Apparently people did not take parent's names generally as a last name, but took on the name of the place they were born, some event in their lives, or a personal characteristic. That approach sounded chaotic but interesting.

Oakheart stood up when he finally finished eating, long after everyone else. "We leave within the hour, miladies."

"Where are you taking us?" Sophy said, rising out of her seat. Aria for once didn't object.

"Why, to Valley Keep," Dellbright said. "Do not be concerned. You will be well cared for."

That comment riled Sophy. "What if we don't want to go there and be cared for?" She failed to keep the sarcasm from her voice.

"Where else would you go?" Oakheart asked.

"Nowhere," Aria said before Sophy could answer. "We are happy to go to Valley Keep with you.

"You might be but I'm not."

"We don't have anywhere else to go, Sophy. I'm prepared to trust them at least.'

Oakheart held open the tent flap. "Do you ladies know how to ride? I can send for a caravan, if you cannot."

Sophy was cornered. Her gaze shifted from Aria to Dellbright and to Oakheart. What if she said no? Would Aria go without her? Would they leave her here by the woods alone in a strange place—abandoned? A sliver of fear pressed into her gut.

"Lady Aria?" Dellbright prompted, smiling that sexy smile of his.

Aria smiled shyly. "Oh...I can ride a little...but I'm not very confident."

Dellbright nodded. "Do not worry. I will see to your comfort." He glanced at Sophy. "My lady?"

"I can ride," Sophy grumbled, though she kept her militant stare on Oakheart. She was no dressage expert, but she had done quite a few trail rides in her time.

Later, when they walked over to where the horses stood in a line, saddled and ready, she thought she understood. Green clad guards addressed Dellbright as my lord prince. Sophy cursed under her breath. Why did he have to be a prince? Aria's smile widened. No wonder he acted annoyed that Sophy hadn't addressed him properly. However, he had not informed them of his status or instructed them on the correct way to address him. It was his bad luck if he was offended.

The men mounted their horses and climbed into their carts, stacked high with tents and equipment.

Oakheart sidled up and introduced her to Merrywillow, a white palfrey. The leg up he gave her into the saddle nearly threw her over the other side. By the look on his face, her slight weight surprised him. "Forgive me, Lady Sophy," he said awkwardly and moved off to his mount.

Riding astride, the flare of the dress covered her legs amply, leaving only her booted feet on show. At that moment she realised why they had been provided with the strange leggings. It meant they could ride astride with comfort. Oakheart swung up easily onto his horse, which was taller than the rest. She could see that he looked at home in the saddle, his broad shoulders relaxed. He was muscled and tanned, though he was nowhere as near as dark as his cousin. He looked about twenty-five in the daylight. She chanced a sneak look at Dellbright, who seemed even younger.

Keeping her gaze on Dellbright surreptitiously, she pretended to arrange her gown, tucking the skirt between her legs and the saddle to prevent it flying up. Dellbright assisted Aria onto the remaining horse. Sophy gaped when he swung up behind her friend, holding her gently around the waist. Sophy's hands turned to fists, but she couldn't take her gaze away.

Aria looked a trifle ill at ease with the close contact. She caught Sophy's look, blushed and looked away. Dellbright talked to Aria, edging her curls away from her ear to speak to her. Dread was building in Sophy's stomach. That little fool, she thought angrily. Had Aria any inkling of what she was doing and of how complicated things could get if she involved herself with Dellbright? Adventures were fine, but they could be dangerous, too. They had no understanding of the situation, the politics or even the morals of this place. Part of her was annoyed that she was more disturbed by the adventure than she thought she should be. Wasn't she supposed to be the brave one?

Oakheart's hail, signalling departure, made her jerk around. The noise of all the men and horses assaulted her and her mount lurched forward to follow Oakheart. Sophy looked over her shoulder, while clutching the pommel of the saddle, to make sure that Aria was indeed following. Dellbright directed his horse after Sophy's and the green and blue clad guards closed in behind.

A pathway of downtrodden grass opened up in front of them. Merrywillow stretched out her gait as she instinctively kept pace with Oakheart's mount. Not dissimilar to the trail riding horses she'd ridden. Sophy held on, clinging to the reins and holding tight with her thighs, conscious of maintaining a good posture despite the irritating dress. If the horse shied she could go flying off its back and land face first into the long grass. Oakheart's powerful arms held the reins of his horse loosely, his thighs snug in the saddle.

As they rode along, Sophy's rear took a pounding. This trek was far longer, and brisker, than any average trail ride. She became tired and began to flop about inelegantly in the saddle while her horse bounded after Oakheart. It must have been half a day of hard riding before Oakheart called a stop to rest the horses. After dismounting by a fast-flowing stream that cut through a meadow carpeted in tiny red flowers, Sophy surreptitiously rubbed her behind on the trunk of a tree. The muscles in her thighs and calves twitched.

Aria, after being assisted to dismount by Dellbright, admired the flowers, the stream, sky and everything else she could lay her eyes on. Sophy could only manage a cruel stare at anyone who crossed her path. Suspicion, as well as her painful behind, was making her miserable. No one had gallantly assisted her off her horse. Oakheart was busy with his men and joking with Dellbright. Aria smiled and gave a little wave as Dellbright again helped her into the saddle. After a few tries, Sophy managed without assistance to gain her seat. She hoped her articulate grunt as she landed on the saddle went unnoticed.

Oakheart led the way after he remounted and sped away. A bit further on, where a smattering of farms dotted the landscape, she could see that the purple haze in the distance had resolved into a mountain range. Oakheart leapt a hedge unexpectedly. Before she realised what was happening Merrywillow decided to follow suit. Leaning forward as her horse jumped, she let out a squeal before settling back into the saddle on the other side. When she crested the next hill, she found that Oakheart had paused. Grinding her teeth, she was ready to shout at him for not warning her about the jump. Then Merrywillow, to her annoyance, walked slowly up beside his mount and gave a little whinny. Irritating horse. Be much more fun if she could control it properly.

Her gaze roamed about the countryside, and then she looked down into the valley, her breath stolen away. Partially obscured by mist was a valley. Further on, she could see the crest of the foothills, nestled below the snow-drenched mountain range. Seated within the valley was a white castle with nine mad spires that seemed more decorative than functional, with pendants snapping in the breeze. As the mist lifted, a small settlement and a smattering of neat farms came into view.

"That is amazing," Sophy said. It was so calm, so green and clean. She heard Aria's intake of breath as she rode up.

Dellbright spoke at last, breaking into their spellbound thoughts. "Behold, Valley Keep, my home and seat."

"It's beautiful," Aria whispered and smiled at Dellbright, her green eyes never leaving his clean-shaven and handsome face.

Sophy glanced at Oakheart. He seemed to notice the mutual attraction, too. When he saw Sophy's look, his face closed over, leaving her to wonder at his thoughts and feelings. Was it possible he was attracted to Aria as well?

The ride through the valley was leisurely compared to the earlier hasty jaunt. Sophy had time to survey the farms, with their fields of standing young, green grain. She smiled nervously at the few farmers, who bowed and waved as their pretty procession passed. It took another full hour before they reached the keep's gate. As they drew closer to the entrance, she realised that the keep's walls glowed softly as if they were made of white marble, lit by an inner light. A faint headache crouched behind her eyes. The surrounding area smelled and looked clean and that surprised her. Castles usually smelled unpleasant from what she had read, because there was no plumbing and horses and people were crammed inside a closed-in building. Yet, there was none of that. She frowned; did this mean it was all an elaborate stage set of some sort? With no real history to it? She looked again, peering around the corners of the out-buildings as she rode by in search of a rubbish heap, but found none. They really were no longer in Scotland.

In the cobbled courtyard, the horse hooves clattered as they rode up before the entrance with its heavy wooden doors. Hands came and held her horse as she dismounted gingerly. Her leg muscles pulled and twitched painfully when she jumped down. She ached to rub her behind, but didn't want to let on that she was suffering. When Oakheart looked her over casually she straightened her spine, denying her fatigue.

Ignoring him, she tugged at her dress, arranging the folds of the skirt until Aria, smiling, joined her. Sophy held back the impulse to smack Aria on the behind.

"This place is magical; made of the stuff of dreams." Aria's complexion glowed richly as she spoke.

"Yeah...bad dreams," Sophy replied sourly.

"How could you? This place is...and Dellbright is so..."

"I know, I know."

❧ 4 ❧

IN VALLEY MIST

ARIA STOOD in the courtyard fighting to contain her emotions. The keep radiated a power that lapped over her in gentle waves. People milled around and she could see that they were good people—actually see it. In amongst them was poor Sophy, looking hollow and out of place.

Into this throng, Dellbright strode. "Willow Reed?" he called to a stout man, who rushed out to greet them. The man bowed low, his white cloak billowing behind him.

Willow Reed opened his arms wide and beamed a huge smile at them all. "Welcome. Welcome. I have been waiting for you." He halted, dropped his mouth open, gaped at Aria and Sophy and said, "'Tis true. There are two of them."

"Willow," Dellbright said, his voice containing a hint of warning.

Willow shook himself and headed over to bow low over Aria's hand. "My lady," he said.

"Pleased to meet you, Willow Reed," Aria said and smiled.

"My Chamberlain," Dellbright said by way of explanation. "Lady Aria and Lady Sophy."

Willow bowed low to Sophy, too, and Aria could see that his

expression hardened as if she was repellent to him. Willow turned away to talk to the prince.

With a puzzled frown on her face, Sophy came up to Aria and commented, "Do I have a sign on my forehead that says disregard at will?"

"Of course not. I...err...don't get paranoid."

Aria was distracted by Willow speaking to Dellbright again.

"How pleased I am that you have come back, your Highness." He bowed to Oakheart as well. "Your excellency."

Dellbright leaned closer to Willow and whispered something. The chamberlain hurried back into the castle with his white robe flaring out behind him. Dellbright offered Aria his arm, and they followed the bustling chamberlain into the light airy vestibule. Here, within the slight shadows, stood a regal lady, who offered Aria and Sophy a shy smile.

"Please meet my mother, Aurore," Dellbright said, standing to the side to allow his mother to come forward.

"I am pleased to meet any friend of my son's," Aurore said, with a voice that was quiet and touched with sadness.

Aria's wide smile was genuine as she curtsied low. "Your highness," she said. Aria was happy to be called a friend of Dellbright's. She nudged Sophy, who, after a slight pause, followed suit with a reasonable curtsy.

"Oh, what charming girls." Aurore was dressed in a simple, brown and cream gown that oozed elegance, her brown hair neatly arranged on top of her head. Her skin was pale in comparison to Dellbright's, though her olive complexion was still evident.

"You are too kind, your highness," Aria asked.

Aurore's smile widened. "Call me Aurore. You will find us informal at the best of times. I was never a princess in the full sense of the word. Please, come this way. I must say, Lady Aria, that your hair is a most becoming colour..."

"Thank you," Aria replied. She glanced over her shoulder at Sophy, who looked pale. Slowing, she put Sophy's hand onto the crook of her elbow. "Come on," she whispered and tugged her along.

Sophy smiled tentatively. Aria could feel her hand tremble. How could Sophy not be enjoying this moment? They were in a prince's castle for heaven's sake. What had happened to her bold, adventurous friend?

⌘

STILL WITHIN THE VESTIBULE, SOPHY WATCHED THE VARIOUS exchanges of glances, although her headache had pounced to her forehead and was trampling her brow with thumps of pain. She gritted her teeth and clung to Aria's elbow. Headache, fatigue and something else was drawing away her energy. Her gaze was drawn to the walls, which were made of the same white marble-like substance as the outside. There were a few items of wooden furniture, chairs, chests and shelves placed in niches or corners. Servants, plump and well-washed, brought wine in gem-encrusted goblets and orders flew around to arrange sleeping quarters, a meal and clothes. Standing apart from the others, Sophy soon became lost in the hubbub their arrival had caused.

Before entering the keep, Sophy thought her headache was caused by the clamour of everyone milling around, talking excitedly, and the servants running here and there. Now her headache clanged like a gong. Through the haze, she heard Aria comment. "The keep's stone walls are amazing and so intricately formed."

Master Willow smiled beatifically in response to Aria's praise. "The material itself is bounty, and it was shaped by the *given* and craft. The blending of these has imbued the fabric of the keep with the life of the land." He moved to the wall of the vestibule, where on one side the stairs led up and opposite was the entranceway to a large hall. "Come, lay your hand or your cheek against it, my lady," he said to Aria. His gaze raked over Sophy. "Please, Lady Sophy, you must feel it also."

Aria strode forward and laid her palm and then her cheek against the wall. Her eyes widened as a smile lit her face. "It's a heartbeat, slow and resounding. So beautiful...so...Sophy you must try it," she said.

Sophy approached the wall and a rhythmic pulse of tension set her teeth on edge. She edged closer, with eyes closed and face clenched.

"Come on, Sophy, it won't bite you," Aria said.

Reaching out her hand, Sophy moved in close to touch the wall. Her fingers made contact. There was a resounding boom and she blacked out.

THE CEILING, PAINTED WITH FUZZY, COLOURFUL FLOWERS, LOOMED overhead. Sophy didn't remember the hall looking quite like this. Blinking helped her refocus her vision. Moving her head made her moan. She was in an airy apartment. There was a rustle of fabric to her left and then the sound of a soft step.

"What happened?" she gasped to no one in particular. Aria came into view dressed even more becomingly than before. Sophy's jaw dropped. Aria's gown was ivory silk, with a bodice embroidered with gold thread and inlaid with gems. Loose sleeves, adorned with a co-ordinated trim of embroidery, floated around her arms. The crystal leaf necklace glittered at her neck like a diamond. The only thing spoiling this fairy tale image before her was a face creased with concern.

Aria's cool hand touched Sophy's brow. "How are you? I was so worried. You fainted when you touched the wall."

"Yeah...well...it's nothing. A headache, that's all," she replied, propping herself up on her elbows to look around the room. The pain had receded somewhat. At least she was conscious now. She was on a bed, in the middle of the room. Through the tall and narrow windows, a slight breeze shifted pale, translucent curtains. "This keep certainly wasn't built for defence, was it?"

Aria cast a careless look in the direction of the windows, pursed her lips and shrugged.

"It's very decorative...but enough of that. Don't you want to know what's happened since you passed out? It must have been ages ago by now."

"That long, huh?" Sophy said.

"I forgot. I'm supposed to let them know how you are so we can decide about a meal. You can eat something can't you?"

"Sure," she replied wearily, her stomach lurching at the thought.

Aria floated to the doorway and spoke to someone there. Then she hurried back to Sophy's bedside. "Are you sure you are well enough to join us? You're still so pale."

Sophy nodded. She did feel better. More importantly though, she wanted to find out what was going on—why the sudden change from prisoner to honoured guest and why did they treat her with distrust when they appeared to accept Aria?

"Help me get up?" she asked in a weak voice, holding out her hand. When she finally climbed to her feet and stood, she wished she hadn't. Her legs and her lower back felt caught in a vice.

"Come into the bathroom," Aria urged, leading Sophy, hobbling and doubled-up, into the adjoining chamber. "You'll never guess what marvels they have in this place," Aria began.

"Ughhh. That hurts." Movement seemed to multiply her ailments.

"There's plumbing and hot water. See," Aria said pointing excitedly to a tub, filled with steaming water, which had an array of flower petals floating on top. She started relating how the pipes worked and how the sun heated the water.

It looked inviting, but as Sophy was feeling miserable; she didn't care how the water came to be where it was. She wanted to soak the soreness from her bones and muscles.

Later, Aria popped her head in. "Let me help you with your hair. There is some special soap in a pot that will make your hair shine. See," she said, flinging freshly washed ginger curls her way.

"Nice." Sophy eased herself down so that the water lapped against her chin then put her head back to wet her hair.

"Everything is so wonderful here." Aria sighed, her eyes losing focus. "Oh, and Aurore is so nice to me," Aria added, helping rinse the soap from Sophy's hair.

"Don't you have any sense of danger?" Sophy asked.

Aria blinked. "No. I told you, I can tell these people are good. If you can't see it, I don't know how I can explain it to you. It is as plain to me as the colour of your hair."

"My lady," said a young sounding voice from outside the door.

Aria's eyes lit up. "That's Rae, the maid. Will you be okay?" she asked, standing up and heading out into the bedroom.

"Sure." Sophy closed her eyes, lulled by the warm comfort of the water.

"Hurry up," Aria called from the other room. "You've got to see this."

"See what?"

"This," Aria said from the doorway, holding up a gown. "It's for you." The fabric had a silver sheen and was trimmed with a black scrollwork design of interlacing swirls. It wasn't encrusted with gems as Aria's gown was, but they would have detracted from the beauty of the fabric and the scrollwork.

"What the hell," she said, hands on the edge of the tub. "What is it with these people? Where do they get these clothes from?"

Aria rushed out, came back in to help her out and wrapped her in a linen towel.

"They make them here at the keep, so Aurore told me."

Sophy lifted one pained and sceptical eyebrow. "Sure they do."

Aria ignored Sophy's cynicism. "It is the local industry. Apparently, there is some plant that grows naturally around here, and they use it to make fibre. Sort of like flax and linen, but not...if you know what I mean."

"No...can't say I do. Sewing and fabric is your interest, not mine. Could never understand why you and Maralain could get glassy-eyed over fabric or yarn."

Aria cast her a hurt look. "Really, there's not so much to understand. There, you look better already." She kept her arm around Sophy and helped her out of the bathroom.

Sophy fingered the cloth, while Aria grabbed another towel and dried her hair. "Is it made from craft or *given?*"

"Totally crafted here at the keep. Aurore told me that they are most famous for their dresses."

Sophy held the dress against herself. "That's a relief. I don't think the *given* agrees with me."

After she put it on, she had to admit that it was heavenly to wear. Too bad there was no mirror to look into. The dress was pretty and at least it gave her confidence to face their captors, or was that hosts?

A swarthy young girl, with a pretty heart-shaped face, came to assist their preparations.

"This is Rae," Aria said. "Come on, sit down and Rae will do your hair and finish mine."

Rae set down a basket of flowers. With Sophy, she dried her hair with a heated metal rod to dry it into long ringlets then wove some of the flowers into them. Rae didn't talk much and smiled sweetly when spoken to. The scent of the small flowers wove a relaxing spell on Sophy.

"Okay, that's enough," Aria said. "It's time."

Sophy followed Rae and Aria down the stairs. Lit with the glow of many candles and lanterns, she could see about thirty people gathered within the large room. A fire burned in the huge hearth and the scent of aromatic wood wafted throughout. Sophy noted how clean the hall was and how the air was not filled with smoke and foul odours. "Aria?" she said, pulling on her arm and pointing at the candles that didn't smoke.

"They're firesticks, not candles. They summon the flame from the wood without consuming it. Same with the fire. It's *given.*"

"Oh. An environmentalist's heaven, then." Fascinated, Sophy gaped at the firesticks. She started when Prince Dellbright came forward and bowed low over her hand. "How do you fare, Lady Sophy?"

"Well, thank you," she replied, gently pulling her hand back.

"You gave us quite a scare," he said, narrowing his eyes. "Are you sure you will not avail yourself of our resident physic?"

"I'm fine, really...your highness."

"Very well. Come, join us." He stepped back and gestured for them to precede him.

The tables, arranged in an arch shape, looked nearly full. Dellbright led Aria to a seat next to Aurore and Sophy to a seat next to Oakheart.

"Good evening, your excellency," Sophy said politely, though tense with headache and uneasiness. She didn't like to be separated from Aria or thrust between Dellbright and Oakheart. Every muscle in her body was crying out in rebellion. Biting her lip in concentration so she would not cry out, she eased into her seat. Oakheart returned her greeting at the same moment Dellbright sat next to her, disconcerting her. The prince had Aria on one side and herself on another.

"I was enquiring after your health, my lady," Oakheart said, obviously annoyed at having to repeat himself.

Sophy swung her head in his direction and blinked. "Much better, thank you," she said, trying to smile and quell her rebellious stomach at the same time.

"You look improved," he commented neutrally.

"Come, let us eat. But first a toast to our guests," Dellbright said, standing with his goblet held high. Sophy frowned at her goblet. Guests? Aria was the guest. She was the baggage. She fingered the goblet, thinking that she really couldn't stomach the wine. Staring over the rim at the people gathered for the feast, she pretended to be interested in it.

"To the Gift of Crystal Tree Woods," Dellbright said, raising his goblet at Aria. He made to drink his wine and hesitated. There was a pregnant pause, in which Dellbright turned toward Sophy, lifted the goblet again, as if in afterthought, and drank his toast.

Puzzled, she raised her goblet. What a strange toast, she thought. Perhaps it was the Argenterran equivalent to 'cheers'.

Sophy played with her food and alternated between that and watching Oakheart's disappear from his plate. Obviously, it did not pay to distract him from a meal. Occasionally, Dellbright intruded, enquiring if she had sufficient food, or if she wanted a certain morsel further down the table.

"Are you not hungry?" Oakheart asked as he reached for more roast vegetables.

"Not really."

"But you are so thin and light weight. Food is a good remedy to that."

"I realise that. What are those?"

"These?" he said, brandishing his triple-spiked eating implement, currently occupied by what looked like potatoes. "Toffelbread roasted with honey."

"Oh, like the porridge? I thought you called it Toffelporridge."

"Yes. A staple food. We eat it sweet, too, baked slowly in milk and honey and flavoured with spice."

"Let me guess...it's your favourite."

He deftly cut some more meat. "Of course. Wine?"

"No, I already have a headache." Sophy said, watching the meat go the way of the rest of the food in the near vicinity.

Sophy hazarded a surreptitious glance at Oakheart. His face was neutral. She had the impression that it wasn't his face at all, but a mask that hid the real Oakheart. It was the same impression she had earlier, and that was puzzling. She should be more accustomed to him by now and able to read him better. She must have been staring because when he turned his green eyes to hers, she blushed. He returned his attention to the food, glancing at her occasionally, sometimes with an expectant look on his face. Just when she thought he was ignoring her, he said, "That there is Willow's cousin, Mayfred and his wife, Vivia. Next to him sits Race, Dellbright's man at arms. The men in blue are mine and the ones in green are Dellbright's."

Sophy nodded slowly. "You know them well?"

He shrugged. "Well, enough," he said returning to his meal. After swallowing a mouthful he added, "I should probably know them better than I do."

Dessert arrived.

"Your excellency," Sophy began.

"Oakheart," he said, reaching for a small tartlet.

"Sorry. I...ah..."

He turned his gaze on her. She could hear her heart thudding, but her words would not come out. She was arrested by the deep green of his eyes as he turned his full attention on her. Something in that look stirred her, made her breath catch. His eyes were at odds with the unremarkable blandness of his face. She gulped, trying to form her words again.

"You have a very nice horse," she said at last, her eyes flicking to her hands clasped in her lap. Drat! I'm an idiot.

"Thank you," he responded, lips curling in a slight smile. He turned his attention to the custard and sweet tarts.

A serving girl walked past. "Please, may I have some water?" Sophy asked. The girl smiled and went off presumably to fetch it. Within minutes, a huge pitcher of fresh water arrived. Several hails for the girl's services precluded her from serving it.

Reaching out, Sophy tried to grasp the handle and pour it, when Oakheart's muscled arm snaked out. He poured some water for her and then some for himself. Her eyes followed his arm, the line of the muscles up to his shoulder, his jaw and then his eyes. She tried to smile, only the attempt failed, so she grabbed her goblet and drank deeply. She spluttered and choked on the wine as she had mistaken the goblet.

Dellbright and Aria looked on in concern, as she coloured to a deep red while Oakheart pounded her none too gently on her back. By the time she recovered, Dellbright was back in deep discussion with Aria. Sophy wished to be anywhere else and couldn't bear the embarrassment a moment longer.

With relief, she watched the dessert cleared away. Aurore walked up to ask if she could escort them to their room. Sophy was out of her chair as fast as her stiff and sore body allowed. Aria halted her and urged her to curtsey and say goodnight to Dellbright and Oakheart.

"If it's no trouble to you, your highness, we are ready to retire," Aria said, curtsying. Sophy copied her movements and then backed away. When Aria followed Aurore to the vestibule, she asked about the keep. "How old is the building?"

"'Tis old," Dellbright's mother replied, as she led them up the staircase to the second floor.

Sophy trailed her hand over the carved, dark stained, wooden banisters, walking carefully so as not to jar her aching head.

"No one knows how old," Aurore continued. "'Twas before the adepts began to gather in Glassy Mountain Retreat and they have been doing that for more than five hundred years now."

"Adepts, your highness?" Aria asked.

"Adepts are special and dedicated people. After much study, adepts are capable of shaping the *given* in more intricate ways than normal folk. Not all adepts work with the *given* though. Some study the ancient texts and seek out mysteries that are beyond even my simple imagining."

"Sounds too much like university," Sophy said, as they walked up to a familiar door.

Aurore frowned slightly at Sophy's remark. "Here is your room. I bid you a good night..."

"Thank you for your hospitality, your highness," Aria said sweetly.

"Please, you must call me, Aurore. It will please me greatly," she said. Aurore smiled at Sophy, too, disarming her suspicion. "You, too, Sophy, must call me Aurore."

Aria bowed her head. "I'm sorry. It is hard to call you that if you are the mother of a prince."

Aurore reached out and patted Aria's head. "If the situation calls for it I will settle for 'my lady'. Yet I hoped we could be more intimate than that."

Aria lifted her face and smiled shyly. "I will try to remember, Aurore."

Aria bade their host good night, shut the door and leaned against it. "Oh, that was a success. You can't suspect them of anything underhand now."

"Oh I don't know," Sophy said yawning and lowering herself to the bed. "I can be suspicious enough for both of us." That earned her a frown and a snort from Aria, who went to the washroom.

❧ 5 ☙

THE MIST THINS

BIRD SONG, horses neighing and the friendly chatter of the keep's inhabitants woke Sophy the next morning. Gauzy curtains filtered sunlight into the room and as she sat up she became aware of the sound of water trickling. Aria's happy singing told her that she was bathing. The new gown that had been placed in readiness for her slid off the bed onto the floor.

Throwing off her bed covers, she retrieved the dress and stared at it for a while. Massaging her forehead, she waited for Aria to exit the bathroom.

Aria opened the door and pulled up short. "You're not still ill, are you?" Her hand brushed the crystal leaf at the base of her throat.

"No," Sophy replied with a careless wave of her hand.

"Do you like the new dress? Pretty, don't you think?"

"I guess." Sophy went to the washroom and came out dressed.

Sitting on the bed, Aria slipped on her shoes and glanced at Sophy with a frown.

"What's the mat—" Sophy began to ask.

A knock on the door interrupted her. Rae entered and curtsied. "Forgive the intrusion, I have brought the mirror you requested. The prince asks that you join him in the sunroom when you are ready." Two male servants carried in a draped piece of furniture and put a stool beside it.

"Thank you, Rae. Please tell the prince we'll be down soon," Aria went over to the draped mirror. "Sophy, I think you should do your hair in front of the mirror this time." Aria flicked off the cloth covering the glass and pulled out the stool.

"Okay." Sophy lifted her skirts gently and sat down in front of the mirror. When she saw her reflection in the mirror, her eyes widened. "Holy crap!" she yelled throatily and stood up in rush, sending the stool backwards with a thump. "I...I....I..."

Aria walked over and righted the stool. "I tried to tell you."

Sophy's hand shook as she leaned in and explored her face. Her eyes were dark, almost black, yet before she'd come to Argenterra, they had been an uncommon dark blue. Her skin, always pale, was faded and almost translucent, and her mouth and nose seemed slightly fudged. It was as if all her beauty had been erased. Sitting down again she said, "Is this what they see when they look at me?"

Aria drew the brush through Sophy's long dark hair. "It's what I see. I'm glad you can see it too. I was starting to worry. Don't you see that is why this place is so fascinating?"

"No." So this is what Aria had meant with those weird comments about her fading. They weren't the result of hysteria. No wonder the Argenterrans looked at her like that. No wonder they warmed to Aria instead of her. Her gaze met Aria's in the mirror. "Look, you go down and talk with the prince. I think I'll stay here." Sophy wished she could access the Internet and get support from her social media buddies. A big greasy pizza wouldn't go astray either.

"No." Aria tugged Sophy's hair. "We're in this together. How many times have I stood by while you flirted and chattered and enjoyed all the attention? Did you ever think about me? How I felt?"

"This is different. You weren't like this, altered by some unnatural means. You were shy." She narrowed her eyes. "You're not shy now, though. How come?"

Aria flicked her curls over her shoulder, revealing a smooth, creamy-skinned neck. "I feel confident and comfortable here. It's like this place fulfils me."

Sophy scratched behind her ear. "And it depletes me."

"Will you come downstairs?"

Sophy wanted to hide away. She had not realised until then how much of her ego had been bound up in her looks and athletic prowess. When she looked at Aria, so happy, so effervescent, she swallowed her self-pity and stood. "Okay. I guess they've already seen me like this. It can only get better. And let's ask Dellbright about what's going on."

"I wish you weren't so suspicious. I think they were being careful, and now they're relaxed."

"But I'm not relaxed. I have no phone, no information. I'm itching to post something on line. "'Modern girl sucked into vortex into land without Internet. Send help!'"

"Grow up! You spent too much time online anyway."

THE GIRLS ENTERED A SMALL STUDY, WHERE THE SUN SPILLED through the long, narrow windows and enlivened the colours in the richly embroidered fabric covering the furniture. Dellbright rose from an ornate wooden desk, instantly forgetting about the large pile of documents he'd been studying. Oakheart, too, put down the stringed instrument he'd been playing and rose to greet them.

Dellbright stepped forward, bowed over Aria's hand and then held it as he led her to a low settee where he placed himself next to her. Sophy plonked herself down in an unladylike heap in the chair. Oakheart looked startled. What did she care? She was ugly. She slouched into the chair and stared at the corner of the study where a shadow danced.

Aria and Dellbright spent some time in idle and uninteresting conversation until Aria coughed and cleared her throat. "My lord prince ..." Aria began and then faltered when Dellbright gazed into her eyes.

Sophy sat up suddenly and leaned forward in her chair.

"Please call me Dellbright."

Aria nodded. "Dellbright, we were wondering if there is something you are not saying about meeting us in Crystal Tree Woods."

Dellbright blushed and looked to his cousin.

Oakheart said, "Perhaps 'tis time."

"What is it? Is Sophy right? There's something going on?"

"As we mentioned before, every one hundred years or so an outlander woman comes to Crystal Tree Woods.'

"But there are two of us," Sophy said.

Dellbright's gaze burned into hers. "Yes, there are two of you, two that heard the call."

Aria was looking at Sophy strangely, as if to say 'what call?'. "And that's a problem?" Sophy asked.

"Unprecedented, but not a problem as such," Oakheart replied.

"Not a problem," Sophy repeated. "So what happens now?"

Oakheart leaned forward. "We have sent for Adage adept."

"Yes, Oakheart thought it best," Dellbright added. "The adept will advise us. Until then please stay with us and enjoy our hospitality."

"We will, won't we, Sophy? Thank you."

Sophy shrugged. What did it matter? They had come to welcome Aria, not her. Aria fitted in. She grabbed her aching head and repressed a moan. It hurt to think.

"You are unwell, my lady" Oakheart asked, sounding close.

Sophy's eyes opened, and she saw his genuine concern. "I need some fresh air."

He stood and held out his hand. "Please, let me be of service to you." He turned to the others, bowed politely to Aurore, who had just entered.

"If you will excuse us, I will escort the Lady Sophy outside for some exercise."

Dumbfounded, Sophy looked at his hand, then gingerly took it. He led her through the vestibule, out the front doors, out the gates and around and behind the keep to the fields and woods beyond. One of Oakheart's men followed them, doing his best to be inconspicuous. Sophy wondered why they had an escort. As soon as she was clear of the keep itself, her headache lifted. Then she debated whether it would be polite to remove her hand from his.

"Thank you, your excellency. I feel so much better already," she said, with a spring in her step.

He let go of her hand. She paused, feeling awkward, and moved ahead of him. The gardens, the woods, the fields brought a smile to her face. From where they stood, she saw the mountains, hung with mist.

"Most people call me Oakheart. You seem better. Sometimes I cannot tell if you are unwell or just do not like company."

Looking back at him, she smiled. "I like company but this place, particularly the keep, doesn't agree with me. I..."

"What troubles you?" he asked softly, as if he cared how she felt. A light breeze lifted a tuft of his white blond hair and placed it on his forehead. He wiped at it idly.

"Tell me about these women who arrive in the woods every one hundred years or so. What happens to them?"

His expression became neutral again. "The Gift of Crystal Tree Woods usually stays at Valley Keep."

"That will please Aria. She loves it here."

"So you think Aria is the gift?' he said, sounding thoughtful.

"Kind of obvious, isn't it? She looks so vibrant and alive here. She is accepted while..."

"You are not," he said, completing her sentence. She tried to read his expression to gauge his sincerity, but he remained unreadable, only his eyes seemed real.

"What would she do here if she stayed? Marry the handsome prince?" Sophy meant it as a joke, but the widening of Oakheart's eyes confirmed her suspicion.

Her hand flew to her gaping mouth. "Oh my god. I must stop her," she said turning away.

"I beg you to do no such thing. Let matters run their natural course." He touched her forearm lightly.

"Natural course? But it is all a set up. The clothes. My god, the dresses. They were all for her. For luring her to stay here."

He blocked her escape. "The dresses are part of the normal course of events that follow the arrival of the Gift of Crystal Tree Woods."

"But we came here together. We're in this together."

He lowered his voice. "Aria told me you were sisters, but not of blood."

"We were friends in school and when my mother abandoned me, her parents took me in and fostered me."

"So she explained. You have a double bond then. One that is not easily severed."

"What am I thinking? Aria would not do anything as silly as marrying Dellbright."

"You think marriage silly?"

"Don't twist everything I say. She hardly knows him, or this place. How can she make such a commitment to some man she hardly knows and in a strange place, one that we don't understand?"

"You confuse love and reason."

"Do I? Well they don't have to be mutually exclusive."

Sophy set a brisk pace to the edge of the woods, trying to calm down. Oakheart suddenly turned toward her. "You must give us time. Things are not always as they seem. You also are a Gift of Crystal Tree Woods. If you are not the one to remain at Valley Keep, there is still a home for you here."

"What do you mean? What would I do?"

He shook his head. "I am speaking generally. The world is a strange place and sometimes things remain hidden. I like to think that we can see beyond our first impressions. You will keep your own counsel about what we have discussed?"

She nodded. "I hope that Aria has more sense than you give her credit for," she said as Oakheart led the way back to the keep.

❧ 6 ❧

THE RIGHT TARGET

FOR THE NEXT FEW DAYS, Sophy's head ached constantly while she was in the keep. Keeping her word to Oakheart about what happens to the Gift of Crystal Tree Woods became more difficult daily. Aria grew distant and spent a lot of time sighing when Dellbright was absent from the room. Sophy took walks with Aria, Dellbright and Oakheart in the pastures around the keep after the noontide meal, or lunch as she still called it. Only outside did her headaches disappear completely. However, they usually sat in the sunroom in the morning, like plump pillows, while her head pulsed and she gritted her teeth. It did not make her good company.

On day five, Aurore came to their room to invite them to meet the ladies of the keep and join the womanly activities. Sophy wanted to barf at the thought. Womanly activities?

"My son is busy this morning and he asked me to entertain you."

"That would be lovely. Thank you," Aria replied before Sophy could protest. As Aria was already dressed, she left immediately with Aurore.

Sophy did her best to delay going to the sewing room but in the end had to show her face. On entering, she was targeted by Dela, who offered her seat to Sophy.

"Thank you, Dela. That is very kind of you," Sophy said, knowing it

53

was important to be polite at all times, even to people you didn't like much. The day before Aria had spent what had to have been at least an hour drumming in the requirements for feminine discourse at the keep. Sophy had to repress snide comments about Aria being the resident expert on the native politics.

Dela held up a threaded needle. "Would you like to sew a few stiches on our tapestry?"

Sophy eyed the needle and then the tapestry. "Ah, no thanks. I'd rather not."

Dela's eyes widened and then her brows arrowed together. "Please, you would honour us."

Aria was in deep discussion with Aurore about the merits of a particular cloth and was therefore unavailable for friend rescuing. Sophy gulped. "I don't sew."

The other women gathered round, giggled, and waved their hands, expressing their disbelief. Sophy realised they thought she was being coy. "I'm serious. I can't sew. I hate sewing."

Dela narrowed her gaze and stuck out a persistent jaw. "I insist you try. This tapestry is a communion among us. All of us have put some small effort into it."

By then Sophy was quite annoyed. Dela was pushy and that made her want to rebel.

"Very well, for you I'll try."

Sophy grabbed the needle, fumbled with it awkwardly and then stabbed an empty section of the tapestry with it. There was a collective gasp behind her. She angled around the tapestry suspended in its frame, pulled the needle through the other side to complete the stitch and tied a knot. Then, with a touch a class, she bit the thread to break it.

The gazes of the women were riveted to the tapestry, their faces a study in abject horror. Sophy shrugged and stepped back to her seat, handing the needle back to Dela. The room was silent, even Aria had stopped talking.

"Oh dear. I forgot to say that Sophy doesn't sew," Aria said gaily.

Dela opened her mouth a few times. "B...but what use is she, if she has no skill?"

Aria walked up and said, "Sophy is family and a good friend. She has no need to sew."

Dela's face turned quite green. With a nod to her gathered friends, they descended upon the tapestry and spent an age unpicking 'the stitch' while discussing it at great length.

Aria went back to her discussions with Aurore. With a fair amount of decorum, Sophy left the room, ran down the stairs and out into the courtyard. She was vacillating about which direction to take when she was accosted by Oakheart. Mortified, she knuckled the tears from her eyes and kept her head down.

"Excellency," she said with a curtsey.

"Lady Sophy. I did ask that you call me Oakheart." He smiled in a bland sort of way. "Do you shoot with a bow and arrow? I will have one of my men bring some weapons for practice." He signalled to a guard decked out in a blue and silver tabard. The guard ran over, listened to Oakheart's instructions and ran into the armoury.

Sophy perked up. Some activity, at last! "I had a lesson or two...but do women here need to shoot with bow and arrow?"

"Need?" He shrugged. "I think not. However, Lady Aria mentioned that you do not like needlework and that your preferences were for more adventurous activities. I do not suppose that archery is as adventurous as you could wish. But I imagine it may be a little more exciting for you than embroidering a cushion."

"You can't have heard about 'the stitch' already. It only just happened."

"Stitch?" His eyebrow lifted. "No, I haven't. 'Tis a good story perhaps?" he said, with a touch of boredom in his voice, hinting that he did not want to hear about it. He gestured for her to follow him.

"I'm sure it will become one," she said with a frown. She was wondering if failure to excel with needle and thread would forever lower everyone's opinion of her. "By the way, I'm not that good at archery."

"Please, do not fret about your lack of skill. I can tutor you, if you do not mind instruction." He turned, took the equipment from the guard, and they continued on toward the practice field behind the keep.

Only the lightness of his step betrayed any emotion. He, she thought, was as happy to be outdoors as she was. They trod the path that led to the woods, but turned to the left where it forked. The woods looked inviting. The scent of trees, bushes, dirt and streams cast an allure. Her headache was almost completely gone, and the memory of Dela's cutting words blunted, she was able to smile with pure pleasure.

Oakheart stopped suddenly and carefully laid the quivers of arrows down. While holding two unstrung bows in his hand, he slid a bag of gear to the ground and dropped it next to the arrows.

"You will find a bracer and gloves in there," he said, pointing to the cloth bag. She bent down to fish them out. Working the gloves onto her hands, she watched him string the first of the bows. With an effortless flow, he reversed the bow, leant on it and slipped the string onto the end. She was glad he had done it for her. Although she could string a bow, sometimes it took a few awkward attempts before she managed it. And Oakheart's bows looked larger and stronger than any modern one she had ever used.

Sophy struggled with the leather ties of bracer.

"Here, let me help you," he said, holding his hand out to her. Silently, she watched him pull the ties securing the bracer to her forearm. "Ready," he said, as he tossed her the larger of the bows. She caught it neatly mid grip. It struggled in her hand as if it disliked her touch. A quick sensation of nausea assaulted her, and she tossed it back to him. He caught it deftly in his right hand, an eyebrow lifted in query.

"What is wrong? Do you like not the bow?"

"It is very beautiful," and it was intricately carved, "but it feels strange, alive..."

"Interesting observation," he replied, lifting the bow and caressing the carvings. "It is carved from a branch a very special tree and was wrought by the adepts with the craft and *given*."

"I see—the *given* again."

"Yes, it was a gift I received on my last sojourn in the Adepts' Retreat."

"Do you go there often?"

"Not as often as I like...'tis like a second home." He passed the second bow, which she accepted gingerly. It was sturdy, wooden and held no *given* as far as she could tell. It was the right size for her, at least.

"You travel a lot, I understand."

He smiled and his green eyes caught the sun and twinkled. "I travel most of the time. I haven't been everywhere in Argenterra, but most places"

"Don't you like to stay in one place?"

"What do you ask me, my lady? Will I settle down? Marry? Wed myself to home and hearth?"

Her eyes widened. Why would he think she asked that? Sophy thought he sounded touchy about the subject. "I was just curious about your job, and what it means to be an ambassador."

"Oh...is that what you ask me?" He let out a breath slowly. "Well...I travel with my comforts, and I have many friends all across the land. The high king values my work and that is enough satisfaction for me. I will not be his ambassador forever, so I value what opportunities this employment gives me, while it does. Now, show me how you shoot."

Sophy braced the arrow, closed an eye and took aim. The target was further than she had ever tried before. She pulled the string, relaxed and let the arrow fly. Although her aim was true, her shot lacked strength, and the arrow only bounced from the target rather than piercing it, as it should have. "Typical. Great."

"You need to keep your arm straight. Your elbow is turning in. Also, your stance is not good," commented Oakheart, handing her another arrow.

She shifted, trying to put into practice his comments, although she resented the fact that she needed instruction. She tried again and again until she had used the full quiver. There was some marginal improvement, some of the arrows stuck. Oakheart withheld comment. Either he sensed her mood or he was satisfied that she had taken his advice. She glanced at him, suddenly noticing that he had not aimed one arrow. Her eyes narrowed suspiciously. "What are you doing?"

"Watching you," he replied. "I will not shoot with bow and arrow today."

"How about you demonstrate for me? Show me how I should do it?"

With a negligent shrug, he hoisted his bow. "You could not copy me, my lady. You are a woman. I am a man. There are differences, in strength as well as in form." His eyes rested oh-so-briefly on her breasts, and then he faced the target. She glanced down. Surely they didn't interfere that much.

His man-at-arms handed him an arrow. Gaze transfixed he placed it, drew back the bow and released in one, powerful and smooth movement. The arrow rode the wind straight and true, thwacking against the target right through the bull's eye.

Sophy couldn't help but sigh. It was like watching a ballet, so perfect and fluid. Even if she practised for a hundred years, she could never shoot like that.

"I will return these to the armoury, my lady. You may like to explore the edge of the woods. I will return shortly to accompany you to the noontide meal."

"I'd love to take a short walk, near the edge, of course,' she said, pulling off glove and the bracer.

He bowed and he and his man gathered up the equipment, unstringing the bows and gathering up the arrows.

She strode lightly over the grass and into the shade of the trees at the edge of the wood. The crisp, moist air cleared her head, renewing her feeling of wholeness. Crunching leaves and twigs sounded in the silence as she moved closer in. Her hand rested on a trunk of a large tree, and she caressed the rough bark. Her foot crunched more leaves as she stepped further in.

The light darkened noticeably, as if a cloud obscured the sun. A mist formed up around her. Thick and cloying, it built up like a wall, blocking out even a glimpse of the tree trunks. It had been a clear, sunny day. The mist was upon her. It constricted, choked. Her heart beat faster, and sweat gathered in the small of her back. All around her was a wall of white.

"Oakheart?" she called. "Hello?"

The mist reached out, a tendril touched her cheek. She wiped at it, frowning at the strange motion. It seemed directed, not random. Its touch was wrong, dirty. Dodging the mist, her foot twisted and a sharp, hot pain shot up her leg.

It hurt to look at the wall of white. Dual red glows appeared, like a pair of eyes. Malevolent. Piercing. She cried out—the eyes moved towards her, straight and true like an arrow in slow motion.

"Sophy?" Oakheart's voice sounded in the distance. "Sophy," he called, louder, closer.

"Oakheart!" she yelled, unable to mask her fear. She heard his heavy tread and the crunch of leaves and branches as he jogged toward her. She swivelled about trying to estimate the direction he was coming from. The mist thinned, hastily evaporating. The glowing red eyes faded.

She saw Oakheart approaching, eyebrows drawn up in a frown. "Sophy?" he said, breathing a little agitated. "What happened? I could not see you."

"I was in the mist."

"Mist?" He was frowning but his eyes were alert.

Her frown matched his. "I was walking, and then all of a sudden there was a mist."

Oakheart looked up to the sky meaningfully. "It is fine. There is no mist today..."

"But there was! All around me. You said you couldn't see me. And what about the glowing red eyes?"

"Eyes?"

"Red eyes."

"You saw something?" he asked, suddenly thoughtful.

"You don't believe me?" She watched his face, his eyes, looking for a sign of disbelief or ridicule.

"I must believe what you say you saw. 'Twas strange that you disappeared from view. I thought at first you had ventured further within the woods or that you were hiding from me...but there you were at once revealed as I drew nigh. You were either hiding or..."

"Or what?" she said, now chilled and rubbing her upper arms.

"Or deliberately disobedient..."

Her head shot up. "Disobedient? Wait a minute, you..."

"Forgive my choice of words, my lady. But if you had strayed further in and harm had befallen you, the fault would have been mine. I took you from the keep, out of Dellbright's care, therefore, I am responsible for your welfare. Young ladies follow instructions so as not to come into harm..."

"Follow instructions?"

"Enough...we must return to the keep. The noontide meal..." He stepped away and gestured for her to walk ahead of him. She muttered under her breath about Oakheart and his stomach. He stared at her, mouth drawn into a thin line, but said nothing. He was silent as they walked.

Sophy let her anger die down. "Oakheart?" she said softly.

"What?"

"There really was something there..."

His gait slowed, as he neared her. "Sophy..."

"I wasn't hiding," she barged in. "Those eyes frightened me. I have no reason to lie."

"Do you not?"

"Why would I invent such a thing? Won't you at least consider that it happened?"

"Of course, I must consider all possibilities...but you will be careful and listen to instructions?"

"I will..." she said tersely, "consider it."

$$\mathcal{R} \quad 7 \quad \mathcal{R}$$

COURTSHIP NEVER HAD A
TRUER RING

ARIA WOKE FROM A RESTLESS NIGHT. Dellbright had asked her to come early to his study because there was something he wanted to discuss with her. Aria had had butterflies the whole night. Could he want to take their relationship further? Her hands shook as she tried to dress. Sophy slept soundly, after a particularly nightmare-filled night. Poor thing. Aria shook her head. They'd shared a room for years, and she'd never known Sophy to suffer from nightmares.

Rae smiled at her as she snuck out of the room. The maid was just starting her duties. Such a lovely girl, Aria thought, so considerate and understanding. Downstairs, the door to the study was ajar. Aria paused, with her hand on the door. This would be her first time alone with the prince. No chaperones. No Aurore, or Oakheart, or Sophy. Her heat thudded. Get a grip! You've been alone with a boy before.

A soft knock, and she pushed the door open. Dellbright looked up from his desk. "Aria," he said her name so softly it made her insides warm. He surged out of his chair and came forward, taking both her hands in his.

"Thank you for coming." He said it as if he doubted she would. Aria couldn't find any words, he looked at her so earnestly, his eyes bright. He lifted a finger and brushed a curl from her forehead and then ran it along her chin, lifting it.

Aria nearly fainted. Her heart beat fast and the pulse in her neck throbbed. His head lowered. He brushed his lips against hers, tentatively, until she relaxed and opened her mouth a little. Lifting his lips away, his gaze roamed over her face and he whispered. "So beautiful, so perfect." His mouth lowered again, and this time there was hunger in his kiss as he grabbed her to him. There was tension in his shoulders, a shuddering restraint as he eased off, releasing her.

"Will you marry me?" he asked her.

Aria blinked. "Yes." This is what she had hoped for but not allowed herself to expect. He'd told her the Gift of Crystal Tree Woods usually married the Prince of Valley Keep but had said there was no expectation that she should. As soon as she heard the story, she knew it to be right.

He grabbed her to him again. "You will be mine," he said his voice changing to low and gravelly. Then he kissed her, devouring her mouth. Aria kissed him back, tried to meet him halfway.

❧

By the end of the first week, Sophy began to fear that at any minute the thing would happen, the dreaded thing that she could not prevent but wanted to stop with all her heart. When she exited the bath, only Rae was around to assist her to dress. Aria's things were neatly arranged, her combs laid out in a row.

"Where is Aria?" she asked Rae.

"Well, my lady. I recall she left before you got up."

"Oh crap."

"What is wrong, my lady? Is something amiss?"

"Nothing. Pass me some shoes," she said to Rae, while she straightened her gown. "Please...thanks," she added as Rae passed them to her. Ramming them on her feet, she made for the door.

"But, my lady, what about your hair?"

Sophy paused and saw Rae's petrified expression. "Darn it." Her hair was sopping wet. She picked up her linen towel, dried her hair roughly and dragged a comb through it.

Rae stared at her, horror written all over her face. "Please, my Lady, Aurore will not like it. She will think me lax in my duty."

"Sorry, I'm in a big hurry." Sophy tugged the door open and ran out. She bounded down the stairs, taking them two at a time. She reached the great hall only to find that Aria wasn't there. Oakheart sat in a huge chair, reading some old book and he looked up vaguely as she hurried back out of the hall.

She darted towards the prince's study and barged in. Time stopped as the thick oak door groaned on its hinges and hit the wall with a loud bang. In the interim, she stood and watched Aria kissing Dellbright, really kissing him. They gasped and separated. She backed up a step as they looked at her, faces full of surprise and blushes.

Oakheart drew up behind her, blocking her exit. Dellbright smiled and love-light shone from Aria's pink face and glowing green eyes. Sophy's heart sank; she was too late. Oakheart put his large hand on her shoulder, preventing her escape.

Dellbright's smile broadened when his eyes fell upon Oakheart and, for the first time, Sophy saw real joy in his look. "My Lady Sophy, I am so glad that you have come." He walked over to her, took her hand in his and led her to the armchair she usually sat in. "I have such wonderful news. The Lady Aria has agreed to be my wife."

He looked at her expectantly. Sophy stared back and opened her mouth.

"But...but..." was all she could manage.

Oakheart's deep voice startled her. "Congratulations, cousin. It took you long enough," he said, laughing at the prince's embarrassment.

Sophy kept her head down, trying to come up with some inane response. At first, she couldn't look at Aria. Composed and as calm as she would ever be, she said, "Well, Prince Dellbright, you could not have chosen better." He seemed satisfied with that, and Aria moved into his embrace.

As her gaze travelled over the pair, Sophy fought the urge to blurt out the truth, that it was a trap, a set up, but the look of love in Aria's face stopped her. Dellbright looked equally smitten.

Sophy ducked around Oakheart and ran upstairs to her room. She hoped for and yet dreaded the moment that Aria would come. Yet when quite a while had passed, Sophy realised that Aria wasn't coming anytime soon. Aria was probably accepting the congratulations of all the keep's inhabitants, the simpering smiles of Dela and her cohorts.

When Oakheart had alluded to the fate of the Gifts of Crystal Tree Woods, she had supposed that Aria had more sense and that the bigger picture would be more important. Yet her foster sister appeared to be accepting of Argenterra. She had no desire to find a way home and had dived into the life at the keep as if she was a fish in a new pond.

Examining her feelings closely, Sophy realised she envied Aria; she could feel the *given*, her looks were enhanced and she was accepted. Accepted and wanted. That was the sticking point. Being the odd one out hurt, and Aria marrying Dellbright made matters worse. There was no way to quarantine the effect. Aria's actions now dictated the direction of Sophy's life.

She gave into the urge to weep. When she finally controlled her emotions, she dozed. It was late afternoon when she woke up. The mirror reflected an awful image. Eyes, bloodshot from weeping, dominated her face. Angry red stains on her pale skin gave her a mottled appearance. She took her time getting ready for the evening meal, changing her gown twice, hoping, at least, to let her red eyes fade.

There was a knock. Rae opened the door to stand nervously to the side as Oakheart came in. "We are all assembled. Will you join us to celebrate the pending marriage?"

"I am getting ready right now."

"Yet you delay." Oakheart's gaze ranged over her dress and her hair, which were perfectly adequate.

"I don't mean to. I can't help it."

"I do sympathise with your predicament, but your friend needs you right now." He turned on his heel and left the room. With one last look in the mirror, Sophy stood up and followed him.

When she arrived in the hall, the prince was standing and looked relieved when she appeared. Aria was seated and cast a concerned look at Sophy before she smiled tentatively. As she took her seat, she looked sideways at Dellbright. The prince coughed nervously and then began his speech. He spoke of the joy that had come to his house and to their land. Eventually, he came to the point, and there was an abounding cheer from those gathered, accompanied by the banging of goblets on the table. The prince bowed low to his followers, and Aria blushed becomingly.

The meal was disagreeable. Sophy wanted to drink wine to wipe out her misery, except Oakheart removed her goblet, and gave her water instead. She tried to fry him with a look, but he took no notice. She tried to stand and leave, but he held her gown so she had to stay. He was really beginning to annoy her so she accidentally-on-purpose spilled the gravy all over her gown.

"Oh?" she said. "I am so sorry." She looked around, encompassing all seated near, including the prince and Aria. "How clumsy of me. Please excuse me, I will have to go and change." She stood and, after a slight tug to release her gown from Oakheart's stubborn grip, left the hall.

When Aria came to their room Sophy pretended to be fast asleep, and refused to stir when Aria nudged her. It was very difficult; Aria was determined.

Early the next morning Sophy jolted out of a potent nightmare. As she drew in a hasty breath to calm her nerves, she noticed Aria standing by the bed.

"It's about time you woke up," Aria began in a no-nonsense tone of voice. "Come on, out with it. Don't tell me you're jealous?"

Sophy threw off the covers and leapt to her feet. "Jealous?"

"Yes, jealous."

"It's not that simple. You realise you're meant to marry Dellbright?"

"You mean the gift marries the prince custom. He told me about that but he loves me and I love him, so it doesn't matter."

Sophy drew her brows together. "You don't know anything about him, about this place. You have done nothing but dribble over Dellbright since we arrived here. There has to be more to this place than Valley Keep. What about trying to go home, and what about your parents?"

Aria's fist clenched and her cheeks began to darken. "My parents? As far as I know we can't go home and so there is no use pining away for my parents. I have to get on with my life. This world is everything. I am complete here, and I am welcome."

That barb sliced into Sophy's gut. "You've always been the logical one, never getting into trouble. Now you're being impulsive." She stopped for breath.

"Impulsive? Me? You don't think about anyone else except yourself...you..."

"Wait a minute," Sophy interrupted.

"No, you wait a minute. You've had your say, and I'm going to have mine. I love him. I'm happy here. There's nothing illogical in what I'm doing. It all makes perfect sense to me."

They stood there glaring at each other. Sophy slumped down on her bed, realising she didn't have the heart to continue arguing. "I'm sorry. I don't want to fight...I don't know what it all means. Can it really be an accident that we are here? Or is there some higher plan?" She buried herself in her bed covers.

Aria came over and hugged her.

"I can't go back. I can't stay here. I don't know what to do. Don't you see, we came here together? We're friends, almost sisters. That should mean something."

Aria rubbed her back and twirled her fingers in Sophy's hair. "Of course, we're friends, sisters always. Nothing can change that. But I love him, Sophy, truly I do. You can stay here with us. Dellbright says so."

"You really love him, then?" Sophy asked.

Aria purred softly, "Oh yes, he is heavenly."

"But it has only been a week. Perhaps you'll change your mind," Sophy said hopefully. "When is the marriage ceremony?"

"Very soon. Six or seven days, I think. The preparations have already begun. You must help, of course, and be my bridesmaid."

"So fast? Oh my God, what would your mother say?"

"I'm sure mother would be pleased for me. Now you won't have to call me princess, and your gown will be very special." Aria was smiling as she talked, her eyes distant as she imagined how it would all be.

"My gown?" Sophy felt out of touch with reality, or maybe Aria was.

"And afterwards you can see me every day..."

Sophy stared at Aria incredulously. Was life that uncomplicated? Sophy had seen enough with her parents to be scared of long-term commitment. And long-term commitment to a virtual stranger in a strange place seemed to be a recipe for disaster.

"Are you really sure?"

"I'm sure. I don't want to discuss it anymore or I will be cross with you. Okay?"

Sophy nodded. "I want you to be happy. Please be happy."

✺ 8 ✺

A GIFT REVEALED

Guilt plagued Aria for most of the morning after her confrontation with Sophy. How was she going to balance things in her new life? If only her foster sister was able to fit in, use the *given*, feel happy and content, then everything would go smoothly. After a while, once Sophy had adapted, Dellbright would find her a husband, and they would all live happily together. Was that such a bad proposition? She tried for a moment to put herself in Sophy's position and found it too difficult.

Aria checked her reflection. She would not like to have her looks degraded like Sophy's had been. She glanced around the room and wondered what it must be like to have the keep cause a headache all the time. Aria experienced nothing but contentment and joy. The feel of the keep was like soft sunlight on bare skin, bathing her in warmth and life.

There were many distractions with a wedding to organise within a week. She wanted to see Dellbright but he was cloistered with Willow. Oakheart was waiting to see him too, which meant she had to wait her turn. The high king's ambassador took precedence, and she believed their meeting was to discuss delaying Oakheart's departure until after the wedding. So with a contented sigh, she wandered into the great hall, which after the morning's bustle was fairly quiet. She found a

69

comfy chair by the window and started to put together a list. Dela brought her some tea and sat with her. They chatted about flowers and what was needed to decorate the bonding chamber. It was a brief respite before Aurore sent her a message to summon her to the sewing room.

Aria joined Aurore in the upstairs room where the keep's womenfolk worked on their fabrics. As Sophy hated all things to do with haberdashery, it was a good thing she wasn't there. Aurore had invited her to go over some fabric designs and, Aria thought, to try to become more acquainted with her future daughter-in-law. Dellbright's mother had a way with design, but more than that she could shape patterns in cloth with the *given*.

"Come sit with me. I'll show you how I made this pattern."

Aria sat close as Aurore leant over a partially unrolled bolt of cloth. She saw Aurore, or more importantly felt her, use the *given* on the fabric. It fascinated her.

"Do you wish to try?" Aurore asked when she had finished embellishing a pale pink silk-like cloth with tiny star shapes. The shapes were in a darker shade of pink, as if Aurore had leached the dye from the surrounding material and forced it into the shapes.

"Me?" Aria shook her head. "I couldn't do anything like that."

Aurore frowned and stared at her for a few minutes. "You can feel the *given*? Is that right?"

"Yes. I can feel it all around me."

Aurore rubbed her chin. "All around you? If that is the case, then you can do something as simple as this with no problem at all. Why not start with a very small piece? We can make ripples in the colour. Then you'll see that you can do it."

Aria nodded. "If you think so. We don't have the *given* where we come from."

"If you can feel the *given* then you can certainly manipulate it."

Aurore cut a square of blue cloth from the end of a bolt. She placed it on the small table between them. "Now, look between the warp and weft. See where the colour holds to the threads. Then push the colour and imagine a wave, a ripple on a pond. You will feel it move as it responds to you."

Aria did as instructed. At first, she couldn't push her awareness into the weave. It seemed too hard, too ridiculous. But as she stared at the piece of cloth, she began to see the *given* threaded through it, like fine spider webs. That was when she began to push and pull the colour. It took a bit of effort before she thought she had managed a wave. When she sat back in the chair, she realised that she must have been staring at the cloth for a long time. Her neck was stiff, and she was thirsty.

Aurore glanced at her with a smile and nodded. "Look what you have done."

Aria sat forward and reached for the cloth. Where there had been a solid blue colour, now there were layers of blues, pale blue, dark blue, navy blues, all slightly rippled to give a beautiful pattern. "I did that?"

"Yes. 'Tis as a wonder to behold, is it not? If this is what you can do with one simple lesson, imagine how learned you might have been if you had been born in Argenterra and trained in Glassy Mountain Retreat."

"Really? I must tell Sophy."

"Your friend still cannot bear any objects formed with the *given*?"

Aria shook her head. "It makes her ill. I don't understand it. The *given* is everywhere. It is part of everything. I am sad for her that she can't feel it, touch it, or manipulate it. I don't understand why, though. We came here together so shouldn't we experience things in the same way?"

"I am a simple woman. I do not pretend to understand the mysteries of the wider world. Your friend is different."

Aria smiled but her heart was troubled. Now that she could use the *given*, Sophy would feel even more isolated. Their experiences were becoming so divergent that they would find it hard to be as close as they once were. She would have new family as well as a husband. She decided it was best to keep the news that she could use the *given* to herself for a while.

❧

I⊤ was the day before Aria's wedding, and guests had been arriving in ones and twos over the last couple of days, with a large cavalcade expected later in the evening. Sophy sat on the grass, surrounded by flowers, and stared at the sunset. She was eager to escape the last-minute panic over gowns and feast, and let the weight of the keep, riddled with *given*, slide away.

Gazing at the sunset, she didn't know what mesmerised her, the mauve sky laced with red as the sun dropped below the mountain peaks, or the melancholy that was growing in the depths of her heart. All around, the scent of roses hung heavy and sweet on the dew-laden air. A tuft of wind tugged on a few petals, lifted them and laid them gently at her feet. She picked one up and rubbed it idly, feeling the soft velvet soothe the tips of her fingers as she inhaled the scent deeply.

The sound of gravel crunching heralded the arrival of Oakheart, who stood on the path in front of her. His blond hair was bound in a queue, and instead of his usual doublet, he wore a dark blue jerkin unlaced over a white shirt.

"My lady," he said, as his eyes assessed her. "What do you do here, alone?"

Sophy tidied her gown. "I'm looking at the sunset."

Oakheart turned to the west and stared for a moment. "Yes, very beautiful. I always wonder what makes it so red. 'Tis almost as if the sky is bleeding."

"I never thought of it quite like that—more like roses, you know, pinks, whites, reds. Here, like this one." She held up a petal that had drifted to her feet. In the growing shadows, it was turning from red to black.

He moved closer and knelt on one knee next to her. He took the petal and sniffed.

"Truly, a flower is the most amazing thing," he said, his gaze far away. "My father says that while we keep our oath to the land, we will have bounty to sustain our bodies, but the flowers are to sustain our hearts. They give joy, healing and beauty. There is a saying I have heard that I think will appeal to you. 'Caress me not, for if you dare, you will soothe away every care, rob not the bud, but let me bloom, and my scent will dispel your gloom.'"

"Hey, that sounds like poetry" she said.

His eyes suddenly focussed, and his green gaze seared her. "Not poetry," he said, standing abruptly, the rose petal now forgotten. "I quote not poetry to ladies."

She saw his colour heighten and was secretly amused. As if he would deliberately try to woo her with poetry. "Sounded like poetry to me. Not that I care for it usually."

The arrival of a young man, dressed in long robes, with layers of blue, green and brown, interrupted Oakheart's reply. The stranger's eyes were clear, ice blue and they seemed to flash within his tanned face. His hair and eyebrows where white.

"Adage," Oakheart said, kneeling quickly and bowing his head with respect.

Adage looked younger than she was, but there was an otherness to him, and his eyes looked straight through her. Sophy stood up and tried not to gape at the newcomer.

Oakheart stood, his bland face smiling. "We are well met, Adage. I did not know that you had arrived...I would have greeted you."

"Yes, just now," Adage said, staring at Sophy as he walked slowly towards her.

"This is Lady Sophy, Adage, the second Gift of Crystal Tree Woods."

After glancing nervously at Oakheart, she curtsied and then stared warily as Adage edged closer, those cold eyes astutely examining her.

"So I see, Oakheart. I received your message," he said, inclining his head in Oakheart's direction but without taking his eyes off her.

"Tell me, Lady Sophy. Did the Crystal Tree gift you with a leaf?" Adage asked in a deep voice that belied his youthful looks.

"Y...yes."

"Where is it? Lady Aria wears hers around her neck on the chain Dellbright gave her. Yet you have no such arrangement."

Heart racing, she began to sweat. Could she tell them? The bodice of her dress was cut low, so she tapped her chest. "It's here."

Oakheart's blond eyebrows rose. "Where, Sophy? I cannot see it."

She rolled up her eyes. No one would believe it. Maybe she imagined it after all.

"It delved beneath my skin. Here."

Oakheart visibly started. Adage held up his hand to silence Oakheart's next words.

"May I, my lady?"

She nodded and stood still. Adage's robes rustled as he moved and warmth radiating from his hand as it hovered above her breast. There was a warming sensation, and then a burning. It hurt to breathe.

"Easy, my lady, breathe calmly and the discomfort will soon pass." Then to Oakheart he said, "Come closer. Look at this." Adage's voice was filled with wonder.

She looked down and all she could make out was a glow that spread in tendrils across her chest.

"What has happened, Adage? It looks as if the leaf is sprouting within her."

"What?" Sophy yelped, pulling back. The glow faded and after a few minutes, she could breathe easier. "What's happening to me?"

Adage regarded her silently, but she could see that he was thinking, calculating.

"Bring her to Glassy Mountain Retreat as soon as you can, Oakheart. More must be discovered of this phenomenon. But speak of it to no one."

"Yes, Adage, I will do what I can," Oakheart replied, his green eyes glinting with curiosity. "The responsibility for the care of her rests with Valley Keep."

"Ah...I see...politics... Do what you must, Oakheart." Adage turned away.

"But what's happening? Tell me," she said, tugging at Adage's robe. "I have headaches when I'm in the keep. Things made with the *given* do not agree with me. Can't you tell me why?"

He turned back to her, smiled slightly. "I do not know, my lady. It is a mystery to me. None of the previous outlanders suffered from your afflictions. I must study this happening and then we will see if the answer is to be found."

"Should I try to go home then? Maybe I am not meant to be here."

"Home?" Adage's white eyebrows drew together. "You mean return to your world?"

Sophy glanced at Oakheart. His face was impassive. "Yes."

"I think you should not venture home, Lady Sophy. I believe you do belong here with us. I invite you to Glassy Mountain Retreat instead. Would you visit us?'

Sophy glanced over his shoulder to the mountains beyond. "Well, if I were able to get there, I would try. I don't know. Will I be all right until then? Is the leaf dangerous?"

"You will come to the retreat, this I have seen. My lady, the Crystal Tree was not made for hurt, so fear not for your health or your life. Even though the meaning of what has happened is not clear to me, it is truly auspicious. It will take time for us to ponder it out. If the headaches leave you when you are outside the keep, then I think there is no permanent harm. I suggest you avoid articles crafted with the *given*, for the moment."

He turned abruptly is a swirl of robes and strode away.

She quirked an eyebrow at Oakheart. "Who was that guy?"

"That was the oldest, most gifted and learned adept from Glassy Mountain Retreat."

"The oldest?" snorted Sophy. "But he looks so young."

"Looks can be deceiving. Come, we must regain the keep. The adept will meditate this night for the bonding ceremony tomorrow. And you must get warm for I can see that you are chilled."

Sophy was chilled, but it wasn't the temperature. It was the thought of the leaf from The Crystal Tree embedded in her chest, growing within her, and the realisation that it meant something. The adept knew, she was sure, and the only way she was going to find out was to travel up into the mountains.

9

WEDDING BLISS AND BLUES

Aria woke riddled with nerves. Today was the day. She was plagued with uncertainty and apprehension left a bitter aftertaste in her mouth. Was it that she needed to belong? Already, she was accepted and she was certain that her decision was so right on many levels. She looked down at Sophy's sleeping form, willing her to wake up so that she could talk over her fears.

She padded around the room and looked out the window. The gauzy curtains billowed out like a pair of angel wings. Streaks of pink and red tainted the mountain mist, signalling that the sun had indeed come up. She sighed. She didn't want to think about it. She had been avoiding thinking about it since she arrived in this fairytale land and met her fairytale prince.

It was too perfect. Her mother told her often that life was full of ups and downs, full of regret and tears. It was the sadness that made the joy sweet. Her mother would not approve of her haste. "Mother," she whispered. "Wish you were here with me. I wish you could tell me everything is going to be all right."

Sophy moaned in her sleep and disturbed Aria's train of thought. She tiptoed over to Sophy's bed and watched quietly in case she was in the grips of a nightmare. Sophy had had several since the wedding announcement.

Sophy was right. Things would be different. She would have duties now, to her husband and to the people of the valley. Aurore had already begun the lessons, training her for her position. She had dragged her friend along mostly to steer her away from trouble, but essentially for company. She was beginning to feel loneliness and a strange form of isolation.

Sophy began to thrash violently, almost throwing herself off the bed. Aria leant down to shake her awake, she didn't want her screaming again so early in the morning. People already thought that Sophy was strange, so she didn't need to give them more evidence.

Sophy sat up with a start, nearly bumping her head against Aria's.

"Sorry, did I wake you?"

"No," she replied gently. "I was already up." Sitting down on Sophy's bed, she cast her worried frown in Sophy's direction, hoping that some sympathy would be forthcoming, but her friend's eyes were haunted with pain, and her face was drawn and pale. "Can you give me a hug?"

Sophy looked at her searchingly for a moment, nodded and then opened her arms. Aria fell into them and hugged her fiercely.

"I know that in marrying Dellbright things will be different, but always remember that when it counts—when you need me, I will come for you. I promise."

"I will always be there for you, too, Aria. Just ask me, and I'll do anything for you."

"Yes, I know you will." Aria pulled back and examined Sophy, noticing the paleness and the loss of weight. Her gown for the wedding would hang on her like a wheat sack. She would have to get Dela to take the dress in. "I'm going to take a bath. You rest."

"Sure. If the red eyes and dreams of blood will leave me alone." Sophy lay back down, while Aria went to prepare her bathing things.

The washroom filled with steam and the scent of rose and lavender. Aria walked in and let her shift fall to the floor. Her foot disturbed the floating petals when it slid slowly into the hot water. Closing her eyes, she tried to quieten her mind. Her head rested on the rim of the tub, and she gazed into the steam, slipping quietly into a half-sleep. A sudden chill woke her. She blinked a few times. The steam was thicker, like a heavy mist.

Inexplicably, it began to shift and mould, as it formed into a hideous face with glowing red eyes. Taken aback, she screamed and reflexively curled into a ball, splashing water onto the floor tiles.

The door flung open, dispersing the mist. Sophy raced in, searching the room for danger or intruders. The red eyes faded to nothing, leaving the vision of Sophy's concerned face.

"What's the matter? What happened?"

"Sorry. It's nothing," Aria said. "I thought I saw something. I must have been dozing." Was it Sophy's mention of red eyes in her nightmares that made her imagine them?

Sighing, she sank below the water line, rearranging the flower petals to hide her breasts. Suddenly she was very self-conscious thinking of her wedding night.

Sophy slumped down the wall and sat on the cool tiles. "I'm nervous too. You would think it was me that was going down the aisle and standing up with Dellbright to say my vows." She closed her eyes and leaned her head back.

"I don't need you rubbing it in. I'm scared. I have only kissed him that one time when you burst in on us. What if..." she said, voice rising and her hands squeezing the edges of the bathtub.

"As far as I can tell Dellbright knows exactly what to do, so I wouldn't be worried that you'll spend all night playing cards."

Sophy came over to the bath, reached down, undid Aria's death grip on the rim of the tub and took her hand in her own. "Aria. It'll be wonderful, magic—everything you've dreamed about. So be happy, okay. I'm happy for you, really."

"But...you," Aria said.

"I can look after myself. Don't worry about me."

Sophy edged back towards the door. "Don't stay in here too long or Dellbright will be marrying a shrivelled up prune."

Aria turfed three large splashes in Sophy's direction, which she successfully ducked.

IT TOOK A LONG TIME TO DRESS. ARIA WAS ALREADY FATIGUED, YET the day had only begun. The apparition in the mist had scared her. The vision of those eyes would not fade. Every time she closed her eyes, they were watching her, burning into her. Shaking herself, she pushed down her fears, unwilling to let that one instant spoil her special day.

Her gown was white and trimmed in gold, with a weighty train that amazed her. They must have used real gold in its making. Aurore supervised the last minute adjustments and the sewing on of golden roses. The poor woman was a bit snappy due the amount of preparation and her desire for everything to be perfect. Aria suspected she had hardly slept since the wedding announcement.

Aria shifted from foot to foot to ease the ache in her calves. Her hair had been elaborately curled and entwined with sweet smelling summer roses and crowned with a golden circlet. Her head felt light and her body heavy. In the same room, Sophy was being dressed in her gown.

"Aria," Aurore chided. "You must stand still or we will never finish."

"Sorry," Aria replied.

Aurore turned a glare in Sophy's direction. "And you, Sophy, keep very still. Your dress needs extra attention—have you eaten nothing in this last week? I swear that you are half the size you were when we measured you for your gown."

"I have been eating," Sophy protested weakly.

"You will shame my house," Aurore added, a touch teary, the strain beginning to show. "The finest gowns in all the land we make. Yet, dangling off your skinny frame they will look as nothing."

Sophy glanced over at Aria, a worried frown creasing her brow. Aria knew that Sophy was conscious that her presence caused resentment. It had been building up steadily since Dellbright had announced his choice, yet Aurore had always managed to treat them fairly equally.

"But my gown is splendid, Aurore," Aria added, eager to turn Aurore's attention. "There is no equal to it and no one will notice...a..." She stopped suddenly aware of how her friend would think if she said no one would notice her. Thinking quickly, she added, "Your fame will spread far and wide. Oakheart will sing tales of this day in those places where he travels."

Aurore stood, suddenly enchanted by her words. "Yes," she whispered. "We are fortunate that he is here to tell of it. Forgive me, young Sophy. I spoke in haste."

"I'm sorry to be so much trouble to everyone," Sophy said.

"Oh but you are not," Aurore said, pursing her lips. "I am beside myself, that is all. Today I gain a daughter."

Aria smiled reassuringly, knowing that she herself would unravel if there were one more short word or instance of frayed temper. At last, after a slight tug here, a pat down there, Aurore smiled. "Come, we are almost done."

"Shoes?" Sophy yelped. "I have no shoes."

The maid began to scurry amongst the piles of clothes at the foot of Sophy's bed. A knock on the door sent Aurore flying about the room checking every little thing. "Hair, faces, shoes, flowers...oh...I must dress myself, excuse me," she said and darted out the door.

❧

THE WEDDING PROCESSION HEADED DOWN TO THE LOWER LEVELS OF the keep, where Argenterra pulsed with life. As they descended, Sophy felt the pressure building inside her head and groaned quietly as she took the next step and the next. It was like walking into a canyon-sized migraine, with pressure waves assaulted her on all sides.

They entered the bonding chamber. Dominating the room was a huge pool, full with dark water that appeared to swallow the light. The pool had raised edges with four niches carved into the marble, with enough room for a person to kneel.

The chamber was alight with the smokeless firesticks. Flowers and leaves hung in decorative arrangements from the walls. People were bowing to someone ahead of her. When her eyes became accustomed to the light, she realised that it was Adage. He looked even younger than he had the day before. His presence unnerved her so she lowered her gaze to hide her reaction.

Dellbright met Aria at the base of the stairs and took her by the hand. He smiled at her, and she smiled back with her eyes shining pools of light. Aria was obviously still nervous as her hand trembled when she placed it in Dellbright's. Sophy sympathised. She didn't know how Aria could go through with it. If it had been her, she would have run in the opposite direction and kept on running. Yet, she noticed how Dellbright's look kept Aria from quailing with fear, and how she smiled back into those dark, mesmerising eyes of his.

"I am Adage Adept. Please take your places." He motioned to Dellbright and Aria, and they followed him to kneel in the first of the pool's niches. Adage's robes rustled in the quiet, their subdued tones and simplicity was in stark contrast to everyone's finery.

"To begin I will recount the tale of Vorn and the First Comers as to all those who take such vows as these should do so as solemnly as those First Comers did when they entered Argenterra. As with the first oath sworn by Vorn and witnessed by the land, so too will your vow be witnessed by the same power and will be as everlasting."

Adage turned, his robes rustling, and looked at the members of wedding party in turn. Sophy cringed, as if a weight was pressing her down. Surely that pounding was not emanating from the inside of her head.

"Vorn led his people through the portal into this world. He, and his kinsman, left behind the evil that had pursued them for countless years and had harried them from every haven. Within the boundaries and walkways between the worlds, Vorn found others who had fled their homes and who looked to him for succour.

"On their arrival, Vorn did behold this very valley from the peak where now stands Glassy Mountain Retreat. Reaching out with his heart and hope, he sought an answer to his peoples' need. Strong he was, and wise, but a greater power dwelled here. He swore an oath to the land to protect it, nurture it and to do no ill. And with this oath he bound all his descendants. All the First Comers took the oath, thereby binding us all. But with the oath the land returned to us a threefold reward. It gave us bounty, craft and the *given*.

"So now we come to this joining, this swearing of oaths, which the land will witness and bind. Who stands with Dellbright in this union?"

Adage said, surveying the crowd with his ice blue gaze. Oakheart moved past Sophy. She hadn't even seen him in the crowd.

Aria flushed guiltily, and Sophy realised that she had forgotten to mention a few details of the ceremony to her. The prince squeezed Aria's hand, and her guilty look disappeared when she gazed lovingly at Dellbright.

Oakheart lowered himself into the niche on Dellbright's side.

"Who stands with Aria in this union?" Adage asked. Nobody moved. Sophy held her breath. She looked at the adept and he nodded slightly. Oh? That's me, she thought. She moved to the niche on Aria's side. She felt weak, but it wasn't the fear. It was being this close to something of the *given*.

Oakheart was in Sophy's direct line of sight. Raising her eyes to his, she put on a brave face, yet she couldn't tell anything from his expression. His eyes though had darkened to the shade of the liquid pool.

The adept began. "Welcome to the union of Prince Dellbright Firemoth, Prince of Valley Keep and the lower kingdom and the Lady Aria, Outlander and Gift of Crystal Tree Woods."

Sophy shivered as he intoned their names. The power was building. The cool air teased goose flesh from her skin. The adept lowered a wooden ladle into the pool and raised it, letting the contents fall out. As the drops of water hit the pond, they set it on fire with crystal shards of light. Sophy 's body resonated with power, painful waves like heat at a bonfire. She grimaced while she stared at Oakheart and then at Aria. Her friend appeared mesmerised by the alteration in the pond and the pure light reflected off the walls of the keep and out of Dellbright's eyes.

Sophy wavered. Luckily, the niche provided her some support. Oakheart held her gaze, slight concern evident. She clung to Oakheart's silent support. When she finally was in control of herself, even though her teeth felt like they were disassembling, she steadied and lifted her chin.

"I call upon Argenterra to bless this union. Behold the power of water," he intoned. The crowd repeated his words.

"Behold the power of the Argenterra." A tree started to sprout from the centre of the pool. Its leaves were clear prisms like the leaves of the Crystal Tree.

The crowd repeated the words and the tree grew larger. Its leaves reached out towards Dellbright and Aria. Soon Aria's hand was encased in leaves and Dellbright's likewise. They smiled with wonder.

Sophy made a strange noise, glad she wasn't the one getting married. The Crystal Tree didn't mesh well with her or indeed any other expression of the *given*. Yet, just as that thought crystallised, the leaf in her breast stirred. Her eyes flew open with alarm. It was hard to breathe. Oakheart's eyebrows lifted but he still held on to her with his green gaze now flaring with colour.

"Behold the *given*," the adept intoned and all followed his lead.

Sophy cringed as the song began. Her pain was a counterpoint to everyone else's joy. Rapturous smiles draped Dellbright and Aria's face. Sophy's teeth seemed to twist in her gums. Her breast throbbed. She thought the leaf was going to tear itself free. Only the fact that her gaze was meshed with Oakheart's gave her the strength to hide her pain.

The adept asked Oakheart, "Do you stand with Dellbright in this union?"

"I do so stand."

"Do you promise to serve this union with love, support and succour?"

"They will have my succour in time of need. Love is mine to give and is *given*, along with the support of me and mine," Oakheart answered.

The adept turned to Sophy. She held her breath. She wanted to say the words only if she meant them.

"Do you Sophy stand with Aria in this union?"

"I...do," replied Sophy with a voice that sounded thin.

"Do you..." Adage hesitated.

Sophy gritted her teeth, holding back the moan that threatened to spill past her taut lips.

"Will you sacrifice all for the fruit of this union?"

Sophy was stunned by Adage's words and the deviation from

Oakheart's vow. She flicked her gaze his way. Oakheart too, looked perplexed.

Everyone was quiet, waiting for her promise. "I will sacrifice all for the fruit of this union," she said, her voice resounding within the chamber. All the while, her mind was spinning because Adage meant children. Did that mean she would lay down her life for Aria's child? Children meant ties, complications and responsibility.

"Dellbright, do you pledge to give yourself to this vow? To hold unto Aria, serving her in mind and in body?" In his hand he held a small plaque with words etched onto it. Sophy guessed it held the specifics of the wedding vows.

"My vow is true and unwavering. The binding oath flows through me and with it the power to fix me to Aria."

Aria repeated Dellbright's oath in a clear and confident voice.

"Then you are bonded, here witnessed by the Crystal Tree and those who are bound to your union. By the power of Argenterra your oath is sealed, none but the final leave taking can sunder it."

A resounding cheer erupted. The leaves of the Crystal Tree shrank back, unravelling from Aria and Dellbright's hands. The wedding participants freed themselves from the niches while the Crystal Tree sank majestically back into the pond. The guests headed for the stairs, leaving the wedding party to follow. Sophy suppressed the urge to push past everyone and elbow her way up and out of the bonding chamber. Her hair felt like it was being ripped from her scalp. Oakheart moved to stand next to her and put his hand on her elbow. She started. "What?"

Oakheart whispered in her ear. "We must ascend together, hands held, and follow Aria and Dellbright to the feast." With that, he held out his hand, palm up. She looked at it, suddenly sick. He squeezed her hand companionably and spoke again. "You did well, this day, Sophy."

"So did you," she returned, smiling as he frowned. "Tell me, why did Adage alter my pledge?"

"I know not," he said, still keeping her hand in his. They followed Aria and Dellbright up the stairs.

"I think you have an inkling and don't want to tell me," she whispered.

"You begin to know me," he said, eyes smiling.

"I doubt that will ever happen." The further away from the bonding chamber she went, the easier it was to breathe. Sophy's brow unclenched and she could even smile.

"Better?" Oakheart asked, watching her.

"Yes, thank you."

They stepped into the great hall. Sophy saw the tables arrayed with every kind of dish.

"Oh, look here is food."

"Yes, as I said. You led me to the feast, so you knew what was on my mind."

Sophy could not help but laugh at this. "You are always hungry. I have no idea what you think about anything."

"I need not explain. We are bound, you and I."

"What?" Her face grew pale. She couldn't help the look of horror that overcame her face. What with weddings and all.

Now, Oakheart was laughing at her. "Not bound that way. At least you could have the grace not to show such aversion to the notion. I meant we are bound together to serve their union—to help them along."

Now it was her turn to redden. "I'm sorry I misunderstood you. I meant no offence"

Oakheart led her to her seat, suddenly serious. "So you think I am undesirable then as a potential husband?"

Caught out, she had to think fast. "It never crossed my mind. If I think about it now I believe we would be incompatible."

"How so?"

"With your appetite, you would eat all the food and I would probably starve before the first six months were done."

His eyes darkened. "As I said, you begin to know me." He sat down next to her, but his conversation was strained. Somehow, her words had wounded him, and she couldn't figure out why. He had no interest in her surely. She was ugly, unwanted and in everybody's way—especially his.

10

LIGHT OF MORNING

ARIA WAS FLOATING IN HAPPINESS. The afterglow of the power of the Crystal Tree left her senses reeling. Her skin was sensitive. Dellbright's hand sent electrical shivers up her arms and up and down her spine. She could barely suppress a shudder of desire. Heat stirred within her. Sexual attraction burned her, making her heart pound. She willed Dellbright to take her to their bedchamber, take her while the power of the tree stayed within her. She could do anything while the power of the *given* was in her.

But first there was duty and the feast. The food never tasted so fine, although she could only taste a bite of each dish. Her eyes, though, devoured Dellbright and his did her.

After an eternity the feast was done, or rather they were done with the feast. The sounds of revelry echoed through the keep as Aria walked to Dellbright's chamber. Aurore, Sophy and Rae helped her disrobe and dress in a fine nightgown.

Aurore wiped tears from her eyes as she helped Aria get into the bed. She had sewn the flowers into the bodice of Aria's nightgown with her own hands. After handing Aria a goblet of warmed wine, her new mother-in-law bade her drink it and then she and Rae departed, leaving her alone with Sophy. Aria sat up in Dellbright's huge bed, with a sheet covering her to the waist.

She'd never been in this room before. Now it would be her room. At that moment she imagined herself to be so small, so insignificant. Tears sprang into eyes, and she wiped them away. She could hear Dellbright's entourage approaching. The euphoria of the wedding ceremony receded, driven away at Dellbright's approach. Her hands clenched the sheets.

Sophy was there. "Don't fret, now," she said, kissing Aria's forehead and giving her a parting hug. She left via the dressing room to avoid the groom and his followers. The main door opened with a creak. Dellbright stepped in dressed in a simple robe. His hair dripped with water around his cleanly shaven face.

He smiled. Aria's heart did a little twist in response and she sank once again into his dark gaze. "Aria," he said and walked up quickly to the bed. "How beautiful you are. Thank you for this day."

"No, it is I who should thank you." Her eyes roamed his beautiful face, drawing courage from the feeling she had for him. He leaned in closer and tilted her chin with his hand. His lips brushed hers, lightly, teasingly and then he seized her mouth, caught it with his own.

She trembled with fear and desire. One kiss and it was enough to melt her. He released her, slipping free of his robe. "You tremble," he whispered into her ear, kissing the lobe tenderly. "I tremble for you, too."

She moaned softly as he nibbled down her neck, sucking gently at the juncture of her neck and shoulder. Her breath caught as excitement snaked through her body, kindling the flame in her.

"Give yourself to me."

His hands were in her hair, holding her in place as his lips met hers.

"Mine," he said.

The kiss went on and on, harder and more demanding.

Breaking free, she said, "Wait." He grabbed for her again, crushing her already bruised lips. She tried to remove his hands from her hair so she could break free. The caress had become a struggle.

Momentarily, Dellbright released her mouth and then with one hand, he seized the front of her gown and rent the garment in two.

Her cry was cut off as Dellbright covered her with his body. Dellbright's smothering kiss stifled her scream but could do nothing for the terror and the pain as Dellbright raped her.

ARIA WOKE EARLY. THE LIGHT WAS NOT YET BRIGHTENING THE window. Dellbright stirred, withdrawing his hand so possessively placed across her waist. She hurt everywhere, but from what she could see of her skin there were no bruises. A numbness settled over her. She didn't want to criticise but her wedding night was not what she had expected. Dellbright had been rough and urgent. He had wept with her afterwards, covering her face with soft kisses.

"Aria?" Dellbright said, pulling her towards him.

It was too late to close her eyes and pretend to sleep. She didn't know what to say to him, as confusion was in her heart and mind.

"Forgive me. I wanted you so badly. I had naught but a kiss to satisfy me...I was desperate for you. I will be gentle, truly. Let me show you. We have time to get to know each other. Please, Aria."

Aria blinked away the tears. Yes, she understood the want. Hadn't she wanted him too? How his hands trembled when they touched her face. She should be forgiving. Were they not bonded till they die? "I forgive you."

Dellbright leaned forward and kissed her swollen lips. With his tongue, he caressed her mouth. Softly, he ran his hand over her skin, across her breasts and lower. Aria sighed as her husband made gentle love to her, and made a mental note to hide the rent and bloodied nightgown before his mother saw it.

❧ II ❧

THE WEDDING WEEK

THE DAY AFTER THE WEDDING, Sophy hung around the vestibule, peering up the staircase with every sound of a footstep in the anticipation of seeing Aria. Eventually, she grew concerned and sought out Oakheart. She checked the great hall but he wasn't there so she ventured outside, nodding to the various guests as they paraded up and down.

In the rose garden, tinkling laughter drew her to the spot where Oakheart and Nella, one of the keep's, elegant and eligible female guests, sat under the shade of a tree. They were chatting amiably surrounded by red and pink roses. Oakheart's voice floated on the air, sending Nella into a fit of giggles. Even her gown seemed attuned to every reflexive twitter as each layer of soft fabric rippled.

Oakheart saw her approach and stood to meet her. "Lady Sophy, let me present you to Nella of WhittleCross."

"Pleased to meet you," Sophy said and curtsied. At least the Argenterrans couldn't be offended by her manners now. She had practised hard to curtsy just so.

Nella smiled. "Pleased to meet you, too, my lady. Oakheart has been amusing me with one of his tales." Nella gave her an appraising look and batted her eyelids at Oakheart.

"Really?" she answered. "I've not heard one of those."

"The wedding ceremony was truly delightful. You must be so happy for your friend," inserted Nella, eager to hold Oakheart's attention.

Taken aback, Sophy thought about a suitable reply. Sizing up Nella's brown eyes, slightly sallow complexion and apricot-coloured dress. The dress was not a product of Valley Keep. She was certain that Aurore would never have condoned the making of such a gown.

"Aria's happiness is important to me."

"And the prince is so handsome. Is he not?"

"Oh yes, very handsome." She caught Oakheart's attention and said, "Speaking of the..."

Again Nella kept on, all the while gazing languidly at Oakheart. "He is not the only handsome one," she said.

"No," Sophy agreed, stifling a laugh. Oakheart's lips tightened. Obviously, Nella didn't need any encouragement from Sophy.

Preening herself, Nella edged closer to Oakheart and looked up into his face. "You looked very well yesterday, Oakheart."

"Yes, well...thank you."

Sophy's smile widened because she detected a faint blush under Oakheart's tanned skin. He noticed her looking and the blush deepened. "Sophy, you came on an errand?"

Nella pouted and cast Sophy an eloquent look. She had been prevented, it seemed, from luring Oakheart to the bonding chamber. Although Sophy had heard that Adage had departed already.

"I came to ask if you knew when Aria would be coming down today."

Nella giggled at her question. Sophy drew her brows into an annoyed frown and glared rather rudely at the girl.

"My lady, the Princess Aria will not leave her shared rooms for a least a week. It is tradition for newly-bonded couples to spend that time in seclusion to ground their union. It is called the wedding week."

She threw her hands in the air. "A week? What could they be doing for week?"

Nella stepped back, obviously wary of Sophy's explosive gestures. Sophy couldn't believe that Aria would leave her alone for so long without even a word of warning.

Oakheart smiled and commented in a low voice, "Do you really wish me to explain what they are doing?" His eyebrow lifted in a copy of her own well-used gesture. Heat clawed up her face. Nella giggled and fluttered around Oakheart, eyelashes working overtime. How dare he embarrass her in front of that silly girl? Didn't he understand what she was going through?

"In that case I'm off to the woods for a walk," she said and started down the path.

Oakheart coughed and replied before she took her second step, "I am afraid, my lady, that you cannot do that unless I accompany you."

"Really?" she replied, turning slowly with her temper moving rather faster. "Since when did you become my guardian?" She stared up at him, hands on hips, and shifted her gaze slightly as Nella gasped at her tone. Not bothering to waste a blink on her, Sophy folded her arms and kept her glare steadily on Oakheart. "I'm free to go where ever I want." Her foot tapped on the gravel of its own accord.

"No, you are not."

"Since when?"

"Since Dellbright passed his responsibility for your care to me for the duration of his wedding week. Besides, you cannot leave since that would not be showing support for their union. You did make a pledge, did you not?"

"Dellbright is not responsible for me, therefore, he can't just hand me over to you. I'm not some piece of property that can be tossed about randomly." Sophy couldn't believe these people. Here she was in a strange land and not even permitted to go for a walk without Oakheart's permission or company.

"As a Gift of Crystal Tree Woods you fall into Dellbright's jurisdiction."

Unfortunately, his attitude and his explanations didn't help her growing anger. Her fuse was lit. Nella was actually looking fearful, switching her gaze back and forth between Sophy and Oakheart.

"If you wait a while I will keep you company on a short walk."

"But I don't want to spend time with you," she said with a sneer. "You're a bore."

Nella fled—from shame or fear, Sophy couldn't tell.

With a quick glance at Nella's retreating form he took a step closer. "You have erred in your assessment of me."

She was too angry to be careful. "Yeah? I am never wrong about things like that."

He actually turned red and unclenched his hands. She had finally made him angry too.

"I give up," she said quickly, taking a step back. "I'll take a walk in this rose garden, if that is all right with you, milord." She couldn't help her sarcastic twist on the 'milord'.

"You may do so," he said calmly but his expression had not changed. "But first I will have your agreement not to go without the bounds of the garden."

"What if the forest looks inviting when I get to the end of the path?" She looked to the distant trees and pointed absently in their direction.

"Well, you may not go if you cannot give me your word. You will return with me into the keep."

"Absolutely not. Why don't you just shove me into the dungeon if this is all the freedom I'm allowed?"

"Sophy?" He sounded pained. "Sophy..." he moved closer, though he didn't touch her. "I am sorry my presence offends you."

"I'd have to care about you for your insults to offend me. Sooo sorry I distracted you from your lady love."

"Sophy," he said with a growl.

She gathered her skirts and fled back to the keep.

✦

ON THE MORNING OF THE FOURTH DAY AFTER THE WEDDING ceremony, Sophy could stand the confinement no longer. She slipped out of the keep early, had almost gained the nearest edge of the forest and was about to step off the garden path, when she heard her name called. She sucked in a surprised breath and hesitated, not quite willing to push things too far by being openly defiant.

Oakheart approached wearing riding clothes and smelling of horse and perspiration. Behind him were two of his men, one holding the reins of his stallion. She smiled brilliantly. "The morning is spectacular, is it not?"

Oakheart stopped mid-stride and seemed to falter. Whatever he was about to say froze on his lips. He looked up into the sky quickly; it was mostly overcast and had actually rained most of the night.

"My lady...? Where do you go?" he asked finally, although her destination was obvious.

He didn't appear angry, yet she thought he would be. His nice manner disconcerted her. "I was looking at the forest. It looks so irresistible today."

"The forest looks the same as it always does." However, there was doubt in his voice.

"You think so?" She arched her eyebrows, thinking that she had the better of him for once.

He relaxed his stance. "In what way are the woods irresistible this morn?" The intelligent glint was back in his eye.

She turned back to the forest seeking inspiration. "The leaves are so green, and there is a certain quality to the shadows today."

Oakheart appeared lost for words. "Would you be so kind as to walk in the woods with me?"

Her eyes flew eagerly to his, and she couldn't repress her instinctive, 'yes'. All of her anger against him was forgotten in that moment. She grabbed his hand and dragged him down the path. One of his men led his horse away to the stables and the other followed them at a distance.

Letting go of his hand, she went ahead of him into the forest. Her step had a spring as she bounded down the path. Oakheart followed closely, though he was so quiet and unprotesting at the path she chose that she almost forgot he was there. Beneath the canopy of trees the weight of the castle walls lifted. Her head felt light. The forest, or woods as Oakheart called them, was not over large so there was little fear of becoming lost. Suddenly she recalled her experience the last time she was there, her encounter with the strange mist. Looking behind at her companion she realised, while Oakheart was with her, she had no fear of its return. He may be annoying and overbearing but she trusted him and he knew his way around this place.

In a small clearing Sophy came upon the brisk stream that fed the lake.

"Come, let us rest for a moment by the water," he said.

"Sure."

She sat on a boulder while Oakheart took up position on a fallen log nearby. He stared at the water in silence, sometimes absently dropping leaves in the current and watching them float away.

The loamy smell of earth and leaves and the fresh tang of the water washed over her, filling her with contentment. The colours enthralled her, rust brown leaves, yellow sunburnt remains fluttered on the occasional breeze. Most of the leaves were green and hung with vigour on the branches of the tall trees. Pale sunlight filtered through the gaps in the branches.

Oakheart stood after a while. "Do you feel better now?"

Shading her eyes with her hand, she looked up at him. "Better, thank you."

"The other day...."

She looked down. "I was rude. I'm sorry."

He knelt down in front of her. "I, too, am sorry for my harsh words. I was unfeeling, Sophy. I forget sometimes that you think you are all alone here. That this place and our ways are strange to you."

"Then you forgive me?"

"Yes, but we must return. Everyone will be awake now."

"Okay."

"Does your head ache all the time in the keep?"

She walked next to him, down the path. "Always. But I'm getting used to it."

He laughed. "I think not. I can tell when it is getting too much for you. You grind your teeth and spit sparks."

Open mouthed with astonishment, she gaped at him, unable to speak.

He gave a full belly laugh. "Forgive me. But your expression is priceless."

LATER THAT DAY, SOPHY HAD AN ARGUMENT WITH WILLOW. "I said, my lady, that you cannot wear those clothes in the great hall."

"Why not?" Sophy had managed to obtain, through Rae, some breeches, a shirt and a jerkin. Her hair was in a ponytail. It was the closest thing to jeans and a t-shirt she could get in this place. She thought a run around the perimeter of the garden would let her burn off some steam.

"Because it does not show proper decorum. The prince would not like it. I must uphold his wishes."

"What is it with this place? I'm not naked or anything. I want to go for a run. I can't do that in a fancy dress. Do you want to see me fall flat on my face?"

Willow threw up his arms, creating waves with his robes. "How can I deal with this? She is so impertinent." A footman scrambled away and a maid ducked back into a room she was just exiting.

"I'm not harming anyone."

"But I am the chamberlain."

"So?"

"Lady Sophy," Oakheart said from behind her.

Sophy sighed. Perhaps Oakheart would see sense. "Hello, Oakheart. Would you please explain to Willow that I am allowed to run around the perimeter as long as I don't step a foot out of the keep's boundaries?"

"No, I will not. You will apologise to Willow and follow his instructions."

"But...I—" One glance told her that Oakheart would not tolerate an argument right then. His fists clenched, his skin darkening under those blond brows.

"Fine." She faced Willow. "Forgive me, chamberlain." Turning away, she said to Oakheart. "I will be in my room." Steering around him, she headed for the stairs. Oakheart's heavy step followed her.

His hand on her shoulder spun her round to face him. "Why do you act like this? I cannot believe you and Aria come from the same place, or that you are even friends."

"Meaning what?" she replied. "Willow was trying to provoke me. Telling me what I should wear."

"Yet, he is the prince's chamberlain. His is the task of making the household run. It is not meet that you disdain him in public or raise your voice to me."

She lowered her voice. "I did not embarrass him on purpose. I just wanted to go for a run." She twisted her hands together. "I miss being active."

"Sometimes I think you enjoy causing discord. Your friend should instruct you in proper behaviour."

"I thought you understood..." Her gaze travelled over his face, seeing no trace of sympathy. No emotion at all. Just his bland face.

"I try, Sophy, but sometimes you go too far. Please try and stay out of trouble for next few days."

Hurt by his words, she fled to her lonely chamber and stayed there until the wedding week was done.

$\maltese$ 12 $\maltese$

EMERGENCE

W AKING FROM A NIGHTMARE, Sophy woke up to a room bathed in the early morning light, the pale walls glowing yellow like freshly churned butter. Massaging the pain of another headache from her forehead, she sat on the edge of the bed and let her gaze roam about the room until it rested on Aria's empty bed.

"It's today," she said to herself. Headache forgotten, she looked through piles of clothes for a dress to wear. After discarding several, she found a pretty, violet-coloured dress with silver leaves embroidered across the bodice and sleeve edges. She found the matching trousers in a chest and hastily put them on. While she remained locked in her self-imposed exile, Aurore had sent her a new set of outfits, designed specifically to suit Sophy's needs. The news of her argument with Willow had obviously reached Dellbright's mother. She had set to work to supply Sophy with garments that followed the keep's dress standards for young ladies but also allowed Sophy to engage in outdoor pursuits with some decorum. Still a beautiful creation, the dress was shorter at the front, ending just above the knees but sloped down to brush her ankles at the back. A matching pair of loose fitting trousers secured at the waist completed the set.

Happy notes floated around the room as she sang to herself while dressing with care. Then she flung open the door and descended the stairs. It was early, and only a few servants were about. Down the corridor, she caught a blur of white out of the corner of her eye, and groaned inwardly. It was too late to retreat upstairs or dash into the great hall to avoid the encounter, so she folded her arms loosely and waited.

Master Willow approached with a jubilant smile on his face. "My Lady Sophy, how pleased I am to see you this day. Surely, the very air is fine and pure. Your smiling eyes add to the lustre of the day." He bowed low over her hand and smiled.

Sophy had to close her mouth as she floundered in forming a reply. She doubted she'd been forgiven.

"Why, thank you, Master Willow," she smiled and curtsied back to him, although her left eyebrow was half-arched in cynicism. Luckily, the gesture was lost on him. "It is a beautiful day," she said. "A perfect day for Aria to re-emerge."

"Perhaps, you are right. I had forgotten that their highnesses were leaving the wedding chamber this day." He made to walk away and then paused dramatically. "I must be about my business. Oh dear, so much to do—there are numerous affairs to prepare for the prince's perusal and the princess must have an odious amount of duties in need of her attention." He patted her on the shoulder. "If you are fortunate," he added in a low voice, his face decidedly smug. "You may see Princess Aria during mealtime, perhaps the eve-tide meal." He turned on his heel, cloak billowing in his wake, and headed for his office.

Sophy stood with her mouth gaping. After taking a few calming breaths, she stepped into the great hall. Inside, the clanging of metal platters, the assembling of bowls, and the banging of large urns of toffelporridge signalled breakfast.

Retreating to a corner, she noted the comings and goings and the increase in the number of servants and guards. The green and blue-cloaked men mingled freely. The sounds of idle chatter and laughter reached her, and she looked over to the guards. A few nodded to her, one bowed with a flourish.

Oakheart appeared. He looked good in tight, dark blue breeches, tied up with leather strips that melded his soft brown boots to his calves. His doublet was dark blue with a central panel of lighter blue. He glanced at her, gave her a slight nod. Obviously, he was still upset with her. He walked over to the table, his breeches hugging his thighs, and sat down. In a flurry of activity, servants brought him bread, cheese, ale and a serving of toffelporridge. Plumes of steam wafted off the huge bowl and he started to eat with gusto, despite the heat.

Their argument and her self-imposed exile from the hall were still fresh in her mind. Even as she ignored him, she knew she looked stupid standing around while people were either eating or serving. She had to move. Placing herself opposite him seemed to be the strategically and politically correct option—close enough for conversation, if needs be, and far enough away to ignore the object of her disregard.

After staring at nothing for five minutes, she realised that Oakheart had not greeted her. His breakfast took priority. "Hail and good morn to you, your excellency," she said, voice ringing with cheer. She smiled, for good measure.

Oakheart had his head down, eating heartily. Her smile began to fade. He kept chewing, swallowed and then lifted his gaze to fix on her. There was something in his expression that she could not make out. She began to fidget. He couldn't still be pissed with her could he?

"Hail and good morn to you," he said flatly and returned to his food without a second glance. Definitely still angry.

She sighed, a big sigh, and drank water from a goblet that a serving boy filled for her. Her gaze travelled around the hall, noting the paintings, the pennons and the sheen of the walls. Servants and porters were rushing about and the place looked sparkling. Master Willow was keen to make an impression it seemed. Then her gaze passed over Aria entering through the doors. She leapt up.

"Aria?" she blurted and ran forward. She pulled up short when she saw Prince Dellbright at Aria's side, an expression of surprise on his face. Sophy quickly dropped a curtsy, hopefully with enough aplomb to not look entirely stupid.

"Prince Dellbright, Aria, good morn to you both. You look well," she said.

Aria came forward, face alight with happiness and grabbed her hand and said, "Thank you. Thank you, Sophy. I'm happy to see you," and then with a quick glance at Dellbright, her expression sobered "I mean, I... have passed my time pleasantly. Please attend me in the sewing room before the noontide meal." Aria then took Dellbright's arm and sauntered off to the table for breakfast, greeting the well-wishers pleasantly.

Something wasn't right, Sophy thought. Something lurked there, under the surface. She shrugged. It was a new life for Aria. One bound to make her a bit uneasy. Sophy put the thought away where it niggled at the back of her mind.

The sound of Oakheart slapping Dellbright on the back drew her gaze back to the scene behind her. Oakheart gave Aria a pretty bow and sweet words. Soon the prince and Oakheart were deep in discussion and, after Aria stopped blushing, she was in earnest conversation with Oakheart too. Sophy felt like an outcast while she watched them. In those few minutes, Sophy was sure that Oakheart had spoken more words to Aria than he had to her in the past week. She lost her appetite and decided to go for a walk, all the while hoping beyond hope that Oakheart was too busy to interfere. She needed to think. Her emotions were in a mess. She also realised that she was pathetic to be so dependent on others for her happiness.

While she wandered around the garden and along the gravel paths, she conjured up Aria's expression that morning and tried to analyse it. Aria looked tired, shy and restrained. She then called up Dellbright's expression and realised she didn't know him well enough. Dellbright looked normal, for him. She walked for hours, dawdling among the roses, thinking and dreaming. The fountains at the rear were in full roar. She trailed her hand in the water of a few them as she walked along. A few times during her meanderings, she walked to the end of the path from where she could see the edge of the woods. She stopped, smelled the trees, and pondered their secrets. She wanted to belong here, wanted to feel a part of everything, but she knew she didn't—couldn't.

At length, she returned to the keep and went straight to the sewing room. She heard the giggles through the door and opened it slowly.

The room was full of light and colour. Gowns in various stages of progress littered the room. Hung in its frame was the huge, partially completed tapestry. Sophy kept her gaze averted from it as it reminded her of one of her most awkward moments. Five other ladies were gathered around Aria, who in turn was protected by Aurore. There was a soft word from Aria and the women burst out laughing. Aria's blush deepened. Hovering at the doorway, Sophy was uncertain whether to enter or depart.

Aurore noticed her and called her in. The women giggled and Aria blushed even more.

"Enter, Sophy. You find us being impertinent to Princess Aria. We must gather and wonder over all the personal details. Unfortunately, your dear friend is leaving us to speculation.'

"Please come in, Sophy, and sit by me," Aria said.

Aurore smiled and beckoned Sophy closer. "Come ladies. We must take our stroll in the garden. These young ladies have secrets to share." The women stood up, curtsied one by one to Aria and headed for the door.

As the older woman walked by her, Sophy clasped her hand. "Thank you, Aurore. I am in your debt."

Giving her hand squeeze Aurore kept moving. At the doorway she paused. "Now, Sophy, remember every word she tells you so you may tell us." The closing of the door muffled the sound of giggles.

Sophy hurried over to Aria and hugged her fiercely. Releasing her hold, they gazed at each other silently. Aria seemed on the verge of saying something. Her eyes looked troubled.

"I missed you," Sophy blurted out, and hugged Aria to her. "It has been a long week."

Aria trembled slightly and released herself from Sophy's embrace. "I missed you too.'"

"What could you have possibly been doing all that time? You must have been out of your mind with boredom."

Aria's expression became strained and spots of pink grew on her creamy cheek.

"Come on, you must've done something else besides that. I mean, there are another twenty-three hours in the day."

"You're not being nice. What I did during my wedding week is my business. It is over now and life goes on. I really don't wish to discuss it with you."

Sophy frowned, feeling chastised. Already things were different. "Oh come on. Tell me. What was it like?"

"Sophy!"

"Well..."

Aria gazed out the window. "I was scared at first," she said quietly.

"Really?" Sophy wondered why Aria would be scared. Dellbright seemed so concerned for her, always watching her.

"But...I'm not sure...He tried so hard to be nice to me. Yes, it was fine..."

"Nerves, I guess," Sophy said sagely. "You seem to like him as much as you did before."

"Yes, yes, I do, of course. He's my prince."

"You're not wearing the crystal leaf," Sophy commented.

Aria picked up her sewing and examined the stitching closely. "I don't need it. I can understand everyone now."

Sophy blinked. "Oh. Good."

Aria still peered at the fabric.

"Don't go all quiet on me. Aria, don't be so exasperating. You have no idea what Oakheart has been doing to me this past week."

Aria's eyebrow rose as she lowered the sewing. "What did he do?"

"Well he wouldn't let me go into the woods, and he bullied me. We had several huge fights, where I...um...lost my cool. Then I locked myself away in my room until today."

"Oh no, you didn't."

"I did," she replied.

"But Dellbright asked Oakheart to care for you. I can't believe you behaved so badly."

Sophy stood up and paced over to the window. "What do you mean I behaved badly? Dellbright had no business taking control of my life. You married him. I didn't."

"I won't hear a bad word about Dell. I couldn't bear it. He did the right thing. You don't know this place, and there could be danger. How would I feel if something happened to you?"

"Look, I know you're married to the prince, but Oakheart's another issue altogether. He is an overbearing bully and a bore."

"You can't have your way all the time. You'll have to change your tactics if you want to succeed."

Stunned, Sophy turned around, hands dropping to her side. "Are you telling me to grow up?"

Aria blinked several times before answering. "I guess I am."

"I see, married for a week and you already feel a hundred years old."

Aria's response was a well-aimed cushion. After that, they talked like old times, until Aurore brought the women back and took Aria away to learn more of her duties.

At the eve-tide meal, Sophy was once again seated beside Oakheart. His mood was different; she sensed his excitement and wondered what the cause was. Dellbright stood, accompanied by the sound of his chair scraping. He waited until the talk died down to a murmur.

"I am sad to announce, ladies and friends, that His Excellency, Oakheart Ambassador from the High King of Silverdale, the Welds and Surrounds, leaves us on the morrow. I am told by my dear cousin, Oakheart, that he has business with the folk of the Gilton Forest."

He nodded to Oakheart and continued. "However, fear not, as he will return once more to Valley Keep within two months."

"So, you are free of your burden," Sophy murmured to him.

"Yes, although in my experience one burden is always exchanged for another." As her eyebrows rose in response, he added, "Sometimes the leaving of one burden makes the next one harder to bear."

"I'm not sure I understand ..." She was interrupted by Dellbright who managed to monopolise Oakheart's conversation from there on. She took a drink to quench her thirst and her boredom. However, after sipping the wine she realised her mistake and felt slightly strange and woozy.

Dellbright noticed her put her goblet down. "How do you like the wine? 'Tis a special brew, seeped with *given*."

Sophy tried to focus on him. She'd only taken two small sips. "That explains why the room is spinning.

But Dellbright was once again discussing trade with the Gilton

Forest and giving Oakheart detailed instructions. Everybody's faces seemed fuzzy and then time appeared to suspend.

After a while, when Sophy blinked, she noticed that the sun had set and that Aria and Dellbright had retired back to their bedchamber. She shrugged. She couldn't remember them saying farewell. Their bed, she thought idly, was probably still warm from when they left it in the morning. She didn't want to go to sleep just yet. Right then, she wished she was at home with full access to Jeff's home theatre system and a stack of her favourite movies. The usual night activities of the keep didn't amuse her. The board games, arm wrestling, sewing, reading, chatting about nothing didn't appeal. Restlessness and unease plagued her. She left the table to stare out of the window. A walk would help settle her down. She had been cooped up in her room for days and had seldom experienced the Argenterran night sky since she had arrived. The room spun again; she needed fresh air to clear her head.

Keen to avoid an escort, she slipped out of the hall, heaving the front door open so she could skirt around the keep to the rose garden. Firesticks lit the path, and the evening dew was heavy with rose perfume. She laughed with the joy of it, kicking up fallen petals and treading on others. The sky was a spattering of silver stardust; so many stars that they looked like a spray of glitter.

She craned her neck to capture the whole of the heavens, until it began to ache and dizziness once again claimed her. She searched around and found a patch of sweet smelling grass large enough for her to lie flat on. Pinching off a rose bud, she lay back and sniffed it.

"Mmm…that's so heavenly."

The cool damp grass pressed against her skin and her dress. Stars twinkling, big blue ones, a red one, perhaps, a planet, she mused. Moonlight spilled over the garden. She frowned at it, realising that its light had a bluish tinge. Then she noticed that the moon was different. Its surface appeared smoother and its size was smaller. She really was in a place called Argenterra.

The wine had her head spinning so she was glad that she was lying down. The rose wobbled in her hand as she twirled it and then she heard a step. She stopped breathing and waited to see if she could hear it again. She wasn't alone. She looked sideways towards the rose bush

"Night," she said weakly to his retreating form. She stood and huffed, defeated.

The spell of the night was broken. It was her fault. Oakheart was right, she always created strife. She couldn't bear to see the stars any longer. Their beauty was wasted on her. She stormed off back to the keep and went straight upstairs to bed. She fell asleep straight away, the effects of a couple of sips of wine still making her head spin.

HARMONY AND DISCORD

SOPHY WOKE up the next morning. "Ohhhhh!"

The door opened and Rae rushed over. "Are you ill, mistress? Princess Aria sent me to fetch you."

"Oh, too much wine," she groaned into her pillow.

Rae raced into the washroom and brought a wet cloth. "There mistress. You will be better in no time."

"Thanks," she replied, not confident of a speedy recovery.

Aria bustled in and let the door bang, Sophy cringed. Peeping through half-closed eyes, she watched Aria march around the room, rearranging Sophy's haphazard pile of gowns, muttering under her breath.

"What are you doing?" Sophy's tongue was thick and dry.

"What am I doing?" Aria looked up, green eyes blazing and her cheeks glowing with pink spots. She threw down the gown that she was holding and marched over to the bed. "You're rude... unsophisticated...arrogant... a pain in the butt."

It hurt to blink back her surprise. "What did I do this time? I haven't even got out of bed yet."

"You missed Oakheart's farewell this morning." Aria flung her hands up in the air and went back to tidying up. "Everyone noticed," she continued to rant as she slammed things around. "You didn't even have the decency to thank him for looking after you."

"I'm sorry but Oakheart wouldn't have cared..." Sophy spoke to the ceiling.

"Don't take that tone with me. He noticed it especially." She marched to the bed, hands on hips with her curls flying about her shoulders.

"Oh no." Sophy exclaimed. Recollections of the following evening replayed in her mind with stark clarity. "After last night, too," she muttered to herself, trying to claw sleep from her eyes. Why did her memory choose to be so good this morning? She felt guilty that she had hurt him, without cause and without meaning to do so.

"Last night? What happened last night?" Aria stepped closer, searching Sophy's face for a clue.

"Nothing important," Sophy whispered.

"He didn't have to take care of you."

When did Aria become her keeper? "Well, I don't care much for his care," replied Sophy sulkily.

"Tsk tsk tsk," Aria uttered. "I can't believe that you can behave in this way. Really, Sophy, you have to try harder. I want people to like you. I know you want them to like you." Then she turned on her heel and left.

Sophy pressed her face into her pillow, but Rae had already drawn a bath for her. She threw off the covers with the knowledge that now her best friend in the world hated her.

❦

RAE HAD BEEN SENT OUT INTO THE KEEP'S VEGETABLE GARDEN TO gather gady root. She did not like the chore at all. In fact, she resented being made to work in this place. It was not how it was supposed to be. If not for those two outlander women, her lot in life would have been different. Kneeling down in the gady patch, she fished out a few roots and shook off the dirt. A shadow fell on her and she dropped them in surprise.

Looking over her shoulder, she expected it to be Dellbright or Master Willow readying some complaint about her work or her dress, but it was Sophy. Rae glanced down, suddenly ashamed of her ill feeling. Sophy was not having a good time at the keep either.

"You wanted something, my lady?" she asked.

Sophy squatted next to her. "Can I give you a hand? You know, help?"

"That would be most welcome. I must confess I do not like digging up gady root."

Sophy picked up the dropped roots and held her hands out for Rae to place some more in her hold. After harvesting sufficient number, Rae stood up and brushed off the dirt. Sophy followed her back to the kitchen.

"Can I help you again tomorrow?" the outlander asked.

"Tomorrow I am going up the valley to visit my home."

"Are you? Can I come with you?"

Rae blushed and nodded before she had time to think about it. Did she want that strange girl coming to her home? Her father would love it. Sophy would make a wonderful addition to one of his tales.

❧

ARIA THOUGHT THAT SOPHY SHOULD REPENT FOR HER BAD behaviour towards Oakheart. However, within a week of the ambassador's departure, Aria had forgiven Sophy for her slight. It took a bit of soothing to get Dellbright to forget, though. She hoped Sophy appreciated how hard she had worked to get her husband to be civil.

"So, what are your plans for today?" Aria said as she visited Sophy in her room. As her gaze lingered on the mess, she realised that she was envious of Sophy's freedom. She had a list of duties that bound her to the keep and a husband to mind...

"I'm practicing archery this morning, and then after the noontide meal I'm riding up the valley with some of Dellbright's men as escort. Rae's family are up that way, and I'm going to visit them with her," Sophy said from the washroom.

"That's nice," Aria commented. "Your flowers are wilting." She stepped closer to the vase as Sophy came back into the room, brushing her hair out.

"Mmm...yes. Rae brought them up a couple of days ago. What are you doing?"

Aria stroked the flower, calling forth its energy and drawing on the *given*. Her eyes closed, and she heard Sophy gasp. Then seeing the neighbouring flower in her mind, she stroked life back into that one as well. When she was done, she opened her eyes.

"You used the *given*. How long have you been able to do that?"

Aria smiled, feeling relaxed. "Almost from the beginning. But this is new." She looked up into Sophy's face, and blushed at what she saw there. "It's all right. I am still me. I thought I'd try it."

"What does it feel like? I'll never know so tell me," Sophy said, sitting down on the stool next to where Aria stood.

"Feel like? I don't know, like an electric current, I think, a mild one. It moves and flows in me then out of me."

"Was it scary the first time?"

"Not at all. It was heavenly. I must be off. I have to meet Aurore in the sewing room. We are working a cloth with the *given*, and I mustn't be late. Have fun, won't you?'

Aria hurried out and almost ran to the sewing room. She didn't realise she had spent so much time with Sophy. Aurore would not approve as it caused the other women to sneer and make hateful comments about her friend. Willow's wife, Dela, was the worst, always noting down when Sophy did something wrong, taking offence at every little thing. It grated on Aria's nerves, but what could she do? This was their home, long before it was hers. And Dellbright, he respected Willow and Dela, and how could she fight that? Dellbright was not to be challenged on any issue, she had found. Unhappy thoughts started to emerge. Aria replaced them with happy ones. She loved her prince, she told herself. She was happy, and she only had to be a better wife, a better princess and Dellbright would be content.

"There you are," Aurore said with a smile, though she was slightly tense around the eyes. The air in the sewing room was full of the echoes of words. Dela looked down into her lap when Aria glanced at her. "We started a few moments ago. Now if you take that end, we will work together. Concentrate now on reinforcing the weave. Yes, that is right. More. More. Enough. Now the next section.'

Aria smiled at Aurore, her guidance valued. The bolt of cloth took all morning to reinforce with the *given*. Then it would be threaded through with fine strands of gold and worked with the *given* again. Aria sighed. Sophy missed so much by not being able to use the *given*.

RAE SAT IN A CART, HEADED FOR HOME TO SEE HER FATHER. RAE gazed out over the mountains leaning over the narrow reaches of the valley, where her home was nestled. It was good to see the house again and all those familiar and simple things. She glanced across at the outlander beside her, who had gazed and exclaimed at everything she saw. Rae could taste the other girl's excitement.

The cart's wheels bounced over the hard clay drive, shaking the cart until they pulled up in front of the house. The outlander entered her home, a simple two-storey cottage. Her father, Kushlan, was still in the fields.

"May I serve you some refreshment?" Rae asked, lifting an earthen wear jug.

Sophy's face was serious as she looked over the cottage, the furniture and their personal belongings. "Thanks, Rae. Can I help you, though? This is your home. I don't want you trying to serve me here. I'm very grateful you let me come with you. I hate being in the keep all the time."

Rae brought milberry juice sweetened with honey to the table and poured it.

"There is nothing to prepare, Lady Sophy. You need only to drink."

Sophy threw herself into the chair. Rae suppressed a smile. Sophy was no elegant lady; no respecter of dress and furniture. When away from Aria's influence, Sophy's wayward manner became even more pronounced. Rae liked to conform to the accepted modes of behaviour and dress, but still could not help admiring Sophy's audacity. It was as if she didn't care what other people thought.

As if to confirm Rae's thoughts, Sophy said, "Please, drop the 'my lady' too. It doesn't fit well and I want to relax." Sophy sat up suddenly and regarded Rae with those dark eyes of hers. "I mean, if that's okay with you. I don't want to insult you or anything."

Rae laughed, a soft, fragile giggle. "You may relax...though I warn you now, if father comes in, he is likely to bore you with some tale."

"I like tales. People hardly talk about interesting events at the keep."

"But they do," Rae said as she sat opposite her. "I guess they do not know where to begin with you. Gifts of Crystal Tree Woods are a tale in themselves, and how can anything our people have experienced mean anything to you? I hear the way you speak, even with Princess Aria, and your ways are strange."

"In what way?" Sophy took a sip of the juice. "Hey...this is very nice," Sophy said with a smile as she gulped the rest of the juice.

Rae thought of a polite and correct way to speak. Something was unseen in Sophy, and it made her unreadable. "We speak much more politely and carefully here. We respect each other so we are not as... open as you.'

"I see. I speak my mind. Sorry, have I offended you, too?"

"Me?" Rae said, with a laugh. "No, not at all."

"That must be a first. I can't seem to help myself. I'm always saying or doing the wrong thing." Sophy stood and began to pace around the small room.

"Yes, others take offence. But not me."

"Mmm..." Sophy replied absently. She was staring out of the door. "Is that your father? The tall, dark man?"

Rae went to the door and caught a glimpse of Kushlan, tidying some baskets as he made his way across the courtyard. "Yes, that is Kushlan, my father."

"Oh?" Sophy blurted and then put a hand over her mouth. She looked at Rae's face closely and stepped back to sit back by the table, cheeks red. "I don't mean to be rude, but you both are so dark skinned compared to the other Argenterrans I've seen. Why is that?"

"Best you not ask, for we will be here all day. Let me say that we have other blood in us."

"If you say so," Sophy said. Rae could tell she was aching to pursue the topic. Obviously, the outlander was not offended by their colouring as some of the Argenterrans were.

Kushlan arrived, filling the doorway. His smiling eyes ran over her and then widened as they fell upon Sophy.

"Company, daughter?" He held out his hands.

Rae rushed over to greet him, placing her hands in his and squeezing softly. "Yes, Father. I am sorry for not sending word first. But Lady Sophy was keen to see some of the valley and to be free from the confines of the keep."

"Welcome, young maid," Kushlan said in his rich and soothing voice, slightly accented from his time with the Puri. His eyes never strayed from Sophy. Rae could tell at once that he was extremely curious about this young outlander.

"Father, we cannot stay long. Can I get you some refreshment?"

He smiled slyly. "Some ale would be nice. You will find it in the cellar...no...in the back shed."

Rae smiled back, knowing full well what he was trying to do. "Oh no, Father. There is some here. You will not be rid of me so easy." She placed the ale in front of her father when he pulled out a chair to sit opposite Sophy. He barely tasted it, because he was so absorbed in studying the outlander.

"So you are a Gift of Crystal Tree Woods."

Sophy fidgeted and her white neck went red. "Uh...yes, so they say."

Kushlan's eyes narrowed, and Rae held her breath afraid of what her father might say.

"Much is hidden in you," he said.

"No, it's not," Sophy said. "What you see is what you get."

Kushlan's eyes widened further, showing the whites, then they slid to Rae's. Uncharacteristically, he laughed, really laughed.

Sophy squirmed in her chair, face reddening while she cast Rae a helpless look. "He finds it funny...my situation?"

"No, I do not think so," Rae said, while Kushlan took a swig of ale to help himself quieten. "I think it is your manner, for he does not act this way normally."

Kushlan stood, gave a quick bow. "Forgive me. I did not mean to offend you. But it is your friend that has married Dellbright is it not?"

Sophy blinked. "You find that amusing?"

Kushlan's face became serious, though there was some merriment still glittering in his eyes. "Of course I do not. But you are so...so refreshing. The keep must be an interesting place at the moment."

Sophy sighed deeply. "Ah well. Yes, I think it is...Rae said you knew tales. Can you tell me one? No one ever talks much at the keep."

Kushlan sat down again next to Rae, while she played with her hands and wondered what kind of tale he would tell. His tales thrilled her, but what would Sophy, a girl from another world, think of them?

Her father cleared his throat. "Very well. I will tell you a tale of this valley. It is said that the valley was first beheld by Vorn. He was drawn to its power and beauty."

"Vorn? Oh—the guy Adage mentioned during the wedding?"

"He was the first high king," he said admonishingly, casting a glance at Rae. "Now the wood from whence you came gets its name from the tree at the centre."

"I have seen it.'

"Have you? It was planted by Vorn. He took a branch from the first *given* tree up in the mountains and thrust it into the ground. From there it sprouted and formed the Crystal Tree. In that clearing around the tree can be heard the song of awakening."

Rae thought Sophy was grinding her teeth. "I've heard it," Sophy commented softly.

"Then you know of the beauty of it. Every one hundred years since Vorn planted the tree a woman has emerged from Crystal Tree Wood. As the woods are within the demesne of the valley, all those who have emerged have been under the jurisdiction and ultimately the affection of the prince. It is not law you understand, solely custom."

"I see. Oakheart told me Dellbright was responsible for me. You don't know how much I hate that." Sophy's gaze looked bewildered. "I mean, I like Dellbright, of course, and I'm very grateful to everyone, but I don't like being told what to do, not being free."

"Would you have wed him?"

"Father!" Rae interjected. She stood, turned to Sophy and curtsying said, "I am sorry, my lady. We should leave now." Rae cast her father a severe look.

Sophy stood at Rae's instruction but her eyes never left Kushlan. "I don't think so…but he never asked me—never really looked at me, so I can't say for sure. He is handsome and seems nice."

Kushlan seemed satisfied with her answer. "An honest answer. I thank you. I will make up a tale of the Two Gifts of Crystal Tree Woods and Dellbright's dilemma."

Rae, though angry at her father, reached up to kiss his cheek. "Father, you should not. Dellbright would not be pleased, if he knew. You know he hates the old tales and even the new ones. They smack of gossip, he says."

"I know, child, but Dellbright has no command over my mouth or my mind." Kushlan held Rae by the shoulders and said, "Are you happy?"

Rae let her annoyance slide away, warmed by her father's concern. "Yes, Father. Aurore negotiates on my behalf. I will be happy. Worry not."

"I do not worry for you, Rae. You are a flower ready to bud."

"Thank you, father. We should go now."

❧

FOR ARIA THE WEEKS PASSED QUICKLY. THE DAYS WERE A WHIRL OF activity, spun one into another as she spiralled into her new life. She learnt her duties and tried to spend time with Sophy. However, she had a husband, who was jealous of her time, as well as servants and a keep to run, so Sophy didn't get that much attention. It was a difficult adjustment for them both.

"Princess," Dela said, approaching her at a run.

"Yes, Dela. Is something wrong?"

"The prince asks you to come to the sunroom." Dela clutched her skirts with tight fists and her face was red from running or anxiety.

"What is it?"

Dela bowed her head. "'Tis not for me to say."

Aria walked quickly, head held high. Her heart was pounding. She prayed it wasn't Sophy causing trouble again. Her friend seemed to be the constant cause of stress, not because she did anything, it was merely her presence. She was in the way most of the time. Dellbright didn't understand their relationship—foster sister or their even stronger bond of friendship.

Master Willow complained on a daily basis, although usually directly to Dellbright. Dellbright had joked that he had a tally board of Sophy's misdemeanours and would recount them to Oakheart when he returned. Even though said as a joke, the comment still worried Aria. Even Aurore, who had the patience of a saint, expressed concern that her friend caused a rift among the women of the keep. She didn't sew, she didn't gossip, never appeared to be grateful and her worst crime was that she said what was on her mind without thought of the consequences.

Aria heard muffled voices as she approached the sunroom. Her hand shook as she opened the door. The voices stopped, cut off like a flick of a knife. As she stepped through, she took in the room. There stood Dellbright, complexion dark with anger, Race, his man-at-arms chastened, Willow's eyes gleamed and Sophy. Lord! She was covered in dirt, her hair muddy tendrils, and what was once a clean white shirt had been ripped, exposing part of a grime-covered breast.

"Aria," Dellbright growled. Aria blinked in reaction to her husband's manner.

"Yes, my prince." She tried to sound calm. "What has happened?" Aria attempted to smooth the incredulous look off her face when she faced Sophy. Her friend's dark eyes glowed with anger and defiance. Emotion electrified the room.

"Your friend..." he stopped and took a breath. "You can see, dressed like a man...she..."

"What?" Her eyes fixed on Sophy, when Dellbright turned to the window, unable to continue. His shoulders clenched with outrage. Aria trembled to see it. Dellbright was not easy to be around when he was angry.

"I...was learning to use a sword with him," Sophy pointed to Race, the embarrassed man-at-arms. "The clothes make it easier. I mean, those gowns are not fit for swordplay, even the ones Aurore designed. Anyway it rained, the ground became muddy and well...the fighting became a little close..." She coughed and the man-at-arms blushed scarlet under smears of grime.

"Yes, princess, I found her in this state and informed the prince," Willow said, indignation evident in the shake of his shoulders. "'Tis unseemly."

"It's not unseemly..." Sophy took a breath ready to launch into a tirade.

"Sophy," Aria warned.

Sophy turned to Aria, hands raised in supplication. "But, Aria, I didn't do anything. I wanted to learn sword fighting."

Dellbright turned back. "You—out," he said curtly to the man-at-arms. "Do not speak of this instance to anyone. Go."

In a softer tone, Dellbright said to his chamberlain, "Master Willow, if you would please excuse us, I would like to talk to my wife and her friend in private."

Willow appeared reluctant to leave, but could do nothing to counter such a direct request. The chamberlain bowed diffidently, then gathered his robe around him to leave.

Aria smiled weakly as he passed her by, though what she saw in his face chilled her.

Dellbright leaned against his desk and regarded Sophy with less anger and more humour than before. "Why would you want to learn sword fighting? I have plenty of men to protect you. If you had any sense, you would ask my mother to teach you to sew. A needle is a woman's sword."

"But I hate sewing. I hate being inside all the time. The keep makes me feel ill."

"How did you get into such a state?" Aria asked.

"I told you, the fighting became close."

"Sophy," Dellbright interjected. "None of my men would have torn your clothes like that or trammelled you in the mud."

"Really?" Sophy replied, eyebrow arched. "They would if you fought dirty."

"You didn't!" Aria lowered herself onto the settee, utterly defeated by Sophy's antics. Her dear friend didn't realise how difficult the situation was, or how much Aria had to do to keep everything balanced. Aria hazarded another quick glance at Dellbright, hoping that his anger wouldn't last till the evening. He was always aggressive when he was in a mood. She closed her eyes, trying to shut the thought out.

Sophy hung her head. "I did a little. Race and the guards were only getting their own back. When I figured out that they were treating me like some little maiden, I turned the stakes. Then it was a matter of pride for them to defeat me. Race would have done so...if Willow—"

"Master Willow," Dellbright corrected.

"—Master Willow hadn't come upon us and run to tell tales."

"I see," Dellbright said, rubbing his chin. The look of horror and disgust had faded. "You have no sense of the inappropriateness of your behaviour, do you?"

Aria thought she saw his lips twitch ready to smile. He coughed into his hand and then his face was once again stern. She let out a breath slowly; perhaps it was going to be all right after all.

Dellbright coughed again and stood in front of Sophy, chin jutting aggressively. "I forbid you to engage in sword fighting with my men, or any man, while you are in my care. You will dress appropriately, behave appropriately and speak appropriately..."

"Or what?" Sophy's eyes glowed with rebellion.

'Sophy, don't?" Aria said.

Without sparing Aria a look, Sophy lifted her chin slightly, gaze never leaving Dellbright's face. "Tell me. I'm interested to know. Will you send me back to my world?"

"That cannot be done," he replied, voice once again shaking in anger. "I could hand you to the next Puri raider I see."

"That would be better than hanging around here."

Dellbright slapped the desk with the palm of his hand. "Care you not for anything? Have you no respect? Do not worry. I will find a way to curb your errant behaviour. Now go and get cleaned up."

Sophy dragged her tear-stained face from his and brushed past Aria in her haste to get to the door. "And," he added to her retreating back. "Keep out of trouble and out of my sight for the rest of the day."

The door slammed. Dellbright slapped his thighs and turned away. Aria didn't know what to say or do. Silence. Then when Dellbright had some measure of composure, he turned back towards her. "Come here," he said softly.

He opened his arms to her, and she hastened to him. She was eager to soothe his anger.

"Oh, Dellbright, I'm sorry. I'll speak to her. I'm sure it won't happen again."

"Yes, I know you will."

Yet, each day little misdemeanours piled up high on top of Sophy's worst ones. Admittedly, Sophy really did try to keep in line, but it seemed she could do nothing right. Aria was torn. She loved Sophy, knew her faults and lived with them. However, she wanted to be accepted by her new family, wanted to retain Dellbright's love. She trod a fine line between harmony and disharmony.

❦

DESPITE FEIGNING INDIFFERENCE, SOPHY WAS EMOTIONALLY drained by the general angst that permeated the keep. It was obvious that it couldn't go on. Something had to give. The next morning, while she sat on the bed brooding, Aria knocked on the door and came in, a bunch of yellow flowers in her hand.

"Morning, I thought these would cheer you up."

Sophy smiled wanly. "Thanks. Look, I've been thinking."

Aria arranged the flowers, trailing her fingers on the long petals. "Thinking? About what?"

"I can't stay here anymore. It's not working out. You know the keep gives me a headache. I can't use the *given*. There is no point in me staying. I'm in the way and making everyone suffer, including me."

"No, no," Aria said with tears in her eyes. "You can't leave. You have to stay here in this place with me. I need you."

Sophy noted the dark smudges around Aria's eyes and realised that she had caused worry and stress for her friend too. "No, you don't need me. I make trouble, without trying. Please let me go. I'll come back again but I need to be free. Release me." Sophy's heart pounded as she said those words—words that had been building up inside, bursting to be free. At the same time, she was afraid to be parted from Aria. But she knew she wasn't responsible for Aria's choices, even though they affected her.

Aria sat down on the bed and leant against the wall, twirling a ringlet in her hand. Sophy watched her and waited for an answer. Aria looked up, her eyes unnaturally bright. "Perhaps you can travel with Oakheart. Dellbright mentioned that he could ask him to take you to the high king's court. Dellbright is sure you would enjoy it. And Oakheart would bring you back again."

"You mean I can go—explore?"

Sophy locked gazes with Aria and saw her nod.

"Yes, if you go with Oakheart I know you'll be safe and happy. But Sophy, don't stay away too long."

Sophy stared speechless for a few minutes, trying to digest this new direction in her life and the impact it would have on Aria and herself. Nodding absently, she said, "Of course, I'll come back to you. Where else would I go?"

"Good. Now that's settled. Let's do your hair." Aria pointed to the stool with the brush. Sophy sat back down and let her friend style her hair. She smiled at Aria through the mirror. "Aria?"

"Yes," Aria replied placing a flower in Sophy's dark hair.

"Actually, the place I really want to go is Glassy Mountain Retreat."

Aria's eyes widened. "The retreat? Why, for heaven's sake?"

"A few reasons. Maybe I can find out why I can't use the *given*."

"But it's in the mountains. It could be dangerous." Aria's expression was a cross between horror and disbelief.

"I kind of gathered that it's in the mountains."

"But it's full of adepts. Why would you of all people want to be around studious, austere adepts? I can't see that appealing to your sense of excitement."

"Aria...Adage invited me. I said I would come. I'm a mystery to him. Perhaps there will be answers there. Though the way you talk about it, I'm getting put off."

Aria stood with her hands frozen in Sophy's hair, her face creased in puzzlement. "Oh, but that means you will be away for an age. The trip to Silverdale could take months and then..."

"Don't worry. I'll come back to see you first. I mean, I'll try." Sophy put her hand on her chest, the quiescent leaf hidden beneath her skin.

❧ 14 ❧

A BURDEN SHARED

OAKHEART RODE into the keep's courtyard and slid off his mount. Surprisingly, Dellbright came forward, pushing through the crowd to greet him. Oakheart was both surprised and suspicious. He watched as Dellbright issued instructions to his men to take their horses away and place Oakheart's belongings in his room. After the immediate tasks were dealt with, Dellbright faced him and said with a large welcoming smile, "Welcome back. You do not know how I have missed you."

Oakheart looked askance as his cousin embraced him, wondering why he made such an effort to greet him after so short an absence. "I am glad to be back, cousin." The rest of his party rode into the courtyard, distracting Oakheart from quizzing Dellbright. He sensed that something was amiss. Stepping clear of the milling horses, Oakheart waited until the rest of the party dismounted. His special guest walked briskly up to them and then waited to be acknowledged.

"Prince Dellbright, I have brought Lillia of Gilton Forest. Please welcome her with the warmth of your hearth and the bounty from your table."

Dellbright bowed low to Lillia. "Be welcome in the *given*. The keep is ready to receive you. The Gilton folk are always welcome here, though rare are your visits."

The forest maiden saluted the prince. "I am happy to be once again in Valley Keep. May I be of service to you in times of need." Willow Reed appeared at the prince's elbow and led Lillia into the keep. Dellbright's gaze grew serious as he watched the maiden pass through the doors. It appeared that he wished to speak to Oakheart before offering him shelter.

"What is wrong? Why these brooding looks of yours?"

"Wrong?" Dellbright flushed, as he turned to lead Oakheart into the keep.

"Nothing...but I have a small matter to discuss with you. Please come into the sunroom. I have some mulled wine ready for you—to ease away the aches and pains of your journey."

Oakheart grinned as he followed Dellbright inside. He had an idea what was amiss—or who was amiss. He mentally prepared himself for Dellbright's discussion. Looked forward to it, actually. Could the political niceties be managed so easily?

"Please, cousin. You must do this. I will have no harmony in my house until you take the Lady Sophy away. Even for a short time. Though she is Aria's foster sister, or more importantly her friend, others dislike her. They make trouble for her."

"That I find hard to believe. The Lady Sophy makes her own strife. You wish to give me the trouble of her, when the responsibility is yours alone." Oakheart enjoyed this discussion. Politics always thrilled him. The custody of Sophy was a matter of delicate politics. He wanted Sophy in Silverdale and then in Glassy Mountain Retreat where the adepts could study her. Yet if Dellbright knew this, he would object to Sophy leaving his jurisdiction. It was the way of things. There was always going to be friction between Valley Keep and Silverdale. Each vied for a place of standing in the world; each leader believed theirs was the greater right, bequeathed by history, to rule all Argenterra.

Dellbright sat staring into his goblet, thoughtfully. "I know," he said at last, "she is my responsibility. Yet, no one ever predicted that I would have two outlanders. You are not seriously suggesting that I should have married both of them?"

The shocked look on the prince's face sent Oakheart into a bout of laughter. He relaxed back into his armchair and sipped at the goblet of Dellbright's best wine. Spiced and warm, it slid like nectar down his throat. He eased the soreness out of his back. It had been a long ride, after all. "No, my friend," he said after his mirth had subsided. "I could not wish such a fate on you. Any man who gave his heart to the feisty Sophy deserves pity and not scorn.

"But I have far to travel, even though Lillia of Gilton Forest is with me and could be a chaperone for her. I fear that even Lillia's warrior's heart would quail with Sophy's ways."

"I beg you. Take her for a short journey first and see the way of it. Surely you need to return to the high king before you take the trek to Glassy Mountain Retreat?"

Oakheart was thoughtful. The mention of the retreat made his path easier. Now he could take Sophy there without raising suspicion. "It could be done," he said carefully. "The adepts should not object to her presence...she may be an object of curiosity for them."

Oakheart liked seeing his cousin at a disadvantage. Dellbright had been so cocky since he wed the beauteous and graceful Aria. "Surely such a favour deserves a special reward," he said, rolling the stem of the goblet in his fingers.

"I have no sister to promise you for a wife. I have a new foal though, if that would suffice."

Oakheart sat giving the appearance of deep thought and consideration. "Well, 'tis a pity for me that you have no sister to offer. A union between Valley Keep and Silverdale is long overdue. Yet, the foal is a very thoughtful gift." It crossed his mind to say that no reward was worth spending time with Sophy. No one had treated him with so little courtesy in his lifetime; no one had ever ignored his charm or his good looks and no one had ever forgot who he was the way Sophy did: regularly.

Dellbright's smiled. "Thank you. Now there will be peace in my household."

"I will take the Lady Sophy with me, and keep her well in my care."

RAE DREW THE BRUSH THROUGH SOPHY'S HAIR. SOPHY CLOSED HER eyes, letting the tension flow out of her. When she opened her eyes, she was startled to see Aria standing there, panting. Aria dismissed Rae.

"Oakheart is back and he has agreed to take you with him." Aria started playing with Sophy's hair nervously and studied her in the mirror. "So, will you go?"

"I'm not sure. Let me see if Oakheart is really willing to take me, or is being forced. That would be worse than anything."

Later in the day, after dodging the high king's ambassador in the great hall, Sophy met him in the rose garden. The scene reminded her strongly of his curt words the night before his departure and her unintended slight. It would be better to come straight out and apologise but she couldn't quite manage it. "You're back. Pleasant journey, I hope," she said sweetly, curtsying impressively before burying her face in a rose bush.

"I am," he said, bowing low. "My journey went well, I thank you."

"That's nice," she said and continued smelling the roses.

He stood quietly for a moment. "I have come to ask…" He stopped and then started again after a moment of hesitation. She did her best not to gape at him in surprise.

"I have come to ask if you would accompany me on a journey. I will be returning to the high king's court for a short time." He stared at her, then added. "Please."

Lost for words, she said, "Thank you for asking me."

"No need to thank me…yet. I am willing to…"

Sophy interrupted. "I'm sorry that the prince and princess have asked you to do this. It must be a real burden." She couldn't discern any emotion in his face. It was bland. She hated not being able to fathom what he was thinking.

"I hope, my lady that you will not be a burden."

With one hand on her hip she said, "I haven't said I would come yet."

"But you will." His voice dripped confidence.

Sophy's hand fell to her side. "What?"

"You will come with me."

Sophy stepped back. "How do you know that?"

"Because 'tis the only option left open for you."

Her fist clenched. "I see. I could return to my own world."

"How?" Oakheart looked relaxed as he bent a knee.

"I don't know...do you know the way?"

"Through Crystal Tree Woods? No, I do not."

"You can be so infuriating."

He smiled. "And so can you."

"Don't I know it."

He laughed softly, running his hand along his hair, brushing loose strands out of his eyes.

"Will you come with me? After the high king's court, I can take you to Glassy Mountain Retreat. You will find some answers there. We all will."

"Yes, I will come with you to Silverdale and Glassy Mountain Retreat and try not to be a burden."

He stood waiting. Then she curtsied low again and said. "I thank you for this honour, Oakheart. Your heart is true." Aria had drummed into her the ritual response for such a favour and, in this instance, she didn't mind so much.

"We leave on the morrow within an hour of sunrise. You will be down in the bailey, dressed, packed and on your horse by that time."

"I think I can manage that."

"Be sure you do. I do not like to be kept waiting, and we must adhere to the schedule if we are to make the crossing."

"Sure."

Sophy walked by his side through the garden in the general direction of the keep. "I must ask you to meet someone who will be travelling with us. She will be your chaperone."

"My what?" Sophy stopped dead in her tracks.

"Your chaperone. You cannot travel with me without one. You cannot travel anywhere without one."

"Oh why? Will it deplete my worth or something?" Sophy ground her teeth.

"Truly you do appear to be intelligent, but at times the evidence escapes me. Not only are you a young lady, you are a Gift of Crystal Tree Woods. Therefore, you must be guarded and protected."

"But I'm not important...and I'm not going to marry anyone here in this place. So who cares about chaperones?"

He turned to face her, eyes serious. "I care, Sophy."

"But..."

"We will not argue the point. A chaperone guards not only a female's honour, but a man's also."

She couldn't repress a smile. "I see...you need protection from me. I like that."

Oakheart frowned, his eyes narrowing. "You are too silly for words. I hope in time you learn more sense. It seems you have lost a lot since I have been away."

In the great hall stood a middle-aged woman, taller than Sophy, wearing green and brown dyed leather trousers and jerkin. Across her chest was a hardened leather chest plate engraved with a leaf pattern. She had a quiver of arrows on her back and a keen look in her eyes as if she could see behind curtains and around corners. Her short-cropped hair and tanned complexion made her stand out from the other women, who were standing nearby. Sophy guessed that this was the 'someone' she was to be introduced to so she walked a little faster. She hadn't realised that there were different peoples here, hadn't thought beyond the boundaries of her own confined experience. Now this forest lady drew out her inborn desire to discover the unusual. She curtsied as Oakheart addressed the older woman, "Lillia of the Swift Arrow, may I introduce Lady Sophy, Outlander, Gift of Crystal Tree Woods."

Sophy's eyebrow's shot up at the title Oakheart had labelled her with. She smiled in spite of herself and saw the answering twinkle in Lillia's eyes. This was some chaperone. Sophy was sure this woman could look after herself.

"My lady," she bowed with a quick dip of the head and kept her expression passive, yet Sophy detected a hint of amusement still in her gaze.

"I'm so pleased to meet you," Sophy blurted out. "Please, I would love to hear of your home, your people, your way of life. Why do you journey to the high king's court? May I sit with you during the eve-tide meal?"

It was Oakheart's turn to laugh and he did, heartily. Without a backward glance, he left the two women to their discussions. Sophy asked forgiveness. Luckily, Lillia found no harm in Sophy's exuberance, and they did not stop their chatter until it was time for the eve-tide meal. Sophy sat next to Oakheart and she could hardly contain her excitement. She smiled at him and at Lillia who sat on the other side of her. "How many times have you been to the high king's court?" she asked Lillia around a mouthful of soup.

"At least thrice. Although I have not been for many years."

"Do the Gilton forest folk travel a lot?"

"Not often. We mix with the overlanders at times. Although our ancestors arrived in Argenterra with Vorn, my people prefer the shadows of the trees and the company and simple ways of our clans."

After a long period where only Sophy and Lillia spoke, Oakheart interrupted politely. Sophy absently drank from her goblet of *given*-brewed wine. "My ladies," he said and looked at Sophy especially as if she needed extra reminding. "We depart on the morrow. Please be packed and ready early. Within the hour of sunrise."

"What?" Sophy squawked. "I forgot that we were to leave so soon. I don't have a thing to wear." His eyes rolled up.

"I will do my best," she added as Lillia nodded like a salute. Sophy drank some more wine nervously. A sudden light-headedness threatened to overwhelm her. Jerkily she put down the goblet, sloshing the contents onto her hand. The cup clattered to the floor and its clang sounded far away. She looked at Oakheart, saw his frown of puzzlement, and fell face-first into his lap.

❧ 15 ❧

LEAVETAKING

A LARGE HAND on her shoulder woke Sophy the next morning. She tried to turn over, groaned and growled low in her throat when her body wouldn't obey. A weight held her down. She tried to open her eyes but they weren't functioning. She was in her bed; she smelt the familiar herb scent of the pillow. That was good, she thought. Reality still floated out of reach.

The hand shook her again. She moaned in protest and opened her eyes, an angry retort on her lips. Her head ached like it had been turned inside out. Her mind was a fudge of slow, half-articulated thoughts. She opened and closed her eyes. There was something she wasn't getting, like why he was in her room.

Oakheart loomed over her and before she could say anything, and before he had voiced the anger apparent in his gaze, a breathless Aria arrived at her door, nudging a nervous looking Rae out of her way.

Sophy realised many things at once: she was naked under the sheets, she was late, Oakheart was in her bedroom, Aria was at the door, her green eyes like blazing daggers and—worst of all—she wasn't packed.

She cringed under the covers, looked from the angry Oakheart to the startled Aria and the horrified Rae. Realising that her hair was standing on end, and that her bare shoulder was exposed and probably other parts of her as well, she couldn't take her eyes off her audience.

Her face started to heat. "Sorry, have I overslept?" Her face creased with pain and her headache, thumped-de-dumped. She tried to pull the covers higher, but Oakheart was poised to pull the covers down. All movement was suspended; everyone had stopped breathing as the situation unfolded.

Oakheart inclined his head, swallowed and moved his hand from her covers ever so slowly, his blush surpassing hers. Aria coughed, shattering the awkward moment. She wasn't a princess for nothing, Sophy thought, letting out a sigh of relief, and then cringing when her head hurt. She was hung over, yet she couldn't remember drinking enough to put her in such a state. Damn that *given*-brewed wine. It must be the reason she was so intoxicated, like everything else made with the *given* it did not agree with her.

"Sophy, come on. I have all your things packed. Please excuse us, Oakheart. We'll be down in a moment."

Oakheart took the opportunity to back down gracefully. After fixing Sophy with a fulminating stare, he swivelled on his heel and left. Sophy noticed a faint blush still on his cheeks although it was nothing compared to the all-over glowing red of her embarrassment.

"Thanks, Aria. You ..."

"We don't have time to discuss this. And now that you have gone and slept in, I can't say all the things I was going to say. It was enough that you flopped dead drunk into Oakheart's lap last night."

"I didn't!" Her memory was blank and that horrified her.

"You did. He had to carry you up the stairs as you were so drunk you were unconscious. I had to strip your clothes off and throw you in the bed. How much did you drink, anyway?"

"About three mouthfuls. I think it's the wine. It does something to me."

"Never mind. You have ruined everything." Aria sniffled as she motioned to Rae to bring the clothes and gave short orders to wash this, move hands, put this on— until they were on their way down the stairs to the courtyard.

Abruptly Aria asked, "What was Oakheart doing in your room? Has he been there before?"

Heat crept up her neck. "Well…It's not usual. I…well…er…I have to make him pretty angry. I think he might have come into my room once before though I was fully dressed—Rae was there."

"Mmm… I see." Aria's eyes assessed her.

"I have to go." Sophy hurried down the stairs, not enjoying how each step reverberated in her head. Then she came out into the bailey with Aria close behind.

The travelling party had assembled near the archway, on a patch of grass strewn with straw. Sophy stepped across courtyard tiles as she followed Aria. A wave of nausea threatened to undo her. "Here is Dellbright and you'd better be quiet. I think you ruined his farewell speech, too," Aria said crossly.

" Sorry," Sophy whispered, embarrassed by all the fuss as well as weak with sickness. This was not how she envisaged leaving Aria. She hurried over to Dellbright and curtsied low, hoping that she didn't topple over.

"Please forgive me, Prince Dellbright. I overslept." Her face radiated heat; she could only imagine how red it was. They all had witnessed her falling dead drunk into Oakheart's lap. Dellbright nodded once, his face grim. Sophy stood and curtsied again to Willow and Lillia. "Master Willow. Forgive me. And Lillia, my humble apologies. Honest, I only drank three mouthfuls of wine."

They all stared —like they were looking through her. Her gaze shifted to Oakheart. He was on his horse, looking everywhere except at her.

"Oakheart?"

He didn't look at her.

"Your excellency, please accept my humble apologies."

Still Oakheart would not look at her. That man was stubborn. "I won't drink wine anymore. Actually, I shouldn't touch the stuff. You must have seen that I only had a few sips, but its effect on me is disproportionate. I did not er…fall on you on purpose or delay our departure this morning deliberately. I can only thank you for your care and your concern."

He was looking at her now. She smiled at him tremulously.

"Very well," Oakheart replied. His tone not very encouraging but at least he was speaking. "Let us depart. Your horse is there."

Sophy was wearing one Aurore's specially designed outfits that would suit horse riding well enough, even though the fabric was slippery and flimsy. At least the long padded trousers would protect her legs from rubbing against the saddle. As she mounted the horse, she realised that she had no idea what clothes had been packed for her, although she did remember to bring her cloak, which she tied under her chin.

They were all mounted. The prince stepped forward and stopped by her leg. He gazed at her with his dark eyes and handed her a cloth bag. "Thank you, Prince Dellbright. What is it?"

"'Tis a talkstone. They are rare, but it is tuned to Aria so she will be able to speak to you over the distances. Unfortunately, no one else may use it. She has gone into the keep to test it. Wait a moment."

Sophy held the bag by the tip of the cloth not at all certain what to do with it. She nearly dropped it when Aria's voice sounded from within. She undid the cord that tied the top, tipped a crystal stone into her palm, and saw Aria's face reflected in it. Then the pain bit into her palm. The talkstone was hot, as if straight from the fire. She juggled it from hand to hand, saying "ouch'. The horse skittered as she wavered in the saddle, until she lost her balance and fell heavily, with the talkstone landing in front of her face.

The assembled party roared with laughter. She looked up and glared. She wasn't quite winded, more like her dignity, what was left of it, was dented. "Hello? Sophy? Why are you on the ground?" Aria's voice issued from the stone. The image of Aria's face floated in the stone's faceted form.

"No particular reason. Bye, Aria. Take care of yourself. I'll miss you." Then she noticed through the stone that Aria was crying. "Don't cry, Aria. I'll be back."

Dellbright bent down and placed the stone back into the cloth bag. "Here, let me help you remount." He helped her rise while she brushed straw and dirt from her clothes. When he hoisted her back into her saddle, he said. "I suggest you leave the talkstone in the pouch and keep the cloth around it when you use it. Show me your hands."

He took her hands in his and examined them. There were no marks but a numbness lingered. "Are you well?"

"Yes, thank you. Give Aria my love and look after yourself."

Dellbright's eyes darkened. "I will." He turned away and headed for a small platform so that those mounted could see and hear him. "Nothing saddens the heart like leave-taking," Dellbright began. "Be true and be well on the journey, for it is not complete until we can gladden our hearts in welcoming you back again."

Oakheart walked his horse forward to halt in front of the rest of the assembled party. "Nothing saddens our hearts as leave-taking," he replied. "But your hospitality and welcome has been beyond the bounds of brotherhood. The beauty of Valley Keep can never be diminished, even when burdens are shared. Our hearts will rejoice when we return and can revel in your welcome." Oakheart smacked his chest lightly in a salute.

"Be well, cousin," Dellbright said.

"And you," Oakheart replied. He turned his horse and the rest of the party followed as they walked the horses out through the gates. Sophy turned in her saddle and watched the keep recede into the background. The green pennons on the nine spires snapped to attention as the breeze blew harder. A lone cloud sped across the sky. In the distance, the far peaks of the Glassy Mountains glowed in the early morning sunlight.

As they rode past the farms, farmers, their wives and children lined the cobbled road. The entourage was large; Oakheart had twelve men in blue tabards arrayed in front and behind. At least six horses carried various loads of supplies and two horse-drawn carts carried other necessities. They rode around the woods and further away from Valley Keep. As they travelled out of the valley the mist descended, shrouding the keep in white cloud.

Oakheart sped up and the rest of them followed. Sophy held on, enjoying the first part of the ride. With the breeze in her face and the sensation of power as the horse trotted beneath her, her heart soared with new freedom. Horse tackle jingled in time to the horses' gait.

Lillia rode by her side and after a time talked freely. Sophy was grateful for the consideration as Oakheart had not looked at her once. Like unwanted baggage, it wasn't a nice feeling knowing that you were only there because someone called in a favour. Oakheart kept his group riding at a swift pace. Even Lillia seemed perturbed by their speed.

"I wonder why his excellency is so hurried," she said, as she smiled at Sophy.

"Probably the late start," she ventured and the other woman nodded.

They stopped to rest a few hours later and Sophy was so stiff, she couldn't dismount without assistance, at least not with any grace. She stayed on top of her mount looking around nonchalantly, while thinking of a way to get down without falling on her face.

Lillia would help her if she would only ask, but she hated feeling awkward. Oakheart's men did not know her well. And then there was Oakheart, after this morning, she couldn't bring herself to ask for his help either. Just then, she noticed a presence by her leg.

Oakheart was standing there, his face neutral and bland as usual. Next thing she knew he reached out, grabbed her around the waist and lifted her down from her mount. He held her aloft then settled her gently onto the ground. She grasped his forearms to brace herself and made an inarticulate noise, a cross between surprise and pain. Grimacing, despite her best attempts to hide her discomfort, she couldn't remove her hands in case she fell flat on her face. It was an awkward moment, she had nowhere to look except at Oakheart.

"Forgive me," he said. His emerald green eyes moved slowly over her face.

"There's nothing to forgive," she said. "I should be asking your forgiveness, not the other way around. I'm sorry I can't explain what happened. Usually the sun wakes me, and this morning it didn't. I'm sure I took only a few mouthfuls of wine."

His eyes narrowed for a second. "So you have explained. I do not rise easily to anger as I did this day. Your behaviour did not warrant my ire. Twice over do I require your forgiveness for I caused you pain with my speed. If there is anything that I can do to aid you, please ask."

She tried not to look stunned. After a few more deep breaths, she was well enough to stand by herself and nodded. She unclasped his muscled arms and he moved off, ending their conversation.

Deciding to work some of the stiffness out of her legs and lower back, she walked around, while the noon meal was being prepared. She ate standing up as it hurt to sit. It seemed Oakheart's remorse extended to prolonging the meal so that she had time to work some knots from her muscles.

All too soon they remounted and when everyone was assembled, they took off. The pace was quick, but not as swift as the morning's ride. They had two breaks before finally settling on a camp for the night.

Sophy walked and rubbed her behind while the evening meal was being prepared, lamenting the fact that she had no pain killers. Again, she ate standing and didn't waste any time struggling into the tent that she shared with Lillia. Once she was horizontal, she fell instantly into a deep and exhausted sleep.

Blood curdling fear stalked her dreams, nameless and formless it tracked her down. Screams rent the air in the still night. She awoke to a rough shaking by Lillia, who was calling out her name. When she shook off her nightmare, she opened her eyes to a candle glow. Lillia's concerned face was distorted by shadows, and Oakheart stood behind her holding a lamp. He was mostly undressed, a fact which Sophy could not help to notice among the chaos of her thoughts. She caught a glimpse of smooth, well-rounded bicep.

"What happened?" her words tumbled out, as the memory of the dream resurfaced. "I'm okay. It was a dream, I think. I'm sorry for waking you up."

"Tell me about your dream," Oakheart asked pushing her firmly back to the mattress and tucking her blankets around her. Lillia stood back in the shadows to make room for him.

"Well," she said, closing her eyes to conjure up the image that had frightened her. "There was a face with red eyes. I don't know what else but it made me afraid."

"That is all of it? No messages or warnings?" he asked, looking at her intently.

She shook her head. "Why are you interested in what I dreamt?"

"'Tis good to talk about dreams of the dark, as it helps to dispel their hold," he explained, getting to his feet. The roof of the tent was low and he had to crouch down to leave.

Sophy was certain he had told her a half truth. "What are good dreams then?"

"Dreams of the light."

"Are there other types of dreams?"

"Yes, dreams of the truth, dreams of the past and dreams of the future. You must rest now, as we will leave soon after sunrise." He squeezed out of the tent flap.

"Sleep well, my lady," Lillia said from her camp bed.

"You too," she answered, unable to prevent the tremble in her voice. With her eyes open in the dark, she wondered whether a dream of the dark was another name for a nightmare or something else. There had been a lot of them lately but that had been the most powerful.

✵ 16 ✵

TO BE SEEN

FOR THE NEXT few days they rode, ate and slept. Sophy became used to being on horseback, especially after Lillia had discovered specially made breeches and a long jerkin with a flared skirt in Sophy's trunk. No more flowing, flimsy gowns. Aurore had made her something practical to wear. Not quite ladylike, but modest enough. She appeared the next morning in her new garb. All the reaction she received was a slightly-raised, blond eyebrow from Oakheart.

The valley surrounds fell away, and the green hills faded like the memory of Valley Keep. The only bane of Sophy's existence was the worsening of her nightmares. By day, Sophy enjoyed her surroundings. Heading north and east, the landscape changed marginally becoming flatter with sparse trees and a plain of lush grassland. There were a few occasional rain showers. At times the rain was heavier in the night. Deer-like animals called yelders ran free. There was little sign of habitation; none of the neat houses that dotted Dellbright's valley.

Oakheart travelled in style. They ate delicious meals and slept in well-supplied tents. Even though Oakheart travelled well, he maintained the pressure by sticking to a rigid routine. He also didn't take delays well, so she learned.

"Why are we in such a hurry?" Sophy asked him, as she and Lillia shared a meal by the camp fire. Around a yawn, she added, "The countryside is so beautiful but we don't get to explore anything."

"We need to cross the Argent Flow before the snows completely thaw and swell the river. If there are storms, too, then the upper reaches will be almost impassable after that."

"The Argent Flow?" Sophy was struggling to stay awake at this time of evening. Her nightly forays into dark dreams disturbed not only her own sleep but everyone's. Even Oakheart had dark smudges under his eyes because her screaming always woke him.

"Yes," Lillia replied, "I remember it well. I don't scare easily but it filled me with fear when I had to cross it. The river is wide and shallow there. 'Tis easily passable using the weir, unless the great thaw reaches it."

"And if it is unpassable, what happens then?"

"We must detour to the Lake of Reflections and take the barge across." His eyes darkened as he lifted them to hers. "I do not wish to detour. It will add a month at least to our journey...but fear not, we have time if we stick to our schedule."

"This lake, where does it go? You've never mentioned it before."

Lillia answered before Oakheart could frame a reply. "It feeds into Brighton Falls, which crash like thunder down into the unknown lands and beyond. We do not venture beyond the boundaries of Argenterra. The *given* fades if we pass too far beyond its borders." She drew a map on the tabletop. Sophy nodded, not really taking it all in. "If we must detour and cross the Lake of Reflections, we will have to back track along the base of the Upper Plateau in order reach Silverdale. The royal seat is placed high above the lower lands."

"I see...why does the *given* fade beyond your borders?" Sophy wondered if she would fare better away from the inherent magic of Argenterra.

Oakheart drained his goblet of wine and brushed a strand of hair out of his eyes.

"'Tis said that Vorn instilled power into Argenterra when the First Comers entered here. He placed trees in places around Argenterra, which fixed the *given* in these places. One is in Valley Keep, which you saw during your friend's marriage. Another is in the wood, one in Glassy Mountain retreat...in Silverdale..."

Lillia sat forward and touched Sophy's knee. "In Gilton Forest we have a portion of the tree only. It was grafted to the great tree, which we now call our heart tree. The *given* is there but 'tis weaker. The Puri have no tree to anchor the *given* to their lands. Though they are close to Glassy Mountain retreat and the original tree, they must work hard to use the *given*."

❧

THE NEXT DAY HER HORSE'S GAIT SEEMED OFF. SHE STOPPED THE horse and slid out of the saddle, easing the ache out of her back. She ran a hand down the legs of her mount. When she lifted the rear hoof, she gasped in surprise. The shoe was gone and it looked like it had been wrenched off, chipping the edge of the hoof.

In the distance, she heard Oakheart's bellow as he called a halt. Lillia leapt off her mount and bounded up. "Are you hale, my lady?" she said, eyes darting here and there to the nearby bushes.

"I'm fine, but Merrywillow has lost a shoe."

One of the young men, Brownlea, stepped forward and held the reins for her. As Oakheart approached, Brownlea stepped out of his way, still maintaining his grip on the horse. After asking her the same thing that Lillia did, Oakheart studied the hoof. He ran his hand up the hind leg and then meticulously examined the horse.

"Is she all right?" Sophy asked. "I stopped as soon as I noticed." She slapped the horse fondly on the neck.

"How did it happen?" Oakheart asked his voice tense.

"I don't know. I said I stopped when I noticed it."

Oakheart frowned and then signalled for the party to make camp. He had one of his men, who doubled as a farrier, prepare the horse for a new shoe. Sophy watched while the farrier worked on her horse, acutely conscious of the delay she'd caused.

The farrier noted that the hoof was tender underneath and said that he would have to prepare and apply a poultice to reduce the swelling before he could fit the shoe. Her horse would not be able to be shod until the morning.

Oakheart stalked away and called for everyone to make camp. Sophy was resting against a tree trunk and with a groan she slid down to sit on the grass. A hot burning sensation flared against her bottom and she leapt up with a yelp.

Laughter filtered round the campsite. Lillia looked up from organising their things. Her laugh was the loudest. "By the *given*, my lady, you have sat on a bunch of firesticks. Surely they do not hurt you, for they need the flame to be called before they burn."

Sophy glowered at no one in particular. "Obviously not in my case. Is there anywhere safe to sit?"

That night, Lillia said across the flames. "Do not be disheartened. 'Tis not your fault we are delayed or the horse is injured. Oakheart is fond of his horses, everyone knows that. He tends them closely, breeds them too. Merrywillow is the daughter of his mount."

It seemed to her that Oakheart did his best to reveal little of himself to her. He'd avoided her since they made camp, confirming to her that he was angry. "He's strange," she said. "And moody...I wouldn't hurt the horse. I can't believe he would react the way he has."

"But he has said naught to you about it...I heard no words of blame from his lips."

"Exactly."

She went for a walk, making her way to Oakheart's tent, where he sat outside by a small pit of firesticks.

"May I have a word?"

"Certainly," he said, putting his bowl on the ground.

"About the horse. I have the feeling that you suspect me of...er... well deliberately ripping its shoe off."

Oakheart shrugged. "I have not accused you."

"But you are thinking it. You're always ready to think the worst of me. Why?"

"Because I cannot see you."

"See me?" Sophy blinked. "Of course, you can see me. You're looking right at me."

He moved an errant lock of hair out of his eyes. "I see a frail girl with black eyes..."

"They are blue, dark blue..." she whispered.

His eyes went to her lips. "And with fragile, pale skin..." Her mouth fell open as she stared into his emerald gaze, mesmerised by his intent look. "But I do not see you."

"Could you mean 'sense' me?"

"Yes, Princess Aria called it that. She said during the bonding ceremony that she could sense everyone, except you."

Both of her eyebrows rose. "She never said anything to me."

"Perhaps she did not wish to distress you."

"Can you see others?" Sophy stared at the rest of Oakheart's men, trying to sense them as Oakheart seemed to do.

"Yes, I can see whether they are true or not."

"And Aria?" she asked.

"Yes, I can see that Aria is true."

Brows drawn together in puzzlement, she said, "I don't understand. But let me get this—because you can't 'see' me, you don't trust me."

He looked uncomfortable with her assessment. "It disconcerts me. I can see everyone else, but not you. I have to rely on other things and 'tis not natural to me to do so. I do not mean to insult you."

"Have you never met anyone you couldn't see?"

"Once only."

"But Dellbright never mentioned that he couldn't see me. Other people didn't seem to distrust me...much—I don't understand."

"Dellbright can sense things slightly, without understanding why, as with many others. I studied with the adepts, thus I have greater...skill."

"I see," she said, her back stiff with affront.

He leaned forward and whispered, "Do you see me, Sophy?"

Now he was trying to make peace with her. "No, I don't see you. I don't see anybody. I rely on what is said to me, what I hear, what I feel and what my eyes tell me. I have instinct. I trust you until you do something that breaks that trust."

"You are very strong then. I am not comfortable with trust without 'seeing'. But I will try."

Sophy stood up, said a quick good night and went to bed, her feelings in turmoil.

When she entered the tent, Lillia rounded on her, cup in hand. "What's that?" Sophy asked, leaning away from the concoction. "Tea?"

"Tea, no. While you were watching Merrywillow this afternoon, I scouted around for some Bell Root. It will help you sleep." Lillia poured some for herself as well. Instead of arguing Sophy sipped the brew, conscious that it was not only her sleep that was broken by her blood curdling screams. She drank the whole cup, hoping the nightmares would stay away.

Sophy slept soundly but woke early; it was still dark outside. She rolled over in her bunk and went back to sleep. Soon after, she had another nightmare. Her heart hammered and when she looked down the crystal leaf was emerging from her chest, bringing her beating heart with it. "No! Nooooooo!" she screamed and thrashed, trying to keep her heart inside her chest. She sat up suddenly, huffing like a locomotive. The lamp was on. Oakheart's head peered into the tent. Lillia was white faced and staring.

"Another dream of the dark?" Oakheart prompted.

Sophy brushed a clump of tangled hair out of her eyes. "I guess. I'm sorry for disturbing you."

"Were you having these nightmares before, Sophy?" Oakheart asked.

"Before when?"

Oakheart sighed with impatience. "At Valley Keep."

"Yes, every night, or morning. I don't remember much about them, except that my moaning often woke Aria. Since then, I don't know. I've slept alone. They are more potent since leaving the keep."

"When did they start?" he asked thoughtfully.

Sophy closed her eyes, trying to recall the exact moment. "I'm not sure...I think when Aria became engaged to Dellbright or maybe a little before that."

"After you entered Argenterra, then?" His brows arrowed together.

Sophy nodded, surprised by his concern. It was probably the lack of sleep troubling him.

"Are you well now?" Lillia enquired.

Sophy dragged her gaze from Oakheart and looked at the forest maiden.

"Yes, thanks for asking. I suppose it's time to get up now."

Oakheart left, dropping the tent flaps noisily as he shouldered his way out. Soon after she heard him bellowing orders for this trunk to be packed, or this saddle to be polished and for someone to heat water.

❧ 17 ❧

A DELICATE WEAVE

IN HER ROOM at Valley Keep, Aria drew her talkstone from its resting place beside her bed. With a quick look behind her to check that she was alone, she called to her friend. "Sophy. Sophy?" she hissed into the stone. Nothing. She called louder. "Sophy? Do you hear me?"

The cool edges of mauve crystal pressed into her palms, yet it remained blank and silent. Closing her eyes, she willed it to work while whispering Sophy's name like a prayer, and although the stone warmed to her touch, it did not reveal her friend's image.

"She cannot hear you," Dellbright said from behind her. She swung round, eyes wide with alarm. The door was ajar and her husband stood there, hand on hip, regarding her with his deep, brown eyes.

"Dell, you surprised me." After quickly replacing the talkstone, she stood up and faced him. "Why doesn't she answer me? One minute it works and the next it does not."

"There is no mystery in that Oakheart's gift is acting so," he said and laid her hand on his arm to escort her out. "Think of what your friend is doing. She would be in the saddle during the day. Her belongings in a cart or tied to a horse. If you want to speak to her, you should call early in the morning or later in the evening when she has her things around her."

"It's that simple?"

Dellbright grinned at her. "Yes. You try to call her every day. Why?"

Aria squeezed his arm companionably. "I wish to speak with her and miss her a great deal. For as long as I can remember she has been with me nearly every day. We can talk for ages about anything at all."

They had reached the bottom of the stairs. She could see Willow waiting in the sunroom, piles of documents gripped in his hands. "Do you tell me that you miss the disruption, the discord, the outrageous activities of your friend?"

Aria's cheeks flushed, but she refused to be embarrassed. "Yes," she said, standing straight. "I miss everything about her, especially the antics."

Dellbright stared into her eyes for a moment. Aria dared to breathe. Then a smile quirked, a dimple appeared. "You are right," he said and chuckled. "It has been rather dull around here."

An impulse to kiss him overcame her. She reached up and planted a small kiss on his cheek, though she wanted more than that fleeting contact. "Thank you, my prince, you understand a little."

"Perhaps," he said as he released her. "But I should be enough for you. I should be your life. I cannot help but envy this relationship you have with Sophy." He turned and entered the sunroom, leaving Aria to digest his words. His manner was light, but his expression was serious and a sense of disquiet grew in her gut.

Later, when working with Aurore on a new batch of cloth, Aria discovered she could work the *given* in even more intricate ways.

"Daughter. Your skill is increasing daily. You are definitely worthy to inherit my place here at the keep as a fine worker of fabric. I warrant that your fame will spread far. I have not seen the *given* worked so. Wait till I tell Dell—"

The smile that had spread over Aria's face disappeared. "No," she said, interrupting her mother-in-law. "Please don't tell him."

Aurore paused, her dark gaze assessing. Then she nodded slowly. "Are relations not well between you?"

Aria looked away, and bit her lip. If Sophy had been there, she could have talked things through with her. With Aurore, however, she could not elaborate. How could she tell her husband's mother all her fears and concerns about Dellbright's behaviour? Aria had already observed how the son dominated her—Aurore was as much subject to his whims as she was. "Everything is wonderful. It is not that. I would prefer to tell Dellbright myself and then we can celebrate together. I hope you don't mind."

Aurore's dark gaze assessed her for a few moments, then she directed her attention back to her work. "Of course. I understand precisely." She sewed a few more petite stitches. "My son has a good heart. Life has not been easy for him. Responsibility was thrust on him early."

Aria forced another smile. "I understand. I have no complaints." Aria went back to work, eager to avoid delving too deeply into her husband's past. Luckily, a group of the keep's women arrived to join in the afternoon's sewing.

"Perhaps this regular routine is boring you at little. You should go out and visit the people of the valley, learn more about them." Aurore smiled as she suggested this.

"I'd love to do that. Sophy is out in the world discovering things. Sometimes I..."

Aurore was grinning, with a too-knowing look in her eye. "I know you miss your friend. I hope we are a comfort to you."

"You are. I do not want you to think that I am ungrateful for your kindness to me. A change of scene would be very welcome."

That night when Aria was preparing for bed, Dellbright came in slamming the door behind him. Aria jumped and turned toward him. He ripped the covers off the bed and then stood, peeling off his clothes and throwing them on the floor. Aria shivered with trepidation.

"Has something happened?" she asked. He had been fine at dinner, but had gone off with Willow afterwards to talk business in the study.

"What makes you ask that? Are you criticising me?"

"No, not at all." Panic quickened her heart rate. She went up to him and tentatively reached out. After a moment of hesitation, he allowed her touch. Then she whispered to him sweetly, "I'm so glad you have finished with your work. Now you can concentrate on me. I have missed you."

Dellbright did not smile, but he did not repulse her. Aria reached up and coaxed his mouth toward her for a kiss. This had to work, thought Aria. I must distract him. Willow must have told him about the work she had done that day with the *given*. It was the only thing she could think of to get him in such a mood, unless it was because he had been brooding about her need to contact Sophy.

Dellbright succumbed to her caresses and began to kiss her in earnest. Aria allowed herself to relax into his embrace. He was rough with her, although not violent, like that first time. Aria went to sleep, hoping that in the morning he would have forgotten why he was angry. Her last thought was of Sophy, enjoying herself with Oakheart and Lillia.

❧ 18 ❧

THE ARGENT FLOW

TWO WEEKS LATER, Oakheart's company camped near one of the rivulets that fed into the distant Argent Flow. Sophy dressed in one of Aurore's flowing creations, as her preferred clothing was being laundered. She decided to take a walk around the perimeter of the campsite, which was dominated on one side by the icy, fast-flowing water. The roar of the rivulet surging over the rocks drew her to investigate. Up close, the water was frothy, white with silver threads shimmering in the sunlight. She walked over casually, and smiled at Brownlea, the guard who assisted her every day. He fetched water, erected her and Lillia's tent, and was generally nice, young and fresh. She thought that perhaps he was even too young to shave. Brownlea bowed his head to her and finished filling the buckets with water for the horses.

The edge of the riverbank felt firm, so she edged forward, carefully placing her feet on a large rock. Crouching down she reached into the rivulet and exclaimed at how cold it was.

Brownlea, laughed at her surprise. "You are lucky, my lady, that it is not all of you in the river. You would do more than gasp with surprise," he said, as his soft, pink face glowed with exertion.

Sophy laughed along with the joke. Then the rock beneath her feet

155

lurched. Her ankle bent, and she dropped into the water. The water rose up to swallow her cry of surprise. Pushing up, she broke the surface and was able to let out a scream of outrage as the chill invaded her clothes.

Fighting desperately for a foothold, she couldn't get a purchase on the bank. The water was deeper and faster moving than she realised. It began to pull her away from the edge and tug her further downstream. The cold made her chest tight. She fought to hold her head above water, but it was so icy she thought she would die from it. Her body began to go numb and her vision dark as she slipped beneath the surface.

❦

OAKHEART SENSED SOMETHING WAS WRONG. HE LEFT HIS TENT AND headed to the river, where he had seen Sophy earlier. As he walked, he heard Brownlea give a loud cry. Oakheart ran, in time to see Brownlea plunge into the river, trying to rescue something or someone caught in the turbulent water. Sophy! Oakheart sprinted, fixing his eye on the pale form with dark hair as it sunk below the surface and then surged up again. The girl was fighting for her life. As Oakheart neared, he saw that the current eddied strangely, and there was a strange disturbance in the air, like ripples in the *given*. He leapt into the water and it was as if it moved on purpose to thwart him. Brownlea shouted desperately for help as he thrashed against the current. "Excellency! Hurry, before she drowns."

Oakheart's gaze raked the swift-running current. He edged away from the bank and let himself be drawn along with it. Sophy's head was already below the surface, and her dark hair floated like waterweed. He dove under the surface, using what he could of the *given* to help him. The water was fresh ice melt and his skin tingled painfully. Sophy came into his arms, her head lolling and her body limp. He lifted her above water level in one movement. The strange sensation in the air dissipated. He scanned the shore and the overhanging trees looking for the source of it but could no longer detect it.

Oakheart carried Sophy to the bank, frowning. He stared at

Sophy's still face in fear: her lips were blue and her pale skin showed veins beneath the surface. He laid her down on her back and called her name. He slapped her cheeks, while Brownlea rubbed her wrists. She lay unmoving, with only a ghost's thread hold on life.

In desperation, Oakheart sat her up and grabbed her from behind forcing air into her lungs. Water and the remains of breakfast spewed forth. She moaned feebly, but remained unconscious. That small sound was a relief and it gave him hope that he had not been too late.

By then, Lillia had arrived, alerted by Brownlea's shout and the general commotion. Still wet from her bath, the forest maiden wailed in dismay when she saw Sophy. "Spirit of the Trees! What happened?" She looked accusingly at both Oakheart and Brownlea, before reaching out to touch the unconscious girl's face and chest.

Oakheart stared back, unable to hide his anger, as he cradled Sophy. Brownlea could only lower his gaze and stare at his sodden feet with shame. Oakheart put his arms under Sophy's shoulder and knees, hitched her a little higher in his arms and stood. "I heard the commotion and came at a run. She was already under the water when I pulled her out." He jerked his head at Brownlea. "He must explain how she came to be there in the first place. She cannot," he said in clipped tones. "We will not leave this place until she recovers...if she recovers."

While calling for hot water, blankets, soup and every other thing he thought they would need, he headed for Sophy's tent. Lillia followed closely along behind, issuing instructions at Oakheart's elbow. Once inside the tent, he gently placed Sophy in her bed and brushed a clump of wet hair out of her face. Her breathing was shallow. Behind him, Lillia was rummaging through her medicines, so he put his hand on Sophy's chest and breathed with her. Buried within, the leaf stirred, coaxed forth by his touch as it had with Adage adept so many months before. Pulling his hand away, the leaf emitted a dull glow. Did that mean that Sophy had hardly any life force left? Right then he envied Adage's knowledge. Refusing to believe she was so close to death, he murmured under his breath. "She has to live, has to."

Lillia bolted from the tent and barked commands for specific supplies to be pulled from supply carts. Acting instinctively, Oakheart placed his hand on Sophy's chest to reinforce the leaf with the *given*, hoping that even the small burst that he could manage would keep her bound to life.

The tent flap opened. Lillia poked her head in. "Why are you wasting time? Take off her wet clothes."

He looked up, surprised. "I did not think it appropriate to undress a maiden."

Lillia entered the tent with a jar of ointment and paused at his words. "Maybe. But a dead maiden does not blush. Here, you take off her shoes and dry her feet." She handed him a cloth. He kept his gaze riveted to her small white feet, while Lillia tore Sophy's gown in strips and covered her with blankets. Then she dried her hair, while Oakheart coaxed a fire out of the small earthenware oven.

"Can you turn her for me? We need to apply this ointment.' Gently, he slid his hands under her small body and eased her onto her stomach. Lillia knelt down next to him and shifted the blanket aside. Sophy's bare back glowed in the firelight. His eyes were riveted to her white, unblemished skin.

"Stop gawking like an adolescent. Any one would think you have never seen a woman's flesh." She thrust the pot of ointment at him. "Rub this in for me, and keep rubbing until you feel her breathing ease. I must tend my brew and then we must get that into her."

He looked down at the pot. Gooseflesh was rising on Sophy's skin. Gritting his teeth, he filled his hand with the pungent ointment and spread it on her back. Then he rubbed it in gently.

Lillia looked over. "Come on Oakheart, you are not wooing the girl, you are trying to heal her. Rub harder than that."

He placed more pressure on his strokes, his large hands almost covering Sophy's back. She was so tiny in his hands. After a few moments, she breathed more deeply as he worked the ointment in.

"That is better. With your strength and my medicines she will be better in no time."

"I hope so," Oakheart replied.

The sound of Sophy's strained breathing filled the tent. Oakheart found that his heart fluttered painfully every time she paused in her breathing, thinking that she was about to leave this world.

For three nights Sophy lay unconscious in her tent, tended closely by Lillia and Oakheart. Oakheart was so disheartened he could only give monosyllabic responses to Lillia's various questions. Late in the night on the third day, Lillia spoke. "Oakheart?"

He looked up, drawn from staring into the embers glowing in the brazier.

"You care for her, do you not?" Lillia handed him some mulled wine, which he took.

He rubbed his chin, which now had a blond growth of beard from his days of vigil, and thought of how to respond. "I am not sure I will ever get used to the forest folks' ways."

Lillia nodded and sipped her wine. "You mean because we know each other's business?"

"And are not afraid to speak your mind," Oakheart added. "I am not certain what to say. I have a duty to care for her. So under that duty of care, I do worry and tend her. As a person, I care for her, as I would any other who is in need." He stopped and looked down at Sophy's pale face and dwelt on it for a moment. "Whatever else you may think I can neither confirm nor deny whether I care for her. I honestly do not know. That she has vexed me on many occasions, I admit. That I have cause to have anger at her ways and doings, that, too, I admit. That she is bright and intelligent, too, anyone can see that..."

"I see," Lillia said and nodded. "You do not know what is in your heart, as does not my Lady Sophy. Although for her the task is harder. She is lost here among us. She struggles for a purpose and a place and finds none. All her attempts end in disaster, as if she is cursed."

At these words, Oakheart's gaze locked on Lillia's. He thought for a while, weighing up the evidence. "Perhaps there is an enchantment of some kind on our young friend, after all. But how and by who?"

"These things are beyond my understanding. Home and my maiden's duty have been my study. Only at Glassy Mountain Retreat will you understand her mystery."

"The Retreat. You are right. But first we must get to Silverdale. If she lives."

"She will rally. I see the improvements in her skin tone and in her breathing."

"Perhaps...but we will never cross the Argent Flow now, we have stayed too long. What other ills will befall us before we make the crossing at the Lake of Reflections? We had plenty of time and now we have little. Her fall into the river brings into sharp relief other strange occurrences. Ones I had dismissed previously."

"Do you know that Brownlea told me something odd about Sophy falling in the river? He said the current behaved strangely when he tried to rescue her, as if it was fighting against him."

Oakheart nodded. "Yes, I noticed that too, and something else. I had the feeling that someone was near, waiting to take her from us. I cannot prove it and as soon as I entered the water, I had no trouble pulling her out. But the incident does add further weight to the idea that there is some force at work to harm her. Yet, I don't know why."

"She is young and harmless."

"Not that young." He rolled Sophy back on to her stomach and rubbed the blend of foul smelling herbs that Lillia had prepared onto her back. Then he tossed the blanket back over her, disconcerted that it still revealed the shapely flare of Sophy's hips. No, he thought to himself, a woman grown, but naive and reckless. As he could not 'see' her, he did not know if she was harmless.

Lillia cleared her throat as she straightened the blanket, covering the exposed flesh.

"As you say. I am so old that all those younger than me seem as children."

Oakheart handed the ointment back to Lillia. "Her breathing has eased, finally."

Sophy coughed. Lillia looked on, nodding "Good, my remedy is working."

Oakheart hoped so, otherwise he did not know what he would do, and he cared not to dwell too deeply on the possible consequences if Sophy died.

19

SILVERTONGUE

The horses' hooves beat against the cobbled road as Aria and Rae headed up the valley. Jostled by the movement of the cart, Aria clung to the sides. Rae sat next to her, with an eager gaze eating up the countryside in anticipation of her visit home. The cart turned, and trundled through a gate as it headed onto the farm.

"Look, princess, my father waves to us. He is so excited by your visit."

"Yes," Aria replied, returning the swarthy man's gesture. The cart turned into the track leading to the farmhouse. Two storeys high, it leant over a tidy yard stacked with barrels, sacks of grain and an occasional red-feathered chicken. When they drew to a rackety stop, Aria could not repress her sigh of relief. The cart was not a comfortable vehicle. Loosened hair obscured her vision, so she plucked it off her face. Rae began to assist her to right her clothes and hair. For some reason, Aria felt irritable, and slapped Rae's hands away.

"Don't fuss. Enjoy your visit." Rae's eyes grew large with shock and shame, so Aria smiled to soften her words. "I don't want you to worry after me. I can look after myself."

"Yes, princess," Rae replied, her small, nervous smile returning. She bobbed down quickly then ran to her father, who was dressed in what appeared to be his best clothes.

Aria smiled broadly, genuinely pleased to be out of the keep and venturing to neighbouring farms. It was her duty to know the cares of her husband's people. Yet, when she looked at the clean and tidy state of the place, she worried about the effort Rae's father had put in to impress her. Her desire to accompany Rae had caused extra work and had put everyone out. Now she stood feeling sickly and cross and wanted nothing more than to return to the keep and lie down.

Rae's father stepped forward and bowed low. "Welcome to our humble home. I am called Kushlan."

"Thank you for inviting me to your home, Kushlan."

"It is to our pleasure and an honour that you have come. Rae, when I see her, talks of you constantly."

He led the way into the house. "If you will follow me, Princess Aria, I have laid out some refreshments for you."

She stepped up into the room, which appeared dark after the bright sunlight outside. At first, shadows loomed and then when her eyes adjusted, she smiled. It was small, but clean and tidy. Hand-worked baskets hung from the ceiling and simple, but expertly wrought, furniture filled the room. On the table was a pitcher, goblets and a plate of sweet tarts.

"This is lovely, Kushlan."

Rae's father stretched out his height, appearing two inches taller. ""Tis home," he said, obviously moved by her praise. "A happy home, happier than the keep."

Rae's eyes darted towards Aria, who quickly masked her surprise at the comment.

"I can see it is a good home and that there is contentment here." Aria sat down and accepted some berry juice and a sweet tart. "Please, you must join me or I'll not be able to enjoy myself."

As Kushlan and Rae sat, she let the cool juice soothe her throat. "So, Kushlan, Rae tells me that you know stories. Do you know any about the keep?" Aria played with her goblet.

"Father, you must not—it was so long ago." Rae looked fearful, and Aria smiled.

Kushlan continued, with a reassuring nod to his daughter. "Yes...it seems long ago, when the prince's father abandoned his oath..."

Aria nearly choked on the tart. She took a drink to wash the food down. "Which oath did he forsake? Not the binding oath?" she asked once she was able.

"It was the oath to Princess Aurore."

Aria did her best to stop her mouth from gaping. She took another sip of juice. "But I understood that the marriage oath cannot be broken."

"Aye, 'tis true, princess..." his eyes glittered with memory. "With deed, he could not betray his oath. He could not consummate his desire..."

"Do you mean Dellbright's father fell in love with another woman?"

"Aye, he did. Prince Daken was smitten by a most fair and great woman."

Aria's skin began to moisten. She clenched her fingers, feeling guilty that they were talking like this, about something Dellbright did not speak of himself. But her curiosity overrode her qualms. "They never talk of it. I always imagined that Dellbright's father had died."

"'Tis as if he had. He has left Argenterra, and she with him, and much sorrow did they leave in their wake."

"They hide it well, Dellbright and Aurore. They seem so content."

"Ware well, princess. Such hurt they bore cut them deep."

"Kushlan, how did Dellbright's father and his lover leave Argenterra?"

The older man shrugged a skinny shoulder. "I cannot say, princess. Such things are not told to one such as me. I only know what I know because I worked at the keep back then. I saw the beautiful Aurore suffer. I saw the change in Dellbright after the events unfolded. His cousin, Oakheart, took the brunt of it."

Aria screwed up her face in puzzlement. "Oakheart?"

"Yes, a more bonny young man there never was, filled with the joy of life. He did pursue them, though no more than a child at the time... but he did not return for some time afterwards. The adepts sent word from the Retreat that he had chosen to stay with them...no more was said or done."

"So that's why Oakheart studied with the adepts. It must have been a shock to everyone."

"Perhaps it was. 'Tis said the Prince Daken suffered from Shabra's curse."

"The what?" Aria was out of her depth here. Her gaze flicked to Rae, who seemed enchanted by her father, despite her apparent embarrassment.

Kushlan's eyes widened and his brow furrowed. "You know not of Shabra, of the early tales?"

"No."

"Father, she has been busy learning how to be the lady of the keep." Rae said for her.

Kushlan's eyebrows rose. He poured more juice into Aria's cup. "I see, a pity you did not venture to Silverdale. Within the palace is a great tapestry. It shows Vorn and his kinsman, Shabra, leading the people through the crystal gate. I have seen it once. Vorn was truly a king among men."

Aria resisted the feeling of regret at the mention of Silverdale. She had been wishing more and more that she had left with Sophy and was away exploring Argenterra, on her way to the high king's seat. "Perhaps I will see it one day," she said brightly. "So tell me, what is Shabra's curse?" Aria leaned forward, with elbows on the table and her chin in her hands.

"In those times, you understand, the nature of oaths was not fully understood. Vorn, we believe, understood them instinctively, but others did not comprehend their binding nature. Some say it is the price Argenterra extracted for providing us with the *given*. We must hold fast to our oaths, whether we want to or not.

"When the First Comers began to settle, Vorn told Shabra to choose himself a wife from among the refugees. Legend has it that Vorn considered long and hard before he bound himself through oath and blood to N'brel. But Shabra, though warned by Vorn's wisdom to choose with care, skited and strutted about, laying his hand on the first woman who suited his fancy. The saying goes... Shabra, ignoring his brother's word, chose a life of discord, in haste a wife he did take, and all peace he did forsake."

Kushlan laughed but Aria could only blush. "I see..." She knew the ramifications of her wedding vows, as she had been lectured on the binding nature of her oath when she wed Dellbright. But what if...no, she couldn't think that. Her stomach flip-flopped and suddenly the room began a heady swing, gathering darkness at the edges.

"My lady?" She heard Rae's distant call. She answered dully, but her words would not take shape.

❧

THE GROUND WAS SHAKING BENEATH ARIA. SHE OPENED HER EYES to see the sun low in the heavens. Her head was on something soft. Putting her hand to her head, she connected with Rae. The maid's swarthy, youthful face peered down at her, brown eyes glowing with concern. "My lady? Are you well?"

"What happened?"

Rae bathed Aria's forehead with a cool cloth and helped her to sit up. "You fainted dead away in father's kitchen. I am afraid he was quite shocked and blames himself. He carried you to the cart and bade me return you to the keep."

"I'm sorry, I interrupted your visit with my weakness. I did enjoy myself."

"Oh, so did Father. He misses the keep sometimes. Aurore visits him, but not often these days."

"Aurore visits?"

"Of course. They are good friends as well as being kin."

"Really? Then you are related to Aurore too?"

"Yes, but everyone is related in some way. I am darker, a throwback to my ancestors," she added, gazing intently at her hands. "My great-grand father was a Puri."

Aria's head came up sharply. "Puri? You mean those raiders from the north that Dellbright talks about sometimes?"

"My great-grandmother was taken in one of those raids."

"If she was abducted how did the family come again to the valley?"

"By negotiation. Heer'Panal was chieftain. He argued that he did Goslien of the Valley an honour in stealing her away. Some of the children of their union, and they were many, were bartered for goods and allowed to return to the valley. We all need new blood, so nobody minded so much."

"But what about the one who was kidnapped and taken away? Did she not want to come home?"

Rae laughed, a tinkle of a bell. "No. He bound Goslien to an oath and sealed it with the blood of their union. I heard it said that she loved him dearly and they lived well together. The Puri live hard lives, and they breed hard, too. She had ten children, which is almost unheard of in Argenterra."

"I see,' Aria replied, thoughtful. Her eyes traced the horizon, to the distant peaks of the Glassy Mountain range. The sun's rays painted the snow-capped peaks mauve and pink and darkened the valleys to indigo. She glanced back at Rae. "Are we related too?"

"Well, princess, by marriage we are. Although we tend not to recognise beyond the second blood splitting, usually." When Aria gazed at her dumbly, she added hastily, "cousins, second cousins. But on the other hand I realise that it is not so straightforward as that. You see, sometimes in the second splitting the blood folds back on itself and you become more related."

The cart lurched and Aria clutched the sides. "I see...most complicated." She stared straight ahead. "We are nearly home," she added. The spires of Valley Keep glowed white in the distance.

"Oakheart is Dellbright's cousin. How is he related?"

"Through their great-grandmother, Rada, I think."

A horse approached galloping hard. She could spy Dellbright in the saddle, wind rustling his dark curls. Her stomach fluttered as butterflies took flight. He looked so strong and brown upon his horse. He yelled to them, though the wind caught the words, and she could not understand him.

Rae leant in close. "I sent word of your illness, my lady."

"Thank you," she replied, patting Rae on the hand. She could not blame the girl for doing so.

Dellbright's horse's hooves battered the cobblestones as he drew in closer to the cart.

"Aria? Are you well?" he enquired with a frown.

She lowered her eyes and then lifted them to his with a smile. "Yes. I felt a bit queasy before but I'm much better now. Sorry for troubling everyone."

"Fool idea to trot about the countryside in this heat. Mother says you should not venture out."

"But I don't understand. She said I should meet the people of the valley. Kushlan was very interesting."

Dellbright's mouth tightened and his eyes flicked to Rae. "Filling your head with yokel gossip, was he?"

She looked away and felt her cheeks pinken. "I...er..."

"Never mind." Dellbright edged his horse away from the cart. With a wave of his hand, he called out, "Driver, move on. I will follow." The cart lurched ahead and Aria once again felt ill. Though she wasn't sure it was heat or fear that twisted her digestion. Something in Dellbright's manner did not sit well with her.

❦

At the eve-tide meal, Aria could not eat. Excusing herself, she went to her room. She had only just sat down when Aurore knocked and entered, followed closely by Rae. "Now Aria, let me look at you," Aurore said, using her motherly voice. She let Aurore gaze into her eyes, and examine her face. "Will you disrobe for me, child?"

Aria complied with Rae's assistance. As her dress fell to the floor, Aurore's hands touched her breasts and fluttered around her stomach. "Have your breasts felt tender?"

"Mmm. Yes," Aria answered as Rae helped her put on her nightgown.

"And the moon's tidings?"

Aria shook her head. She had not had a period at all since coming to Argenterra. At first, she thought it was the journey, the shock and excitement. Now, she didn't need to guess where Aurore's questions and conclusions would lead.

"This is very good news. You are with child, and so quickly too. Will you tell Dellbright?" She helped Aria put on a robe.

"Tell me what?" Dellbright stepped through the door. "Tell me why there are so many women in my bedroom?"

Aria smiled nervously. She had hardly had any time to digest the news. However, she did know what the consequences of unprotected sexual intercourse were, so she shouldn't be that surprised. "I'm...er... pregnant. We're going to be parents."

Dellbright stood stock still, eyes wide and staring. Then as if life had suddenly been gifted him, his eyes sought his mother's face. Aurore nodded and he ran forward to clasp Aria's hand. "I cannot believe it. So soon! I never expected that was why you were feeling poorly. You have made me, us, so happy."

20

TRAVEL'S TOLL

Faint sunlight crept in through the tent flaps and the lukewarm rays tickled Sophy's eyelids. A band of constriction bound her chest. When she tried to push at it, she realised it was a large arm. Confused, she gaped as her gaze travelled up to a shoulder and the sleeping face of Oakheart.

Edging up onto her elbows, she caught sight of Lillia asleep on her other side. She tried to pull her thoughts together, but it was as if she had ceased to exist for a time.

She moved feebly under Oakheart's weighty arm, but he didn't move or wake. Prying her arm out from under the blanket, she lifted it towards his face. Her arm was heavy and clumsy and it took two or three tries before she could get it close to his face. That did not wake him so she tried stroking his face and her fingers brushing the bristle of his beard. She had never touched him before, not in this way. Had she ever touched a man on the face before? Perhaps when she was little. Thoughts of her father when she was very young came to mind.

Oakheart's eyes flew open and his hand automatically grabbed hers. He looked disoriented for a moment and then he sat up quickly. His abrupt movement woke Lillia.

"I told you she would live," Lillia cried and hugged Sophy fiercely.

"What happened to me?" Sophy asked in a thin voice. "Have I been sick?" With a bewildered expression, she met Oakheart's, then Lillia's gaze.

Oakheart shrugged, got out of bed and struggled from the tent. Once outside, he called out that all was well with Sophy and then requested some broth. A few moments later, he was passing Lillia a bowl full with steaming liquid and then he was gone.

While Sophy sipped her broth, Lillia related the tale of her excursion into the river and its aftermath. Sophy shuddered. "How awful. And I've caused another delay! This means you won't be able to deliver your message to the high king in good time. It's all my fault. And Brownlea, is he all right? He didn't catch cold, did he?"

"He is well," Oakheart said, as he re-entered the tent unexpectedly. Sophy thought that he was back to his bland self except, as expected, he was angry. She could tell from the set of his shoulders and the smouldering of his green eyes. From being the cause of so much angst, she could readily detect the signs.

"Now," he said with a stern edge to his voice, which snagged her full attention. "You will be careful, very careful, from this moment. I do not need any more mishaps. You will get up and walk gently around the camp and then you will rest. We leave on the morrow."

Lillia assisted her into a robe and helped her with some slippers. With Oakheart and Lillia's assistance, she made her way shakily out of the tent. The men called greetings and well wishes. Sophy nodded her thanks, her gaze searching for Brownlea. She caught sight of him walking towards them with his head bowed. When he caught up, he tried to apologise to her.

"No, Brownlea, I am to blame." He looked to Oakheart. On receiving Oakheart's nod, he ambled off to clean his gear and ready things for their departure on the next day.

Her strength had returned marginally by the time she had walked two circuits of the camp. She was able to walk unaided to her tent where she collapsed back on her blankets exhausted and slightly dizzy. That brooding presence she detected in her dreams was close to her. As she fell into an exhausted sleep, she sensed those red eyes watching her.

In the morning, Lillia woke her and helped her to get dressed. Sophy felt heavy, as if her body was dragging her down. She tried to be optimistic and respond to Lillia's chatter and Brownlea's teasing, but she was still too ill to ride.

When Brownlea and Lillia propped her up so that she could eat breakfast, Oakheart took one look at her. "We will not leave this day. You are still too sick," he said with his gaze resting on her for a few moments, before he left. Sophy coughed her lungs out most of the day. Lillia plied her with herbs and broth until she could hear liquid splashing in her insides. She managed three laps of the camp after noontide meal with the assistance of Lillia. They passed Oakheart, who did not once look up when she went by. Sophy felt the blame weighing her down further. Without even trying, she was being the burden she said she wouldn't be.

The next morning Sophy felt improved, not completely whole, but sufficiently restored to chance mounting her horse and moving on. Although Lillia looked doubtful, she readied their things and went to inform Oakheart that they were ready to travel that day. Sophy wanted things to go smoothly; Oakheart's brooding looks upset her. And every day that she lay about here, the longer she delayed Lillia. But the forest maiden never complained of being prevented from carrying out her duty and was an unfailing friend. So Sophy dressed comfortably for a hard ride. She had finished dressing in her breeches and was wrestling with her boots when Aria's voice echoed from the talkstone.

"Sophy, are you there?"

Elated, Sophy dashed to the stone and unravelled the covering. "I'm here," she said to the cloth-wrapped stone she held in her hand.

"How are things? You must be near Silverdale by now, so Dellbright says."

Sophy thought hard. "Um, well, things are fine, but we are taking our time. Not quite at Silverdale yet. The scenery has been breathtaking to say the least. Everything is so green."

Aria's face peered through the stone. "You look awful. Are you sure you're okay? Oakheart is looking after you, isn't he?"

Sophy had to pause to blow her nose. "Of course, he is. I have a cold—nothing to worry about, believe me."

"I'm glad it's nothing serious?" Aria lowered her voice. "Guess what? I have something to tell you."

"Don't keep me in suspense. You know I hate it when you do that." Sophy smiled at her friend's image, wishing they were together again.

"You are not going to believe this. I'm pregnant."

Sophy made her features bland, even though her surprise nearly made her drop the stone. For her it was the worst possible news and not in the least unexpected due to the circumstances. "Pregnant? Ahh...that's wonderful news," she said, though Sophy could hear the doubt in her own voice that she couldn't adequately disguise.

"Well, I have been a little sick, you know, throwing up all over the place. Dell is so happy about it, I cannot help but be happy too. Aurore and everyone are spoiling me. I hope your slow going won't prevent you from returning before the baby is due."

"Of course, I'll be there if I can. But, Aria, I don't actually know anything about having babies. I might get in your way."

"Don't make excuses. You must be here. I need you ...need you here. How can I go through with this without you?"

"I want to be with you. I'll try to make it, even though I don't make the decisions." Inside she was quaking with fear: babies, responsibility, permanence—it was all too much. Aria with a husband and a baby meant things would never be the same.

"I need you here. I can't do it without you. I have a feeling..." Aria glanced behind her then peered back into the stone. "I must go now. Look after yourself," she added as her image faded.

Sophy stared at the stone, though Aria was no longer there. Her thoughts were awry. Aria sounded happy, but there was something in her manner, something furtive in how she called to her on the talkstone. Shaking her head, Sophy wrapped the stone and placed it with her personal items. With a heavy heart, she threw the rest of her belongings into her chest and pushed past the tent flaps.

Outside her tent, Oakheart was pacing up and down, grumbling about how Sophy needed throttling about the neck for making him wait. Lillia stood by frowning at him, while she held the reins of two horses in one hand. When Sophy emerged, she coughed into her hand. Turning on his heel, Oakheart stopped mid-grumble at the sight of her and almost threw her into her saddle. Merrywillow stepped back when she settled. Sophy patted its neck and spoke soothingly. Oakheart signalled his men, and they collapsed the tent.

Standing by the horse, Oakheart looked her over casually, not bothering to comment on her looks or her clothes. "Sorry about the delay," she said. "Aria called on the talkstone."

His left eyebrow rose. She wasn't sure if he was mocking her or was surprised at Aria's call. "All is well at Valley Keep?" he asked after a slight pause.

"Yes, I understand they are. There is news, too. Aria is going to have a baby," she added.

He smiled, the light twinkling in his eyes. "That is good news..." then he frowned. "The high king will be pleased to hear it, if he ever gets to hear of it."

Sophy blushed, wondering if he would ever forgive her.

Oakheart nodded to Lillia, who had already mounted. "Let us move on. The carts can follow us. I am keen to put some distance between me and this place."

❧

Oakheart led them relentlessly toward the banks of the Argent Flow, although daily he told them they were too late. When they arrived, Sophy dismounted and stood staring at the river. It was wide, wild and voracious, as it hurled itself over the weir to the rapids below. Spume curled up in wide swirls to paint the sky like tongues of white flame. The sound of the water rushing, like a thousand horses stampeding, exhilarated her. It was impassable, as Oakheart had said. The sight of it was so awe inspiring that she couldn't fathom how it could be passable at any time of year.

Cold and hot at the same time, Sophy felt light-headed as they made camp. At the noontide meal, she wandered around with Lillia in close company. The ground was full of abundant green; spinach, silverbeet and asparagus grew wild everywhere. "One would never starve here," she said as she pointed out the growths to the forest maiden.

"Perhaps, my lady. Look there are toffel plants a plenty. We will need to gather them before we leave. It will take many days now to reach the Lake of Reflections."

The call came to mount up again. Feeling weak, Sophy struggled to mount. Brownlea helped her up and tucked her feet into the stirrups. Oakheart was obviously too angry to take any notice. He had stared at the rapids, lost in his thoughts, for most of the stop.

Strange lights flickered at the periphery of Sophy's vision as she gained her seat. The sunlight warped into crazy angles, shafts broken and fuzzy. She closed her eyes to shut out the sight as it caused her stomach to clench and clench again. She clung to Merrywillow mindlessly, until time became a monotonous blur of passing thoughts streaked in red. She looked up in her daze. The sky had changed from azure to grey. The sun glowed red and painted the edges of the clouds vermilion. It was as if her essence was being sucked away. Smells made an assault on her senses; the scent of the trees, the river, and the horses in such a manner that made them out of proportion with everything else. The clenching of her stomach became a throbbing that peaked in full-fisted punches. She doubled over and groaned into her saddle. The pattern of the leather smeared across her fevered gaze and then mono-chromed like the sky. A voice called her name from very far away, then she fell a long, long way down.

❦

"Your excellency? You must stop."

Oakheart heard Lillia's call and saw that she had leapt from her mount to run back to where Sophy lay senseless amongst the greenery.

Oakheart galloped back, sliding off his mount a few heartbeats behind Lillia.

"What happened?" he said tersely. His worry over Sophy was driving him to distraction. He needed to get her to Silverdale so that she could be looked after properly. He had seen how pale she had become, how thin, how lifeless...

Lillia stared at him, tears standing in her eyes. "I have failed. She is with fever and very sick. That recovery after the river was none such at all. Forcing her to move on has probably made it worse."

"There is no time for recriminations. We must decide what is best for her. Is her care beyond your skill?"

"I do not know. I would not risk it. I could not bear it if she died because of my failure."

Oakheart blew out a breath as possibilities shuffled through his mind. Halfway between Silverdale and the valley, he was hard pressed to change direction. Surely there had to be an alternative. Sophy would not make either trip in her current state. An idea occurred to him.

"Triversmeet is not far from here. We have to diverge from the main route a short way, but there is a physic stationed there to treat the families of surrounding farms. There is also a hostelry where she can be housed in some comfort."

"Triversmeet? I do not know it. If we make up a litter we could carry her there safely."

Oakheart bent down to scoop Sophy's frail form into his arms. "There is no time for that. I will despatch a messenger, now, to ensure the physic is forewarned of our coming." Oakheart summoned his fastest rider, Gilde, gave him a short set of instructions and sent him on his way.

"I will carry her with me. There rest of you can follow in your own good time."

"I am coming with you, Oakheart,' the forest maiden said, in a tone that brooked no argument. "How long will it take to reach Triversmeet?"

Oakheart did not wish to prevent her accompanying him. She was a fair horsewoman and would not delay him. "A few hours, no more. I had hoped to withhold news of her presence until we reached Silverdale. But that cannot be. Word will get out."

Lillia leapt back on her horse and took it out of line to follow Oakheart. The second in command, Sedge, saluted once and began organising the remainder of the swain to follow them.

"You will take a guard?" Sedge asked.

Oakheart agreed to the suggestion. He was not convinced the fall in the river was not some kind of attack. There had been some strange presence there that he could not explain. Whether guards could assist or not, he did not know. Brownlea brought up his mount followed by one other, Tal, an older, more experienced retainer.

Making sure that Sophy was well wrapped for the ride, Oakheart sent his mount into a trot and then eased him into a canter. Thankfully, the horses were fresh that morning so that he could make Triversmeet with ease. He hoped the physic could deal with Sophy's inability to use or receive the *given*.

21

THE PRICE OF A PROMISE

TRIVERSMEET WAS a small settlement with a few buildings, a combined inn and supply store, storage sheds for crops and a small pier to collect goods coming down the river. Just a bit past the pier Oakheart saw the physic's house, next door to the hostelry.

Gilde ran up to Oakheart's horse where he cradled Sophy. "The physic is at the hostelry, lighting a fire to warm the rooms. He said to bring her there as soon as you arrived."

Lillia slowed her horse and levelled it with his, nodded quickly after hearing Gilde's instructions.

Inside the hostelry, Oakheart stood in the long room, Sophy draped across his arms, eyeing the twenty or so bunks lining the walls. Beside him, Lillia assessed the room methodically and issued instructions to Brownlea on how to screen off the end of the room for their privacy. After placing Sophy on the bunk Lillia had chosen, Oakheart turned at the approach of footsteps. The physic was a young man, whom Oakheart had not met before, but he thought he knew the man's predecessor.

Gilde introduced him. "This is Sage Silvo, renowned physic, formerly of Silverdale."

Oakheart greeted the man. He had not heard of him, and grimaced at the use of the honorific Gilde had accorded him. The man's vanity did not inspire Oakheart to value his healing skills, but he chided himself on judging the physic on appearances rather than his ability to heal.

Lillia began peppering the man with a list of symptoms, what cures she had already tried and the final announcement that the *given* did not agree with Sophy.

"No *given?* If I am thus restricted, I can offer you no assurances. It is part of our healing lore. I will examine her first and give you a prognosis."

Oakheart and Lillia watched the physic examine Sophy. Oakheart kept glancing at Lillia, while the forest maiden chewed her lips. He saw her flinch when the physic moved Sophy in a particular way. He could see that she itched to shove the man out of the way and treat the girl herself. She shared a look with him but kept silent. Sage Silvo muttered under his breath as he checked Sophy's heart, breathing and pulse. Her eyelids were peeled back and her mouth inspected. With a final humph, Sage turned to them.

"It is a nasty infection that has been left to smoulder in the body. The only treatment I can suggest is a tonic of mine. But be warned it was augmented with the *given*. I cannot tell how she will react to it."

"But in her weakened condition could it be fatal?" Lillia stated, as she knelt next to the bed and grasped Sophy's hand.

Silvo spread his hands in mute appeal to Oakheart. "Quite possibly, but, the girl will die without it. It is up to you, your excellency."

Oakheart's gaze lingered on Sophy and then locked with Lillia's. She nodded slowly.

"Very well. We will try your tonic. But start with a small dose."

"If I am to treat this woman, I must decide the course of treatment and the dosage. A small dose will do nothing. She could die within the day if she is not helped."

Oakheart took his gaze away from Sophy's still form. "Do what you must."

From a small cauldron dangling over the fire, Sage brought a cup full of steaming brew. With a nod to Lillia, who raised Sophy to a sitting position, the physic spooned small amounts into Sophy's mouth and urged her to swallow. Lillia placed her back on the bed and smoothed the hair from her face. Brownlea had brought a sheet to screen the end of the room off and proceeded to hang it up. Once that was accomplished, Lillia covered Sophy and undressed her carefully. In silence, the physic watched the proceedings. There had been no reaction so far from Sophy.

After Sophy was settled under the blankets, the physic spoke. "I will give her another dose in an hour. We should see some improvement after the second dose."

"And if there is no improvement?" Oakheart asked.

"There is nothing I can do but try another and another until she recovers—or dies. If you do not like my remedy, you may as well let the forest maiden tend the girl with her grass and leaf remedies."

Thankfully, Lillia ignored the tone of derision in the man's voice and words Oakheart was offended on her behalf but held back a retort. There was no point in alienating this man. They had to trust him or no one.

"If you have no other need for me, I have a meal waiting for me. Send your man to the inn for provisions and if there is any change in her condition let me know."

With a slight bow in Oakheart's direction, the physic left. Brownlea hovered near the edge of the curtain he had erected. Oakheart sent him to fetch provisions, water, bedding and whatever else he thought they would require. At least, if Lillia had water to boil it would keep her occupied. Anything was better than the forest maiden's distraught look and constant fussing with Sophy's bedding or hair.

The afternoon passed slowly, with no discernible change in Sophy. Sage Silvo returned hourly to feed her more doses of tonic. Oakheart was sure her insides had to be swimming in the brew by then, but still there was no change.

As dusk gathered, he dozed in a seat next to Sophy's bunk, while Lillia took the opportunity to sleep. The forest maiden tried to hide the fact that the ride that morning and the constant attendance on Sophy had taxed her strength.

A sudden movement disturbed him. His eyes opened with start.

The firesticks crackled in the corner fireplace and light flickered around the room. All he could hear were the snores of the men as they slept elsewhere in the bunkhouse. Then he saw Sophy's foot jerk and heard her heel smack against the bed. Sitting up quickly, he placed his hand on her leg. Then his gaze travelled up her body. Her jaw was locked and her hands curled into claws.

"Lillia!" he called.

The forest maiden opened her eyes, groggy from sleep. "What is it?"

Tremors travelled along Sophy's body and into her limbs. "Sophy," he replied.

Lillia threw herself to the floor next to Sophy's bed. "By the trees, she is reacting to Sage's tonic."

"Should I send for him?" he asked her. Lillia shook her head and chewed her bottom lip.

"What should we do then?"

Lillia grabbed Sophy's hand that flew up into the air, nearly hitting the forest maiden in the face. "Keep her from harm and pray her body tolerates the *given*."

For the best part of an hour, Sophy convulsed so much that they were hard pressed to hold her on the bed. Oakheart saw her body jerk and had barely enough time to warn Lillia, so they could direct the gush of regurgitated tonic into a bucket.

Lillia screwed up her face. "That appears to be all of it and more."

Lillia eased Sophy back onto the bed. Her breathing ranged from harsh gasps to faint wisps that were barely detectable. Oakheart was at loss what to do. Lillia had run out of options, and they both agreed that Sage Silvo was no use at all. His tonic sat in a bucket, reeking of bile. Oakheart could sense the life seeping away from Sophy's pale face. There was a course of action he could take, but it was an option that came with a high price.

"Leave me alone with her."

"Why?"

Oakheart focussed his gaze on her. "Do not ask me things I cannot tell you. Trust me and leave me be."

Lillia shifted her gaze from him to the still form of Sophy, then nodded slowly. Lillia put on a cloak and pushed past the privacy curtain.

"Make sure no one disturbs me," he said

He closed his eyes, meditating on what he was going to do. Fear made his hands tremble. He knelt next to Sophy and lifted her into his lap. Securing the blanket around her, he sat back in the chair. Huddled over her form, he placed his hand on her bare chest. Her skin was cool to the touch, and he tried to ignore how deathlike that seemed. The crystal leaf took a lot of coaxing to respond to him. It would take more than a small amount of *given* to cure her. It would take an oath, one of careful wording, an oath that could be made only once, without killing him.

Oakheart pushed his awareness into the leaf, sending the *given* into it. The leaf emitted a weak glow. Taking a deep breath, he whispered to her, to the world around him. "As the *given* is my witness, Sophy will not die while I live." Then the oath worked its will. Oakheart's heart shuddered, followed by a bone-wrenching weariness that near smothered him. He wept as the land took the price of the oath from him. It was the equaliser. He did not know whether such a gift would shorten his own life in the longer term, but the wording was the best he could come up with at short notice. Sweat broke out on his brow as he placed Sophy back on the bunk, covering her bare flesh with a blanket.

The curtain flung back instantly, Lillia eyes going directly to Sophy. "Oakheart?"

He raised his head. "Some of your broth, perhaps. For both of us."

Lillia knelt by him. "What have you done? Will you not say?"

He shook his head. "Do not ask me. Just bring Brownlea to tend me. I fear I cannot walk."

"Are you secretly an adept, Oakheart?" she whispered.

Oakheart sank back onto his bunk, unable to answer before he fainted.

SOPHY WOKE TO THE SOUND OF THE RAIN. THE DROPS PIERCED

through the haze of her dreams, and her eyes opened to the beat of them on the roof. A lamp flickered, sending its quavering light across the pillows. She lay on her side. Her eyelids were heavy and her vision was dreamlike, surreal. Oakheart slept a hand width away with only a medallion around his neck to adorn the naked skin of his chest. She was in a strange place, a room. Her gaze travelled around her, to Lillia on the other side and the fire in the grate.

"Lillia?"

The forest maiden jerked awake as soon as she spoke. "Are you well?"

Oakheart appeared to be sound asleep on his bunk as he did not react to her voice.

Sophy smiled tentatively. "Yes. But I don't remember much."

A strange man lifted the curtain and entered the area. He smiled unctuously and rubbed his hands. Sophy let out a squeak of surprise.

"Well, well, my cure worked very well indeed."

Lillia sat up, looking fierce. "Sophy, dearest. This is Sage Silvo, the physic of Triversmeet."

"Thank you for helping me, sir," Sophy said, in what she hoped was the correct way.

He moved closer to her bunk. "Let me take a look at you." Sophy let him examine her. Her gaze rested on Oakheart. It was unusual for him to sleep so soundly. Wasn't he interested in her feeling better? She must have been terribly ill. Her body was weak. Sage Silvo pronounced her fit and well and recommended further bed rest before they recommenced their journey.

After thanking the physic and showing him out, Lillia stuck a bowl of broth under her nose. Sophy smiled. "Thank you, Lillia. I suppose it tastes foul."

Lillia sniffed and her tired eyes twinkled. "Bad taste is a prerequisite of good medicine so drink up."

❧❦❧

Two days later, Lillia pronounced Sophy fit enough to be moved. Since she had first awoken to the sight of the physic, Lillia had plied her with various concoctions every time she opened her eyes. The sole break in drinking them and the monotony of sleep was her need to relieve herself. Oakheart had slept almost the whole time while Sophy remained in bed. He slept so deeply he hardly moved at all and did not even snore. Sophy had the impression that Lillia was nursing them both, though her friend would not explain what was wrong with the high king's ambassador.

After Lillia's announcement though, Oakheart dragged himself wearily from the bunk and issued orders to prepare for departure the next day. Sophy was still very tired. Her limbs were weak, and her head ached if she tried to stay awake. Oakheart reappeared in the alcove, whispered something quietly to Lillia, then, without warning, he was back in his bunk, fast asleep.

"What is going on? Did he catch my illness or something?" Sophy asked.

Lillia frowned. "No. It is fatigue, I think. He helped in the nursing of you. He will be fine tomorrow. You'd best go back to bed. We will leave early."

Sophy groaned but complied. As she drifted off to sleep, she hoped she would be much better the next day.

The movement of the cart woke her the next morning. Sophy had no recollection of being moved and loaded on the rickety contraption. She managed to get a brief glimpse of Triversmeet but there were not many people about. When Lillia saw that she was awake, she pulled out two carved forks, or what passed for forks in Argenterra, and showed them to her. These were sticks with two prongs, which the locals called spikes.

"A gift for you," Lillia said, as she packed them away again. "A local farmer carves them, and when we dine out at Silverdale we can eat elegantly."

The cart ride was not comfortable. It seemed that Sophy was rocked off to sleep, only to be regularly jerked awake again. By the end of a week travelling that way, Sophy felt worse. Her arms, legs and back ached. Lillia inspected her, after Oakheart placed her in their tent. "Bruises," Lillia pronounced. "The cart is hurting you. Though I am not sure going slower would help."

About an hour later, Oakheart came in, passing Brownlea on his way out. The guard had brought her a meal and made idle conversation for a few minutes. Lillia explained the bruising to him. Oakheart had dark rings under his eyes, and he pushed a chunk of hair off his face. "Very well, I will take her with me on my horse. If that does not work we will have to camp until she is fully recovered."

Sophy said nothing. What could she say? Sorry for being a nuisance? She thought they had heard that already—quite a few times. Lillia nodded, agreeing with Oakheart's suggestion.

For two weeks, Oakheart carried her in front of him on his horse, while Lillia plied her with remedies. Sophy was asleep when they made the banks of the Lake of Reflections. Oakheart set up his pavilion on the edge of the lake and commanded that a signal fire be lit. To celebrate their arrival at the lake, Oakheart had a special meal prepared and Sophy was well enough to enjoy it.

The Hilson's Barge drew up the next day after their arrival to ferry them across. Sophy was still in bed, when Lillia and Brownlea came to put her in a litter. She fell asleep still inside the tent and did not wake up until they were making the crossing. She lay in the middle of the boat staring straight into the blue sky. Oakheart watched her. Their eyes met briefly, and then she was lulled into a natural sleep by the motion of the barge.

❧

OAKHEART MADE CAMP ON THE FAR SIDE OF THE LAKE AND WAITED for the rest of the party to cross. He was still bone weary from the effects of the oath. Although Lillia did not know or understand what he had done, she instinctively knew that he had been weakened. Hopefully, the way forward would be swift and he could deliver Sophy to Silverdale safely. Although weak from illness, Sophy did her best to help set up camp. Not that she could do much more than hand Lillia items from their luggage. Oakheart was tempted to make her sit still, but she looked so determined he did not attempt to halt her efforts.

He heard Sophy sniff herself theatrically once or twice. "I need a bath," she said to Lillia in a low voice, so unlike the lively Sophy that had left Valley Keep that Oakheart 's gut twisted. His care of her had been so lax, she had suffered for it. He could only blame himself and now he had made an oath, in which there could be difficult and unpredictable complications.

Lillia went off to talk to one of the men that had travelled with them. Soon after, Brownlea arrived with buckets of hot water at Lillia and Sophy's shared tent. Oakheart frowned as he watched the women go in. As Sophy seemed so subdued, so weak, he worried whether a bath would be good for her. Would she ever be well again? At least he knew she would not predecease him. That thought was cold comfort.

Camping near the lake for a day and a night, Oakheart waited for the three barge trips needed to bring everyone across. He had to force himself to wait. Sophy sat on a rock watching the last barge approach the shore. Due to her illness, she had not strayed far from the tent, which was a relief, as he did not like the prospect of fishing her out of the lake. Who knows what the magical properties of the Lake of Reflections would do to her. Sophy's eyes were dark and had a faraway look. Oakheart wondered what the strange outlander was thinking and feeling.

"Are you well, my lady?" Brownlea said as he draped a blanket over her shoulders before squatting next to her with an easy smile on his face. Oakheart watched them for a while. Sophy returned Brownlea's smile and thanked him. It was like the old Sophy was there for a moment.

"Yes, thank you. I'm feeling better hour by hour. You are so attentive and kind. Thanks for that."

Brownlea laughed. "Me? Pray do not say so. Oakheart has been very attentive to you."

Sophy's face reddened and her voice carried. "You're joking. He is distant and cross and barely speaks to me."

Brownlea sucked in a breath. "You could not be more wrong if you tried. My lord Oakheart has carried you every day, has he not? Plied you with Lillia's concoctions and watched over you closely while at Triversmeet."

"Really?" she said, laughing. "I thought it was Lillia who looked after me."

"How can you mistrust me so?" Brownlea asked, looking wounded. "I speak the truth." He stood up and walked away to continue with his chores. He nodded to Oakheart as he passed by.

Lillia arrived and handed Sophy another brew. Sophy pushed away the bowl the forest maiden had held out to her. "Lillia...I don't need it."

The forest maiden shoved the bowl back at her. "Nevertheless, you will drink it."

Lillia squatted by the fire, her eyes bright as she watched Sophy nod and take small, hesitant sips. "In what way do you mistrust young Brownlea?"

"He said Oakheart looked after me and wouldn't let anyone near me."

Lillia's eyes were sharp. "The lad speaks true. Oakheart barely let me near you. I came near to wrestling him..."

"What?" Sophy blurted out.

Oakheart walked closer, coming up behind Sophy. He felt no guilt in letting her speak her mind while he listened in. She had a right to abuse him. His care of her had been faulty and that was all about to change.

"I thought the better of it though," Lillia added. "He is a little too large for me."

"Oh stop. He probably wanted to throttle me because I caused another delay."

Oakheart coughed politely to announce his presence. He smiled when he saw her cringe. Was he offended that she disregarded his care the way she seemed to do? Was she truly so disbelieving of his good intentions? "You best sleep now, my lady. We will depart early."

"Oh...of course." She stared at him uncertainly. He pointed to her tent. Her gaze followed the direction of his finger, realising he meant right away. With a quick, embarrassed glance at Lillia, she struggled to her feet and lurched toward the tent, muttering all the while. Oakheart couldn't resist a smile. Perhaps she was recovering after all.

❦ 22 ❦

TEA AND A CHAT

THE AFTERNOON SUN filtered through the narrow windows and a light wind fluttered the curtains. From her seat, Aria gazed out to the mountains in the distance, watching the clouds build.

"My lady?" Rae enquired softly, peeking in through the door. "May I enter and bring you some rose-scented tea?"

"Yes," Aria replied wanly, nursing her nausea. She could barely eat, but Rae's tea and company helped her through the worst of it. "Come and talk to me. I'm feeling a bit sorry for myself this morning."

Rae bustled in, wearing a pale lemon dress with pretty, embroidered sleeves. Aria had made sure that Rae was treated well in the keep. Not that Aurore neglected her young relative, but Aria found in Rae a friend, something she missed a great deal now that Sophy had gone. Every day Aria could feel the error of letting her friend leave and did her best to not dwell on the possible repercussions. In a different light, her treatment of her friend shamed her. When Sophy had needed her most, she had effectively abandoned her to be with Dellbright. Aria suspected she would regret this more and more as time passed.

"Why is that, my lady?" Rae poured some tea into a delicate clay cup and handed it to Aria.

Aria put a stray curl behind her ear and took the cup. With a sigh, she reclined back into the chair and stared at the ceiling. "I don't know. I guess I feel awkward and out of place. I am too ill to attend my duties and now Aurore is doing them."

Rae sat close by on a stool. She took Aria's hand in hers. "Do not let it worry you, princess. Aurore is happy to do them. And you have nothing better to do than rest and grow the heir to Valley Keep."

Aria laughed at that and met Rae's dark gaze. "Will you talk with me a while? Tell me some more of the early tales, about Goslien of the Valley."

Rae's smile was radiant. "Yes, it would bring me great pleasure. She was not the first Goslien, you know. Here, let me adjust your cushion."

"Really? It's a pretty name." Aria sat forward then eased back into the chair. She liked Rae's pampering. Sophy was far too energetic to worry about other peoples' comfort. Aria experienced another twinge of guilt and longing when she thought of Sophy. She pushed the feelings away and listened to Rae. She could do nothing about Sophy's absence now.

"Goslien, my great grandmother, was descended from Goslien the Gossamer, youngest child of Vorn, through Shabra's line."

"Vorn. I know a little of him. Your father admires him greatly."

"He does. Father likes to collect tales about Vorn. I often thought that my father wished he had been alive in those early days, when Vorn and the First Comers were settling in Argenterra. Vorn became the first high king and is loved and revered by all. There was no one as wise as he." Rae had a distant expression on her face, as if she saw Vorn in all his glory. Aria couldn't help but be enthralled by such enthusiasm. It seemed it was not only the father that dreamed of days long ago.

"I see…tell me then. If I close my eyes, it's only because the light hurts them… I'm still listening.

Rae glanced behind her out of the window and sighed. "The legends tell of Shabra's choice. You know father mentioned the curse?'

Aria nodded but couldn't quite allow herself to smile. The thought of Shabra's Curse sent shivers down her spine. She couldn't and wouldn't think of it.

"Shabra's wife was Lilt of the Blue Eyes. Vorn spurned her advances so she wed his kinsman, Shabra. 'Tis said that she made a torment of his life afterwards and that she practised secret arts. She taught her daughters, Tineal and Shareal, all she knew and it is said that no man could withstand these arts, except for Vorn, of course. After many, many years, Lilt of the Blue Eyes gave birth to another she child, who was fair upon fair with bewitching blue eyes. Some say that she did conjure the child, for Shabra was ever in want of the marriage bed."

Aria opened her eyes, a smile creasing her face. "This is great, Rae. How do you know all this?"

"My lady, families tend to cherish and hoard the stories about their ancestors. Family members will hunt stories out and write them down. You will find other tales that bear no relation to mine. Some tales are about people, some about places. Father says these stories enrich our lives, give us meaning and teach us something about who we are. Shall I pour you more tea?"

Aria shook her head after taking another final sip of tea. "No, thank you. But please continue."

"Very well, if you insist," Rae responded with a smile. "Shabra named his youngest child S'Vorn, in honour of the high king. Though by that time both Vorn and Shabra were in their elder years. S'Vorn, still in the thrall of youth, was sent by her mother to seduce Vorn. N'Brell, Vorn's wife, had died a few years before, so he was free to choose again. It is said that Lilt wished her daughter to be the high queen and, through that alliance, she could control all of Argenterra. The tales talk often of her great ambition. What is said is that through some art S'Vorn did manage to bring Vorn to her and the blood of their joining stained the earth. But Vorn would return no vow, thereby vexing Lilt's attempt at entrapment. When S'Vorn bore the child from that one union, Vorn took it and named her Goslien. He raised the child himself, and she grew to be wise and fair."

Aria was wide awake, her hands clenching the arm of her chair. "What of her mother? Where did she go?"

Rae, who had been staring out the window as she related the tale, turned and gave Aria a shy smile. "It is also said that S'Vorn cared not that her child was taken. There is one tale that says she later seduced the high king's favourite son by N'Brell. Although, as if by some curse or other, she bore him no children."

"And Goslien? What about her?"

"Goslien the Gossamer was named for her hair so fine and pale it glowed like finely spun silk. It was rumoured that her eyes were crystal-clear and so pale a blue they glowed in the dark."

"Fascinating. I love these tales."

Rae sighed once as she gathered up the tea cups. "She lived a good and true life."

Aria was watching Rae pack up the things, making ready to leave. "And that is it?"

"Yes, for now. You are looking tired. Aurore will be angry if I wear you out with my quaint tales."

Aria grabbed her hand. "I like your stories. What about the Puri? You have family among them?"

Rae looked at Aria's hand. Her dark eyes widened. "Yes, I do. Goslien's blood runs through Hanal of Puri, the leader of the Puri. I have not seen him, though he is a kinsman of mine. I have heard it said that he has inherited Goslien's clear and bright eyes and that he can see into peoples' hearts."

Aria let Rae's arm go gently, conscious of the girl's discomfort. "You sound wistful when you speak of him..."

"Do I?" Rae blushed becomingly. "Aurore has written to him to see if he will take me for a wife. If that proposal is not acceptable, she asks him to find me a husband among his people."

Aria stood up suddenly, almost knocking the tray of tea things from Rae's hands. "But that means you will leave here. You can't leave me. I don't want to be alone."

Rae's face stilled, her smile all but disappeared, as she put down the tray and grabbed Aria's outstretched hand. "But I can't stay here. I was sent to..."

Aria knew she was overreacting but couldn't help it. "There's something you are not saying. I would hear it, Rae, if you are a friend."

"My lady, do not distress yourself. Sit down, and I will tell you all." Rae patted Aria's hair, arranging the curls. "You have made me your lady-in-waiting and that is good for me. I am grateful for your kindness, but I was sent to the keep to be considered by Dellbright as a wife."

Aria stared disbelievingly. Rae nodded and her cheeks burned with shame. "Yet by then he had heard you were coming. He did not even look at me and bade me to serve at the keep. Aurore could do nothing, or would do nothing, as she, too, was caught up in the excitement of the arrival of the Gift of Crystal Tree Woods. Once Dellbright has made up his mind none can sway him."

"Dear God no, I am the cause of your unhappiness."

Rae shook her head and smiled. "Not you. I can see that he loves you. Although I was shamed by his treatment of me, he has not injured my heart."

"Oh Rae. This is terrible." Aria's eyes watered with tears. "How could he have treated you like that? Even if he didn't wish to marry you, how could he make you a servant, ignore you?"

"He did not mean to, my lady. 'Tis his way. And Hanal of Puri has as much merit. I will have a husband among the Puri. They do not mind the colour of my skin there, and I will be able to live as one of them."

"You do not have to seek a husband among the Puri," Dellbright said from the doorway.

Aria started, and Rae's eyes widened as they both stared at Dellbright filling the doorway.

"Willow's son, Brookfell, is a good candidate. Good enough for you, Rae." He tossed his gloves onto the bed, his tone betraying his anger.

Rae rose, curtsied to Aria and turned to face Dellbright, who had stepped into the room.

"Brookfell is a child still, Prince Dellbright. I have no interest in him, or he me."

"Then we will find you another..." Dellbright ran his hands down Aria's hair and sat on the edge of the bed near her.

Rae sucked in a breath and squared her shoulders. "No, there is no other to be found in the valley that suits me. I have my heart set on Hanal of Puri, or whomsoever he chooses for me. Your mother has already made the arrangements."

Aria, alarmed by Dellbright's tone, made to intervene. "Dell...your mother has already arranged things..."

Dellbright glanced at her, his expression mocking. "Do not interfere with this. Mother had no business arranging anything. I will speak to her about it."

Rae glanced to Aria, her eyes filled with tears. With a nod, Aria let her go, fearing to add to her embarrassment.

When Rae had left the room, she said, "Dell, she doesn't wish to stay. I don't wish to part from her, but in the circumstances I can comprehend her desire."

"What circumstances?" Dellbright asked, his voice raised and cheeks reddening as he stood.

A tendril of fear curled in her stomach. Aria tried to put it down to nausea and braved Dellbright's anger. "I think you know what those are better than I do."

Dellbright glared at her, turned on his heel and left, slamming the door behind him.

Aria stared at the closed door and chewed her bottom lip. She tried to rearrange her opinions, re-order her thoughts and bury her disquiet. It wasn't easy to learn that the one she loved had faults. She hadn't quite added them into the love equation.

23

TIME FLIES LIKE AN ARROW

SOPHY STRUGGLED out of her tent and stretched luxuriously while gazing at the scenery. She felt so good after her bout of illness. It was joy to be able to fend for herself. It was early, and mist lay like lazy sunbathers over trees and in the hollows. She turned towards the grassy hill that had appeared only as a dark space the night before. She blinked. It was actually three hills grouped together like triple breasts. Mist obscured the clefts between, giving the impression of dark moist secrets.

"Good morn, my lady," Brownlea said as he placed a pail of heated water in her tent. "I see that Faruni's Triplets have caught your eye."

"Faruni's Triplets?" she repeated, drawing her gaze from the hills to Brownlea's young, fresh face. He smiled shyly and looked down at his feet. "Would you like to hear the tale?"

"Yes, of course I would." Sophy stepped over to a low stump and sat down.

Brownlea squatted next to her. "Faruni was a First Comer, but she was already aged when she arrived in Argenterra. A young man called Nu Ranl asked her to wed him. Affronted, she scoffed and cuffed him around the ears. Not to be put off, he pursued her until she became so enraged she went to Vorn to protest . But Vorn was wise and bade her to wed Nu Ranl. It is said that Vorn's endorsement of Nu Ranl's suit made her even angrier, so in spite she wed Nu Ranl, thinking to make him miserable all his days. But to her surprise, she enjoyed her husband even though he was many years the younger. And from her aged womb did spring three children—triplets."

Sophy frowned. "Did she have them there on the hills?"

Brownlea laughed softly. "I think not. 'Tis only a tale that goes with the naming of the hills."

"That is a very interesting story, Brownlea,' Lillia said, emerging from the tent. "I have often wondered about those hills. Now I will pass that tale on. Thank you."

"You are most welcome, but I do not own it. The tale comes from Oakheart. He told it to me when we first passed this way."

"That is even better for Oakheart has read the histories, so there must be truth in the tale." Lillia aimed her dart-like stare in Sophy's direction. "Come Sophy, you must wash and prepare yourself for our departure, lest you earn Oakheart's ire."

"Yes," Sophy replied, waving to Brownlea before she re-entered her tent. There was little time to dress and eat breakfast before it was time to depart. Avoiding upsetting Oakheart was high on her list of things to do.

⁓

"So my lady, shall we continue?" Brownlea said, over the clip-clopping of the horses' hooves. "Some words from you that rhyme with sky, pray."

Sophy laughed as they passed out of a copse of trees and entered a narrow cutting. Brownlea had been working hard to lift her spirits with silly rhymes that meant absolutely nothing. "Brownlea, you wear out my brain. This will be the tenth rhyme and all of them so bad."

"Well, do not give up on me now," he replied, eyebrows rising in appeal. "I must stumble on one stroke of genius...eventually."

Unable to resist his enthusiasm Sophy said, "Mmm. Sky, fly, but that is obvious. Try, by, lie, cry, dry, my..."

Brownlea frowned, easing the reins as the horse walked beside her own mount. "My is not suitable...but let me try, to rhyme the sky, without a lie, lest you cry and your face, by the by, will remain dry."

Lillia's laugh sounded over the sound of jingling tackle and the murmur of men.

"Truly, master Brownlea, your hard work to cheer my charge has worked a charm. Her looks have so improved."

"Hail!" came a shout from the rear. Sophy chilled by the fear in the voice, looked around. Bows were strung and curses filled the air as horses' hooves chewed the rocks and soil. Her gaze flicked upwards. In the sky, dark, arrow-like shapes approached, heading straight for them. As they drew nearer, she saw that they were birds with large, pointed beaks. The thrum of bowstrings filled the air as arrows were set loose to intercept them. Horses and men milled together. Sophy looked left and right, her mount pacing nervously. What was going on?

A bird fell with a thud next to her. She stared at it, caught by sight of the thin beak as sharp-looking as a dagger. Oakheart's hail as he violently swung his horse around and headed towards her sounded over-loud. He pushed at the rumps of the mounts standing between him and her. In slow motion, she saw Brownlea gasp and drive his horse towards her. He leapt, flinging himself onto her mount and nearly toppling her from her seat in the process.

Her scream was swallowed as she clung to her saddle as Merrywillow lurched under her. The reins were torn from her hands when Brownlea threw himself in front of her. Merrywillow began to buck, and Brownlea went limp. An agonised groan wheezed out of him, while she clutched at him, grabbing his jerkin to hold him steady. There was blood everywhere, on her hands, on her lap where he lay. She shook him, and his head lolled, bringing his body angling towards her. A fountain of blood erupted over her and his clothes. The arrow shaped bird dislodged in the spurt of blood fell with a splat onto the ground. Her knuckles turned white as she gripped Brownlea's jerkin, and while she screamed incoherently, the light faded from his eyes.

Birds dropped from the sky around her. Oakheart's men sent a volley of arrows into the thick of the birds. Yells and curses surrounded her. Lillia held her mount steady, her bow thrumming as she launched arrows at the deadly birds, deftly picking them off one by one. The more she killed, the more seemed to take their place. The ground was black with the strange looking creatures.

The smell of Brownlea's blood sent Sophy's mind reeling. Those blood red eyes surfaced in her mind. She was mesmerised by their malice. "No," she whispered as that presence oozed close to her. Then she noticed that Merrywillow was tipping to one side. She was sliding out of the saddle in slow motion.

Oakheart called to her. She couldn't respond. The nearness of that presence had taken her volition. Oakheart tugged her out of the saddle and draped her over his lap. Her eyes never left Brownlea's body; she watched in horror as his body slid to the ground in a heap and then Merrywillow, too, fell sideways, the beak of one of the birds puncturing his chest.

Horses and arrows and blood filled her vision. Her mind went numb. The shaking of the horse's gait loosened her stupor. She screamed and struggled against Oakheart's hold.

"Go back. We must help him." She tried to escape from Oakheart's lap but he gripped her firmly, pushing her down so that she could hardly breathe. He made for the cover of trees, keeping her steady. The sound of battle lessened. When one of his men shouted an all clear, he helped her climb into the saddle proper.

She turned to face him. "What are you doing?" she screamed into his face. She pawed at him with her blood stained hands, eyes wide and heart beating. "Go. Back."

Oakheart's face was impassive. A muscle in his jaw twitched. Her fist banged on his chest, followed by the other. "You bastard! We've got to help him!" she shouted, her voice hoarse and breaking.

"My lady?" Lillia said.

"We can save him...we can," Sophy said, her voice overtaken by sobs. Brownlea was dead. He'd been smiling at her and talking to her, and now he was dead.

Oakheart reached for her and pressed her to his chest as she cried. He whispered to himself as he held her. "Your mother's grief will cut deep, as you pass into the final sleep..." He rubbed her back, attempting to gentle her sobs.

She brought herself under control and used her hands to push back off him. "We have to go back. We can't leave him there."

He grabbed her by the shoulders and looked deep into her eyes. His throat worked, his Adam's apple sliding up and down. There was grief in his eyes. "We cannot go back. 'Tis is not safe. He is gone now and 'tis too late."

"But—" Sophy was cut off.

"There is naught we can do. Come!" he called to his gathered men. "We must ride to shelter, lest more arrow birds are sent against us."

They rode without a break to the base of the plateau where there were caves useful for refuge. Exhausted, they huddled in several of them where they could see the by-way that led to the upper plateau. Oakheart's men rubbed down the sweaty horses and settled them in one of the caves.

Sophy sat in the larger of the caves. It was damp and smelt of decay. Numb, she huddled against the wall, nursing her grief. She couldn't understand their attitude. Why did they leave Brownlea's body behind? She was so confused and upset that she wouldn't even look at Oakheart. Lillia squatted down next to her.

"Here drink this. It will warm you," she said as she stroked Sophy's hair back over her ears.

"No, don't want it." Sophy pushed the cup away from her. Lillia grimaced as she successfully saved the contents.

"Sophy." Oakheart's voice was a hiss.

"Don't speak to me like that." Sophy glared at him. "Don't you dare. What sort of place is this? What were those things?"

"I told you, they were arrow birds..."

"Yeah, after they attacked us. I mean, what other creatures do you have here? Care to tell me about those? When am I next to have my life threatened?"

"My lady," Lillia interrupted. "I know you sorrow for Brownlea...but arrow birds have never attacked in that way before."

"What Lillia says is true," Oakheart said as he sat on the floor of the cave, looking defeated, his complexion ruddy from reflected firelight and anger. "They were discovered a long time ago, by accident. Their beaks are poisonous but they have never attacked in force. Not like that."

Sophy kept glaring at him, unwilling to let her anger fade. He kept staring at her, his eyes roaming her face. When she continued to glare without talking to him, he stood up and left the cave.

Sophy turned to Lillia. "But I don't understand why we couldn't go back and get Brownlea, even if..."

"My lady," Lillia said. 'You do not understand our ways. Your life was in danger. There was nothing to be done. Brownlea knew the bird was poisonous when he threw himself in its path. He was dead before he touched the ground. Oakheart did what was right. There is no use railing against him for saving your life. Overlanders believe that the heart leaves the body at death and that only an empty shell remains. Where possible they care for and revere the dead but in a time like this...well it is not meet that it be done. It does not mean that the Overlanders feel any less for their fallen comrade."

She listened to Lillia and then slowly understood that she had been the focus of the attack. "It was heading for me? Someone wants me dead? I can't believe it. Why? It doesn't make any sense?"

"It does seem the attack was centred on you," Lillia pointed out.

Sophy collapsed against the wall of the cave. This land, so beautiful, hid something, a secret, a terror. She didn't know what. And Aria? Was her dearest friend okay? Was that the something that Sophy sensed in Aria's eyes, in her expression, something that Aria hid from her? The dark shadows in the cave, disturbed by firelight, seemed alive. She shook her head. "I'm nothing, no one. I can't believe someone tried to kill me."

"Yet, it may be so. Remember the river, the horse's shoe."

"Accidents..." Yet Sophy had drawn the same conclusion, no matter how much she wanted to disregard it. She wiped at a stray tear on her cheek. Fear clenched her gut. This was too real, too dangerous. Brownlea was dead because of her. What about the rest of Oakheart's men and Oakheart himself? She was responsible for their lives. Sophy buried her face in her hands, trying to block out belief.

Lillia patted her on the head lightly. "Perhaps they were accidents —it grows late and this subject disturbs you. Drink this. It is cooler now. It will help you rest. Nothing can be proven for the moment, but you must take care in future."

Sophy glanced at her friend and tried to smile at the motherly ministrations. Lillia mopped Sophy's tears with a cloth from her bag. She paused at Sophy's expression.

"What is it, my lady?"

"I think I want my mother..." she replied as she was drawn into Lillia's strong embrace. Sophy hadn't wanted her mother since she was ten years old. Aria's mother, Maralain, was the best mother she had ever had. How she wished that Maralain was there with her to tell her not to cry and to get over it. Sophy let her tension ease and dozed fitfully against Lillia's shoulder. The forest maiden's strong hands helped Sophy to the ground where she could stretch out and rest.

❧

Brownlea's death was a terrible blow to Oakheart. How was he ever to know whether his death was due to the vow he had made to save Sophy's life or misfortune—chance. Riddled with guilt, he could barely face his men. To make matters worse, Sophy blamed him as well. There was enough blame to share around. How had arrow birds been gathered and then directed in such numbers? As he re-entered the cave, Oakheart saw that Sophy was asleep. He was relieved, as he wanted to share his thoughts with Lillia without Sophy listening in. Stepping closer to the forest maiden, he placed a pot of salted meat stew by her.

"How is she?" he asked.

The forest woman sniffed and spooned some of the stew into a bowl. "Her health improves, though the loss of Brownlea wounds her spirit."

Oakheart retied his hair and let out a sigh. "As it does the rest of us. There was something terribly wrong in that attack." He searched the forest maiden's face, knowing that her senses were keen enough to sense it as he did.

"Of course it was wrong, unnatural, strange. Were they controlled by some misuse of the *given?*"

Oakheart shook his head. "No, not the *given*, something else. I cannot help feel a sense of foreboding. Sophy is closed to me. She wants me to trust her but 'tis so hard. And now this."

He hated to voice his fears, but he could not 'see' her and, try as he might, learning to trust by sight and action alone was too alien to him.

When Lillia spoke, he could see the truth in her. "I have not your abilities...but I tell you this. She is true in heart and deed, and she could no more see Brownlea harmed than she could you or me."

Lillia spoke with conviction and he could see she believed what she said. Oakheart wondered how Lillia could befriend Sophy without being able to 'see' her in the *given*. At that moment, he wished he had Adage's great wisdom and foresight. Oakheart was like a blind man blundering his way across the land and falling deeper and deeper into an abyss.

⁂

A GREY SKY GREETED THE TRAVELLERS THE NEXT DAY. SOPHY blinked away sleep as she squinted out of the mouth of the cave. Lillia held another brew under her nose. "Drink this now," Lillia said.

Dazed from sleep, she sipped the hot liquid. Its warmth flowed into her, and she grew more aware. Then she gagged. "That's disgusting. What it is it? Fermented tree droppings brewed with horse piss?" she said sourly.

Lillia huffed a little. "I will not reveal the recipe. 'Tis an old one passed on through countless generations. You need not insult it. You look much better already."

The sound of movement drew her attention. Horses were milling, and men talking. Sophy edged out of the cave mouth. "What's happening?" she whispered to Lillia.

"Oakheart sends half of his men on to Silverdale. He will not move until he has extra protection."

"Why? For me?" Sophy's mouth hung open.

"For you and the rest of us. The climb up the plateau can be treacherous at times. If something untoward happened then it could result in injury or death."

"I see," she said, frowning. Stepping outside where the slight breeze blew her dark hair around her face, she watched the proceedings.

Oakheart looked up. "Sophy, go back into the cave."

"What?"

"I said go back into the cave," Oakheart repeated coming up to her.

She backed up. "Why? It's safe here." She took another step back, unable to confront him further.

It appeared that he was not in the mood to argue either. "Do as I say." Then he turned to the forest maiden. "Lillia, make sure she stays inside."

"But..." Sophy said to his back.

Lillia tugged her arm and urged her back into the cave. "Come, my lady, now is not the time to discuss it." Lillia guided her back inside.

Oakheart appeared at the cave mouth about an hour later, accompanied by the remainder of his men. They trooped in, arranging supplies and belongings until the large cave felt crowded.

"We will camp in here together. The other caves are not hospitable and 'tis easier to keep watch," he said.

"Can't we go out at all?" Sophy asked.

Oakheart shook his head. "No. We will stay here. I will take no further risks."

"But..."

He swung round toward her, chin jutting. She leaned back against the wall as his anger washed over her.

"Do you think that people in Argenterra are attacked every day?"

Dumbstruck, she could only shake her head and watched as he paced.

"It was a sore deed, one that shakes the oath... You may not like it that I husband my people, protect your life. I care nothing for that. So no more complaints, no more opinions."

Lillia came forward and drew her back to her spot. When offered hard bread and dried meat, she stared at it and shook her head, her appetite had fled. Silently, she watched the rest of them. Lillia organised and reorganised their things every hour or so. Oakheart stared moodily into the dark corners of the cave, occasionally muttering to one of his men. When the sun finally faded, he set the watch. He brooded silently for the rest of the evening. Occasionally his gaze met hers, but Sophy could read nothing from his expression. Her own eyelids weighed heavily, and she drifted off to sleep.

The days in the cave became a blur of boredom and dull food. Lillia was the glue that kept the group together. She tended Sophy, encouraged Oakheart and rallied his men, even though their food situation worsened during the second week.

"I don't think I can eat this hard bread anymore…I'd kill for a pizza," Sophy said quietly to Lillia. Oakheart edged closer and sat down.

"You will when you are hungry enough," he said, plucking the bread from her hand.

"Hey," she protested when she saw it disappear into his mouth.

"Why do you complain? I will not see it tossed aside. There is scant enough for us to waste."

"But I didn't say I wouldn't eat it."

"Come, share mine," Lillia said, trying to head off another argument between them.

"Thanks, but I'll take only a little. You need your strength, too." Sophy chewed the bread while treating Oakheart to a haughty stare.

She swallowed a mouthful. "Can't someone go outside and find bounty or use the *given* to bring us fresh food?" Sophy said to no one in particular.

Oakheart shook his head.

Lillia said to Oakheart, "I would gladly venture outside to glean what I could."

"No. I will not risk you." Oakheart took his green eyes from Lillia, and stared accusingly at Sophy, silently daring her to contradict him. Sophy pouted and did her best to ignore him.

Everyone's spirits were low. The supplies ran down to the extent that they ate only hard bread and water for the last few days. Sophy felt weak and slept a lot. At first, she didn't mind. It was a chance to heal, but as time drew on the enforced inactivity had an effect. Even Lillia's stamina was fading. Being locked up in a dank, smelly cave was a terrible burden to the forest maiden as she needed trees and dirt and sun to thrive.

24

A RIPPLE OF LAUGHTER

IT WAS late in the morning, and most of the group were dozing, when they heard a call from the watch. Rousing themselves at the sound of hoof beats, they struggled from their bedclothes. Oakheart bounded to the mouth of the cave and after a moment's hesitation was gone. Dreary eyed, Sophy trudged towards the opening with Lillia in tow. She blinked rapidly and held her hand up to block out the bright sunlight. Still masked by the haze, she saw a tall, lithe man with dark hair and a reddish-brown tan leap down from a horse and embrace Oakheart. He wore an immaculate uniform and his smile was wide under his straight, perfect nose.

Oakheart, obviously relieved to see the man, pounded him on the back. The newcomer turned and shouted a greeting to the accompanying men. The man walked towards Sophy and Lillia and slapped his soft cap against his thigh as he bowed to them.

"Fern Ripplebark at your service, ladies," he said with a smooth voice. "Hark, look what the cave has expelled," he added as the rest of Oakheart's men came out to greet the newcomers. They were all dirty and pale from two weeks in the cave. Some of the men stretched and eased their joints. After a few more of Fern's quirky comments they ended up smiling and giving him cheek back.

When Fern's eyes passed over her again, Sophy was suddenly conscious of her dirty gown and straggly hair. When she glanced around at the rest of her companions, she realised she wasn't alone in her dishevelment. Lillia squinted at the newcomers, but her face was neutral. Only Oakheart looked like he had kept some discipline. He had a slight beard, but at least his clothes were clean. He introduced Sophy and Lillia.

Seemingly without pause, Fern continued to bombard them with absurd observations. "What are you? Ground worms slithering through caves?" Fern said as the strutted around them. "Come, fear not the light of day. I am come with a force of men to accompany you home."

His humour was lost on Sophy. Fern had grey eyes, like the colour of storm clouds. They sparkled to the extent that they spread cheer among the group. He faced Oakheart. "Knowing you, old friend, I guessed you must be feeling poorly, so I have brought good food."

Oakheart quirked his lips into a lopsided smile. "Good, we will eat and then talk. I admit to being heartily sick of hard bread and water." Oakheart's gaze passed over Sophy, although there was no hint of a smile in his look.

Miffed, Sophy turned to Lillia. "I think I'll clean up before we eat. Do you think Oakheart will allow us to walk around for a bit afterwards? I don't think I can bear the stink of the cave again."

Lillia's smile was reserved. "He is relaxed now, my lady, with the extra men for protection. I think it will be fine. Come let us amuse ourselves while the men cook."

Sophy managed to change her gown and grimaced as Lillia brushed and braided her hair. Although it couldn't be washed, she looked presentable. The attention to her clothes and hair, combined with the open air, helped lift her mood. A sense of trepidation hung over her, mixed with grief. Argenterra was not everything it seemed—and someone, or something, wanted her dead. She thought back to the river. The rock had been firm under her feet. Perhaps it had moved of its own accord. A shiver passed over her. What an alien idea. As alien as the *given*, she supposed. Yet she saw the *given* used around her every day, even Aria could use it. Heavens was Aria safe? Sophy ached to speak to her. Yet she had Dellbright to protect her and pushed back her worry. When Lillia finished arranging her own clothes and joined her as she neared the fire, Sophy covered her anxiety with a smile.

Fern was in deep discussion with Oakheart when she walked up to the campfire. Fern said to Oakheart, frowning into the flames, "Alas, poor Brownlea. His mother will not take it well. He was her only child and a joy to all who knew him. You say that the attack was aimed at the Lady Sophy. Do you know why? Or who?"

Oakheart shook his head carefully, averting his gaze from Sophy. "I do not know the why of it, or even the how. The Lady Sophy is an Outlander, a Gift of Crystal Tree Woods. The *given* rejects her and Lillia thinks she may be cursed." He lifted his eyebrow at Fern, as if daring him to contradict what he was saying.

Sophy put her hands on hips and looked askance as Lillia. "Cursed? You never said."

The forest maiden looked embarrassed. "My lady, I meant no insult."

"And what do you think, Oakheart?" Fern asked, his grey eyes surveying Sophy minutely as she and Lillia took a seat next to them.

Oakheart sat back, easing the kinks out of his shoulders. His men were on lookout. Sophy noticed that his gaze often flicked to where his men were stationed. He was still wary of further attacks. Sophy swivelled her head around, checking for herself that all was well. When Oakheart began to answer Fern, she focused her gaze on him. "There are too many happenings to be coincidence. The birds were definitely aimed at Sophy. Three of them hit the mark. Brownlea was struck by one and her mount Merrywillow by the other two. If I had not reached her before another struck, she would be dead now."

Sophy went weak at the knees and butterflies took alarming flight in her stomach. She hadn't realized how close it had been and how brave Oakheart had been in snatching her from her horse's back. And she had treated him with disdain, blame and anger. Her cheeks burned with shame.

The meal arrived and interrupted their talk. "So there are two Gifts of Crystal Tree Woods," began Fern, when the edge had been taken off his hunger. "One with surpassing beauty and wed to Dellbright, so 'tis rumoured." His gaze rested on Sophy. "These times are full of surprises."

"Strange times indeed," Oakheart replied, helping himself to his third portion of meat. Sophy rolled up a blanket, rested it on a large rock, and laid her head down. She was tired, now that her stomach was full.

"So, my friend. Do tell of this beauteous gift you left behind in Valley Keep."

Sophy dozed slightly, but still heard the conversation around her.

Oakheart's voice took on a husky quality. "Princess Aria...how sweet and true she is. Dellbright was felled by her the very second he laid eyes on her. I cannot fault his taste."

Fern guffawed. "Do not stint in your description, Oakheart. 'Tis not like you. At present, I know not if she is tall, or short and stout..."

Oakheart chuckled too. "Well then...her hair is like a fiery sunset, beset with twining ringlets and curls that fall to caress her shoulders and back. Her eyes, forest green, glisten with laughter and honesty. Skin, creamy soft and unblemished, catches the moonlight..."

Fern was quiet while Oakheart spoke. "Sounds good so far...and?"

"Her figure is pleasing. She is about Sophy's height, within a hands breadth. Her manner is what is most becoming. A true lady, one born to be a princess. Her smile sets one's heart abeating..." Oakheart filled his plate with more food.

Fern's voice was eager. "And you let Dellbright snatch her? Did she not fell you with one look?"

Oakheart did not answer for a minute. Sophy heard rustling as someone jostled the firesticks to give more light. "Aye, she did but she was not for me...her heart was Dellbright's too, in the same moment his was hers."

Goblets banged together. "Well, I would not have let Dellbright have his way, no matter what the legends and traditions dictate."

Sophy stirred, making it obvious that she was awake. Fern was watching her when she yawned.

"What say you, my lady?" he asked. "Did you hear Oakheart's description of your friend? Did he do her justice?"

"Yes, I heard, and no, Lord Fern, he did not. He understated her beauty…"

Her reply seemed to stun him. Perhaps females of his acquaintance didn't compliment each other's beauty. But Sophy had never been envious of Aria's looks. She was attractive too, or had been before she came to Argenterra. She certainly didn't envy Aria's marriage to Dellbright, or the prospect of children. Beauty had hindered Aria in this place, the same way that plainness had hampered her.

Fern shut his mouth over his next retort. Oakheart laughed quietly, though his eyes regarded her under his blond brows. Was there some admiration in that gaze? Sophy didn't know, or care.

Lillia sat down and Sophy began to drift off, lulled by good food and a warm blaze. The night air was slightly damp but refreshing. It was quiet in the immediate surrounds. The camp sounds were punctuated with the crackle of the fire.

"I fear, my friend," Fern said, his voice ringing loud in her sleep-filled mind, "that you have the worst of the bargain. I would have left this one at Valley Keep and brought the Lady Aria to the high king's court."

"You will hold your tongue," Oakheart hissed. "What I do is my business. I will hear no more words against Sophy. She is in my care and that is all you need know. Come, Lillia, I will carry Sophy to her bed."

He knelt to pick up Sophy. "Come, little one,' he said tenderly. Sophy still heavy and dazed from sleep didn't protest and she hung like a dead weight in his arms as he carried her easily to her bed within the cave. Sophy was awake enough to be excited by Oakheart's gallantry and concerned about Fern's obvious dislike. What would Silverdale bring? she wondered, as Lillia helped settle her to sleep.

❧ 25 ☙

SEPARATE WAYS

Once again Rae combed Aria's hair, while she sat in her chair by the window, looking out to the valley.

"That feels good, thank you, Rae," Aria said rather wistfully.

"It gives me pleasure, my lady. Your hair is like the evening sun as it sets over the fields, all gold and red. I could only wish my hair to be so."

Aria rubbed her extended abdomen and tried to move into a comfortable position. The child kicked her, under her ribs where there was no avenue for escape. At five months it was big, and Aria was petite. The ache kept her awake at night and made her irritable by day.

Aria's gaze was drawn to the window when she heard the sounds of movement, horses' hooves, shouts and bustling. "What is that, I wonder?" Aria said, her brows drawn together. She stood with hand on the chair arm to steady herself.

"I know not, my lady," Rae replied as she edged to the window, in front of Aria.

Aria had a strange thought, more hope than a logical assumption. "Maybe Sophy has come back to me." Aria took two steps towards the door. "I will go down and see..."

Footsteps in the corridor heralded the arrival of Aurore, her colour heightened by excitement and exertion. Her eyes skimmed over Aria and settled on Rae. "Rae, child," Aurore said breathily. "Hanal has sent his brother to fetch you. You must come down and greet them. I have Dela packing your things. You will depart within the hour."

"Oh no," Aria said, tears beginning to swell. She latched onto Rae's arm, her eyes pleading with Aurore. "Not just yet... I...I...don't want her to leave me."

Aurore faced her, eyes and smile full of tenderness. "You would not stay her, Aria. Rae has served you well. She must find her own destiny, her own happiness. Hanal will watch over her. He is an honourable man."

Aria smiled tremulously at Rae. "Of course, she must." Aria hung her head. "But can they not stay awhile, take some food?"

"I see what you think, child. But that cannot be. They ride under a flag of truce. Dellbright would not allow them succour in his home, and they in turn would spurn a feast if offered. They sleep in the open, in tents or in caves, and not in constructions such as this. To shape the earth as we do offends them."

Aurore moved forward and took Rae's hand. "Quick, you must go down to the bailey and greet them. I have ceremonial refreshments to offer and your wedding gift to give. After that, you will depart." She bustled Rae out of the door and followed after. As the door shut, Aria looked up and weighed the sorrow she felt in her breast. The door flung open and banged loudly against the wall. Aria startled, stared wide-eyed at Dellbright as he stood there with a scowl on his features. "Are you happy now?"

Wiping the tears from her eyes, she stood to face him. "I'm sorry. I don't understand what you mean."

"I said are you happy now that my kinswoman is to go with those... those animals? That her offspring will be darker and fouler than those of her ancestors?"

Aria was shaking. Dellbright's manner scared her. It was as if she didn't know him anymore, but she refused to be cowed. "I'm not happy to parted from her. And I'm shocked that you speak that way about the Puri, when their blood also runs through your veins. Rae is proud to join with them, and I'm happy for her." Her chin rose slightly, daring Dellbright's anger.

"Speak not so to me." Dellbright went to the small table and splashed some wine into a goblet, his posture and movements radiating his discontent.

Aria took a step towards him. "There's no shame in it. Why do you deny any kinship with them?"

His dark eyes smouldered. "That is for me to know and to feel. You understand nothing of the history of this place."

"I would if you ever spoke of it. Why do you not share it with me?" She spoke softly, quietly and reached for his hand.

"You will not side against me again," he whispered harshly, squeezing her outstretched hand. "It is me you must obey. My mother understands how it is and at least she understands my heart."

"I thought I understood your heart and my place in it. You wound me when you speak like this. I have bound myself to you and no other. Can't we be at peace?"

He lifted his other hand, caressed her cheek with the back of his fingers. "So much beauty and grace in you. I am a lucky man. But you are not so satisfied in me. I can sense it. Even now, your eyes speak your disappointment."

Aria shook her head.

He dropped his hand and took another mouthful of wine before dropping the goblet to the table.

"You prove it daily, especially by needing your friend and again twofold by worrying over a troublesome girl, who should never have had your notice."

Dellbright strode past her to peer out the window. Yet she knew he wasn't interested in what was going on outside.

"I'm...I'm satisfied with you. I love you. It hurts me when you are angry with me."

He appraised her with a charming look, taking her in from head to foot, weighing her up.

"Truly? But you only have to do the right thing and then I won't be angry. I will be sugary sweet to you, caress you tenderly, whisper sweet words."

"And what is the right thing that I should do? Please tell me."

He sat down on the edge of their bed. His smile dissolved and his expression became calculating.

"Cease yearning for your friend."

Aria gasped and her stomach became as heavy a lead.

"Call her only when I am in your presence and at the times I prescribe."

Aria's eyes grew round with shock. "Does it mean so much to you?" her voice shook with emotion.

"If you give me this undertaking, my love," he replied, moving closer and running his fingers through her hair, "I will be the most content and loving husband..." He drew her to him, nuzzled her neck, kissed her earlobe. He pulled back, lifted her chin and captured her mouth with his. The kiss was penetrating and she responded in kind. His urgent hands pursued her, rubbing along her back, along her neck, pressing her close to him. "Tell me," he whispered seductively against her neck. "Tell me, you will love me."

"I do, Dellbright. I love you. I won't call Sophy unless you are there. I'll do my best not to miss her."

Those lips came down and sealed her words.

While Rae, shared ceremonial refreshments with Aurore in attendance, Dellbright stripped away Aria's clothes. "I love the shape of the child in your belly," he said as he kissed down the length of her body. "You will never leave me. Our child will grow big and strong surrounded by his loving parents."

"Yes. I will be here for you." She moaned as he made love to her.

"Say it again. Tell me you will always be here."

"I will always...be...here."

Then when his passion cooled and he dressed, Aria lay sprawled naked on her bed, hair in total disarray. She rubbed the mound where her flat stomach used to be.

"Your words please me, Aria. Now it is time to farewell Rae."

Eyes alert, Aria sought her clothes. "You have distracted me, my prince. How will I show myself looking like this? Everyone will know what I have been doing. You must help me."

Dellbright smiled like the day they first met in the forest. Aria recalled the memory and the feelings he had inspired. She clung to that, anchored herself to it. "Very well then, turn and I will reclasp your clothes."

When he had finished doing up her gown and tugged the various wrinkles to a semblance of neatness, he regarded her hair. "Here, let me turn this brush on you." He drew the brush through her hair in swift and efficient strokes. Her hair fluffed up and spread out like wings.

She caught her reflection in the mirror. Her hair was wild, her lips puffy and Dellbright had left marks on the smooth, creamy skin of her neck. "I can't go down looking like this." She found a scarf and wrapped it around her neck. With her hands she tried to flatten her hair. "We must control it somehow."

Dellbright went over near the bed to his wooden chest and rummaged about. "How about this?" He held up a tiny filigree tiara, shaped like a replica of a branch of the crystal tree.

"How beautiful! May I wear it?" Her fingers touched the exquisite headdress delicately.

"Of course. 'Tis yours—part of the bride price for the Gift of Crystal Tree Woods." He placed it on her head and kissed her forehead. "I should have presented it to you earlier. Mother only reminded me about it this morning."

In the bailey, amid the milling horses, Aria embraced Rae fiercely. "I will miss you. You have become a good friend."

Rae smiled through her tears, hardly suppressing her excitement. "I will think of you often, princess. Be happy and look after that child for me," she patted Aria's growing middle.

Aria smiled sadly. "I will. Do not accept anything less than your heart's desire from this Hanal of Puri. Do you know why he did not come himself?"

Hanal's brother, Tarkel, who was a tall, dark, Puri man stepped closer, towering over Aria and Rae, assessing them with his inky black eyes. "My brother was far from home when our kinswoman's message came. I act in my brother's stead. He will decide Rae's fate when he returns. That is all I can say to you." He walked proudly back to his mount and took the reins as if another moment near the keep would sully his person forever.

Aria walked carefully towards him, her arm linked with Rae's. "I thank you and pass Rae to your care."

"Come," Tarkel said to Rae.

With one quick glance back at Aria, Dellbright and the keep, Rae climbed onto a Puri horse and one of the Puri tied her things to the saddle. Fleeting as the wind, the rest of Puri flew to their mounts, and, with a cry, Tarkel led them out of the gates.

Only then did Aria cease waving and let her tears fall. When she heard Dellbright's step behind her, she wiped them away hastily and threw up a happy face. "Come, we should see what cook has in store for the eve-tide meal," she said with false happiness. "I have a particular craving for milberry pie and custard."

26

A PURI DESTINY

RAE CLUNG to her mount and did her best to quell the trammelling of her heart. She was finally moving, heading into the hills with the Puri people of her father's tales. As soon as they left the surrounds of the keep, the party split, the mysterious, dark-skinned men slipping away one by one. Rae stayed with Tarkel. She had no choice for he kept a leading rein on her horse. Clinging precariously to her mount, she despaired of presenting a good figure to her soon to be adopted people. Not an experienced rider, she felt sadly lacking and clumsy.

The robes of the Puri men flared in the wind as they galloped out of the valley towards the hills. They seemed at one with their mounts, lean and muscular, as they increased the pace. Rae knew that soon she would enter Panal's Pass, the narrow cutting that led to the wider expanse where these people dwelled on the fringes of Argenterra.

The steep cutting was shadowed in the setting sun, making the plains beyond look grey, flat and barren. As the fading light left an orange blush along the edge of the hills ahead, the pace slowed. They wound around a cluster of large boulders, until they came upon a camp. Women came out of makeshift tents, dressed in colourful trousers of red, green and yellow, with their heads wrapped in bright, patterned cloths. Rae could only gape at the beauty and the strangeness of it.

Horses milled. The party of men that had left Valley Keep together converged from five different directions. Slim, swarthy youths came to take their mounts at the men's orders. Rae's gaze flicked in all directions as she tried to take in what was happening around her. In her confusion it took a while to notice that Tarkel stood by her mount. "Get down. We will rest here and leave in the morning."

Rae nodded and eased herself out of the saddle. His manner was curt. Feeling out place and wanting to belong, it was difficult to hide her disappointment. While she loosened the ties holding her possessions to the saddle, she sensed a presence behind her, like a prickle up her spine. She hesitantly looked over her shoulder and was greeted with a waft of spice scented air.

Dark eyes peered out of a beautiful face. Lips reminiscent of dark, rich wine smiled around neat white teeth. "I am Umri, wife to Tarkel. You will share our tent until Hanal decides your future."

Rae smiled and curtsied to the tall and thin woman. "I thank you for your hospitality. May I repay you and yours in kind."

Those eyes were unrestrained in their scrutiny. Large, dark, like a midnight without stars, she seemed to stare right through her. Rae looked down, blushing.

"I see," Umri said, wistfully. "That it is you who will decide your fate."

Sweat slid down her backbone, though she was chilled. "What do you mean?" Rae asked, surprised by the woman's tone.

"I see you," Umri said, jabbing her finger at Rae. Then her expression unclouded, a smile lingered sleepily on those dark lips. "I see the future...sometimes. I hear voices on the wind. I am Hanal's seer."

"His what?" Rae nearly dropped her bundle of possessions.

Umri walked around her, nodding vaguely to the youth who took away Rae's horse and looked her up and down. "I advise him...that is all I will say," she said after a moment.

Rae was uncomfortable with the scrutiny. No one, not even Dellbright, had assessed her this way.

Umri smiled sweetly. "Come, food awaits." Umri glided away, her headdress flapping in the light breeze. Rae traipsed after her somewhat reluctantly, the travelling cloth bulging with her possessions hugged to her chest.

As they huddled in the tent, the wind shifted and ballooned out the sides. "Eat. We do not have to spare food for Tarkel. He will eat with the men."

"Thank you, Umri." Rae put a portion of meat on her plate.

"I heard Aurore gave you a huge bride gift, four bolts of the best of her cloth."

Rae smiled with remembrance. "Yes, my father, Kushlan also cedes me his Puri lands."

"That should buy you a husband. Kushlan's lands are well placed and suitably large."

Rae glanced up, trying to keep the hurt from her face. "I do not want to buy a husband. I want to belong."

Umri laughed softly. "I meant no offence. You belong to yourself... that much I see. I hope Hanal does not disappoint you."

Rae paused before taking a bite of her food. "How could he?"

Umri's gaze turned serious. "In every way...be warned." Her eyebrow rose. "Or should he be warned?" She laughed as she cleared away the food and scraped the plates clean with sand and cloth.

"Where do I sleep?" Rae asked eventually, after Umri had gazed unspeaking into the fire for half the night.

At her words, Umri looked up and the distant look evaporated. "There, to the side. I would face the wall of the tent if I were you. There is a curtain so let it drop behind. Be warned, young maiden, my husband will share my bed this night."

Rae nodded, removed her outer clothing and lay down. The wind puffed the tent, sending ripples up and down above her head. Already she was homesick for the keep, for Aria's sweet voice, and the sameness of it all. Letting out a slow sigh, her eyelids grew heavy and sleep came in a moment.

A sound in the night woke her. Holding herself still, she listened with eyes closed. The sounds of Umri's marriage bed filled the tent. Rae willed herself back to sleep, scrunching her eyes closed. Sighs and moans lingered. She heard them over the quavering beat of her heart. Rae cursed herself. She was no child, but her mother had died in childbirth. At the keep, such a thing would be frowned on. The sound of flesh upon flesh filled Rae's mind and, even though it was cool, she began to sweat as Umri's passion flowed over her. She tried to shut the couple out, but it appeared to go and on and on. Awareness came with the morning sun, but Rae was uncertain as to when she actually fell asleep.

"Wake," Umri said.

Rae turned, still wrapped in her covers, startled by Umri's voice. She lifted the bottom of the curtain to peer at the woman.

"Come here."

Dropping the curtain Rae drew on her gown and adjusted her outer clothing. "Yes," Rae replied, careful to make her voice low and humble. Umri's ways were strange to her. The Puri woman appeared capricious and changeable, and Rae did not know how to proceed.

Rae lifted the curtain and shuffled forward on her knees. The contents of her travelling cloth were laid out in front of Umri; her clothing separated into piles. Umri looked up. "These are your possessions," she stated, running her hand over the piles.

Rae nodded dumbly.

"These you will not need." She indicated her pile of gowns, gifts from Aria and Aurore. "Unless you come on a visit and not to live."

"No. I come to the Puri to live." Rae kept her expression neutral, showing neither pleasure nor regret.

"Then these will be traded." Umri lent backward to pick up a pile of Puri clothes and then placed them in front of her. "Take these. They are mine, but Tarkel bade me give them to you."

Another pile appeared next to it. "These are new and the trade price for your Argenterran clothes will pay for them. Do you accept?"

"Yes," Rae replied. She gazed at the colourful clothes and fingered a red vest.

"Now, what is in here?"

Rae's eyes focussed on a bundle wrapped in cloth. She had never seen it before, but it had Aurore's seal on it. "I know not."

"May I open it?" Umri's expression was eager, like a child with a gift.

Rae nodded. She dared not refuse. As the cloth parted, Umri gasped. "I do not believe it." She stood up and dangled a robe down the length of her body. "This is cold cloth."

The robe was beige, the cloth thin with fine threads laced through it. It had been wrought with the *given*. Rae could sense it from where she sat. "I did not know it was there," Rae replied, somewhat awed even though she did not know what cold cloth was.

Umri sat back down, folding the cloth back into its neat shape. "This," she said. "You do not trade. It has no price."

"Yes. Aurore must have gifted it to me." Rae reached forward and brushed the cloth with her the tips of her fingers.

Umri's eyes glazed as she caressed the robe. "Yes, she made it, every part of it. Her thoughts are woven in between warp and the weft." She laughed softly. "I see the way of it. Kushlan is her lover. She thought of him as she made it for you."

"That is a lie," Rae cried, shock rocking through her. "Aurore is honourable and my father would not..." Rae did not like that Umri could see things that she could not.

Umri smiled. "Believe what you will, but it is here in the cloth for those like me who can read it. Let me tell you what I see."

Horror filled Rae. She wanted to flee but Umri's voice, distant and haunting, began:

"'I cannot', she says with tears in her eyes, trying to push the tall and handsome Kushlan away. But Kushlan embraces her, kisses her cheek and whispers urgently in her ear, 'But he is gone, the oath is broken. I am free...come to me...come to me...' Aurore pulls out of his grasp, though it breaks her heart, she steps away. 'My son needs me,' she says, sobbing like a lost child. 'He is grown and will soon be a man,' argues Kushlan. Tears leak from his eyes, heartbreak written on his face. 'No, I will not go with you. I cannot leave him and bring more shame on my house...'"

Umri's eyes refocussed. A sure and steady smile greeted Rae's stunned expression. Rae opened her mouth, throat working to form words but none would come. Her cheeks radiated warmth but the ring of truth stopped her denial.

"How sad it is," began Umri. "Do not fret, child. They never joined in the flesh...she denied him, though her heart ached to be with him. You never knew?"

Shaking her head, Rae sniffed.

Umri's graceful hand caressed the cloth again. "There are other secrets here...but you are not ready to hear them." She placed the robe aside. "The rest of the clothes are acceptable. They are fancy and flimsy but you may wear them for your husband in the privacy of your tent. The cold cloth robe will keep you warm, even in the coldest winter. The cape that you brought is useless compared to it. But retain this, too. It may come in useful for a curtain, or a cushion, or to wrap your child."

Rae's mind was awash with turbulent thoughts. So much had happened so quickly. How different it all seemed from Kushlan's tales and her own imaginings. She never thought she would feel so adrift emotionally. Rae watched mutely as Umri efficiently rebound her possessions, leaving the used outfit for her to change into. Umri dumped the pile of clothes in front of Rae. "Put these on and give me the ones you are wearing. We will wash and ready them for trade."

Behind the curtain, Rae slipped off her gown and her underclothes. A shallow bowl and a cloth stood just on the other side of the sheer curtain. "May I use the water to wash?" she said quietly to Umri, who was packing away utensils and other belongings.

"Yes, though use it wisely. Our life is harsh and water is a gift. I have scented it for you."

Taking Umri's words to heart, she wiped the scented water across her skin, careful to husband every drop. Then she slid her legs into the trousers, her feet into her boots and the shirt over her head. The red vest she eased her arms into, and then studied the headdress. "I do not know how to wear this. Will you show me?" Rae asked as she parted the curtain and shuffled across the floor of the tent.

Umri stopped her packing and looked over her shoulder. "Unmarried women wear it so," she undid her headcloth and arranged it so a section draped down her back like a long braid. She tucked hers back in and kept working.

Rae tied hers in an approximation of what Umri had shown her. Then she edged closer to her again and bowed low. "I thank you, Umri. I am your kin. Please let me help you."

Tarkel entered the tent, all quick movements and bustling robes. "So little sister, Tu Raenal, daughter of Kushlan, you look like one of us now."

Rae gaped at him, then bowed low as she had to Umri. Tarkel said over her head.

"Carry those to the horses. We leave after we eat."

"Yes, Tarkel. I thank you."

❧ 27 ❧

ON THE TRAIL TO SILVERDALE

ONCE THEY LEFT the stale caves behind Sophy's mood lifted. She kept gazing behind her to catch a glimpse of the Lake of Reflections. Lillia had not stopped talking about the wonder of it, which only made Sophy increasingly annoyed that she had missed it. The group of riders rounded a bend and, in the setting sun, the water glowed silvery pink. Squinting, Sophy tried to see more but it was too far away. With a shrug, she faced the front and concentrated on the road ahead.

Each plod of the horses' hooves counted out the days as Oakheart led them slowly to Silverdale. Sophy hated having to let the horse walk because she felt every lift and step of its gait. Squeezed between so many mounted men, it was like riding between two brick walls. Every guard was tense and alert and forever watching for more arrow birds or other forms of attack.

In general, Fern's voice spiced up the meals. He could be so smooth but his words slipped beneath her armour like a well-placed dagger. She did her best to avoid his notice, often without success.

Ten days after leaving the base of the plateau, Sophy was shovelling stew into her mouth, trying to ignore everyone. Walker moon rose, piercing their camp with light that brought the tents and men into sharp focus. Oakheart sat across from her, clean-shaven, with his hair neatly tied back. He appeared lost in thought. Gazing at him from beneath her lashes, she wondered if Brownlea's death had affected him and how he dealt with the loss.

While she sat there deep in thought, she realised that she had let Brownlea's violent passing slip from her mind. It was as if the movement of air as they travelled along chased her grief away. But now when she looked at Oakheart, hair glowing silver in the moonlight, the pain renewed, accompanied by grief and guilt. Brownlea had died because of her, and Oakheart carried the burden of responsibility.

The dreams of the dark that had tormented her had stopped as if the hand that placed them there was busy elsewhere. That night though, memories of Brownlea, his face smiling, his silly chatter, the blood welling from his chest, plagued her. Her tossing and turning, denied her meaningful rest. When morning came, bleary eyed and mind-numbed, she decided she had to talk to Oakheart although she didn't know whether it was for own sake or for his. After breakfast, striding around the camp and trying to avoid getting in everyone's way, she sought an opportunity to catch Oakheart alone. Fern was directing the men to break camp. Distracted, it took a while for her to catch sight of her quarry. He had a smile on his face after one of Fern's jokes, but somehow it didn't reach his eyes. Something was bothering him and she suspected it was Brownlea's death.

Oakheart sat down and leant against a log while he sorted his gear. No one else was close by. Leaning down to tug her boots higher, she pushed a stray lock of hair behind her ear and then went up to him with her eyes lowered. He was cleaning a dagger. The hilt was black and gold and etched with a leaf pattern. The motion of his hands slowed when he noticed her presence and he quirked his eyebrow at her.

Sophy's face heated, and her throat decided not to cooperate. "Uh hem," she cleared her throat. "Oakheart...I was wondering how you were."

His mouth straightened, not quite a frown and not a smile. "Are you asking me how I fare, my lady?"

Sophy nodded eagerly. "Mmm...are you feeling...happy?" She crouched down beside him.

He looked askance at her. "You mock me..." Oakheart shoved the dagger into its sheath.

"No, I don't." Surprised, she nearly overbalanced. It was hard to be dignified with her hands in the dirt. Wiping them off, she said. "I'm concerned—with Brownlea and everything. You seem a bit down."

"Down? I am seated." He stood, stowed his dagger away and began to throw items into a chest with his back to her. "Are you concerned for your safety or the quality of my care?"

She bolted upright to her feet. "I'm not worried about me, or my safety. I'm worried about you..."

"Why?" He turned to face her, his expression serious.

"Because I...why what?" Her eyes narrowed when she realised he was scamming her.

"Why do you not worry about your safety? It should be upmost in your mind. I know it is upmost in mine."

"I think I'm going to scream," she said through clenched teeth. Looking down, she realised that she had dug a hole in the ground with her foot. "Never mind." She turned away, fist balled, and headed back the way she had come. What a waste of time trying to talk to him, she thought crankily.

"Sophy," Oakheart called after her softly. She slowed but didn't turn back. "Thank you for your concern. I grieve for Brownlea but I am well otherwise," he said.

Perplexed, she sped up and reached her horse, which had been saddled for her. She checked the girth and played with the stirrups while trying to calm her racing heart. She had no idea what had just happened or why such a simple thing as talking to a friend about how they were feeling had become so complex.

Fern headed her way. "My, you do look dark," he commented. "Are there thunder clouds in the sky, perchance?" He began to scan the sky, which was blue and clear.

"No, my lord," she ground out as she tugged at the saddle blanket and checked the girth strap again. She reached for the pommel, ready to mount. Her new horse wasn't as cooperative as Merrywillow. He sidestepped, causing her to hop.

Fern smiled, though his grey eyes coolly appraised her. "May I assist you into the saddle, my lady?"

"Thanks," Sophy replied, with enough force to part his hair.

Fern assisted her onto her horse. "Angst, my lady? Is your favourite giving you trouble?" He looked meaningfully at Oakheart, who was checking his own mount, carefully examining the hooves.

Sophy glanced over her shoulder in Oakheart's direction. "Fern..." she began tersely, then changed her tack, puffed out a breath and said, "I mean, Lord Fern. You don't even begin to be funny. His excellency," she said over-loudly, "is not my favourite. And if you must know, I spend most of my time being the unintended annoyance of his life. So you will do us all a favour if you would quit the boring innuendos."

Fern bowed, chuckling. "Very well. Here comes your warrior chaperone. The *given* will need to favour any who dare to cross her."

"Do not test me, Lord Fern. You will find me a relentless opponent." With a sour expression, Lillia mounted her horse swiftly and stared at him crossly. Fern headed off, bellowing orders and questions to the men as they finished stowing away gear.

"Thanks for that, Lillia," Sophy said, genuinely grateful. "You don't know how trying his constant teasing can be."

"You are welcome, my lady. And I do know how trying it can be. I have to listen to him until my chest burns with outrage. I do not understand it. Truly I do not."

Sophy was surprised by the virulence of Lillia's response. "It's not that bad, is it?"

Lillia glanced askance at her. "If you do not think it is bad, my lady. Then how can I take offence?"

⁂

IT TOOK FOUR MORE DAYS TO REACH THE TOP OF THE PLATEAU. Sophy was sure they could have covered the distance in less than half that time, but Oakheart's constant precautions slowed their progress. Once the last cart lurched up the path to the plateau, Oakheart decided to make camp, even though it was still early. Oakheart wandered off and let Fern organise the camp and setting the watch.

Sophy dismounted when Lillia did, stretching her tired legs and back. Lillia went off to supervise the unpacking of what was left of their things, leaving Sophy to stroll around the borders of their now expanded campsite.

The general hubbub made her feel out of place. Turning full circle, she paused when the view expanded over the lip of the plateau. The distant mountains were backlit by the red blush of sunset, dark shadows spread, crawling across the land to cover, forests and lakes. She hadn't realised that they had come so far. She had no idea where the valley was, where Aria was. When Oakheart's muscled arm disconcertingly circled her waist, she nearly jumped out of her skin. She pushed down, trying to dislodge his hold. "I'm nowhere near the edge, Oakheart."

"For a normal person that would be so, for you, no," he said softly in her ear. She slapped his arm in frustration, and he eased his hold enough for her to breathe at least. "You may gaze upon the land from here, a safe distance from the edge and within my grasp. You like views, do you not?"

All sorts of butterflies had taken flight in her stomach at his closeness. She swallowed hard. Confused thoughts flitted, making her frown. The dying sunlight created even more contrast in the landscape. Low cloud draped over the distant hills and the sun's rays painted the landscape with shades of red, burnished orange and mauve. The Argent Flow was a pale streak in the far distance as it cut through the green and browns. "I don't think I've seen anything as beautiful as this. When I first saw the valley, I thought it was beyond imagining. This is art."

She felt, rather than saw, him smile. When she relaxed into his embrace, he did not pull away as she expected. Then she remembered the incident when she had tried to comfort him over the loss of Brownlea. Perhaps Oakheart was as confused as she was. It was hard to be angry with him when he was this close to her. His voice vibrated in his chest. "The view from Glassy Mountain is even more spectacular, especially in the morn and at eve-tide. You will see for yourself and compare which is the superior."

"Oakheart," she said, turning to face him. Releasing her, his arms dropped to his sides. "It's a very long trip to Glassy Mountain Retreat. It feels so distant, so remote. I wonder if I will ever see it and find out about this leaf..." She rubbed the place where the living crystal leaf grew within her and lifted troubled eyes to his.

He glanced to where she touched the spot. "The way is long, yes. Do not fear the leaf. I know that it has worked to preserve you when you would have otherwise failed."

Her eyes grew wide. "What do you mean? How would you know that unless you touched me..."

"I did, and beheld the leaf. It bound you to this life...However, it is not as you—" Red streaks of embarrassment began crawling up his neck.

Sophy gaped at him. He backed up a step, while Sophy decided whether she should run and hide herself away for a while. "I should find Lillia now."

He moved to block her escape, so she tried to dodge around him. He put a hand on her arm, and her gaze returned to his "One moment, before you go. Your dreams—I have not heard you cry out for many weeks now. Have they left you?"

"M...Mostly. I still have them, but not with as much force."

She took another step, and he fell into step with her. "I smell food cooking. Perhaps 'tis time to eat." Oakheart sounded light-hearted, so Sophy responded in kind, grateful for the opportunity to overcome that awkward moment—a moment that suggested an intimacy that wasn't there.

"Let me guess...toffelbread?" she said archly.

"Yes, and with gady root sauce..." He waved his arm, gesturing for her to walk ahead of him.

"Your favourite," she added with a laugh. How could trouble and morose thinking get in the way of a good meal?

Fern was frowning at her when they approached the camp. Oakheart headed to his tent, which his men had erected in his absence. She slowed her steps. "Is something wrong?" she asked him.

He started and looked down as she approached. "No, my lady, I was just overcome by your beauty."

She came to a halt. "Fern,' she said in warning. "Please do not start…I know exactly how I look."

"Perhaps," he replied, his tone short and hard. "His excellency seems enamoured of you…he cannot seem to keep his arms from you."

"Oakheart? Enamoured of me? You're joking. He was making sure I didn't fall off the edge. That's all."

"I think you tell untruths. You think your ploys will capture him."

"My ploys?" Again, blood burned her cheeks as she stared at him, open-mouthed. Turning away, she scanned for Lillia's and her shared tent, but with the men milling around she couldn't see it. So much for a quick retreat.

"Yes, I see your tactics," Fern said to her back. "Drawing him off to woo him. It will not work though. Oakheart sees through such paltry tricks."

For some reason, Sophy's eyes watered, a precursor to tears. However, she didn't want the shame of crying, so she found anger instead and swung back to face him.

"Tricks, ploys…Fern you are so wrong about me and about Oakheart. If I stay out of trouble, sometimes we are friendly. That is all."

"How smoothly you utter those words, but your actions speak clear. I have seen so many women throw themselves at Oakheart. To no avail. He will not be drawn in by your devices…especially with your looks."

He turned on his heel and left her standing there. A few guards close by had obviously overheard their conversation as they looked away when she glanced around. Sophy, with her colour heightened by embarrassment and anger, was ready to punch something. Burning with indignation, she went to find Lillia.

Later, as Lillia and Sophy ate, clouds covered the moons. Fern waltzed over, his mood still dark. Sophy cringed in anticipation.

"Cloudy moonlight becomes you, my lady," Fern said, lightly, though his voice had an edge. "Perhaps when the sky fills up with storm clouds your true beauty will spill forth and dazzle us."

Lillia sucked in a breath and glared at the young man.

"Thank you, Lord Fern," Sophy replied tightly, trying not to glower at the fire.

Lillia hissed at Fern and he held up his hands in a gesture of surrender. Sophy lost her appetite. She sat staring at the flames, trying to work it out. She was not throwing herself at Oakheart, and he definitely had no interest in her. Well, no interest other than keeping her safe from harm and finding out what mystery she represented.

"My lady?" Fern said.

"I'm sorry, my lord," Sophy replied to Fern. "I'm tired. I'm going to bed. Night." She stood up hastily and stepped away from the fire, wiping her hands on her breeches.

Fern stood and called after her. "You will not hear the apology that Lillia has pressed upon me. Alas I am sorely wounded." Fern was back to his theatrical self.

"Night," she repeated.

She passed Oakheart on his way to join them and nodded. He slowed, trying to catch her eye, but she kept walking straight for her tent.

"Is Sophy well?" She heard him ask.

"I think so, Oakheart," Lillia replied.

"Her manners are appalling," Fern said clear enough for her to hear.

"Fern. Enough." Oakheart's voice was faint, though she detected the admonishment.

Sophy entered her tent and threw herself on her bed. She refused to let tears flow. Fern would not get the better of her.

❧

By mid-morning the next day, Sophy found that the track they had been following became a wide and flat road. Fields ran in all directions, full with ripening grain. A breeze brought fresh air to lighten the smell of horse dung and human sweat. What trees there were seemed few and far between, although they offered shade to grazing animals. Sophy was relaxed, and even Oakheart seemed less eager to crowd her with men and arms. If they were to be attacked, they would have plenty of warning in this open space.

Over the next day, houses appeared, grouped together and hugging the road. Oakheart's smile was genuine when the residents waved and called out their hellos. "How is the harvest?" he called out to a farmer bent over a sickle.

"Ah well," replied the farmer, teeth showing white against his weathered skin. "'Tis not all in yet but it should be good. There will be enough to keep you city folk plump."

As Oakheart guffawed, sun-browned children ran alongside the horses, their happy faces full of excitement. When Oakheart picked up the pace, they ran off to play in the fields. Orchards, ponds and farms crowded around the road and on toward the town, its outline growing up ahead on the horizon. Carts with cloth, grain, pots and other produce headed down the road, presumably to supply shops and stalls and the castle. The hard packed road made way to a cobbled surface with large neatly packed stones. The sound of horses' hooves clicking made conversation difficult.

Lillia leant over and yelled, "Look, my lady, see that cloth."

"Which?" Sophy bellowed back, while she shaded her eyes with her hands, looking at the market just outside the walls of Silverdale.

"The green one. 'Tis the colour of the forest at sunset."

Sophy saw the cloth and others. She gave Lillia an appraising look. "Really, Lillia, I didn't know you were partial to clothes and fabrics."

Lillia smiled slightly. "I must confess to a little vanity. 'Tis not often gratified in Gilton Forest, but when I come to court I do try to uphold appearances...for the Queen's sake, of course."

"I see...we will have to investigate the markets then. If you can bear it."

"Mmm...yes, I may be prevailed upon."

Houses, not quite crammed together, backed onto the walls of the town. Dark stone towers stood at the four corners of an imposing castle. Sophy had to blink. It wasn't what she was expecting. This town and castle were built for defence. There was nothing romantic or overly artistic in its design, unlike Valley Keep.

"What troubles you, my lady?" Lillia asked.

Sophy shook her head, dislodging her puzzled expression. "I am surprised by Silverdale, that's all. Do you think the castle is made with the *given* like Valley Keep?"

"From memory, no. But it would be unusual for there not to be one part or another enhanced with the *given*. The bonding chamber, for example."

They passed through the gates in single file. With the traffic and people milling about Sophy had to walk her horse carefully. Laneways criss-crossed, revealing three-tier houses leaning over the streets. People gaped and pointed at them as they traversed the town.

At that moment, Sophy felt a sense of foreboding. Fern's taunts rose up in her memory. How would she cope in the high king's court? She had outraged Valley Keep at every turn. Silverdale was different, bigger, grander and, to her at this time, very important.

It wasn't fair, she decided. Oakheart had not taught her how to behave. Yes, it was his fault. Jolted out of her reverie by the wild neigh and jerk of her horse, she saw several creatures. Fascinated, she slowed her horse to watch the small hairy creatures scramble close. Lillia kept going unaware that she had slowed down. She was considering how cute the creatures seemed, when they growled and then gnashed double rows of teeth. She struggled to control her horse, which continued to rotate its head. Suddenly, it reared up and dropped her into a pile of muck. The creatures, round balls of fur with four spiral horns disappeared as quickly as they had arrived.

Oakheart and the others turned around at the commotion, while Fern rode up from the rear. By the puzzled looks on their faces, they had not seen the creatures or her horse's reaction. Oakheart dismounted and headed her way, leading his mount by the reins.

From the saddle, Fern looked down at her, a sneer evident. "A rather inept way to ride your horse, or is it the fashion where you hail from."

Words failed her as she struggled to stand. Fern laughed as he dismounted, obviously pleased at his own wit. He grabbed her horse. Her traitor mount appeared calm, although she glared at it meaningfully. Oakheart walked up to her, looking angry, yet she could not fathom why.

"What were those things?" she asked as she gained her feet, pushing at the congealed muck clinging to her clothes.

Oakheart was about to say something, seemed to think better of it, and paused. Taking a deep breath, he opened his mouth again. "What things?" he asked.

Sophy waved her hand vaguely to her left. "Didn't you see? Those fluffy things with the horns."

Oakheart screwed up his face. "Warren beasts?" He became tense, his eyes slanted left and right.

His manner made the hair on her arms stand up. "What are they?" she asked suddenly wary.

Oakheart shrugged then turned to Fern and said, "Warren beasts never come to the town...never this far north. Do they? I have heard naught of them beyond the Lower Plateau."

Fern looked at her as if she was crazy.

"What are you talking about?" she asked.

"Warren beasts are those creatures you described," Oakheart said to her at last. "Yet I cannot account for you seeing any in Silverdale."

"Neither can I. They were there one minute, spooked my horse, and gone the next. Perhaps someone is keeping them as pets."

Taking a cloth from his saddlebag, Oakheart tried to wipe the drying mud and gunk from her clothes. She snatched the cloth from him and did her best to tidy herself up, muttering to herself at the same time.

"When we reach the castle, you will have time to clean yourself and dress before you are presented to the high king. I should warn you that you may not get an audience for a few days. I hope you will not be insulted. The high king is busy. Do not worry, Lillia will keep you company."

Sophy nodded. "That's fine by me." At least she didn't have to appear in front of the high king smeared with grime and rubbing her wounded rear. Fern, for once, kept silent. Lillia came up to stand next to Oakheart, her expression was sympathetic, yet she coughed once. Sophy took the hint. "I mean...Thank you, Oakheart. You do not know how relieved I am."

Sophy hopped back on her horse without assistance, and they

continued to the outer courtyard. Her hands shook, and she kept her gaze lowered. As far as she could tell, no one took much notice of her. In her current mood, being ignored was a blessing. She dismounted. Straight away Lillia and three guards encircled her, serving to screen her dishevelled state from curious onlookers.

Oakheart loomed over Lillia's head. "Excuse me. I must leave you now. Filo will direct you to the guests' quarters. I will send word to you soon."

"We thank you, your excellency. You have cared for us well," Lillia said with a formal bow. Oakheart bowed in the same way and left with Fern. The chaos of men dismounting, and the unloading of clothes and provisions, soon obscured them from view.

A servant dressed in green and gold livery appeared in front of them. "My ladies, I am Filo. I am to take you to your quarters."

"We thank you for your service to us," Lillia said, as she grabbed Sophy's hand. "Stay close to me, my lady. I do not wish to lose you."

ALONE AMONGST FRIENDS

WHEN SOPHY PASSED through the massive entrance way, it was as if she had been swallowed by the castle. Soon, after so many twists and turns along the grid of passageways, she lost all sense of direction. Awestruck, she plodded behind Lillia through bare halls and rooms draped in tapestries. She passed through tall, thin doorways and out into a quadrangle garden, which contained tranquil ponds. Finally, Filo stopped in front of a wide door, and pounded his fists on it. Steps sounded and the door swung inwards. A large lady, with grey hair neatly arranged in a bun, looked them up and down.

With a quick nod of his head Filo said, "Mistress Tilla, I pass these guests into your care. Please excuse me." With a bow, a swirl of green cape, he was gone.

Lillia stood taller, tilting her chin up. "Good Mistress, I require a suite with two bedrooms for me and my charge. We are here with His Excellency Oakheart Silverbow. The Lady Sophy is in his care."

"I see," Tilla replied in a surprisingly deep voice. Lillia's performance didn't appear to impress her and the woman's eyebrow had quivered slightly at the mention of Oakheart. Tilla stepped out, pulling the large door shut behind her. "We are quite full, miladies. I will see what I can find for you. If you would be so kind as to follow me."

Again they walked down passageways and turned so often that Sophy began to feel dizzy.

"This should suit you," Tilla said as she fumbled for a key. She swung the door open and led the way in. "'Tis light and airy. Not large, but sufficient for your needs. You appear to have no servants of your own." Her gaze swept their dishevelled and road stained appearance. "Belle is the maid for this section. Pull the rope there if you need any assistance." She walked back towards the door, her large hips brushing up against the doorjamb and paused. "If you need anything else, you know where to find me." Then she pulled the door shut behind her and left them alone.

Sophy flung up her hands. "Did she say find her? How could we do that? I couldn't find my way out of a closet in this place."

Lillia stopped frowning. "Pray do not worry, we may ask anyone for her, and they will give directions. You must be tired. You will need to bathe before you rest, though." Lillia sniffed theatrically, then scrunched up her face. Sophy was still covered in muck from her fall from her horse. "I will ring for the maid, Belle, I think she said her name was." She jerked the rope pull once and then walked to the bedrooms and examined the view from the windows. "Oh this is very good, Sophy. The suite is exactly right for us."

"I don't know what you mean. It looks ordinary to me." In her dirty state, she couldn't sit on the sofas in case she left a stain so she stood around idly.

Lillia's expression was eager. "You do not understand. We are up a level. We have a view to the gardens. The sitting room here is generous, not grand, but ample." She pointed to the bedrooms. "They are fine, too. Yes, we are reasonably well respected at least."

Sophy chewed her lips while she mulled over Lillia's assessment of their accommodation. Lillia could tell all of that from what kind of room they were allocated? She wandered around the room, examining the furnishings. She had no experience with being a guest in a castle.

There was a knock at the door. The maid, Belle, entered. "You called for service, my ladies," she said with a curtsy. Belle looked a little older than Sophy. Her complexion was pale and her brown hair was set with plaits that wound round her head.

Lillia tugged her leather jerkin down, drawing attention to the leaf pattern engraved there.

"Yes, thank you, my dear. The Lady Sophy needs to bathe. Will you prepare the water for her?"

"Yes, certainly, my lady." Belle went through to the washroom, which lay off the sitting room and between the two bedrooms.

Lillia hovered behind the maid, but was still talking to Sophy. "The plumbing here is not as civilised as Valley Keep, but will be sufficient to your needs." Sophy nodded to Belle when the bath was prepared and waved Lillia out of the room. Before she could disrobe, the main door swung open and four porters brought in their chests and other baggage.

Lillia efficiently directed the baggage to their respective rooms. Sophy had hardly any time to blink when Lillia started rummaging around in Sophy's clothes trying to find something for her to wear.

Walking into a cloud of scented steam, Sophy shut the door, feeling a sense of joy. She had forgotten luxuries such as hot, perfumed water. She shucked her clothes eagerly and eased into the tub. Her muscles had hardened from the months of travelling, but that did not mean they couldn't be softened by a long soak.

When she finally exited the washroom, Belle and Lillia had unpacked all her things.

"Look, Sophy, all these gowns that Princess Aria packed for you are still safe. How lucky."

"Yes, very lucky." She fingered the cloth of one of the gowns absently. Too bad Brownlea didn't make it too. Her stomach rumbled noisily. Sophy blushed, hugging her middle.

"Oh my," Lillia said, blushing deeply. "I forgot to order some food. Belle would you be so kind as to fetch some bread, cheese and wine for us."

"Of course, my lady. Are you sure that will be sufficient? The refectory will have other food available. You could still go there—"

Lillia interrupted her. "Of course they will. But we are too weary to make our way there. And we would not like to impose. No, a few morsels will tide us over, and then I think we will sleep."

Belle left and by the time she returned about twenty minutes later, Sophy could barely keep her eyes open. Lillia forced her to eat and when she could swallow no more she crawled into her bed. She luxuriated in being in a real bed. The comfortable and firm mattress, the feather light quilt, and the sweet smelling pillow lulled her off to sleep.

Her sleep was peaceful until she dreamed of Brownlea. The images were so strong, so powerful and immediate, it was as if the event was happening right at that moment. She sensed a darkness, awash with surreal swathes of colour. Her dream vision distorted and then cleared, opening to Brownlea's death scene. She wanted to hide from what was coming . However, she was helpless as Brownlea dived, taking the poisoned beak in his chest.

The smell of blood was thick. She moaned, trying to fight the dream. Blood bubbled and spurted from Brownlea's nose and mouth, gushing over her until she was red with his blood. The sound of her screams rent the air and hurt her ears. She was at one with her dream self, reliving that moment. Oakheart appeared huge, overbearing and sweating blood lust. His gaze was hard, and he looked ready to slay her. Then as she begged for help, he sneered at her and yelled at her with words laden with derision. At first, she couldn't make them out, and then she heard him clearly.

"You should have died. It should have been you. Not Brownlea. I want you to die. Why do you not die?"

Horrified, she gazed at Oakheart, mesmerised by his once-green eyes. Light flared out from his unnatural orbs like flame. Tongues of red fire licked her skin. She screamed and sat up panting, wet with sweat that reminded her of thick and sticky blood.

It was dark and cold. She could hear her own breathing echoing loudly in the room. After so long in close company, she didn't like being alone. That was it, she thought. The power of the dream was still with her, as if she was close to the source of it. She awoke with the question in her mind—could Oakheart hate her that much? She eased out of bed and made her way to the next room.

Lillia was awake. "Are you well, child?"

"Yes," Sophy said, though her voice sounded timid. "May I bunk in with you?"

"Mmm...yes, here," she said sleepily and moved over to make room. At length, Sophy fell asleep wrapped in the referred warmth of Lillia's body and comforted by her presence.

OAKHEART MADE HIS WAY TO THE HIGH KING'S PERSONAL AUDIENCE room, after dispatching a palace guard to advise of his arrival and to request an urgent meeting. By the time he got there, courtiers were exiting the main audience chamber, some grumbling about their abrupt dismissal. It was with relief that Oakheart saw the high king enter the small homey chamber. "You are back, finally. Only a month or two late." The high king walked over and embraced Oakheart and then slapped him on both shoulders. His blue-eyed gaze bored into him. "Well?"

"A long story. We have a lot to discuss. First, I am sure you have heard that I bring with me one of the Gifts of Crystal Tree Woods?"

The high king nodded. "Yes. Adage sent word from the retreat months ago. I cannot survive without that talkstone you gave me. Very useful. I also know that you sent your men to fetch Fern with a troop to provide protection up the by way. What in Vorn's name is going on?"

"Brownlea is dead, killed by a coordinated attack of arrow birds."

The high king walked across the room to stare out the window, picking up a goblet from the table. He shook his head and took a long draught of wine. Frowning to himself, he walked back toward Oakheart. "This is not good at all. And to make matters worse, your timing is off. It is not safe for this outlander, or you, in Silverdale at this time."

Oakheart did not bother to hide his surprise. "Have there been attacks?"

The high king lifted an eyebrow. "Attacks? Here? No. Hanal of Puri is here with his sister Lyant."

Oakheart did his best not to blush. "And?"

"Do not come the innocent with me. You let that barbarian trick you into a compromising position with his sister. I have put him off, but cannot avoid the pending interview without creating an irretrievable diplomatic incident. I must meet with him soon. You must leave straightaway."

"But Sophy?"

"That outlander will be safe enough here. If I pretend she does not exist maybe Hanal of Puri will too."

Oakheart's mind was racing. Perhaps the high king was right about Sophy, but the treatment of Hanal he could not agree with. "Is there no chance you will consider Hanal's proposal? Long have the Puri suffered for Shabra's actions. They are not so barbarian as you think. A marriage between the Puri and Silverdale would do much to heal the breach."

"Never. I am the high king here and I will not let that dark, untrustworthy...You know my thoughts. I cannot and will not change my mind. Surely you would not consider marrying such a..."

"For peace between our people I would. Lyant is intelligent and cultured. If only you could see. It would be so easy to take this opportunity and secure all our futures."

"Bah. You overestimate the threat they pose. I will not have them in our lands. Nor will I ally myself with that upstart with his dubious parentage. Pfaah! to his claim that he has as much of Vorn's blood as I do. Besides, they breed too much and will outnumber us in a generation."

Oakheart shook his head. "Argenterra will regulate their birth rate as it does ours. I believe all will be equal eventually."

"Oakheart. I will discuss it no more. Off you go, straight away." He made shooing gestures.

"Where will you have me go? What excuse will you give?"

The high king refilled his goblet and sat heavily in his chair. "Go to the lookout at Brighton Falls. Wait for me to send for you."

Oakheart wanted to argue further, but he knew Veld, the high king, would not budge. The bitterness went too deep. Oakheart could not understand it. "I see. So you will have me sit around in Brighton Falls doing nothing?"

"Not nothing. The new tower is almost complete. I want you to oversee the last of it. Make sure there are no more accidents."

"And may I, at least, bathe and change my clothes?"

The high king guffawed. "Yes, provided you do it quickly. I will look out for the outlander."

"And Brownlea's mother? May I at least see her and offer comfort?"

Veld nodded into his goblet. "Of course. Give her my condolences. Her husband died when the lookout tumbled down the cliffs at Brighton Falls, you know. Best not tell her where you are going...in fact, best not tell anyone except those few who you take with you."

Oakheart left the high king on his second goblet of wine. He had very little time to organise his affairs and send a few messages before he had to leave. He hoped Sophy and Lillia would forgive him. At least he could ask his friend, Fern, to show them around while he was gone.

❦

THE NEXT DAY SOPHY SOUGHT OUT TILLA, THE MISTRESS OF THE Visitor's Hall, to send a message to Oakheart. The fat, old lady looked at her wearily, her jowls wobbling. "I am sorry miss...I have a new lot of visitors expected and another lot departing."

"Please, it's only a short message...to Oakheart. You know, the high king's Ambassador."

"Of course I know Oakheart. Known him since he was a lad...but I am still far too busy to take a message. You had best find him yourself or find one of his men to deliver it."

"But I don't know the way. Please...Oakheart will be pleased if you brought him the message. I'm one of his special guests."

The woman eyed her, and wiped her hands in her apron. "Do you know how many young maids want to send messages to Oakheart?"

Sophy stared at her blankly, at a loss to understand her. "No. I don't. But that's the only message I'll be sending him if this is all the effort it takes."

"Very well," Tilla said as she ambled off, muttering about young upstart maids being kept in their places. Sophy stared, feeling her anger rise.

Her time in the high king's palace would be disappointing if her first day was any indication. She turned on her heel and stomped away to fill Lillia in on the Mistress's rudeness. It took quite a while for her to realise that she couldn't find their suite. In the end, she had to ask a footman to escort her.

Lillia, of course, took her complaints about Mistress Tilla in her stride. "Now, my lady, you must understand that she is labouring under a big responsibility. I am sure she meant no offence. We must try and fit in."

"I'm trying to fit in, Lillia," Sophy replied, throwing herself onto the rose patterned sofa. "Everyone hates me, makes fun of me, insults me..."

Lillia clucked her tongue. 'Now my lady...no insult was intended, I am sure. I treat you well, do I not?"

Later in the day, after finishing a light meal, a tap sounded on the door. As Lillia opened it, the maid, Belle, stepped into the room. "Please excuse me...I am sent to tell you that his excellency, Oakheart, has been sent on an urgent mission and will not return for some time. He sends his apologies for his rudeness and asks that you enjoy Silverdale's hospitality in his absence."

Sophy's eyes searched Lillia's face, and the forest maiden seemed to take the news well.

"Thank you, that will be all for now," Lillia said, shutting the door on the maid.

Sophy crossed her arms over her chest and huffed.

"Do not pout, Sophy."

"But what does it mean? How can he bring us all the way here and then dump us like this?"

"I imagine the high king sent him elsewhere. He would not abandon us willingly...but now I know not what to do." Lillia went to pour some wine for herself and handed Sophy water. She gulped down the whole goblet without pause. It was then that Sophy began to realise that something was amiss. "What is it Lillia? Is there something wrong?"

"Yes and no. 'Tis of no great moment. I have other contacts here in the palace. However, it will take time to get an audience with the high king. With Oakheart, I would have had direct access. I would have been able to deliver my message, get my answer and return to the Gilton Forest. Now I am delayed. Already, so delayed."

"Why can't you request an audience with the high king? Aren't you an ambassador or something yourself?"

Lillia chuckled. "'Tis not that simple. This palace is much more complex than Valley Keep. There are politics here, ploys and counter ploys. I do not have the stomach for such things. Oakheart is clever and knows his way around. He also has a close relationship with the high king. With him gone, I will have to use other means and it could take me at least a month to get my audience. Unless, of course, Oakheart comes back before then. I should not despair." Lillia paced as she spoke and stopped when she saw the look of horror on Sophy's face. "What is it, my lady?"

"A month for you to see the high king? But what about me? I have no message or importance. I'm just Oakheart's guest. I... I..."

"Now, my lady...Sophy do not upset yourself."

"I think I will go to my bedroom just for a bit." Sophy turned and headed through the doorway, dragging her feet. What was she to do while Oakheart bounded away on some mission? Throwing herself down on her bed, she groaned into her bed covers, thumping them, too, for good measure.

After a few minutes, she grew bored of taking her anger on the bedding and rolled over to stare at the ornate ceiling instead. She thought of Aria and began to fumble through her belongings in search of the talkstone. Gingerly, she undid the strings of the cloth bag and shook the crystal out on the small table. She touched it lightly with a finger and snatched it back, as it singed her. She would have to wait until Aria called her, and Aria had only done that infrequently.

Sophy leant on the windowsill, gazing out. The sky was blue and the tops of trees nearly reached the level of her room. Leaning out further, she saw people walking in the garden below, courtiers, she imagined, in many coloured robes, some even looking as if they hailed from elsewhere entirely. Darn Oakheart, she thought. Without acquaintances, they could go nowhere, and they couldn't be introduced to the courtiers. "Rats!" she said to the sky.

When Lillia called her to eat with her in the sitting room, she feigned sleep.

⁂

"Come," Lillia said after days of moping around the suite. "We must socialise, so get dressed and we will brave one of the eateries."

They had kept to eating in their rooms since their arrival, much to the strange looks of Belle, who took away their empty food trays.

"But we don't know anyone. I thought you said that made us social outcasts?" Sophy replied as she ducked into her room to tidy herself up.

"That does not signify anything, Sophy. We may, perchance, luck upon an acquaintance and then we may not. We have each other for company, and I will not sit here day after day with only quick parades in the quadrangle garden. I pray, at least, that I may find someone I know to assist me."

Sophy emerged, tugging a crease from one of the fantastic new gowns that Aria and Aurore had sent with her.

"You look fit enough to meet the high king himself," Lillia commented. She wore her traditional forest gear, brown and green leather pants, this time with her chest plate embossed with a leaf pattern.

"You're joking," Sophy replied. Lillia looked at her blankly. "Jest?"

"Jest, no. Overstate, yes," Lillia quipped as she swung open the door and led the way out.

"Do you know where to go?" Sophy asked as they walked through a set of ornate doors, and passed by a few important looking people. A large tapestry, gracing a huge wall, depicted a well-muscled, large, tall, blond man with arms outstretched in supplication to a gate that shone like a rainbow. Pictured around him were a bedraggled bunch of people with awe stretched across their faces. As Lillia dragged her along, she read the inscription it said: Vorn, First-Comer and High King.

"I have an impeccable sense of direction," Lillia said with a frown.

Her face twitched as she turned left and right at the end of a non-descript corridor.

"What are you doing?" Sophy asked, altogether embarrassed by Lillia's queer behaviour.

Lillia kept up her strange routine, barely acknowledging Sophy. Then as Sophy looked up and down the corridor she said, "I know... you're sniffing for food." She could barely contain her laugh.

Lillia frowned, not pleased to be found out. With a tilt of her shoulder, she angled round to the left. The number of courtiers thickened and the smell of roasting meat grew stronger. "There, you see," Lillia said with satisfaction as a double-door opened and spilled out some well-fed and slightly tipsy courtiers.

"That was easy, even I could have smelled my way here," she said, following Lillia inside.

The clatter of metal plates and the chatter of many voices overwhelmed Sophy for a moment. From the look on the forest maiden's face, it did her too. Trying to discern a spare place amongst the scraps and spills on the tables was a difficult task.

"Hark, look there," Lillia said with a decisive step in the direction of some seating.

Lillia propelled her along towards their goal, but shifted her gaze sufficiently to catch sight of Fern, chatting amiably with three palace guards, who looked very smart in their uniforms. His eyes met Sophy's for a split second, flicked to Lillia and then back to the men to whom he was talking.

"Lillia? Is that—Fern?" Sophy said. Her gaze sifted through the crowd. She noticed him leaving. Darting around the diners, she made it to the door he had exited from and wrenched it open. She heard steps and saw a figure retreating down the corridor. "Lord Fern?"

A whirl of a blue cape, those grey eyes briefly met hers, and then he disappeared around the corner. Puzzled, Sophy stared down the hall. Other diners entered, edging around her immobile body. With a shrug, she pivoted on her heel and re-entered the refectory.

Lillia looked up from the table, where she held their spot. "Where is Lord Fern?"

Sophy sat down. "He ran away."

"Sophy, you exaggerate. A courtier such as Fern Ripplebark does not run away. Perhaps he did not notice you."

"No, Lillia. Listen to me. He saw me, twice, and ran away. He must really hate me to avoid me like that."

"Hate? That is too strong a word. Perhaps he was busy and means to meet us at another time. I do hope so, for though his connections are not as good as Oakheart's, they are many times my own."

"I'm doubly sorry then. For you and me."

❧ 29 ❧

FRIENDLY FOE

THE DAYS MERGED into one long wait. Neither Sophy nor Lillia sewed, a usual pastime for ladies, so they had little to amuse them. Occasionally, Lillia would dress and leave in search of some contact and would come back in the evening disheartened. They were both restless and took walks in the garden courtyard. They passed others among the mossy paths and received polite nods of acknowledgment. Sophy's anger with Fern brewed as each day passed. They never met accidentally again, and even Lillia on her expeditions, neither saw nor heard from him.

The various peoples represented at the high king's castle fascinated Sophy. Lillia didn't know all of the cultures, but she pointed out those that she did know. A very tall and thin man, arrayed in multicoloured feathers came from Glasshiver, the land beyond the Glassy Mountains. He was followed by a bevy of women, who were his brides, mother, aunts and sisters. Sophy could not tell which was which, as they all looked the same age and their feathers were all of the same colours. Lillia explained that the way the colours were arranged displayed the relationships. Glasshiver did not have access to the *given*, so items crafted with it were greatly prized by their people. "So these people didn't come with Vorn?" Sophy asked.

"I know not. I only know that the *given* is centred in Argenterra. My son, who is studying to be an adept, told me that Vorn's power, which he thrust into the land, is what enables us to use the *given*, that and his oath, which all swore.'

"So the people from Glasshiver could have come with Vorn and chose not to make his vow and then left?"

Lillia shrugged. "You would have to study the early writings to understand that."

With that, the family for Glasshiver passed out of sight and were replaced by another family from the upper wastelands. These were Puri, dressed in ankle boots and plump trousers. Both the men and the women wore brightly coloured headdresses and embroidered aprons. Lillia said the Puri travelled the land as the seasons changed and relied on the *given* for sustenance, especially for water. In the upper wastelands, the given was hard to summon and, though the lands were barren, it was adorned with a colourful people. To their surprise, the Puri showed open acknowledgment of them, nodding as they walked past and the man, who appeared to be the leader, gave Lillia the ritual Gilton forest greeting. After three weeks of passing each other in the garden, they at last stopped in their walk and spoke with Lillia.

The man bowed low. "Greetings fair forest maiden. I am Hanal of Puri." He spoke the same language, but he pronounced his vowels differently and rolled his 'rs' among other things.

Lillia smiled and bowed in the same fashion. "You honour me, venerable Hanal of Puri. May your waters flow with the *given*. May I introduce my young friend, Lady Sophy of Valley Keep."

Sophy tried to copy their bow and did a fair imitation of it. She was about to speak when she was arrested by Hanal's eyes. They were a clear, pale blue that sparkled like crystals. His swarthy skin enhanced the visual impact of his eyes. Taller than her, he was broad, clean-shaven with a full mouth and a nose like a mountain peak. A colourful headdress hid his hair, which added to his regal bearing. She gaped stupidly until Lillia coughed.

The Puri man looked toward Lillia, finally lifting his mesmerising eyes off Sophy.

"Your friend is not of the Silverlands or the wider expanse. She is an outlander, if my guess is right."

"Yes, venerable Hanal of Puri, I'm an outlander. And you're not guessing, you can tell."

Those eyes shifted back to her and then moved away. Sophy breathed in again after the shiver of his gaze left her. "Of course, I know what you are. We live close to the land in Puri. We know when we see a foreign element." He bowed again and said, "Forgive my words. No insult was intended. I would be pleased if you would both join me and my family for a meal this eve."

Lillia thanked him at length and accepted his invitation after getting a nod from Sophy. It was a relief to speak to someone other than each other. When they returned to their suite, word arrived that Lillia had been granted an audience on the next day. The forest maiden's tension evaporated to be replaced by excitement, while they dressed for dinner. Sophy was less lucky. She was no emissary and had no purpose other than to lay about the suite of rooms they had been allocated, until Oakheart once again graced them with his presence.

While they dressed with care, Lillia explained what she knew of Puri ways. "Now my lady, you must speak only when you are addressed directly," Lillia began as she buffed her chest plate.

"Not too hard I think," Sophy replied.

"You must eat what is presented to you and, most important of all, keep your gaze down."

"Why? Hanal looked at me. Stared at me quite rudely, actually."

"That may be, but the Puri believe that the eyes are the soul and only those who are mates can share their soul."

"Does that apply to foreign elements like me?"

"Yes. And if you want to avoid getting married to Hanal, you must avoid looking into his soul."

⚜

Sophy walked closely behind Lillia as they entered Hanal's apartments. Sophy expected great food and interesting conversation

249

from what Lillia had told her about Hanal. He was the leader of his tribe and had a reputation for excellent hospitality.

The room smelt of citrus and spices. The subdued lighting set the mood. The Puri had brought soft furnishings made with rich fabrics to adorn their suite, which was twice the size of the set of rooms allocated to them. Sophy watched and copied Lillia's movements and words, doing her best not to slide off the plump cushion she sat on.

"I have had my audience, finally," Hanal said as he served them wine. His gaze brushed over Sophy, and he was careful not to touch her when she took the goblet from his hand.

"How lucky for you," Lillia said, her face animated and happy. "I will have the honour to speak with the high king tomorrow." She relaxed back into her cushion, as if she met with the Puri every day and sighed. "The wait has been long, I must admit."

Hanal did not give the impression that he considered himself lucky. He frowned. "My party will leave by the end of the week," he said his voice dropping a level.

"We will be sorry to part from such friends so soon. You have added much to our daily routine with your hospitality," Lillia said as she nodded to the young woman who entered. Sophy acknowledged her in the same way, and watched while the woman took a seat behind Hanal. Puri men, dressed in plain robes, brought platters of food, spicy meats, coarse grain in a piquant dressing and flat breads. Hanal encouraged them to eat. Sophy chose the same things from the platters as Lillia did, but Hanal pressed her to take other titbits, singling her out for special attention. Remembering Lillia's instruction Sophy took them with an awkward smile.

Hanal swallowed a mouthful of chopped spiced meat and wiped his mouth with a napkin.

"I waited two long months for my interview with the high king, which is reasonable considering my purpose. Though it is a big investment in time and we had limited success."

Lillia nodded. "So protracted…I hope your business was not urgent. 'Tis a long time to be distant from home."

"When things are important the waiting is tolerable. It could have been longer. I could have been ignored completely." He gestured to the young woman, who had entered previously. She placed a stringed instrument on her lap. "This is Lyant, my sister. She will play for us."

Leaning back on his elbow, he observed them from under his dark lashes. Sophy saw his crystal-blue gaze riveted on her. Ignoring his scrutiny as best she could, she exulted in the exotic food and studied Lyant surreptitiously. Lyant's complexion was unblemished and softly tanned. When she stroked her stringed instrument, an ornately carved and painted gourd, the sleeves of her robe swayed gently. Sophy thought she was in her mid-twenties and couldn't help being awed by Lyant's air of contented, self-assuredness. Lyant sang then, a quiet song in a sweet voice that only added to her charms. Sophy suddenly felt untalented and ugly.

"It is a shame," Hanal said over his sister's song. "That his Excellency, Oakheart Silverbow, was not present at our interview. Matters would have run much more smoothly, if he had been."

Sophy thought he referred to Oakheart's statecraft until Lillia commented, "Yes, venerable Hanal, Oakheart would have surely seen your sister's beauty and pure soul and agreed to a betrothal."

A strangled sound escaped Sophy's throat. Lyant wanted to marry Oakheart? That would mean Oakheart couldn't show her the land. There would be no travelling to the Glassy Mountains if he had a wife. Her heart sank. She realised how selfish she was. Here I am thinking only of myself, she thought. Of course Oakheart would want a wife, and Lyant was a beautiful creature. She would have to find her own existence, her own place in this land. If his absence had taught her anything, it was that she needed to develop some self-reliance.

Hanal chuckled, though without any real joy. "He has seen both her beauty and her pure soul."

Lillia spared her a quick warning look. Sophy looked down quickly, eager to escape notice for she had been stupidly gaping at Hanal.

"You journeyed to Silverdale with Oakheart Silverbow, did you not, Lady Sophy?' Hanal said, his eyelids drawn down over those eyes.

Sophy spoke to the cushion, not daring to lift her face. "Yes, we did. He was in Valley Keep...'

"And the Gilton Forest," Lillia interjected. "I also accompanied Oakheart to Silverdale from the valley."

"And how was he?" Again Hanal addressed Sophy. Her cheeks flushed with guilt. He had so much presence, she felt intimidated.

"Err...he was well..." Her gaze flicked to Lyant, who had stopped strumming and studied Sophy while pretending not to do so. There was nothing in her expression to betray any deep feeling that Sophy could discern.

"I heard, you understand, through court gossip, that two of you emerged from Crystal Tree Woods. One of you was said to be exquisitely beautiful."

"That would be Aria, I mean Princess Aria," Sophy said. She looked over to Lillia nervously as she didn't understand where the conversation was leading.

Lillia, picking up on her confusion, said, "The Princess Aria married Prince Dellbright, and they are expecting their first child."

"The land gives its bounty freely. I am pleased to hear of their impending joy," Hanal replied and there was a slight smile as his eyes rested on his sister. "Oakheart was not ensnared by her beauty then?"

"No," Lillia added. "Not by Aria's beauty."

Once again, Hanal's eyes rested on Sophy and her skin prickled. Was he assuring himself that she was not beautiful enough to tempt Oakheart and lure him away from his sister? She played with her hands until his attention shifted elsewhere.

"Regretfully, venerable Hanal, we must leave you this night," Lillia said, rising and bowing in the Puri way. "It was a great honour to share your meal. One day I hope to repay you or your kin."

Sophy copied the forest woman's movements and hurried after Lillia.

❧ 30 ❧

A PLAGUE OF DREAMS

ARIA STARTED FROM ANOTHER NIGHTMARE, one filled with blood and defilement. Thankfully, this time she did not cry out. Her breath heaved within her chest, and she tried to quieten it before she disturbed Dellbright. Her husband lay quiet and oblivious beside her.

Envious, she watched his untroubled sleep, wondering why nightmares plagued her so often. This last week they came on every night, potent and real. It seemed that the absence of Sophy, and now Rae, left her vulnerable to this onslaught. Sophy had experienced nightmares, particularly after she had announced her plans to marry Dellbright. She did not look back on those days with joy. Sophy probably had the nightmares because her best friend had abandoned her.

As much as she loved Dellbright, she missed the closeness of others. Thoughts of her mother flooded in, nearly making her weep. How good it would be if Maralain were here with her to support her through the pregnancy and the birth. Aurore was kind, but she wasn't her mother. And she was always on Dellbright's side so there could be no confidences shared between them.

Now that Dellbright kept the talkstone to supervise rare calls to her friend, she couldn't talk to Sophy either, not freely. They had shared so much in their lifetime, first as friends and then as sisters. The separation was hard to bear. If only she had known then and had not been so caught up in herself, Sophy would be there with her and not away travelling the land. It was not without envy that Aria contemplated how different her life would have been if they had gone together, herself unshackled by an oath. She loved Dellbright but he was difficult. Fear effectively ruled her relationship with him.

Staring at the ceiling helped to pass the time until the sun came up. Getting up too early would draw criticism, and she was too desperate to fit in to attract adverse comments, particularly from her husband. The child moved within her. She patted her abdomen and thought about her life with a child and a husband who was jealous of her time. Perhaps when the child was born her husband would feel more relaxed and give her more freedom.

Shadows in the corner of the room writhed. Her gaze flicked to the curtains but they were still. After the dream she had just had, the illusion of movement made her heart rate quicken and the baby kicked suddenly. An unseen presence lurked. She closed her eyes, experimenting with the *given*, hoping to pinpoint it. There was nothing there, yet she sensed it still. It was the presence that infiltrated her dreams. The presence slid away, and Aria did not know she had slept until Dellbright shook her awake. The echo of her scream still lingered in the room. She had dreamed again, an ill dream.

Light blared in from the open curtains. "Why do you insist on screaming all the time? You are making my life a misery. Is it to take revenge on me perhaps? Do you like torturing me?"

Aria's heartbeat hammered in her chest. She could barely pay attention to Dellbright's accusations. Her mind was full of blood, so much blood. It was the same dream again, this time with more detail. She was beginning to understand that it was some kind of premonition. It had to be.

"Sorry. I don't know what makes these dreams come on. Maybe I shouldn't eat so much before I sleep. I'll be careful from now on. I'm sure it won't happen again."

He nodded. "Mother sends word that she wants you early in the sewing room. There is much to be done."

"I'll head there as soon as I can." He left her and went into the washroom. She was drained and tired. She disturbed others with her cries—but they did not live with her fear.

❧ 31 ❧

WITHIN HIS GRASP

WHEN THEY REGAINED their own suite, Sophy threw herself on the sofa with an exaggerated sigh. Lillia had a quick look around the room. "That went very well did it not, Sophy?"

Sophy sat up straighter. "Yes, very well. How did you know that Hanal wanted Lyant to marry Oakheart?"

Lillia sat next to her. "You do not know do you?"

"Know what? That Oakheart is a ladies' man?"

"No, no. Oakheart is...er. Hanal aspires to further the prosperity of his people. Let us say that the marriage of Lyant to Oakheart would give Hanal a great advantage politically."

"Yes, but that doesn't explain how you knew..."

"Oh, rumours fly around the land faster than the wind. Everyone knows of Hanal's desire—of his ambition. It is as famous as his eyes."

"They were...daunting. And Lyant? Does she wish to marry Oakheart?"

"Of that I do not know. Oakheart may be able to tell you. If I understand Hanal, Oakheart has certainly met her, gazed upon her face..." Lillia frowned as she turned the corner.

"Why would I ask him? It's none of my business."

Lillia laughed, her concern dropping away. "Just so, we should go to bed."

Alone in her room, Sophy lay awake. Her heart felt desolate. She struggled with her feelings, knowing that she was being selfish. Aria's face loomed large in her mind. It made her heart ache. Why did she leave her dear friend behind? What was she running from? Why hadn't she stuck it out and made things work out at Valley Keep?

Her dreams were full of Aria. Her heart beat painfully in her chest. The leaf in her chest pulsated unnaturally. In the dream Aria was crying, blood everywhere, leaking from her eyes, staining her beautiful hair.

"My lady?" Lillia queried, hovering by the door.

Sophy bolted upright, barely able to draw breath. The leaf throbbed in her chest, preventing speech.

"You were moaning..." Lillia said as she stepped through the doorway.

"Aria—I dreamed of her. Something terrible happened to her in the dream."

"Yet, it was only a dream." Lillia didn't hide her disquiet quickly enough before she sat on the edge of the bed. Oakheart had always questioned Sophy about her dreams of the dark.

Sophy shivered. "Only a dream... I'm sorry I woke you." She glanced to the window. It was still dark, though an early glow indicated that the sun would soon rise.

Lillia patted the top of Sophy's head. "It will be well," the forest maiden whispered like a prayer, then stood up. "I will take a leisurely bath. You should try to get more sleep."

Sophy dozed until she heard Lillia readying herself for her audience. She flung off the bed covers and darted out to help. Lillia was fully dressed though her hair was still damp. Drawing closer, Sophy inhaled the scent of rose and lavender. Lillia then bent over to tie up her soft knee-high boots.

"What are these?" Sophy asked, as she traced her finger along a leaf pattern embroidered onto Lillia's sleeve.

"Oh, that is a second Mark. It signifies my relationship to the

Queen of Gilton Forest." Lillia shoved the sleeve in question through the loops of her chest plate.

"Second Mark? Are you royalty then?"

"Not like here. I am Queen Ryssa's second cousin, but so are about fifty others with the same kinship connection. The forest people like to breed. And as the *given* has less sway in the forest our fertility is not moderated as it is in Argenterra."

"You mean that the *given* dictates how many children people have?"

"Something like that. I do not think it is proven but more a theory based on observation. My son, who is studying at the Retreat, told me about it. He said that when the First Comers arrived they had lots of children. As the population grew, they had less. It is rare for families in Argenterra to have more than three children. Help me, will you?"

Lillia turned around, and Sophy tied the breastplate and then stood back to admire her handiwork. "You look like a warrior princess."

Lillia beamed in response to her comment as she placed a crown of twined oak leaves on her head. Sophy inhaled the fresh forest scent and wondered how the leaves still looked and smelt fresh because they had been picked in the Gilton Forest many months before.

"Well, you are ready?" Sophy said.

Lillia looked at her, tears in her eyes, and nodded.

"It's okay," Sophy said as the forest woman embraced her. "I'm fine. You go along now and say the right things to the high king."

Lillia straightened up and looked Sophy seriously in the eye. "You stay out of mischief while I am away. I do not want to find you married to Hanal and on your way to Puri before I return."

Sophy's heart leapt at the mention of that name. "Hanal? Me?" She hated to admit it but something about the Puri leader was as interesting as it was frightening.

Lillia looked herself over in the mirror one final time. "You may not glow with beauty as does Princess Aria, but you have a deeper beauty within." Lillia then opened the door to leave.

Sophy smiled weakly. "Thanks, I think. Good luck. I'll be here when you get back."

The door shut behind Lillia, and Sophy stared at it for quite a while. What would happen after Lillia had had her audience? There would be no need for her to stay in the palace. Then she would be friendless and alone. And Aria, what would she think? Sophy, the embarrassment, the weight that dragged everyone down.

"Stop it," she said aloud. She wiped at her eyes angrily. "I will not cry! I am pathetic." Turning on her heel, she went to bathe and dress.

About an hour later, after some breakfast, Sophy gazed out the window and looked down at the people strolling below. She idled her time by speculating on what they were doing and saying. A flash of colour drew her attention. Crystal-clear, blue eyes met hers. She drew back. Too late, Hanal of Puri had seen her. Why was she afraid of him? She stepped forward and peered out of the window again to search for him among the people she saw congregating, chatting in groups or racing by on mysterious errands. When she saw no sign of Hanal, she relaxed.

Sophy grew bored of this activity so she strolled around the suite, running her hands across the back of the sofas, twirling the goblets on the serving tray and straightening the bed covers. While in her bedroom, searching for something else to do, she heard a noise. Thinking it was Lillia already returned from her audience, she rushed out of her bedroom only to be brought up short by the sight of Hanal of Puri standing tall and proud in the sitting room. She was so disconcerted that she stood gaping until he said something.

"Forgive me," he said simply and inclined his head. "I have imposed on you and startled you. The maid said you were within."

The sense danger tainted the air. Sophy wasn't sure how to act. She waved her hands vaguely in the direction of the sofa. "Belle let you in? Please, take a seat."

Her heart throbbed so loudly she was sure he could hear it. If she ever was in need of a chaperone, this was the time. He took a few steps to the sofa, and Sophy walked slightly behind him. Belle had not let him in she was sure of it, because she would have announced him if she had. Why was he here? She wanted to ask but...did not think it was the right way to behave with Hanal.

"Thank you." With a rustle of robes, he sat like a prince in the small sitting room. His deep purple, loose fitting coat crossed at the front revealing smooth skin and a smattering of black chest hair. Sophy lifted her gaze, and flushed when his eyes met hers briefly. Clearing her throat, she hastily looked away. "Would you care to offer me some wine?" he said casually, lifting a dark eyebrow slightly.

The air crackled with tension and suppressed excitement. Sophy had never been so aware of someone before. "Of...course," she said. He watched her as she moved to serve him. The red fluid twisted and caught the light as it fell from the pitcher to the goblet. She filled it halfway intentionally, because she didn't want him lingering. Part of her wanted to run from the room, but another part, the stronger part, wanted to stay and ride out the moment.

With the goblet in hand, she stepped up to where he sat and stood confused while she tried to remember the correct etiquette. Those eyes shifted to her again. She dared not be drawn into that stunning blue gaze. She bent her knee and offered the wine up to him. While she glanced at him through her lowered lashes, she thought she caught a hint of a smile on his full, maroon-coloured lips. His hand reached out and those strong fingers stroked hers as she released the goblet.

Her reflexive gasp at his touch escaped before she knew she had uttered it. Now her cheeks radiated heat as she stood awkwardly. Mentally, she berated herself for feeling so young and gauche; surely, she was more sophisticated than this.

"I cannot drink this alone, my lady," he said quietly, though every word seemed to curl around her insides.

"Oh...yes...sorry." She walked back to the sideboard and brought her goblet back to her seat. It had a splash of wine only, yet she knew even this amount of the *given* brew was enough to overwhelm her. Suddenly the room seemed too warm. Her dress felt uncomfortable. Her eyes darted from corner to corner and, all the while, her mind was racing. She was out of her depth. Then as her eyes passed over Hanal, she saw that he was staring at her again.

Remembering Lillia's words, she lowered her eyes. "Please drink," she said breathlessly, raising her goblet. The wine tingled on her lips and slid languorously onto her tongue and down her throat. The effects glided through her body, making her burn. She put the goblet on the side table.

Hanal raised the goblet to his lips, though his eyes stayed on her.

She was as conscious of his gaze as she was of her own breathing. "The forest maiden is out, I see," he said, after finishing the wine. "I must apologise for intruding on you."

"Yes, I expect her back at any moment."

Hanal was standing, she noticed all of a sudden. She stood, too, although she caught her foot on the hem of her dress. Those hands caught her and then held her. His fingers encircled her wrists, powerful and firm. He drew her to him, but did not touch her anywhere else, except for that gaze and those hands on her wrists.

"Why do you hesitate to look at me, young maiden? Am I offensive to your eyes?"

His breath brushed against the skin of her neck. Her eyes flicked up to his; she lowered them quickly.

"You are not offensive to me, Hanal of Puri. But I...we...should not be alone ..."

"You are no Argenterran maiden. Have I harmed you?"

His grip did not lessen, if anything it tightened. "I am under Oakheart's protection. He would not like it."

"So," he said, pulling her closer so that the warmth of his body and the scent of his spiced skin washed over her. Her hands, now free, grasped onto his cloak and glanced off his chest. "He has pledged himself to you?"

"Of course not," she said, trying to pull free. "I cause nothing but trouble."

His hand grasped her chin and he lifted her face. "Do you speak true?"

"Yes. The *given* rejects me. Lillia thinks I am cursed."

This close to him, something primitive and strong called to her. The hands that had sought to draw her near pushed her back gently. The river of tension ebbed, like a long breath exhaled.

"Cursed? By the waters that flow with the *given*. Your words belie what I feel about you. By rights, I should take you with me. Veld and his cohorts hold too much power. I would have something to bargain with you in my hand or in my bed. Yet, look at you, at the rooms you occupy. No one of importance has come near you. You are neglected and forgotten. You confuse me, young maiden."

"You want me to be more than I am. If you had seen Aria, you would have been in no doubt. All of Argenterra would have fought for her return. But for me they would be grateful that you had taken me away."

"Enough. I will leave you in peace. For now. I thank you for being so candid with me. You are no courtier bent on manipulation. You believe what you say, so I will leave you in the hands of the forest maiden. Though I doubt even she would dare to follow you into the lands of Puri."

His eyes lifted to hers once again and then they travelled down the length of her as if he was putting every detail of her shape and form into his memory. Again the tension in the air rose. The thought that he might grab her and kiss her came to mind. Then he said in a voice like a caress, his accent making him sound husky, "You are as ethereal as moonlight and your figure as perfect as sunset. We will meet again, though a maiden you will not be afterwards."

He turned, his robes billowing, and headed out of the door. The moment had passed. His intensity no longer surrounded her, and she felt release when the door shut behind him. Plonking herself down on the couch, she wondered about Hanal and those poetic words of his. It had been a dangerous and exciting moment. She knew that instinctively. The flutter of her heartbeat had yet to fade. Had she looked beautiful, she knew that would have swayed him. Something about her ordinariness bothered the Puri leader. His ambition to take something of importance to High King Veld nearly overcame that ordinariness. Yet the way he had assessed her figure gave her pause. That gaze seemed to have peered through her clothes, caressed all of her secret places.

She had no idea how long she sat there contemplating her surprise encounter when Belle entered to deliver some food. It was early afternoon, she realised. After picking at the stew and bread for a few minutes, she went to have a nap. At least it would pass the time. She dared not tell Lillia that Hanal had come to her room, because she predicted the forest maiden would fly about in a fit of remorse, labouring the point about her chaperonage and the dereliction of duty her absence had been. No, she thought, best forget it ever happened.

Sophy didn't realise she had been asleep until a familiar voice called to her.

"Sophy? Sophy, are you there?" Aria called from the talkstone. Dazed, Sophy slipped to the floor so that she was eye level with the talkstone on the table.

Rubbing sleep from her eyes, she said, "Aria? It's so good to see you."

"Well, you must be having fun," Aria said.

"Fun? Oh fun—Yes, lots of it."

Aria's face hovered in the crystal, slightly plumper than previously. "There must be parties and balls. You must be meeting new people. What is he like?"

"Who?"

"The high king? Were you scared when you met him?"

Sophy didn't know what to say. "Umm...He's just like any other high king."

"What does that mean? What about balls and parties?"

"Parties, well...too many of those to count. And the balls, well they are...um crowded with people and it makes it too hard to dance without treading on people's toes." A thought occurred to her. "Aria, there are other kinds of people here, foreigners compared to who we've met in Valley Keep. I was introduced to Hanal of Puri."

"Hanal of Puri...so that's where he is."

"What do you mean? Have you met him?"

"No," Aria said with a shake of her head. "Rae wishes to marry him."

"Rae? The maid?"

"Yes," Aria whispered. "But she shouldn't have been a maid serving us. She's Dellbright's cousin. Hanal's, too."

"So that's what Rae meant by other blood," Sophy replied. How would little Rae deal with Hanal of Puri? He would have her for breakfast and forget she existed by lunchtime.

"I should have been the one to take you to Silverdale. Now, Dellbright says you won't be back in time for the baby's birth." Aria wiped her eyes, then glanced off to the side. "Oh Dellbright. I'm sorry I started without you."

"I thought..." Sophy paused, wondering why Aria had disappeared from view.

The Prince's face hovered in the talkstone, though Aria's hand was visible. "Lady Sophy, excuse me for interrupting your private chat. In a few weeks, the festival of Oomra begins. Oakheart will have to stay for that I am sure. Afterwards, you will be free to return."

"Can't you come to the festival?"

"Alas, no. We received an invitation, of course, but cannot attend. Aria does not have the strength to travel and, if something should happen, we could not have our child on the road."

"Oh I see. Thank you. I must offer my best wishes on the imminent birth of your child. I hope all is well within the valley also."

"You are most kind, Sophy. I will return Aria to you."

"Aria?"

"Yes, Sophy," Aria said in a slightly strained voice.

"I miss you. I wish I could be there with you, especially when your time comes."

Aria's voice shook when she spoke. "Me too. I'd better go, Dellbright's waiting. Goodbye."

Aria's image faded. Sophy still had that eerie feeling that something wasn't right, but couldn't put her finger on it. Aria looked well enough, but had dark smudges around her eyes.

"You did very well, my Lady Sophy," Lillia said, from the doorway. "You were unselfish to disguise your pain."

She started and blushed. "You're back."

Lillia nodded.

Sophy pulled herself to her feet. "I lied though. That's not right, is it?"

"It may be true that to tell an untruth is not right. Yet your intent was to spare your friend concern, was it not?"

"I guess so. I didn't want to destroy the image she had of what I was doing. I realise that the prince convinced her to let me go on the pretence that I would have a great time compared to the quiet life of Valley Keep."

Sophy stood to help Lillia take off her formal clothes. "How did you get on? Did the audience go well?"

"It did. Yet I must wait for Oakheart to return. The high king's aid is to be provided by Oakheart."

"Then you won't be leaving straight away?" Sophy paused and then sat down heavily on her bed.

Lillia turned and gaped at her. "What would make you think so? Oakheart placed you in my care. I could not abandon my duty. I can only surrender you to him."

"Oh...but."

Lillia knelt by Sophy as she sat on the bed. "My dear friend, we will be together for quite a while yet, I think. Oakheart cannot..."

"Cannot what?"

"Take charge of you by himself...so I think perhaps that you will see Gilton Forest..."

"Really?"

"Yes...Unless..."

"Unless what, Lillia?"

"The high king sees fit to marry you off."

"What? You can't be serious."

Lillia laughed. "I hope I am not. Come help me out of the rest of this gear and we will go for a walk."

❧ 32 ☙

THE HIGH KING'S PLEASURE

A couple of days after her clandestine meeting with Hanal of Puri, Sophy and Lillia strolled around the courtyard garden, treading along the moss covered stone paths. They paused on a bridge arching over a fish filled pond. "Look at that one. It is so fat," Sophy said, pointing. She looked about and noted a few folk walking leisurely amongst the trees. None of them wore the Puri's colourful robes. "Hanal is not walking here today."

"That is because he departs for his home at this very moment."

The blush that stole up her cheeks took Sophy unawares. Lillia's eyes narrowed, and she was about to speak when footsteps sounded on the path. They turned to see a liveried guard standing at attention.

Lillia looked up. "Yes?"

"A message for the Lady Sophy of Valley Keep and Gift of Crystal Tree Woods."

"That is me," Sophy replied, with an embarrassed smile.

The guard saluted, then stood at attention again. "You are commanded to the presence of the high king."

Sophy broke eye contact with the guard and glanced nervously at Lillia.

"At what time, pray?" the forest maiden asked.

"An escort will call at your rooms within the hour." The guard swivelled on his heel and departed.

"Thank you," Lillia said to his back. "Come quickly, we have no time to waste."

"I can't do it. I never expected to be presented without Oakheart. I've nothing to say to the high king."

"Where is your nerve?" Lillia's eyes flashed angrily. "Do you want to break Oakheart's trust by acting like a coward? I thought you had more courage than that."

Sophy felt as if Lillia had slapped her. "Tell me what to do, to say."

"First we must get to our rooms." Lillia bounded up the stairs with Sophy following close behind. By the time she reached their door, she was winded. However, Lillia dove straight through the door and pounced on Sophy's gowns. After rummaging through them, she came forward. "Here, you must wear this," Lillia said. "Quick take off what you are wearing."

Hurriedly, Lillia dressed Sophy in Aria's wedding gown. "Why am I wearing this one? I'm not getting married."

"Yet, it is the custom. You are unmarried. The high king may choose a husband for you. Young women are presented ready for marriage."

"You were serious before? But I don't want to get married. What if he has someone in mind?"

"Do not worry. I think in your case there are complications, being an outlander and all. I think Oakheart mentioned that you are still the responsibility of Prince Dellbright. Any arrangement will need to be approved by him. That is the way the politics work between the valley and Silverdale. However, I am not sure if he approves before or after." She shrugged.

"That's not very comforting. Has he ever married someone off straight away?"

Lillia paused in arranging her dress. "One or two that I know about."

"That doesn't make me feel very comfortable."

"Hush and be still." Lillia attached the heavy gold trimmed train and Sophy wobbled on her legs. Some of the gold roses were still attached. Lillia placed the others with quick stitches. Sophy looked at her reflection wistfully. Her colour had not improved. "I can't wear this. I look sick in white."

"It will be this dress and no other. The choice is yours."

"That's no choice."

"Take heart, Sophy. This dress is so beautiful in itself that you will only be secondary to it."

Sophy blinked back her surprise. "That won't boost my confidence."

Next, Lillia arranged her hair, splashed her with scent and pushed her out the door into the charge of the waiting escort.

"Be strong and true, Sophy. I will be waiting for you on your return."

"Thanks." Sophy tried to smile but gave up the effort. Soon she was walking at a slow place through the palace halls with her escort. Her procession consisted of two short guards with green-skirted uniforms with sleeves adorned with gold epaulets. The palace occupants stopped and stared at her as she passed. She raised her chin high and her steps gliding and even, like a bride to the altar.

A wooden door embossed with a grey metal flung open at her approach. She stepped across the threshold and stopped. The room was small, dimly lit and laid with worn carpet. She had been expecting a grand throne room, yet this appeared to be a private and well-used sitting room. She took another tentative step and saw a large, old man sitting in an ordinary chair.

"Come in," the high king said. "Let me look at you."

Sophy walked up and curtsied deeply to him. "Stop that," he said with a wave of his hand. "I said let me look at you. How can I do that if you are down there? I put up with that nonsense all day. I do not need it now in my private chambers."

"Please forgive me." The high king's behaviour had thrown her completely off guard.

"Nothing to forgive." He stared at her intently, and Sophy returned his regard. He looked familiar; he had a red face, grey hair and wrinkles. He had been drinking, and his goblet still rested in his hand.

A servant handed her some wine. She took a sip, thought better of it and held it instead.

"So," he continued, "you are the stranger from another world. There were two of you, so Oakheart tells me. Mmmm...unusual for Crystal Tree Woods to be so generous. Never happened before. You have caused quite a stir among the adepts. How do you like my castle?"

Before she could frame a polite, non-committal answer, he answered for her. "Yes," he coughed as if embarrassed. "Very boring for you, I am sure. Sorry about that, but necessary. I had to send Oakheart away to avoid a certain person. Otherwise I would have been obliged to enter into a betrothal agreement I had no wish to sign."

Was that Hanal and his sister, she wondered?

"Oakheart is due back on the morrow and, then perhaps, he can introduce you to some other young people. You are presentable enough for marriage. I am sure I can find some poor chap to suit your taste."

Her eyes nearly popped from her head. "Your majesty, please, I beg you not to do that."

His eyebrow lifted at her outburst. "It is my privilege. Do you suggest I stop my most favourite pastime?"

"No, I don't, but..."

"Good then. See you some other time. Perhaps tomorrow's feast to welcome Oakheart back from his exile."

"You are very gracious, your majesty."

"Piffle..."

She paused mid-curtsy. "I'm sorry?"

"I said piffle...wasted on me that. I am a bad host." His white eyebrows rose up and down, then he buried his nose in his goblet.

A servant showed her to the door and the escort led her back to her room. So Oakheart was returning. She had mixed feelings about that, but she couldn't wait to tell Lillia the news.

❧

It was dark in her bedroom. Aria sat crying silently in the

dark. She wiped her tears and moved her hands to her distended abdomen. The child kicked, and she soothed the spot.

Dellbright's words after her surreptitious call to Sophy echoed in her head. "Why do you wish your friend to be here? You have me and my mother and that should be enough for you. You insult us both by asking for more."

Dellbright didn't understand her need. Sophy understood. They were in this together. They were bound like twins to a purpose and the separation was a physical ache. Footsteps approached and she struggled to sit up and wipe her face. The door opened and there stood Dellbright framed in light. "Aria? Are you in here sitting amidst the darkness?"

"I'm here."

He walked towards her with the firestick in his hand and placed it in its holder. He knelt next to her, bringing her hand to his mouth to kiss. "Please, Aria, join us downstairs. You cannot be constantly fretting for your friend. She is safe with Oakheart and her days are full of pleasure. Surely, you do not wish that she return here so soon."

Aria squeezed his hand. "But Dellbright, you could send for her, have her escorted back. Please, I need her with me. Please understand."

He stood abruptly, dropping her hand. As he looked down at her anger stained his cheeks. "You will not ask me that again. You wound me with your request. Is your love so weak that I cannot suffice for you?"

"No, my love is strong. Please understand..."

"No, do not say it. Your constant harping about your friend strikes me to the heart like a dagger's thrust." He slapped his chest for emphasis. "All other outlanders came alone to Valley Keep. None made such a fuss as you. You with your nightmares and screaming, trying to gain pity from all of us. You will cease asking for your friend from this moment."

Aria stared up at him in disbelief and buried her outrage. "I will not speak of it again. I can hardly help the nightmares though."

And she washed and dried her face and took Dellbright's proffered arm to return to the great hall.

Later, while she prepared for bed, her mood became sombre. She did not know where her joy had gone.

"There you are," Dellbright said, entering their room and shutting the door behind him. Although his voice was mild, it held an undercurrent of impatience. "Come to me," he said.

Aria stilled her hand, caught in the movement of brushing her hair. She didn't want to comply. His manner and his voice were not welcoming. Her brush continued through her curls.

"Aria, come to me. Now," his voice hardened.

Aria's hand shook. What was happening? He was her dear prince and yet he made her tremble in fear. The voice that once was a caress was now knife sharp. She placed the brush on the table and straightened. Edging towards the bed, she took in Dellbright standing naked in the light of the firestick.

"Take off your night gown."

"But..." She hesitated. His eyes, once warm, were hard glints. Her senses rebelled. Shaking her head, she backed away. But he was there, arms like steel, holding her in place.

"Do not deny me. I have been patient with you, too patient it seems."

"I deny you nothing...I'm with child...I don't feel..."

"No more excuses. Being with child is no reason to refuse me my rights."

"Rights?" The room seem to darken, to close in.

"Yes, you are bound to me. I want you...now."

Her frightened eyes stared at his. "Not like this. You are angry with me." She remembered their wedding night and the blood. Oh no, she thought, not like that again.

"Yes, like this. Anger or no." Her reached for her, grabbing the front of her gown. She heard the rip of the fabric as he yanked it down and tore it apart, releasing her breasts.

"Oh god, no," she said, her heart beating like a club against her rib cage.

Then he was kissing her, smothering her cries with his lips, crushing her flesh against her teeth. She tasted blood. Hands that had been soft and caressing became firm and demanding. Whimpers of pain leaked out of their sealed lips, as his hands crushed her breasts. He pushed her back against the wall, lifted her and was inside her, urgent, angry and violent. Aria screamed with a voice full of fear and disillusionment. It made no difference. Dellbright took what he thought was his.

RAE STRODE NEXT TO THE HORSES. THE AIR WAS FILLED WITH DUST and the quiet steps of hooves. Umri walked beside her, eyes bright and dancing. The men rode their mounts, often breaking off into ones or twos to scout ahead and behind.

Rae was tired. It had been a long trek over the foothills of the Glassy Mountain range, through Panal's Pass and up into the wasteland. Each night she had fallen into bed and risen the next day to continue the walk without complaint. Now up ahead was circle upon circle of tents. Multi-coloured cloth flapped from tent poles and dark-skinned children wove between the rows, playing games in the sand.

Umri pointed. "These are our homes. Here we wait the return of Hanal." Umri's eyes assessed her, then the otherness came into her expression. "Yes, we have time to prepare you."

Something in her gaze made Rae blush. Umri had dropped vague hints as to what preparation Rae needed, but had never been specific.

Umri's husband called to them, urging them to hurry. Tarkel was ever distant during the day. He never spoke to Umri unless to give her orders. A casual observer would not even guess that he was Umri's husband. But the nights, Rae went into a blush, were full of their joining. They talked at night, whispered love words and poetry, as they moved together. Rae had asked to leave, to sleep in a separate tent, but the attempt had sent Umri into a pout and brought harsh words from Tarkel. She was in their care. No other would take her in, and she could never sleep alone. Puri women slept with their families and then with their husbands. To do otherwise was to risk ostracism.

"What preparation do I need, Umri?"

Umri glanced at her sideways, a slight smile tilting her dark, dewy lips. "That depends on what you want. If you want Hanal of Puri in your bed then I can help you. If you want Hanal to give you to another for a wife, then I can help you."

"I want to be Hanal of Puri's wife," she said.

"I know and with that I cannot help you. I will tell you now that you have nothing to offer him. He has nothing to gain from binding himself to you..."

"I do not believe you. He is my kinsman and an honourable man. I have put my fate in his hands."

Umri turned and pointed towards a large tent with a dark green cloth fluttering in the wind.

"That tent is mine—ours. Kushlan Silvertongue has filled your head with stories. If he ever returned to Puri lands, he would earn his way by telling tales around the campfire. The image of Hanal you hold is not real. He is ambitious, and you should understand that. I can only get you into his bed, not bound to an oath."

Rae sped up to keep pace with Umri as she headed for her tent. "How? What must I do?"

"First sleep facing away from the wall. When Tarkel comes to me, watch and learn."

Rae gasped. "No. I could not." Her face burned with shame.

"Do not act so. How do you think I learnt to please my husband? I watched my mother. It is an art. You are not in the valley with those simpering women of Argenterra anymore. You are in Puri now. If you wish to survive with some control over your destiny, you will do as I say. Then we will talk strategy."

"Yes, Umri," Rae replied as they entered her new home. Her heart raced. She must forget the old ways. Puri was her home now. There was no going back. She thought of Aria, so chaste and so pure when she arrived at the keep, in the arms of Dellbright and how their eyes glowed with desire. Would Dellbright ever have looked at her that way? No, she thought, he would not. And Sophy? Where would that strange outlander maid end up?

The world was changing and constantly stirred by people and their decisions. Now she had to make her own choices. In what direction would her humble choices send events? Would she even cause a ripple?

❦ 33 ❦

NEITHER JOUST NOR JEST

Oakheart's familiar, deep tones woke Sophy the next morning. After throwing off her bedcovers, she flicked water over her face, climbed into a fresh gown and put on some slippers. Opening the door to her room, she paused on the threshold. Oakheart looked up from where he sat on the sofa and waited for her to speak. Feeling unsure of herself, she hesitated.

"Well, do I not get a welcome?" he asked her. Then when she didn't move, he stood up and bowed quickly, a shy smile on his face.

That was prompting enough. She launched herself at him and hugged him tight. He patted her on the back. Sophy let go of him and stepped back, suddenly aware how exuberant her greeting was.

He grinned at Lillia. "I see that your time must have passed tediously to welcome me so heartily."

"Yes," Lillia said. "At times we were at a loose end, your excellency. We did meet some people though, some that claim an acquaintance with you."

Oakheart looked curious, and raised an eyebrow in query.

"Hanal of Puri and his sister, Lyant," she supplied.

Oakheart let out a sigh. "Yes...I do know them. They were well when you met them?"

"Yes," Sophy said. "Although a little disappointed that you were not there to agree to their arrangements." She could not detect any sign of love or relief. "Hanal is impressive, isn't he?" she added.

A frown clouded Oakheart's brow. "Yes, he is formidable. It was a pity that I was called away. Surely you met more than Hanal. Did not Fern show you the sights?"

"Fern?" Sophy blurted out in a voice full of contempt. She was ready to give Oakheart a run down on his friend's slight but as she drew breath, Lillia sent her a warning look and cut her off.

"Unfortunately we were unable to connect with Lord Fern," Lillia said.

"Oh?" Oakheart said, his expression thoughtful. "But I understood..."

Lillia shrugged. "No matter, I must return to Gilton Forest soon, Oakheart."

"Yes, I do know it. However, I must beg you to remain until after the Feast of Oomra. I cannot leave until then, and Lady Sophy must have her chaperone," he said.

"Yes, of course, excellency. It will be as you say."

"Well, we must not dally. Come, I will take you to meet the courtiers and a few of my friends. After the noon-tide meal, we will have a tour of the surrounding countryside."

Lillia and Sophy bounded unreservedly from their respective chairs and assembled a range of attire and belongings they would need for their excursion.

Having satisfied both Lillia's and Oakheart's exacting standard of dress, Sophy and her companions set out. Eyes that once ignored Sophy now followed her as she strode down the halls, accompanied by Oakheart, who stopped often to explain points of interest, a painting, a mural or a tapestry. Sophy couldn't suppress the surge of happiness that came over her. Even Lillia seemed overflowing with joy at Oakheart's attentiveness.

By the time they met up with Fern for a tour of the town, neither Lillia nor she could recall a name above two courtiers. Sophy was unable to question Fern about the incident in the food hall, because he still teased her continuously, and rather than have a verbal duel she kept quiet. The more Fern talked, the less Oakheart did, and that put a dampener on the afternoon.

All too soon, the sun was setting, and they were headed back to the palace through the town. Sophy was wary, remembering her mishap with the warren beasts. Fern was reiterating some exaggerated flaw of Sophy's when the warren beasts struck again. Sophy held her mount steady, but Fern's horse reared and threw him to the ground. The warren beasts disappeared. Fern landed in a pool of mud, a remnant of recent rain. Only the whites of his eyes showed through and his curses were loud and colourful.

"Lord Fern? Are you hurt?" Sophy asked solicitously.

Oakheart could hold back no more. He let go a loud guffaw as he dismounted to assist his friend.

"Up you come," Oakheart said.

"Warren beasts. Cursed creatures," Fern muttered as he pushed at the slime clinging to his clothes.

Oakheart's brow furrowed thoughtfully and his eyes narrowed. "There is no sign of them. Lady Sophy, did you see?"

"Yes. There were about seven of them, I believe."

"Curious, someone must have brought them here. Fool thing to do. I will mention it to the city guards. Perhaps they can search them out."

"Do what you will. I must away now," Fern said, wiping his feet on the cobble stones and grabbing for his horse.

After he mounted and took his leave, Sophy sighed loudly.

"I agree with that sentiment," Oakheart said and remounted. Somehow, Sophy had the impression that Oakheart was not pleased with his friend's behaviour.

That evening Oakheart took them to dine at one of the refectories bursting with smartly dressed courtiers, who chatted continuously and loudly. There was music and dancing and although Sophy didn't join in, she revelled in the atmosphere. What a change from quiet evenings with Lillia. Oakheart was often called away to talk with other diners, setting groups of them laughing with a well told joke or tale.

Lillia and Sophy retired early and, as they moved to leave, Oakheart came with them to accompany them back to their rooms. All eyes turned towards them as they walked through the crowd, and

Sophy realised that Oakheart did them a great honour. It was true; his company meant she was no longer a non-person. Now people recognised her as the outlander and were keen to be introduced. Contentment filled her voice as she said good night at the door. Oakheart bowed with a flourish and left. Sophy, head in a swirl, leant on the closed door, wondering at the speed things had changed.

Sophy's days and nights were now filled with activity and the Hall of Visitors was beginning to fill up in preparation for the big Oomra festivities. She had formed many new acquaintances, although she kept with Lillia most of the time. Having felt alone herself, she did not have the heart to leave Lillia in the same position. Court happenings, the ladies gossip, the love intrigues and minstrel's lullabies and love poetry didn't impress Lillia much, but the forest maiden bore it well and kept her spirits up.

When Oakheart could accompany them, they went to the town. The market was explored, the farms visited and orchard trees lazed under. Always extra guards accompanied them, due to the risk of attacks. There was always that undercurrent of danger, but the sunny skies and the laughter and busy days overshadowed it all. Sophy hoped the threat wouldn't resurface.

❦

THE MAIN EVENT OF THE OOMRA FESTIVITIES WAS A GRAND, ROYAL ball. Lillia and Sophy locked themselves away preparing their attire. Both of them had acquired a few extra pieces of wardrobe from the markets, and Sophy persuaded Lillia to borrow from the vast store of gowns that Aria had provided.

The forest maiden was taller and had a fuller figure, but the gowns lent themselves to easy adjustment, especially with the added fabrics from the market stalls. Lillia was most becoming in a green gown with a leaf pattern in a darker shade of green. She wore her oakleaf crown and a shawl, woven with silver thread, which hid her cleavage from general view.

"Lillia, you look wonderful. You will have a hard time holding the courtiers at bay, I think."

"They had better stay away or they will feel my dagger." She tapped her trusty blade strapped to her shoulder. "I have a husband at home, who would not take their attentions kindly. Though I must admit a bit of admiration at my age would not go astray."

"You never mentioned you had a husband. I feel guilty keeping you from home."

"Nonsense," Lillia said, as she gathered Sophy's hair up and secured it in an elaborate style. Sophy noticed something odd in the mirror. Her face seemed less fudged. Sophy wanted to ask about it but Lillia interrupted her. "I am here because it is my duty to be here. My husband will be more pleased to see me when I return and the homecoming will be twice as sweet. Now we should curl these short bits. What do you think?" The hairstyle that Lillia fashioned made her appear more elegant and mature.

"Do you notice something peculiar about me, something different?"

"Not particularly, except you do look well in that gown."

Sophy pivoted in front of the glass to see the fall of the hair from the woven bun.

"Yes, I feel pretty in it. They way you've done my hair is fantastic. I really like it. Thank you."

"I have not finished yet. Please sit down." Lillia wove some silver ribbon through the layers of Sophy's hair and sat back to look at her handiwork.

"Well, my lady, that silver and your dark hair go well together. And it sets off your gown becomingly."

Sophy wore a dark blue dress woven with silver threads that caught the light as she moved. The bodice was trimmed in silver too, and it was so tight it held her breasts high.

Lillia placed a shawl with silver threads woven through it across her shoulders. "Now you truly look like a princess."

"Thank you, Lillia. The dress does look well, doesn't it?"

"It does. Come, we must go."

They walked arm in arm to the great ballroom. When they arrived it was already full with palace guests, some of whom were already dancing.

Oakheart found them easily. "My, you two look elegant," he said with a pretty bow. "Lillia, you truly astound me with your transformation." He flushed a little when he looked at Sophy, and inclined his head. "You look becoming in your gown, too, my lady."

Sophy noticed that he pushed at an imaginary strand of hair and nervously tugged on his doublet. When she curtsied to him, she couldn't help noticing that he looked exceptionally handsome in his dark blue breeches and blue doublet edged in silver. He often wore those colours, which meant they might be part of his heraldry or some such. Dismayed, she looked down at her gown then and realised that she was probably wearing his colours.

He was on the verge of speaking to her when he was called away by a group of courtiers.

"Excuse me."

Sophy cursed herself for a fool, but there was little she could do about her clothes now. Let them all think she was wearing his colours on purpose. What did she care? He didn't have a patent on them. Well, she hoped he didn't. Sophy wandered around the edge of the room looking at the dancers. The high king sat on his throne looking vague, or sleepy, it was hard to tell. While she watched, she saw Oakheart go up to the high king and whisper in his ear. Both of them looked in her direction so she looked away.

A new round of dances began. Ladies with full-skirted gowns circumnavigated the floor on dainty feet, led on by the guiding hands of their dance partners. Sophy smiled at the goings on. This was some dance. Hundreds of firesticks dangled from six ornate chandeliers that filled the ballroom with a golden glow. Sophy found the rich fabrics and music exhilarating.

A gap appeared in the crowd. Her breath caught and her heart beat slowed. She saw him— a pure, white winged angel at the far end of the room. Strains of music and the rumble of voices faded into the background. Those pink eyes of his locked onto her hers, drawing her to him. Sophy stepped forward, angling through the dancers as if in a dream. Miraculously, she avoided colliding with any of them. White feathered wings fluttered as she approached. Her gaze never faltered, travelling from the top of the angel's head, along the fine white hair that fell to his shoulders, the immaculate weave of his loose robe, to his bare feet. Sophy felt as if her very cells were singing.

"My Lady Sophy, how pleased I am to meet you at last," he said, his voice whispering like a flute.

"You know my name," she said, breathlessly. Her head felt light and her voice sounded distant.

"Yes, the whole land sings your name." He moved closer.

"It does? What's your name?" She wanted to touch him, wanted him to touch her. Now she was close to him, her heart beat double time. She licked her lips and noticed how his eyes watched her mouth.

"I am called Rufus."

"Rufus," she breathed his name. "You are very beautiful." She sighed, lifting her hand to touch his hair, but he edged away and her hand fell to her side.

His laugh was soft. "I know...And I can see your true beauty. Beyond doubt, you are lovelier in person than in my visions."

His words caressed her, spreading numbness up her spine, until her knees began to buckle. No one thought her beautiful in this place, no one trusted her except this angel, Rufus. How she wanted to hear those beautiful praises again.

"I see you..." His wings shimmied as he stepped closer. Unafraid, she stood her ground as he brought his wings forward and cocooned her within them. His sweet scent spilled over her, sending her senses swirling. A soft finger touched her face and her pulse throbbed as if drawn to his flesh. His other hand ran down her arm, bringing her towards him. Instantly, her skin was alive as if he had run his tongue over her. Her eyes grew heavy, so she closed them. Languidly, she allowed his feathered wings to caress her back, sending her shawl drifting to the floor.

"Oh, my lady, you are a gem beyond all beauty," he said, his breath fanning the soft skin of her neck. "How easily you respond to my touch..."

"Rufus," she said huskily. "Touch me..."

A large hand fell on her shoulder, jerking her out of Rufus' embrace. The air cooled around her. "No," she yelped.

"Sophy?" Oakheart's voice was a slap and his touch like ice. She stared at him uncomprehendingly, mouth opening but no words forming.

"Your excellency. How good to meet you again," Rufus said, his wings rippling with unease.

"Rufus," Oakheart returned, barely acknowledging him with a nod. "My lady, the high king wishes to speak with you."

"He does?" Sophy was perturbed. She wanted to melt into Rufus's arms, but Oakheart's presence prevented it. Why was Oakheart here? Why was he insulting Rufus so? How could he treat an angel that way?

Out of the haze of her mind, words flew into her mouth. "I have already met the high king, thank you."

Reaching out for Rufus's hand, she stepped towards him. Oakheart grabbed her hand and held her in place. The tip of Rufus's wing touched her shoulder, and she moaned slightly, as if he was stroking her. She began to slip away into ecstasy.

❧

OAKHEART FROWNED. SOPHY'S ACTIONS WORRIED HIM, ANGERED him. "Sophy, what is the matter with you? Tell me?" he demanded, pulling her out of Rufus' embrace and into his own. Her head rocked back, and she stared dazedly into his face. Her eyes were glossy, as if she was drunk. He shook her once or twice. "Sophy?"

"Yes, Oakheart," she spoke dreamily. "Isn't he the most beautiful creature you ever beheld? Just like an angel. I think I am in love."

"Enough," he said, letting his frustration show. A few people nearby looked up in surprise.

Emboldened by the scrutiny of others, Rufus stepped closer, placing a possessive claw onto Sophy's arm. "Come, Oakheart, the girl wishes to be with me."

Reacting quickly, Oakheart stepped back with Sophy in his arms and called on the *given*. Rufus reacted as if struck. This was a creature he could not 'see'. Sophy's true self was hidden from him too, but he knew her and could trust her.

"I mean her no harm," Rufus said, backing up in reaction to Oakheart's belligerent posture.

"You insult the lady with your conduct. Stand aside."

"Your lady friend's virtue is in no danger."

"I will be the judge of that. You will cease communicating with her."

Rufus's eyes glowed red. His mouth chewing anger, he said in a loud voice, "She is becoming in your colours, is she not?"

Oakheart's temper frayed. Rufus appeared bent on creating a scene, so be it. He would not let her fall into Rufus' hands. Then to his horror, Sophy said in an outraged voice, "I'm not in his colours!"

Oakheart ground his teeth together as those surrounding them began to mutter, sending a wave of gossip around the room.

The longer Oakheart held Sophy in his grip, the more awake she seemed to become. He squeezed her arm and shook her slightly. Her eyes flew open, lucid and less glassy. She turned toward the creature and said, "I would wear your colours, Rufus, if you told me what they were."

Oakheart could not believe his ears and then, to his further horror, she fluttered her eyelashes like some come hither maid.

"See, excellency, you are tramping on my ground. She is mine." Rufus's triumphant smile provoked him.

"Enough," Oakheart growled out. Rufus's triumphant smile disintegrated. Oakheart dragged Sophy to him and lifted her chin so he could talk to her. "You do not know what you are saying."

Sophy smiled stupidly in answer.

With his arm around her waist, he drew her close. "Rufus, begone from here. You will interfere with Lady Sophy no longer. She is under my protection."

With that, he wrenched Sophy away and dragged her towards the nearest alcove. Rufus slunk off. The onlookers recommenced their talking or drifted off to dance. Oakheart knew he had made a scene, but cared not at that moment what people thought or said. Sophy was not acting like herself and that meant danger.

He reached the alcove, flung open the curtain and the two lovers within fled beneath his angry stare. He twisted Sophy around and let her flop down onto the bench. Her head lolled. When he saw the unheeding dark eyes, he thought of the leaf. He placed his hand on the bodice of the gown. The neck was too high; he would have to undo it somehow. He sat down next to her and drew her face down over his lap. He undid the ties of her dress half way down and eased it off her shoulders. He tried to hurry because he did not wish to be discovered in this predicament. Being caught with a partially dressed lady could lead to all sorts of complications. Yet his need was dire.

The dress gave way suddenly and Sophy's right breast eased out, surprising him. He placed his hand on her chest and summoned the leaf. He gasped as responded, glowing with power. The leaf had spread its tendrils within her. It now snaked across into her arms and one strong taproot seemed to descend through her trunk. He reinforced it, hoping that it would jolt her out of Rufus's hold.

Her eyes opened with a start; he had indeed wakened her. He hastily removed his hand as she sat up and instinctively grabbed at her gown. It took her a minute or two to take in her situation. She gaped at him, the alcove, and at him again.

"Oakheart? Oh my god!" Her rapid movement as she stood made him get off the bench and step back.

"Sophy...are you well?" Sweat gathered in the small of his back. The full focus of those dark eyes were on him.

"What do you mean am I well? What were you doing? Why is my dress undone?"

"'Tis not what it seems. Here, let me help you. Quickly." He gestured for her to turn around. She nodded, as if she actually understood her situation. He fumbled with the ties and explained himself. "You were not yourself. I had to use the leaf to rouse you."

"Nonsense. You ruined everything. Let me go back and talk to Rufus."

With the ties finally fastened, he swung her around to face him and seized her shoulders.

"You will not go near him. Sit down and explain to me what you were doing."

"I was talking to Rufus...that angel...he's so handsome. Please let me go back." She tried to pull his hands off her shoulder.

Uncertain, he knelt in front of her, taking her hand in his. "What do you see when you look at Rufus?"

She opened and closed her mouth a few times. "He is a glorious, winged angel, pure white, with flowing white blond hair, and a strong, well-built body...Why what do you see?"

"Sophy, I see a grey, hairless being with bat wings and red glowing eyes. He has a face of the dark and a black heart. Somehow, he has bewitched you."

"Oh—I don't believe you. Rufus is beautiful. I want to be his."

Oakheart grew more and more frustrated. He grabbed her by the shoulders again and shook her gently. "Think about what you are saying. You are acting wanton. That is not like you."

"Wanton? You must be mad to think it."

"No, not so mad. Do you think me a simpleton? I see what effect he had on you. How you moaned your pleasure when he touched you. Aye, you were bewitched, for I have never seen you act so."

She stared at him, an angry expression clouding her features. "Me, bewitched? I act that way because I have never seen anyone so beautiful, so handsome, so good..."

"Is that so?" Oakheart held back his indignation. "Your words do not ring true. Dellbright is handsome, is he not?"

She frowned. "Yes, very handsome...but he did not like me, could not love me. But Rufus loves me...I can tell. He desires me."

"As I said, bewitched."

"Stop saying that. The *given* doesn't work on me or for me. How can I be bewitched?"

"I know not. But I do know that Rufus is not what you describe. Be careful, my lady. Come and see for yourself." He motioned to her to stand by him. "Do not look directly at him. Catch a glimpse of him out of the corner of your eye."

He held the curtain apart and pointed. She looked, gasped once with her hand going to her chest and stepped back. "Oh god."

"Sophy..."

Her eyes were troubled and her hands shook. "He looks like you said. I don't understand it. His eyes, they burn like in my dreams." She shook her head. "I don't know what this means. Is it his eyes I see? He said I was beautiful, said he could see me..."

Flecks of tears fell upon her cheeks. In an attempt to comfort her, he ran his hand down her back. She shivered at his touch, her eyes dark and round.

"Come. Let us dance, my lady. Otherwise people will begin to talk if we stay in this alcove any longer."

As she blushed deep red, he wished he could have unsaid his words.

"Yes, you're right. We don't want to give people the wrong idea." He held the curtain open for her as she stepped out. With some skill, he steered her through the onlookers and made their way to the dance floor. When he grabbed her hand to twirl her around, she asked, "I thought you said the high king wished to meet me. You lied to me."

"I did not lie. The high king did say that, but you told me that you had met him already, so I thought there was no need. Perhaps he had forgotten that he had met you."

He took her hand, ignoring her incredulous look and led her around the floor. There was something sinister in Rufus' interest in Sophy. The eyes—Rufus' eyes were in Sophy's dreams of the dark. Could it be him?

❧

As they danced, Sophy tried to put Rufus from her mind and smother her embarrassment. She would have done anything Rufus had asked her too. While Oakheart held her around the waist and moved her along with the dance, she closed her eyes. Images of Rufus kissing her naked skin assaulted her. "Oh my god!" she choked out.

Oakheart regarded her silently, eyebrow raised in query. She had to look away, lest she betray herself. Rufus's taint was still on her, and on one level she wasn't sorry for it. He had offered acceptance, something she craved.

Some of the women called out to Oakheart as they danced. When she looked around, she noticed them smiling and waving to him. Her eyebrow challenged him, and Oakheart pretended not to notice.

"Please dance with me next, your excellency." A pretty, young lady called.

"No, with me, I can dance better than anyone at court," the young lady's friend said boldly.

Sophy noted Oakheart flushed a little at the comments. She couldn't understand his popularity. She examined him closely, trying to see what they saw in him. When he caught her strict analysis, she blushed profusely. Now he would have reason to think her brazen and wanton towards anyone, including him. She looked out to the crowd, noted the looks, the constant scrutiny. He was passable looking. There was nothing ugly about him, and he did have a great body, she allowed, but so had some other men she'd seen. Fern, if his mouth didn't get in the way, was very handsome; nearly to Dellbright's standard.

Their dance was interrupted when one young woman in a sumptuous red gown stopped Oakheart by standing in his way. "Why, your excellency, I thought you did not dance. Yet here you are," she said as she looked Sophy up and down with a sneer. Sophy smiled sweetly back and arched an eyebrow at Oakheart. He danced with practiced ease. Obviously, he was not averse to telling a few fibs if it suited him.

"Rossette, how good of you to notice that I am dancing. If you will excuse me, I am still dancing."

He took Sophy's hand and twirled her around in time with the dance, leaving Rossette in the way of the other dancers. A few muffled groans and curses followed her from the dance floor.

At the end of the dance, Sophy curtsied prettily and said, "Such an honour, your excellency," she said, fluttering her eyelashes in an approximation of Rosette.

"Very amusing. Now I have to take my leave. Stay out of trouble. If you will excuse me." He bowed, turned on his heel and left. Sophy looked around for Lillia and saw her talking with the high king. After curtsying to the high king, she waited quietly for them to finish speaking.

"There you are," the high king bellowed. Obviously, thought Sophy, he never spoke in a normal voice. "Saw you there dancing with young Oakheart. Now there is a good lad if there ever was one. What say you?"

She remembered their discussion. "I...er... your majesty. His excellency is well respected and sought after. I assure you that he... a... would never think twice about me."

"Nonsense, nonsense. Just needs the right idea in his head. I am up to putting it there, say the word." He looked her up and down, measuring her and seemed to note the colour of her gown as he thoughtfully rubbed his chin.

"Please don't. He's a good friend, and I would like it to stay that way. Besides I'm too young to marry."

The old King looked her up and down. "Not too young by the looks of you." He chuckled to himself.

Sophy silently implored Lillia to assist. Luckily, the forest maiden was quick on the uptake and changed the subject. Sophy's breathing relaxed somewhat. She was confused. The angelic vision of Rufus stirred her. She desired that strange creature and the two images of Rufus plagued her. She excused herself and went to get some air. She found her way out to a patio with a balcony beyond. Going up to the rail, she peered over the edge. The sky was full with stars.

"It's so beautiful," she whispered to herself.

It wasn't long before she heard someone walk up behind her. A heavy tread and then she felt a presence. She swung round hoping it was Rufus, but Oakheart stood there.

He looked at her strangely. "Are you well, Sophy?"

"Perfectly. Thank you."

"Here, I brought you this." He placed her shawl around her and drew it higher over her shoulders. His touch was sensuous, and she didn't know what to say. What was happening to her? Was this some potent sexual awakening she was experiencing? She grabbed the ends of the shawl and snuggled into it.

"My lady?" said a flute-like voice.

"Rufus?" She took a step back and quailed at the sight of his red gaze. His apparent anger scared her. She was so startled that she stumbled and nearly toppled over the balcony rail. Only Oakheart's quick thinking saved her. He grabbed her and her gown tore.

Oakheart growled low in his throat. "You will leave us." There was so much power in Oakheart's voice, the embedded crystal leaf resonated within her, making it difficult to breathe.

Rufus's eyes glowed keenly, and he reared up as if afraid. He drew his bat wings in closer to his body. His eyes glowed like embers as he backed away. She couldn't forget the look of hatred he levelled at Oakheart. When Rufus was out of sight, she sighed.

"Come," Oakheart said, grabbing her hand roughly and tugging her along behind him.

"Where are we going?"

"You are going back to your suite. Only there will you stay out of trouble. I will have guards placed outside your door and Rufus escorted from the castle. Lillia will meet you there shortly."

Her feet barely touched the ground as she scrambled along behind him. At his command, four guards fell in behind them escorting them down the various passageways. When he reached her door, he swung it open, tumbled her in, and nodded curtly. "Forgive me. Your safety is my excuse. Good night."

Sophy stood open-mouthed as she stared at Oakheart's retreating back. The broad shoulders, topped by that blond head, turned the corner. She went inside and the guards looked unseeingly at her as she heaved the door shut.

When she finally did fall asleep, Oakheart, the high king and Rufus fought for precedence in her dreams: Oakheart chased her, like a ghoul pursuing her through dark and endless caves; Rufus's red eyes set her skin on fire and made her writhe and the high king pronounced her as someone's bride.

❧ 34 ❧

A BRAVE AND QUESTING HEART

THE OOMRA FESTIVITIES continued throughout the week with no further sign of Rufus. Oakheart said that he was a guest of one of Silverdale's nobles and that the high king had issued a decree for his banishment. Rufus's effect on Sophy had not waned, despite knowing he was some kind of strange creature. It was a relief though to not worry about the incident further.

The final event of the festivities was a tourney, and she was surprised to find that both Lillia and Oakheart were competing, though in different events.

"Can I join you?" Sophy asked, while she watched the forest maiden prepare her archery apparel.

"Alas you cannot as the lists are full. I believe Oakheart is on the quest and needs followers. Perhaps you can prevail upon him to allow you to join his party."

Sophy huffed. Prevail was about the right word. At that moment, Oakheart knocked on the door and entered. He was decked out in hunting clothes that didn't leave much to Sophy's imagination. He wore a sleeveless jerkin that crossed in a big vee at the front of his tanned chest, and around his neck hung a medallion that Sophy thought looked familiar. His pectoral muscles bulged underneath his smooth skin. She began to blush when the looking became thinking. What was wrong with her? First Hanal, then Rufus, and now she was acutely aware of Oakheart's physical attributes. She looked down and studied the carpet, which had very interesting patterns woven into it.

"Good morn to you, your excellency. You are ready, I see," Lillia observed.

"Please call me Oakheart. Sophy hardly ever uses formality with me." His smile encompassed them both.

"Well, Oakheart, young Sophy wishes to join your quest party..."

Sophy watched his smile freeze at Lillia's words.

"I see," he said. "And does young Sophy not wish to ask me herself?"

That remark made her look up. She was sure her uncertainty and confusion showed on her face. "I...I err...I have caused so much trouble that I thought I would be a hindrance rather than a help."

He laughed heartily and when he'd finished, he wiped his eyes and sat down opposite Sophy.

"If you wish to join me you had better prepare yourself—now," he added for emphasis.

Sophy shot from her chair and bounded out of the room. Over the sounds of her preparations she heard their conversation.

"Are you sure you know what you are doing?" Lillia asked.

"Of course not. Only somehow, I cannot refuse her desire. If I cannot prevail, even with Sophy's little errors, then I am not fit for anything; to win the quest, to be the high king's ambassador or to—"

Her approach interrupted their conversation. Lillia glanced her way, doing a quick assessment of her clothing. Sophy wore one of Aurore's creations, an ensemble suitable for riding, but elegant enough for Silverdale's social niceties. The trousers were dark green and the over-tunic was patterned with leaves of pale green and yellow.

Oakheart held the door open as Sophy embraced the forest maiden briefly. "Good luck and strike true, Lillia."

Lillia chuckled. "Go well and be bold, Sophy."

Sophy found that funny and laughed as she went ahead of them into the corridor.

Oakheart submitted himself to a hug from the forest maiden and then she slapped him on the shoulder heartily. "And good wishes and luck to you, Oakheart. Take care of her."

"I will," he replied, smiling. Sophy wondered whether his smile was forced.

❧

It was dark in the forest and the quest party slowed to a halt behind Oakheart. There were five: Oakheart, Fern, Sophy, Leda, who was Fern's sister, and Mane, one of Oakheart's guard. The forest was damp and a mist rose, obscuring the debris that carpeted the ground. It was quiet. A tree branch creaked and one of the horses snorted. Sophy nocked her arrow in anticipation. Oakheart had a dagger and a sword in a scabbard on his back. Fern had what looked like a small axe dangling from his belt. They had been trailing a gnarlet, which was a cross between a pig and a wild dog, except it had triple spines on its head and long claws on its forelegs. She had only glimpsed it a few times, once when it was released into the forest, and a couple of snatches as it rummaged through the undergrowth.

The quest was a competition. An item had been placed within the gnarlet's territory. The quest party were to use their collective brains to locate the prize in the time allocated. The gnarlet would inevitably attack every time they closed in. It had attacked the party twice already and, from the pattern of the attack, Oakheart had been able to pinpoint the general whereabouts of the item.

Oakheart made a sign to prepare for their next foray into the target area. A horse nickered nervously, and Leda's horse baulked at the mist. Fern's sister struggled to quiet her mount. Fern reached out and pulled on the reins and led Leda into the mist. They had to walk the horses carefully to avoid injury on the mist covered forest floor.

Oakheart's head moved from left to right and down and around, his eyes alert. He stopped and the gnarlet sliced through the mist. Sophy took aim and released her arrow. She struck home, but not with enough force. Her arrow bounced against one of the spines and the creature fell back into the undergrowth.

It was quiet again. Sophy tried to prepare another arrow in case the beast came back. Before she was ready, a piercing wail came from the forest floor. Looking up, she saw triple spines approaching. Her mount reacted as if struck and sent her tumbling to the ground in a tangle of arms and legs. The confused movement of hooves, shouts and growls deafened her. The gnarlet had scented her. The mist fell away from its hunched body as it sprung forward. She tried to move but Oakheart landed in front of her, his two feet planted firmly on the ground. He ripped out his sword from the scabbard on his back and struck. Hot, sour blood stung her face. She spat it out in disgust.

After Oakheart had cleaned his sword, he re-sheathed it and bent down to help her stand.

"That was a terrible shot, my lady," Fern began, leaning on the pommel of his saddle. "You should have let another, more skilled, take aim. We wanted it wounded, not dead. Now we have lost the quest. We needed the beast to locate the prize."

"Fern,' Oakheart said in a low voice. "You will cease in your attempts to ridicule the Lady Sophy." He did not raise his voice but it was clear as he enunciated each word that he would stand for no more comment. "The quest is lost when I admit defeat, and I have not done so."

This time Sophy agreed with Fern. It was a bad shot. She wondered why Oakheart was so touchy. Leaning down, he grabbed Sophy under the arm and practically threw her up into her saddle. "She acted bravely, although unluckily. Let us move on."

Sophy avoided looking at Oakheart, grabbed her reins and settled her mount by slapping its neck and speaking soothingly.

"Ride behind me, Sophy," Oakheart said, quietly. "The rest of you follow us in single file."

They walked the horses through a rough path in the tangled undergrowth. The sound of falling water sounded off to the right, and Oakheart led them in that direction. They had tried to penetrate this area in three places.

The sound of falling water grew louder and soon the air was full of water particles lifted from a waterfall. The light cut into the gloomy forest around the falls and when Sophy looked up she saw that the rock face was pockmarked with holes.

"Fern, take Leda and Mane further downstream. Cross over where the stream narrows and search among the rocks." Oakheart signalled them as he gave the command.

"You, follow me," he said with a nod to Sophy.

Slowly, he walked the horse around bushes and fallen tree trunks. Sophy was careful to follow his every movement. He headed to a basin in the rock, where white froth collected from the cataract above. The water settled in the pool, the current making large ripples in the surface. Soon they were at the base of the rock face, standing directly underneath the cave-like holes. Once dismounted, they climbed over the slippery rocks on foot, leaving the horses to graze at the water's edge. The impact of the water hitting the rocks was loud. She opened her mouth to ask Oakheart something when her voice turned into a screech. Oakheart whirled and unsheathed his sword in one swift movement. Hundreds of warren beasts poured out of the holes in the rock face above them, landing indiscriminately on Oakheart and on her, cutting with their teeth and claws. It was like a moving mass of fur, roiling and sliding on the rocks.

She tried to fling them off when the creatures leapt onto her arms and thighs. Numerous cuts and scratches rent her clothes. Blood flowed down her arms, hands and legs. Oakheart thrust a dagger into her hand. She clenched it willingly. Waving it about, she knocked two of the beasts from her. She fought mindlessly, in a panic, slashing and ripping at the little furry bodies. The creatures stopped falling from the caves above and regrouped, looking like a wave of fur and horns. Sophy had barely any time to draw breath before they began snarling in unison and gnashing their strange teeth.

They surrounded Oakheart and lurched forward with one mind to attack him. Her voice was hoarse from screaming. She dove after them, stamping down with her feet and slicing the furry things with the blood-slicked dagger. She nearly lost her grip when a persistent little beast wrapped his jaws around her hand. She flung her hand backwards, crouching as she did so, and smacked it against an upthrust of rock. A slight whimper escaped its throat before it went limp and slid off her hand. She savaged another ten more before she noticed Oakheart was bleeding from many wounds. As the beasts attacked anew, she threw herself against the throng, heedless of her own welfare. She picked up the squirming things and flung them behind her into the falls. A few fell against the rocks, leaving globs of blood and gore. She was frightened that Oakheart would soon go down under the weight of the attack.

Fern was suddenly there, the air thrumming with the sound of his axe, which made quick work of the nasty beasts. With the next intake of breath, the remaining creatures retreated as quickly as they had attacked. While she watched, they scrambled up the side of the rock face, some into the caves and others over the top.

Sophy staggered to Oakheart, who leaned his back against a boulder, eyes shut, panting and bleeding. She was terrified that he was mortally wounded and that she had somehow killed him. Her eyes ranged over his body. There were a couple of deep gashes on his thigh. Blood welled through his fingers where he pressed them against his flesh to staunch the flow.

"Oakheart?" she wailed as she collapsed by his side. "How bad is it?"

He opened an eye and looked at her. He let out an angry wail himself when he caught sight of her and grabbed her to him with his free hand. She sobbed on his wounds, releasing her pent up fear.

Leda and Mane arrived. Hurrying, they began ripping cloths and unpacking medicines from the saddle packs to bathe their injuries. Leda carried healing bark, enough to seal Oakheart's largest rents. When Oakheart took his hand away from the worst of his wounds, Leda squeezed the bark, dropping the juice in. Oakheart pressed the severed flesh together and held it. The blood stopped pulsing through the slash in his skin. He put his head back against the rock, ignoring Leda as she spoke softly to him and wiped the blood from his lesser wounds. Then he breathed out and let go of the larger cut in his upper thigh. It was now sealed, an angry red line marking the spot. Next, Leda bound the rest of his cuts with cloth ripped from her clothes. Leda nursed Oakheart tenderly, stroking back his blood-soaked hair. The sound of her cooing to him echoed over the chaos of the falls and the clop of horses hooves.

With the help of Mane, Sophy's wounds were bound. Her cuts were minor, although her bruises were not. She had various painful scrapes, especially along the backs of her hands from where she had flung the warren beasts against the rocks. By the time Mane had helped her and assured her she was not dying, Sophy let out her breath. Her heartbeat slowed and her forehead was clammy. Shock was settling in.

Fern stood around as if surveying the scene, holding back caustic remarks if the expression on his face was anything to go by. Leda stood back quickly and blushed when Oakheart said tersely, "Leave off, Leda. I am well enough." He sat up. "Fern, something is not right."

"That is an understatement. Let me send Mane for a litter. You cannot ride."

"No, I will ride. We may have lost the quest but we fought bravely. We will return no less the victors when the truth is known."

Sophy stood wearily and walked to a quiet, secondary pool that filled from the overflow of the falls. With her hands cupped, she brought up some water to splash on her face. She needed that coolness to refresh herself, to let it restore her calm. While she washed the blood away, she saw light glinting off something beneath the surface. Curious, she reached down towards it. The distance was deceptive. She slipped into the pool and dived under to retrieve it. The object was a goblet with the high king's emblem on it, two prancing Yelders. She kicked up to the surface and bounced around in the water with the goblet held high.

"This is it," she shouted exuberantly. She looked over to Oakheart, who stood on wobbly legs, shaking off Leda's ministrations. He returned her smile heartily. They were battered and bloodied, but they had fulfilled the quest.

It didn't take much brain power to decide that the trip home was going to be uncomfortable. Sophy had many cuts to her upper thighs and buttocks, which made riding an unwelcome proposition. She decided that walking would be better and tried leading her mount. Oakheart wouldn't have it though.

"You will ride with me," he said.

"But you are wounded too," she pointed out, fretting that her sitting with him would add to his hurts.

"Do not argue with me. Come." He reached down to help her onto the saddle. She could hardly walk away from his outstretched hands without delivering an insult. She swallowed deeply, put her foot on the stirrup and allowed him to lift her in front of him.

After he settled her in place he said, "We ride triumphant, together."

The horse began to walk at his command. His sharp intake of breath when she moved suddenly made her guilty.

Fern sidestepped his horse closer to them. "Let me take Sophy. You are hurt." He frowned at her, not hiding his dislike, and then he slid his gaze behind her share a look with his sister.

"Please, your excellency," Leda pleaded. "You will injure yourself further and undo all my hard work."

Oakheart turned a deaf ear to their pleas. "Keep the peace now. I will return on my own terms."

The gentle sway of the horse's gait and the rhythmic beating of her companion's heartbeat lulled her off to sleep before she could fight her fatigue.

Sophy jerked awake when she felt herself falling, but Oakheart was handing her down to Lillia and they were already back in the castle grounds. She ached and throbbed all over. She saw Oakheart dismount gingerly while a crowd began to gather. Their murmuring increased when they saw the signs of battle. The noise prompted the high king to stride over from his pavilion, his face creased with concern. When he caught sight of Sophy and Oakheart covered in blood, he let out an expletive that hushed the crowd mid-murmur. "What in the *given*'s name happened to you both?"

Sophy blushed and deferred to Oakheart to answer. The high king's ambassador gave a weak chuckle. "Your majesty, we ran into some unexpected trouble. If it pleases you after I have taken the Lady Sophy back to her suite, I will meet with you and tell you all."

"Very well," the high king said in a moderately quiet voice as if reading some code in Oakheart's words. He swung his heavy frame around and headed back to his pavilion, while bellowing generally to the people standing around. Some ran off, presumably sent on errands, others bowed and looked away from Oakheart and Sophy.

Oakheart whispered Sophy's ear. "Come, my lady. I will escort you back to your chamber."

Sophy tried to struggle out of his grasp. "That isn't necessary."

"Be still," Oakheart said curtly. "I say 'tis necessary. You fighting with me will completely destroy the effect of my gallantry." He smiled when he noted her affronted stare. "That is good. I like to see you lost for words."

He marched through the crowd and kept on going until he reached her rooms, then he scooped her up and carried her over the threshold. He walked through the sitting room and placed her gently on her bed. He was clearly exhausted by this time and knelt with his head down, panting into the bed covers. When he looked up, she saw that he had bruises on his face and one eye was beginning to swell shut. He looked as if he had been in a brawl.

Sophy reached out and lightly touched his face. She wanted to ask what it was all about, but her mind was tired.

Oakheart looked up at her touch and squeezed her hand. "Thank you," he whispered.

"You're thanking me? I should think you should curse me, yell at me, blame me. I endangered you..."

"No," he interrupted. "You fought bravely, without thought for yourself. I will never forget it until my dying day. You could not have known the warren beasts were lying in wait."

"Were they? Don't they live there?"

"No. They live a long way from here. Warren beasts are said to be the minions of Rufus," he said. "He can control them."

Sophy drew in her breath. "Rufus?"

"Yes, my lady. I would deduce from the attack that it is he who is responsible. Perhaps for all the attacks on you."

"But they were after you. They did not keep attacking me once they scented you. There may not be a connection between the attacks on me. Why would Rufus want to hurt me seeing how he liked me? Are you certain?"

Oakheart's expression darkened as she spoke. "As certain as I can be." He stood up to leave and then leaned down to pick up her hand and kissed it.

Sophy smiled wanly, not sure how to take his show of affection. It made her feel warm on the inside. Oakheart still held her hand when Lillia arrived to interrupt their private conversation. Gently, he placed her hand back on the bed cover and walked out of the room. Sophy lay back against the covers, desperate to sleep and forget the images of blood and gore and death she had seen that day.

DREAMS OF BLOOD

ARIA SCREAMED in the dead of night. Her time had come. She cried out in pain and terror. Dellbright started from his sleep and tried to comfort her as they waited for Aurore to come and assist with the birth. Aria would not be comforted. Fear controlled her in the dark well of misery.

"Please," she begged. "Make it stop. Make it go away. There is blood, so much blood!"

"Stop such talk, you make no sense. There is no blood." Dellbright pleaded, trying to force her to be still on the bed. Aurore arrived with a bevy of the keep's women. "Thank the *given* you are here, mother. I do not know what to do with her."

Dellbright made way for his mother, who stroked Aria's brow and spoke soothingly to her. Yet as the labour progressed, Aria became wild. She writhed and spat at anybody who approached her. She shoved at the bulge in her abdomen, as if trying to purge the babe from her body.

"Son. Help me."

Dellbright rushed to the bed to hold Aria's hands to prevent injury to their child. His eyes were wild with fright. Aria did not care. They did not understand. There was so much blood. She could see it everywhere around her, a pool of it.

Through her hysteria, she heard them talking. "I do not understand, Mother. 'Tis like the gentle Aria I married has disappeared. Has she lost her senses?"

Aurore looked up, her expression worried. "No, not her senses, but she is afraid. I hope that is all that it is. Sometimes there are complications. Aria is an outlander, who knows what that may mean at a time like this."

Aurore stroked Aria's brow. "There my little love, all will be well," she crooned. "Be calm, calm now. All will be well..." She repeated her litany, yet as each contraction took control of her body Aria fought it savagely. Her cries, filled with denial, woke the entire keep.

Dellbright brought wine to her, and Aria refused it. Frowning, Aurore shook her head, as he downed it in one gulp. "Why do you look at me like that?" he asked as he tossed the cup onto a tray.

"She would be calmer if her friend was here, my son. They share a bond we cannot understand," Aurore whispered.

"Do not accuse me, Mother. I made the right decision. 'Tis too late to change it now."

"Yes, I know. Perhaps you could send for Sophy. Then your lady wife would be comforted after the birth. The news that her friend was coming would give her hope, too, and may calm her a little."

Aria wailed in pain and her breathing became hoarse as the contractions intensified. Suddenly squeamish, Dellbright walked away. He gave his mother a long thoughtful look and left the bedchamber with Aria's howls stalking him like a shadow.

"Please," Aria begged Aurore. "The blood. I don't want to see the blood. It fills my dreams." She groaned, as she pushed. The agony was more than she imagined as she struggled to push her baby out. Her skin tore and she screamed. Her mind was filled with red. For a time it was as if she no longer existed.

Aria gained her senses when Dellbright nudged her awake and handed her their son. She smiled weakly. The room's lighting was muted, with dark shadows lurching in the corners. The terrible visions were still there beneath the surface.

Dellbright touched her cheek. "Come smile. 'Tis over. Look what a bonny son you have whelped."

Aurore reproved him for his choice of words, but nothing could remove the smile of pride from his face. He lay next to Aria and stroked her hair with their son nestled between them. The sun's ray broke through the curtains and threw dappled light into the room. Aria had survived the night, something she didn't think would happen.

"Smile and greet the day with your son, Aria."

Aria smiled through her tears, taking no comfort in Dellbright's presence. The sunrise filled the room with red tinged light. Aria could see only blood.

❦ 36 ❦

SEDUCTION'S ART

RAE PRAYED that the *given* would give her strength. Hanal of Puri had returned from Silverdale two days before, and Umri was preparing to send her to his tent. For weeks Umri had been instructing her, and Rae had tried to learn, but Puri ways were so different. Rae could not bring herself to go through with it. At that moment, she could easily walk back to the valley on her own and scrub pots in the keep's kitchen for the rest of her life. Her father, Kushlan, had brought her up on tales, fanciful stories woven with *given* lore and heroic feats. He had never dwelt on the realities of love making, on the different arts employed by Puri women to seduce a man. Rae's thoughts had been romantic and pure until Umri's lessons were in her head, swirling and multiplying in time to Umri's voice instructing her while Rae bathed in spiced water.

"Rub it in well, Rae. It is a special mix, subtle but effective."

"Yes, Umri." Rae's hands shook as she squeezed the cloth and then soaked it in the water again. Tree bark floated in the bowl, part of Umri's special blend.

"Now, remember to be humble but firm. Hanal will try to send you away. He may say things to hurt you, but continue as we have discussed as if your life depends upon it."

305

Rae lifted her painted eyebrow. "I am frightened. He may not desire me."

"Nonsense, any woman can make a man desire her, if she knows the way of it. You are untried, which is how it should be...he will like that and yet you will know how to please him. I have taught you so you can bend him to your will...at least get yourself in his bed."

A passer-by chatted to another as he walked between the tents. "Ssssh. Someone will hear."

Umri gave a careless wave of her hand. "So what if they do? Many have tried to catch Hanal, but he is devious. You are in his future, this I can see. Now go. Tarkel waits to escort you to Hanal."

Rae stood and let Umri fuss with her overdress and trousers, which was one of Aurore's flimsy designs made with sheer cloth with filigree lace edges. Umri had held it back from sale at the last minute, as her plans took hold. Rae tried not to shiver when Umri took her by the hand and lifted the tent flap. Tarkel nodded once and grimaced. Umri lowered her eyes and stepped back into the tent. Rae followed slowly and dutifully behind Tarkel.

In the centre ring of the Puri camp was a large pavilion, consisting of smaller co-joined tents. Lyant, Hanal's only sister, lived in one of the smaller tents. Rae did not know who shared the others. Tarkel proceeded to the centre entrance that was flanked by two panels of dark-red with a yellow slash down the middle.

"Older brother!" Tarkel called, opening the tent flap for her. Rae stepped through, blinking hard to get her eyes to adjust to the dimmer lighting. Heat rocks glowed in the brazier, and rich carpets covered the ground. Seated before them was a shadowed figure.

"Hanal, great leader, I bring you Tu Raenal, daughter of Kushlan of the Valley, whom we know as Silvertongue."

Tarkel backed out of the tent, leaving Rae on her own. She stepped forward, knelt and bowed, put her forehead on the carpet and waited.

"Rise," a deep, rich voice said. From where she knelt on the floor she saw his dark skin glowing in the reflected light.

Hanal said nothing more and then proceeded to unwrap his head cloth. As he removed it, fifteen long, dark braids fell to his waist. He wore a loose robe that opened across his dark, lightly-furred chest. Rae lifted her head and studied him, for she wanted to imprint this moment in her mind, every exquisite detail of this man.

Licking her lips quickly, she said. "Greetings, Hanal of Puri. I come as your kin, seeking succour." Those eyes washed over her. She could not help herself. "The eyes of Goslien!" she whispered. Rae stared at his face, willing him to look at her with those eyes. She wanted to sink into his soul and never leave.

"Umri told me your head was full of old tales. We have no time for them here."

Rae smiled shyly, but was emboldened enough to speak her mind. "Yet, they enrich our lives and bring us the wisdom of those who lived before us."

Those eyes again fell upon her face and looked away. "You are outspoken. I do not like that. Aurore presents you ready for marriage. I have no need of a wife. What say you to that?"

He was blunter than she had expected. "I would serve you in any way I can, honourable Hanal of Puri. You are my only kin now. I throw myself on your mercy."

He smiled, white teeth contrasting with skin that was only a shade darker than her own.

"You are persistent. What if you serve me by marrying one of my clan? There are a few old widowers in need of a new wife and mother for their many children. With your tongue, though, they will drive a hard bargain."

"I will do anything," she said with emphasis, though blood ploughed through her veins. She saw his eyes widen then narrow, glad Umri told her to look for that reaction. "Anything, to repay you for taking me in." She bowed low again to the carpet and waited. She prayed Umri's plan worked as she had no intention of marrying some old herder and becoming a work horse for his fifteen offspring.

Silence hung in the air. She peered up from her place on the floor, when her heart rate had slowed enough. He slid his outer robe off his shoulders, letting it spill to the carpet beside him. Her eyes were drawn to a bowl of water next to him.

Without a word, she stood and carefully trod to where he sat. Her hands were shaking so she squeezed them. "May I undo your braids,

Hanal?" Her voice was soft and buttery, in the way Umri had made her practise.

"You may," he said, though his voice was quiet like a soft breeze. Lifting a braid, she undid the weave, separating the strands of hair gently. She had never touched a man in this way before. She could not quite suppress her awe at how brazen she was being. When the last braid was undone she began to massage his scalp. He did not move or speak but he relaxed and the aura of tension slowly evaporated. Rae had breached the first barrier; she had touched him.

Next, she took the cloth from the bowl, wrung it carefully in one hand and wiped his face. His skin smelt of spice. His eyes bored into hers as she worked the cloth down his neck. Dipping the cloth in the scented water again, she began to clean his chest. A muscle twitched slightly, and her hand stilled. Her pulse beat in her neck again, stronger and more powerful each moment her hands were on him. Surely, he would sense her fear.

"You try to tempt me," he said with a voice that was hard and flat. Her eyes flew to his face, then dropped. The pulse in his neck rapid. She saw it, and the sweat beading on his upper lip.

"I do not try to tempt you, Hanal of Puri. I do tempt you..."

Surprise was written on his face, his gasp a thin whisper.

Rae rocked back on heels and stood slowly. With a tug, the ornate trousers slid to the floor, leaving her standing in the sheer tunic. The light from the brazier emphasised the shadows of her breasts and the scalloped front gave Hanal a view of her upper thighs, glistening with oil and spice.

Sweat gathered on Hanal's forehead and he licked his lips. His eyes were riveted to her hands as she reached up and pulled the tunic over her head, all the while willing her body not to tremble. There she stood, in a halo of dark and soft light, as naked as the day she was born, trying to find the courage to do as Umri had taught her.

"Your body is like a summer's night," he began, edging closer. He ran a hand down her hips. "Dark, warm and moist. Your skin is like gossamer silk." She smiled in the way Umri had made her practise, not like a child but like a woman, a woman full with desire, a woman full with love. She also smiled because Kushlan was right. The Puri were poets in their hearts. They just never admitted it.

Hanal's hot hand traced a circle around her nipples. She inhaled deeply as her blood stirred. "Ripe fruit ready for the harvest," he said as his lips touched her skin. "Now I will taste your honeyed pear."

Rae groaned softly, trying to keep the exultation from her expression, as Hanal of Puri, drew her down beside him and made love to her.

37

FAMILY BUSINESS

THE MORNING after the attack by the warren beasts, Aria's voice boomed out of the talkstone. Groggily, Sophy leaned over so Aria could see her face.

"Aria?" she asked, her tongue rather thick.

"Sophy! My god, you look like you have been partying too hard."

Sophy groaned in response. It was proving difficult to wake up. Aria chattered on. "Never mind that, I have news for you. I am a mother—Dellbright and I have a son."

Rolling onto her stomach, Sophy shifted the pillows obscuring her view. "Already? Are you are all right? Did it hurt much?"

"Yes, I'm fine now, though still tired. Here is little Gillcress," she said as she lifted the baby to the talkstone.

Sophy leaned in closer and saw the tiny wizened face. It was strange to think of Aria as a mother. Had it been that long already? "He is very cute, I think. It's hard to tell. Are you sure everything is all right?"

"I am. I only need you to make everything right. When will you be coming back?" Aria asked.

"I'm not sure. The festival is over so we should be leaving soon." She did not want to talk about the attack on Oakheart and herself.

"Unfortunately, I think we are accompanying Lillia back to Gilton Forest before Oakheart can bring me back to Valley Keep. I'm not sure how long that will take."

Aria turned her face to the side. "Dellbright, how long do you think it will take?"

Dellbright's faced loomed into the talkstone. His proud smile dominated his face.

"It could take at least two months, maybe three, before you reach Valley Keep. I am sorry. The going will be tough, as winter will be upon the land on the last leg. How is Oakheart, Lady Sophy?"

"Well. Very well. I wish I was there already."

"You will be here in no time at all. Now Aria has something besides our son and me to make her happy, the knowledge that you are returning to her. Farewell, Sophy."

The imaged faded from the stone. Again, she sensed something wasn't quite right. Aria had black rings around her eyes and she acted timid with Dellbright. She mulled over Dellbright's words. There was an undertone there. Did Dellbright not want her back? Sophy sighed loudly and dozed. It was too hard to figure out. She must have fallen into a deep sleep because next thing she knew Lillia shaking her out of a bad dream.

"Come, my lady, you must wake," Lillia said as she shoved a dreaded herbal concoction under her nose and helped her sit up. "You must prepare. There is a feast in your honour."

"God, I can't even walk. Tell them to have a good time without me. I don't want to move." Sophy tried to huddle back down into her blankets.

Lillia put her concoction down and tugged the blankets off Sophy. "I am sorry, my lady, the high king has commanded it. He has his servants dragging poor Oakheart from his bed as we speak. It appears that the high king has no patience for healing bodies."

Feeling slightly chilled without her blankets, Sophy glared a Lillia. But when she saw her no-nonsense expression, she nodded, and let Lillia help her into a sitting position. Straight away Lillia waved the concoction under Sophy's nose and stood guard while she sipped it. "This is far worse than any of your other medicines."

Lillia sniffed. "It will make you heal so do not insult it."

Sophy blocked her nose and gulped the liquid down, gagging afterwards.

"Come, young maid, we must get you bathed and dressed."

Groaning and complaining all the way, Sophy stopped whinging when she realised that Lillia had scented the water with healing herbs of spruce and pine. She actually felt better as she lay in the bath. Too bad she had no time to linger. Lillia called loudly and often for her to hurry up, and then the forest maiden dressed her in a flowing gown of pale blue with a pattern of dark blue and silver flowers. At least it was loose fitting so it did not irritate her injuries.

Outside the door, guards stood to attention and the fell into step with them as Lillia paraded Sophy through the corridors.

Sophy entered the same chamber that she had met the high king in before and then was ushered through a connecting door. Lillia patted her on the hand, a smile crinkling her eyes. Sophy gasped in surprise. It was not a formal banquet that she was attending but a quiet dinner. Before her stood a normal sized table set for six people. Candles lit the room and the welcoming aroma of roast meat wafted in from a small kitchen. Oakheart arrived on the arm of the high king, walking stiffly, his bruised face turning yellow in places. The swelling of his eye was less and some of the other larger cuts had been healed with bark and showed as fine pink lines on his face and hands.

Sophy was greeted warmly by them both and shown to a seat. Lillia sat next to her and then the high king joined them. Leaning over the table he said to Sophy, "This is my private dining room, and I will sit where I like." Then he stood and shoved Oakheart down in his seat and bellowed for his servant to bring the food and wine.

"And where is Mallow, the bard? I wish him to entertain us, but I promised him a meal first." He turned to Sophy and said, "I cannot get the bard to do anything I ask unless I feed him first. Apparently, 'tis a trick of the trade. He is always getting into my cellars and recommending to me which are the best of my wines. If I am lucky he tells me before he polishes them off."

He guffawed and slapped the table; Sophy jumped in spite of

herself and looked nervously at Oakheart. He tried to smile, but grimaced instead. Apparently his face hurt.

A scruffy-looking, thin, old man came in. His clothes were well worn, but appeared to have been of good quality once. He sat down without so much as a by your leave. Sophy guessed this was the weedy bard, Mallow, and the flush around his cheeks indicated he had already been sampling the high king's wine.

There was one other chair still vacant and Sophy wondered who the other guest was going to be. She looked around and then smiled. The servant plonked huge platters on the table. She was a robust, middle-aged lady, and not a servant, Sophy guessed. She took another look at her clothes and did a double take. Definitely not a servant, but what? The older woman sat down in the remaining chair and glared at the high king until he had the grace to look away.

"Oh?" he said, as if only just realising that he had failed to introduce her. "This is Vola, my sister and good friend. Sometimes she deigns to cook for me. Thank you for the meal, Vola."

"Eat up, everyone. I have not spent these long hours preparing this feast to have it go cold while you flap your lips."

The high king looked at Vola without changing his expression and then burst into a fit of belly laughter. Oakheart tried not to laugh, as it appeared to hurt.

Next, the high king lunged with his eating dagger and skewered a huge portion of meat. Oakheart followed suit and everyone relaxed and ate and talked. After a while she forgot that she was tired, sore and in royal company.

Later, they sat around the fire, listening to the bard play idle notes from his harp and sipping some sweet and heavy wine that tasted of overripe berries. It was delicious, although she was cautious not to drink too much of it lest she embarrass herself. It did not appear to have any *given* in it, which was well and good. Then the bard sang a song, a melancholy ballad about a dream of Vorn in his last days. Sophy listened and sipped her wine, her eyes travelling over the other guests. The ballad talked of strange days when the land would become un*given*. His deep voice intoned the foretelling of the ancient evil reaching into Argenterra and breaking the binding oath. She caught

Oakheart staring at her, the firelight reflecting against the green of his eyes. He appeared deep in thought.

The high king stood suddenly. "I do not think I have heard that tune before, Mallow."

"I do not spend all my time below drinking wine. That was the result of several days of research and creativity," the old bard replied.

"Maudlin. That is what it is."

The bard continued to pluck his instrument, his eyes drifting closed.

Not long after that, the high king bellowed a good night. Startled from her reverie, Sophy rose wearily. "Thank you, and good night everyone."

Not getting out of his chair, Oakheart waved, smiling with his eyes. Vola hugged Sophy carefully and kissed her cheek. The bard was asleep on the sofa and hadn't reacted to the king's loud farewell. When the doors closed behind them, Sophy couldn't help thinking that the high king was the strangest host and king she had ever met. He barely talked below the volume of a shout all night. Perhaps he was deaf.

38

THE BEAUTY REFLECTED WITHIN

A WEEK later and it was time for them to depart from Silverdale. Amidst the crowd of travellers and onlookers, Sophy searched out Oakheart. She called out when she saw him with the horses, checking them all for travel readiness. He turned around as she approached. Most of his facial swelling had gone, though he still moved stiffly. Sophy was feeling fine. She and Oakheart hadn't talked much since the meal with the high king, mostly due to their respective recuperations. "Did I mention that Aria and Dellbright have had a son?"

Oakheart finished speaking to one of his men and stepped up to meet her. Lillia came nearer too.

"No, you did not." He smiled then without cringing. "All is well?" he asked, while patting her horse's hindquarters. Oakheart had provided her a replacement mount from his own stock of horses; another white filly, named Flywell.

Sophy couldn't stop herself watching his large tanned hand, as it gently, but firmly stroked the horse. "Yes, so Aria said. They called him Gillcress."

Lillia clapped her hands once. "Oh! Gillcress is a good forest name."

A wave of homesickness for the valley and for Aria swamped Sophy.

She would not be convinced that everything was all right until she saw her friend. At least they would be on their way soon.

Oakheart nodded. "Very well, we will mount up soon. Wait for a moment."

Sophy chatted with Lillia while they waited for the group to form up. The entourage had doubled in size from the one that left Valley Keep and it took longer to organise. Sophy spotted Oakheart headed in her direction, carrying a sack.

"Sophy, come here." Puzzled, Sophy quirked an eyebrow at Lillia and strode over. As she neared, he upended the bag spilling a pile of what appeared to be bronze chest plate and leggings to the ground by his leg.

"Yes?" she said and smiled nervously, an eye on the pile of armour.

One of Oakheart's shoulders lifted as he eased an ache, but his gaze remained steady. "I want you to stand still while Lillia and I put this on you."

Her gaze fell to the pile on the ground. "I don't think that is necessary. It looks very uncomfortable."

Lillia clicked her tongue when she strode up to join them. "Sophy, you must mind your manners. Oakheart leads this troop and you must comply with his request."

Oakheart picked up a piece. "You will not accompany me unless you wear this armour," he said, without a smile.

"But Oakheart..."

"Enough," he bellowed. She closed her eyes in shock, gulped back her retort and nodded once. Then she spread her arms and stood with her legs apart so they could tie the armour on.

Lillia bent down and deftly strapped on the leggings. Oakheart grabbed her arm and tied on the arm bits. "Turn around," he instructed.

Mutely, she followed his command, though her anger was building. He held the chest plate with his hand, while Lillia did up the ties after placing them under her arms. She straight away started to itch.

"This armour is made with the *given*. I can't wear it," she said beginning to push and scratch around the edges of the of the chest plate. Lillia had finished tying on the back plate.

Oakheart's green eyes blazed with anger. "You can and you must. 'Tis true there is some *given* worked within the outer layer, but I am assured that it will not cause you harm. A little irritation, perhaps."

He turned to walk away. Lillia stood behind her, waiting to go back to their mounts.

"Can't we discuss this reasonably? I don't see why I have to wear this."

He stopped dead in his tracks and confronted her. "You only have to look to your scars and the attempts to injure you. You will wear the armour or remain here in the palace under the high king's protection."

"But..."

"You try my patience. If you are left behind, it will be for many months, perhaps a year, before I come back. Many things could happen in that time."

Her mouth fell open. "You're threatening me."

Oakheart leaned in close and lowered his voice. "If you see it that way, then I am. Now go and mount up." He glared her into submission. Backing up, she didn't dare speak another word. The armour was unwieldy, and she fumbled as she tried to mount her horse. He must have noticed her difficulty. He strode over, heaved her up onto her mount and placed her feet in the stirrups. His assistance didn't mollify her mood, nor did his manner. She sniffed and looked away. He waited by her side, perhaps for thanks and, when none were forthcoming, he stalked away. The bearing of his shoulders told her he was angry and, at that moment, she really didn't care.

"Bully," she muttered as she scratched under the breastplate.

"My lady," Lillia chided. "Have a care."

They rode out aiming for the by-way that led down from the Upper Plateau. They would cross the Lake of Reflections within the month and, provided she was uninjured and conscious, she would see the wonder of it. They could cross sooner but Oakheart was taking extra precautions. Again.

During the first part of the journey she had little opportunity to question Oakheart about why they were attacked and why he made her wear armour because he was still angry with her. It didn't help that she was generally surly and rude to him whenever he tried to help her dismount.

Surely, he hadn't expected her to like being strapped into some very ugly and uncomfortable armour.

"Why won't he speak to me, Lillia?" she asked one day as they were heading out of camp.

"Well, you have done nothing but abuse him to his face, complain about the measures taken to protect you, and been thankless when assisted. If I were him, I would not speak to you either." Lillia kept her gaze on the road and twitched the reins.

Sophy nudged her horse so that she was abreast with Lillia again. "But you speak to me all the time."

Lillia glanced at her, a fleeting smile on her lips. "That is so. But I am not he. I do not carry the burden for this party. I do not bear the burden for the lives in his hands as he does."

Sophy tugged at the armour, which kept rubbing against the saddle. "Are you saying that in order to get him to speak to me, I must first apologise to him for making me miserable—"

"For attempting to shield you from harm—"

"For being the bane of his existence these past weeks.... that is impossible."

"Not so...difficult, yes, to swallow your pride, but it can be done."

"It is easy for you to say. You are not me."

"I am not him, and I am not you, so it is easy for me. Thank you for pointing that out."

That evening when the camp was settled for the evening, Sophy headed over to Oakheart's tent. She walked awkwardly as her leggings banged together.

"Oakheart?" she called out. Silence. "Oakheart? I need to talk to you." Still more silence. She tapped her foot on the ground while she waited. This was really hard, she thought.

"Look, I'm sorry for giving you a hard time. I understand you are doing your best. I don't like fighting like this...can we be friends?"

"Certainly," said a voice from behind her.

She swung round and nearly overbalanced. He was standing behind her with a pot of hot water. "I thought you were in your tent." She backed away from the opening as he moved to enter.

"Obviously."

"Well?" she asked.

"Well what?"

"Can we be friends again? Will you talk to me?"

He stopped and looked into his pot of water. "Yes." He opened the flap of his tent and entered.

She stood waiting. He didn't come out again. "Oakheart?"

"Yes, Sophy."

"So, can we talk?"

"Not now, after the eve-tide meal."

"Oh. All right then. See you later."

She stomped back to her and Lillia's tent. "Success, my lady?"

"If you can call it that. He said he would talk to me this evening."

"Good. Why are you so cast down?"

Sophy locked gazes with Lillia. "I have to stay in this armour until I go to bed. I will go crazy by then."

❧

SOPHY LOOKED DOWN AT THE STEAMING STEW. CAMP FOOD AGAIN, she mused. No more fine wines and chef prepared meals, eaten off pretty little plates like they had in Oakheart's company. Just then, Oakheart's bulk lowered to the ground beside her. "You wished to speak to me about a particular matter, my lady?"

Her gaze settled on his face, taking in the green eyes, darkened with night shadow, and his complexion ruddy from reflected firelight. "Yes, I do. I want you to tell me about Rufus."

He shrugged. "He is not liked."

Sophy leaned toward him. "That much I can see. Why not? What did he do?"

Oakheart held himself still, light reflecting in his eyes as his gaze travelled over her. The hand resting on his knee closed into a fist. "Rufus lives in the warrens beneath the Lower Plateau. He has lived there for a long time, before Veld was high king, maybe even before his father was high king before him. No one has actually witnessed any foul deeds or, should I say, and lived to tell of it."

"That's it? That's all the reason you have for treating him so badly? Why would you think he meant any harm to me? There is no proof that he has a black heart like you said."

"I do not need proof." Oakheart threw his head back, loosening his hair from the ties that held it in place, a chunk falling across his right eye.

"You can't condemn him for no reason. Surely you can see that."

"That is the truth of it, Sophy. I cannot 'see' him. He is not bound by the oath."

"But you can't see me either. You do not know if I am bound by this oath. Yet I think you trust me now…a little." Then she recalled how careful he had been with her at first. How everyone reacted to her in different degrees, depending on what they could perceive.

"You must understand. I have my reasons, and I do not have to share them with you."

"So you don't really trust me either? That's why you don't tell me things. Why you won't tell me about Rufus now?"

"'Tis not like that. You have proven yourself in many ways."

"I don't understand. Why would you think that Rufus wanted to harm me? I had the distinct impression that he liked me." She was about to elaborate when she heard him suck in a breath and once again clench his fist.

When he spoke, she clearly heard the undertones of disgust. "My lady, I saw what effect he had on you, and I can guess what you felt. That is enough to convince me that he means to harm you. If he was true, if he was honest, why did he not show you his true form? Why did he enchant you? There can be no other explanation other than he means you ill and that his heart is black."

"Maybe he is lonely because everyone despises him and he sees me as a friend."

Oakheart bounded to his feet, leaving her sitting by the fire gaping. He was about to stalk off and then paused, turning once again to face her. "I cannot speak with you any longer on this topic." Then changing his mind, he took a step closer to her and knelt on one knee. "If he had good faith, he would approach you openly. If he desired you, he only had to ask who had the care of you and seek permission, but he did not."

Sophy crossed her arms over the chest and glared at Oakheart. His gaze travelled over her face for a few moments and then he was up and striding away from her. After staring in the fire for a few minutes herself, she stormed off to her tent and went to sleep.

The rest of the trip down the by-way she stayed out of Oakheart's way. Fern was nice to her, while Oakheart stayed angry. She expected the usual twist of the verbal knife every time Fern spoke to her, but it never came.

Twenty days since departing Silverdale, after an uneventful and very slow descent, they reached the lake crossing. Some of the guards gathered fruit from a small orchard. Moving among the trees, the men caressed a branch, murmured, and fruit would grow and ripen. It was a slow process as the trees had already been harvested. She noted that only one branch per tree was taxed this way. As the *given* did not respond to her, Sophy was unable to help.

She sat by the side of the road, kicking the dirt. Lillia, sensing her mood, remained close by, silent but watchful.

"Sophy," Oakheart called out as he navigated across the lines of men and horses.

She scrambled up clumsily. "Yes?"

While she wiped the dirt from her hands, Oakheart strode up to her. Fern had also heard and came trotting up behind. "You will accompany me on the first trip across the lake. Lillia, take charge of the second load, and Fern you take the third."

When it came to embarking Oakheart was overly cautious. He lifted her bodily into the ferry. Although she was highly embarrassed, she dared not struggle unless he dropped her in. The thought did occur to her that Oakheart considered her incapable of doing anything properly. Once on board and left to stand on her own two feet, the sight of the lake amazed her. The surface was silver-coloured and appeared to have the consistency of mercury.

Oakheart stayed next to her as he supervised the loading of men and horses for the first trip. As the barge eased away from the shore, she kept to the middle while Oakheart moved to the side. From her position, she could see that the water reflected sunlight. Impossibly, it looked like a mirror, flat, silver and smooth. Entranced, she edged next to Oakheart, who stood near the rails, gazing out over the lake.

"It's so beautiful," she breathed and mist swirls of breath curled around her face due to the cold.

"Yes," his voice was a touch dreamy. His gaze lingered on the water as he spoke. "'Tis said that the Lake of Reflections defies even the *given*. Nothing can be hidden from it and its surface reflects only truth."

"Really?" Sophy leant over the edge and her breath caught at the sight. Her reflection showed the face she had before she came to this place—pale, smooth complexion with dark, blue eyes rounded by awe. Then a handsome face appeared next to her image. Transfixed, she wondered who it was. Sparkling green eyes, a smile that could sever a heartbeat greeted her gaze. Oakheart blew out a loud breath in her ear. She jumped. Dragging her gaze away from the lake surface, she gaped at her companion. Oakheart stood next to her, plain and bland as ever and then she looked to the image again.

"Oakheart...is that your face?" she asked, as she pointed.

He appeared puzzled by her question, started to say something, then thought the better of it. "'Tis me. You do not recognise me?"

"No." She frowned, looking between him and his reflection. The lake showed only truth. Then that had to be what he looked like, and why he always appeared to be masked. Like her own face. "That is not what I see when I look at you. You have no colour, you are plain, ordinary, even uninspiring. Yet, your reflection is handsome, colourful and alive. What is going on?"

"Mmmm. 'Tis puzzling. I think the truer image is the reflection." He leant over the side and stared at her reflection.

"You do not look like your reflection either," he said, after staring her reflection and her face repeatedly, his expression grew more and more shocked.

"I know, but I have looked the same since I came here. That is how I looked before I arrived in Crystal Tree Woods." She sighed. "Now I see how others see you. It explains the women...er...I mean, what I want to know is why do I see you differently?"

He looked at her for a while, perhaps trying to see the beauty so casually reflected in the lake. "I cannot answer."

"Cannot or will not?"

He shrugged. "Anything I said would be a guess. But I will think on it and let you know when I have come up with a theory."

With no choice but to accept his answer, Sophy spent the rest of the voyage entertaining herself by looking at their reflections in the lake. Oakheart complied by standing near. His true face shone with humour and intelligence, which she had glimpsed once or twice since meeting him. How different their meeting would have been if they had seen each other's true faces. As she stared in wonder, she noticed that he stared at her, too, thoughtfully. It was if they were seeing each other for the first time and yet not, because they were no longer strangers.

When the barge hit the pier, she realised that she had been captivated by Oakheart's reflection for the whole journey. Coughing awkwardly, she stepped back as guards and horses began to move at his command. Their gazes met momentarily, and she noted that he was blushing, before he stepped back into the throng of guards. Had he been looking at her, too, for the whole crossing?

AFTER THE FINAL GROUP HAD COMPLETED THEIR PASSAGE, OAKHEART ordered the camp to be broken down and they continued on. They travelled on for days, and Sophy withdrew into a cloak of melancholy. The lake had changed something for her. It had brought the threat against her into sharp focus. She was now certain that she was enchanted. She hadn't changed her looks at all, rather, they had been disguised. But how and why? Even more puzzling was that Oakheart's true face had been hidden from her.

As they rode, Lillia tried to rally her spirits but nothing worked. Sorrow and self-pity swirled about her. One day, when they stopped for the noon-tide meal, Sophy could hold her fears and frustration back no longer. When sliding from her horse to dismount, her thigh piece snagged on the stirrup and she nearly toppled head first to the ground. After righting herself, she tugged viscously at the ties, ripping the offending piece from her body and slamming it the ground. At the same time she yelled to no one in particular. "I'm sick of these things."

Growling, she tried to wrench off the rest. Oakheart's heavy tread sounded behind her. Anger washed over her. In a small part of her mind she knew she was being unreasonable focussing on him, narrowing down the blame but there was a pleasure in wanting to hit him, smack him right in that chest, which he so proudly displayed before her. With her feet parted and clenched fist raised, she faced him

"Sophy?" Lillia's worried voice drew closer.

Beyond being obedient and polite, she ignored the forest maiden and concentrated on Oakheart.

He ignored her belligerent stance and let his gaze travel over the discarded piece of armour, his mouth a grim line. "You will put it. Back. On. Now," he yelled at her. "We leave soon—"

"I. Will. Not," she snarled. "I'm sick of leaving places. Do you hear me? I won't wear the damn things any longer. I don't care who attacks me. Let them try. I've had enough of this evil place." Her eyes watered as she heaved in one breath after another.

Oakheart moved nearer, putting his face close to hers. "You will put the thigh piece on now, or I will put it on you."

"I'd like to see you try." They were eye to eye, Sophy breathing hard.

Before she could blink, Oakheart dropped into a crouch, flipped her over to balance her on his lap and started strapping on the thigh protector. Too stunned to even struggle Sophy held herself rigid. When the thigh piece was in place, he let her drop to the ground and stood up, walking away without a backward glance.

By then, Sophy was fully aware of how stupid she had been to let her temper get away from her. What had she achieved except humiliation? Aghast, the assembled guards and Lillia stared at her, while she limped back to her mount. Even though Oakheart hadn't hurt her, he may as well have smacked her behind. Fern snickered in the background and Sophy bit back the impulse to smash him in the face. Then she let out her anger, breath after breath. That little episode had achieved nothing. Lillia mounted up and moved her horse beside her. She didn't need to say anything, the question was obvious. Why did she take out her anger on Oakheart? He was only trying to protect her useless hide. Sophy nudged her horse forward, not able to look the forest maiden in the eye.

It wasn't easy going for the next few weeks. Shame hampered her. Fern's sly comments when Oakheart was absent prodded her. She fixed Fern with a baleful glare, wishing that she could pummel his chest, or his face, certain that she wouldn't feel shame afterwards, only satisfaction. She was almost to the point of very impolitely wiping the smirk of Fern's face when she caught Oakheart standing still and looking at her. She unclenched her fist, smiled sweetly and walked away.

After her tantrum, it was difficult to approach Oakheart. He sat most evenings with Fern and his men, talking and laughing quietly by firelight. Sometimes they sang sweet songs; songs of love, beautiful maidens and of daring deeds. Fern had a pleasant voice and so did Oakheart. Sophy lingered on the edge of the camp one evening listening so that she could put faces to the voices. Her armour still annoyed her and the only place she was allowed without it was in her tent, so that is where she usually went straight after the eve-tide meal.

She watched the landscape as the days passed and the green fields faded. What started as a smattering of trees became more consistent. The season was turning, the leaves transformed into a tapestry of colour, yellows, reds, oranges and browns.

The forest began to thicken. The trees were larger, thick-trunked and old, huddled together for warmth, their backs to the cool breeze. As they progressed, the clumped old trees grew closer together. Long trunks with high limbs, entwined in a heavenly embrace, stood neck to neck. The forest breathed with one breath, Sophy thought, after they had travelled within the trees for a few days.

The weather grew cooler, day by day, and a chill began to harden on the breeze. Rain drenched them for three days running, and the wind became colder. Sophy's lips were blue and her teeth chattered, yet she had no voice for complaint.

"Do not fret, my lady," Lillia said, breaking into her thoughts. "We are nearing Gilton Forest and once inside we will be sheltered. The forest provides some protection from the elements."

"Do you mean this isn't Gilton Forest?"

Lillia inspected the trees with a quick glance. "The edges only. Soon we will reach the heart of the forest and safety."

"I see," Sophy replied. She scratched idly under her breastplate and tried to ignore the urge to scratch elsewhere. The armour had burnt her skin, only the damage was not severe. Red marks had appeared, but they didn't worsen.

Within the week, after slow going, they neared the inner layer of the ever-thickening forest and Sophy could hear the pleasant song of birds. This forest lived. Gilton Forest was massive and the trees stretched high above, nearly touching clouds. They made camp in a small clearing, which Lillia called the Oaks Glade.

"You may take off your armour here. We are safe," Lillia said as she dismounted and breathed in a deep lungful of forest air.

Sophy looked over to Oakheart in case he had some argument, but he astutely ignored her. She shrugged and quickly unlaced the ties, throwing the various bits of armour aside as if they were serpents rather than protection. She had to beg for assistance from Lillia for her thigh piece; it was in such a tight knot.

Lillia clucked her tongue while she applied herself to the knot. "My lady, do not be so quick to show your feelings. Have you learnt no decorum? Truly, you shame me. Have I taught you nothing?"

Sophy's happiness at being free of the tedious armour quieted. "I'm sorry. I'll try harder."

Lillia's lecture suddenly made her feel worse and her joy was tugged away like the armour from her body. Things didn't improve as she watched the camp get set up. Feeling low made every joint ache, and the thought that she might sleep better with the help of wine crystallised. A few mouthfuls would deliver oblivion. However, she couldn't ask for some, she had to wait for the meal.

Sophy edged closer the main fire, joining the others as they sat around and ate a stew of dried meat with hard bread. The supplies were nearly at an end, so they ate the remainder. The forest folk would meet them and even if for some reason they didn't, Lillia knew where to hunt in this place.

Wine was passed around. Sophy usually didn't take it, so she had to be careful not to attract attention to herself. She lifted her goblet to Fern, who filled it, splashing the golden liquid around the rim. She peeped at Fern from under her lashes. He hadn't noticed anything unusual in her actions and continued to chat to those around him. She sighed, relieved that he had ceased actively taunting her since her fight with Oakheart. At least she thought it was that had taken the edge of his ire, but perhaps there was some fundamental flaw in her that repulsed the courtier. An idle recollection of the way young men used to look at her came to mind. It seemed so long ago. She had been in this land for so long that her past didn't seem real at all. But it was real, as real as the wine she drank, as real as the Lake of Reflections and as real as the blood that spilled from her and Oakheart's wounds when they were attacked.

Sophy sipped her wine slowly. She wanted to get drunk, but had to be intelligent about it. Keeping quiet, she sat back in the shadows hoping to go unnoticed. If the wine had *given* in it, she would not need to consume much.

The fire burned, the blue flames contrasting with the yellow, orange and red. Real wood this time and not firesticks. She stared into the fire for what seemed like moments but when she next looked up, she thought she was alone. She started. She had been so absorbed that she hadn't noticed anything. Fern had gone to bed and so had Lillia. She took a large gulp of wine and then stopped.

A presence lurked nearby. Oakheart sat there, watching her through the flames. Their eyes met. She could feel the wine's influence on her, always exaggerated. While she gaped at him, he crept closer, reached out and took her goblet away, gently releasing it from her pliant fingers. He placed it by him on the ground and took her hands in his. She was too surprised by his approach to move or speak. Perhaps he was going to lecture her now.

"Let there be peace between us," he said, making eye contact.

She couldn't think of anything to say. The world was not behaving. He was so close she could see the pores in his skin; the slight scars of old scratches and cuts; and the flecks of gold in his green eyes. His breath feathered her face as he slowly exhaled. After swallowing the lump that had formed in her throat, she nodded dumbly and dropped her gaze. Suddenly everywhere was warm, her skin damp with perspiration that had sprung up with the flame of his closeness.

Through her wine-numbed mind, she knew she wanted to be his friend. Their silent war had been taxing. The realisation that she had discovered Oakheart on the Lake of Reflections and then lost him again through her own ill will hit hard. There was no true reason to be fighting. It was as if they drew together only to fly apart like opposing poles on a magnet.

Sophy raised her eyes to his face, searching for the handsomeness that was hidden from her view. Edging closer, she reached up slowly and stroked his cheek. His pupils dilated and then contracted with the surprise of her touch. He didn't pull away. How had she gotten so close to him? Kneeling, she reached up and pressed her lips to his. He must have been surprised because his lips were, at first, unresisting. Encouraged by this she pulled his head closer and deepened the kiss. Then with his hands on her shoulders, he pushed her gently but firmly away.

His gaze travelled over her face. "No, Sophy," he said harshly. "You will not play games with me. No drunken advances from you. That is not for me."

When he released his hold, she sat back on her heels dumbfounded. Games? Advances? Her mind spun with the ramifications of what she had done and what he had said. It wasn't the wine, she wanted to say, but the words stopped in her throat.

He stood quickly and strode purposefully to his tent, shoulders hunched. While she stared as his retreating back, she realised the bounds of friendship had been breached. He did not care for her romantically and now he couldn't even treat her as a friend. It was only a kiss, she told herself, nothing special. Yet as she touched her fingers to her lips, she wasn't so sure.

Sophy had coped with the land rejecting her, the *given* repulsing her, Fern's sneers and others overlooking her, but Oakheart's rejection over a kiss left her feeling bereft.

39

HANAL'S SEER

WHILE THEY DISCUSSED BUSINESS, Hanal, Umri and Tarkel drank hot brewed tea. Rae had been sent away to prepare a small meal, as Hanal had not wanted her listening in. Rae did not mind. Hanal was everything she had ever wanted, except he was not her husband. Right then her body sung in remembrance of his lovemaking and his sweet pillow talk. Yet she knew there was no turning back, she had shared his bed without an oath.

"Tu Raenal, come here," Hanal's voice echoed in the tent. Rae took the small pot of food off the fire, wiped her hands and hurried. She parted the curtain, came forward and bowed low to Hanal.

"Come and sit by me, little sister," Hanal said, tenderly. "I wish you to tell me of those that you know at Valley Keep."

"Yes, Hanal. Greetings, brother Tarkel and sister Umri," Rae said as she knelt at Hanal's right hand.

Umri smiled, her dark eyes assessing how Rae moved. Tarkel ignored her, as he had done since she had joined Hanal's household.

Hanal turned towards her. "I heard in Silverdale that there were two women who came out of Crystal Tree Woods. One married your intended, Dellbright." Rae blushed at his words and wondered how he knew about that.

Rae glanced at Umri. Hanal's seer smiled broadly, arching her sculpted eyebrow. Rae lowered her head and answered Hanal. "Yes. There were two—Aria and Sophy."

Hanal rubbed his clean-shaven chin. "Sophy, I have met. She was an outlander through and through. Tell me of the other one…Aria."

Rae relaxed and let her mind fill with memories of her time at the keep. "Princess Aria is a kind and beautiful woman—"

Umri moaned suddenly and her eyes glazed over. All of them stopped moving and talking while they waited. Umri shook herself, fluttering her eyelids. "She is not the Gift…" she said, her voice distant.

Gooseflesh rose on Rae's arms. Umri was using her seer's sight and it felt as if the wings of death had passed over her.

Hanal sat up straighter. "What did you say?"

Umri shook her head as if to clear it. Then she lowered her lashes. "She has the mark of the binding oath." Again she went into a trance, her chest heaving until she opened both her eyes with a start. "It is not possible that she is the Gift of the Crystal Tree Woods. You have been deceived."

Rae's eyes widened. "No. It cannot be. She is. They all said so. I am sorry to argue with you, sister Umri, but they all believe her to be so. What I saw and heard leads me to that conclusion, too. Aria and Sophy were good friends and talked about their world between themselves."

Chin lifting, Umri's eyes flashed with anger. "She can work the *given* can she not?"

Rae, confused, shrugged. "Yes, she works it better than Dellbright, I think. Yet, wisely she does not do so in front of him. Kushlan says if she had been born in Argenterra she would have been an adept."

"No," Hanal said as he stood and paced. Rae scurried to move the earthenware cups out of the way of his feet.

"What is it, Hanal?" Umri asked, bowing low to the carpet. "Have I said something amiss? Has my sight displeased you?"

He swung around, fist clenched. "No, Umri, it has not. You have opened my eyes to other possibilities. I have been tricked by Veld, that much I know. He may say he will try to negotiate a marriage between Oakheart and Lyant but it is a ploy. By Oakheart I have been betrayed and my authority flouted. He did gaze upon my sister and saw her soul but did not marry her. Between those acts alone it is enough to wage war on them..." Hanal's eyes flashed as his gaze swept over them. "What a fool I was to fall for their trickery. I had her in my grasp."

"Who?" Rae and Umri asked in unison. Rae hid her embarrassment by pouring more brew in his cup, hoping that he would sit and be calm. He had never been so full of anger in her presence before. "Sophy, the Outlander, the Gift of Crystal Tree Woods. I thought, because they ignored her, that she was unimportant. But it was a scheme to deflect me from the real Gift of Crystal Tree Woods. Oh how well they spread the rumours of Princess Aria, the beauteous and gracious gift and wife to Dellbright."

"Pray excuse me for speaking out of turn again," Rae said, her voice wavering. "But Princess Aria is all those things and more. She is married to Dellbright. It was a real bonding. I saw the blooding of the marriage bed myself, for I was the one to change their sheets. Sophy, on the other hand, was barely tolerated. Oakheart only took her to Silverdale because Dellbright begged him to. I overheard them arguing about it. The whole keep was in an uproar at her unseemly antics."

Hanal lowered himself to the floor and took a fresh cup of tea. "So you say, but you do not understand how long these Gifts of Crystal Tree Woods have been hoarded by the princes of Valley Keep, supported by the high king in Silverdale." He took a sip of tea and swallowed. Umri watched him closely and Tarkel barely moved. "I was tempted to take her...so close to taking her. How she quaked in my presence. She would have yielded to me easily—so out of her depth, so overcome by my presence alone. One caress and she would have followed me anywhere... one kiss and she would have opened to me.

"However, Oakheart's slight had me in a rage. I wanted to take him, too, and force him to marry Lyant. It did not happen that way. They tricked me well."

Rae's eyes fell to the floor as her heart plummeted. Sophy would replace her in Hanal's tent if he captured her. That much even she could see. If Hanal could not get Oakheart to marry Lyant, then possessing Sophy was the only way to satisfy him. It would be Goslien and Heer Panal all over again. Yet this abduction would not be motivated by love, as it had been with Heer Panal—it would be motivated by cold, hard ambition. Either way, Rae would have to give way to Sophy. Umri had spoken of Hanal's desire to raise the Puri from their lowly status and to place himself equal to the high king. The animosity between the Puri and Silverdale stretched back to the First Comers, she knew. Back to Vorn's kinsman, Shabra, and his manipulative ways.

Umri again consulted her sight, head slanted to the left and moaning slightly.

"Yes," Umri said, her voice distant. "They hid Oakheart from you. They know you tried to trap Oakheart with Lyant."

"I did no such thing," Hanal replied as put down his now finished tea and arranged his robes around him. "He chose to talk with Lyant, chose to gaze into her eyes…I provided the opportunity. Now I must make other plans."

❧

RAE HID HER FACE AS SHE PICKED UP THE CLOTHES SHE HAD BEEN washing and piled them into a basket. The Puri women shunned her. To them she was an outcast, a woman who lay with her lover without an oath and without dignity. Rae blinked back the tears. She loved Hanal and wanted to be oath-bound to him, but he would not discuss it.

"There you are," Umri said, placing her washing next to Rae's. "All alone?"

Rae turned towards her, angry. "You knew what would happen. No one will speak with me. Only Lyant will spare me a word or two, and you. But the rest…"

"What did you expect? The Puri are no different to the Argenterrans in that respect. They like oaths to be sworn."

"I wanted so much to be accepted."

"And you will be when you get Hanal's oath. Then you will see their attitudes change." Umri dunked one of robes in the water. "Tell me, does Hanal's seed grow within you?"

Rae blushed to the roots of her hair. Avoiding eye contact, she rewashed a napkin, scrubbing it hard against the rock.

"It does not," she said at last. "He chooses to withhold his seed. He said he did not want complications."

Umri sat thoughtfully, idly rubbing her cloth together. "He is wily, I will say that. But it is important to have his seed within you. I have an idea."

Rae looked up puzzled. "How can you do anything about it? He spills his seed on the sheets."

"We must do this before we go to the caves for winter," Umri said, lowering her voice and leaning towards Rae. She pulled a fine square of silk from her robe and placed it in Rae's hand. "When you lay with him next place this underneath you. As soon as you can afterwards, gather the cloth up, keeping his seed within it, and bring it to me."

"But...how?"

Umri smiled slyly. "When does he make love to you? Morning or evening?"

Rae could not respond, only her face grew more heated.

Umri's smile turned to a chuckle. "I see. Lucky you." She pursed her lips. "Place it under you in the morning. His seed is strongest then."

Rae could not ignore the guilty feeling. "I cannot do it. I love him too much to go against him like this. I could not bear his anger."

Umri gripped her hand. "Would you have him cast you out? Marry you off to some old widower? He will do it when he is tired of you. You have seen his ambitions. Only by bearing his son will you secure him."

A shiver of fear laced through Rae. "I am afraid. I would die if he cast me out. I will do as you say. For the love of Hanal, I will do it."

"Good. See you in my tent early."

Rae picked up her basket of clean clothes and went to place them on the rocks to dry. She avoided the rest of the women, choosing to walk farther afield. Her thoughts weighed heavily on her mind.

The next morning, still warm from Hanal's bed, Rae crept towards Umri's tent. She squatted outside and listened for Tarkel. From what she could tell he was absent. "Umri?" she whispered.

The tent flap opened and Umri's hand beckoned to her. Rae slipped inside, shaking with anticipation.

"You brought it?"

Rae nodded and lifted the silk square tied in a knot. Umri took it.

"Take off your trousers and lie down over there." When Rae stared at her, Umri added. "Come on. We must be quick. You do want Hanal's child?"

Rae quickly undid the tie to her trousers and let them drop to the ground. She stretched out on the bedding as Umri instructed. Umri scraped Hanal's seed into a metal cylinder. "Now relax. I am going to put it inside you. It may feel strange."

Rae looked to the tent roof. "Are you sure about this? It seems unnatural."

"Some say so. But I have done it before with success. Puri must breed to survive. When a man is injured or unable to sire a child, they ask one of their kin to give of their seed. It is done in secret, mind you. I am bound by promise not to speak of it. Only those involved know of it. This," Umri held up the cylinder, now empty, "was passed to me from my grandmother and from hers before that from Shareal herself."

"The Shareal, daughter of Lilt of the Blue Eyes and Shabra?"

Umri's eyes narrowed. "The very same. Now lay there for a while so the seed will take. By the time we reach the caves to shelter for the winter we will know if it worked. The signs are good, though. You are fertile now."

"You can tell?" Rae asked, fascinated by the woman's knowledge.

"Pfft! Of course. I told you I was Hanal's Seer. That encompasses many things."

40
A BINDING OATH

SOPHY LEFT her tent before dawn. She had not slept well and was keen to avoid the scrupulous eye of Lillia, who had the knack of knowing when Sophy was not herself. There were only a few guards about and, with a nod, one of Oakheart's men indicated that he would follow her. Without argument, Sophy bore the intrusion, even though she wanted to be alone. At least the guard kept a discreet distance.

It was good to be free of the armour as she walked beneath the trees, running her hands along rough bark. Yet, she was troubled. How was she going to face Oakheart? She didn't know how.

Walking on, she tried to quiet her mind. A small clearing opened up ahead. It had a portion of fallen tree trunk, which she headed for, and a large tree to one side with branches that drooped to the ground. A good hiding place, she thought.

Leaning against the trunk, she brooded. Surely kissing Oakheart was not as terrible as pummelling him with punches. She had been tempted to do that in the past. Yet, the kiss was an affront, an apparent trespass on his person beyond forgiveness.

Oakheart left his tent and went in search of Sophy. After some enquiries, he discovered she had left the camp. Awake most of the night, thinking, he now thought he had a good understanding of what she was going through—and what his actions had cost her. He located the guard who was responsible for Sophy's safety that morning. After receiving directions from him, he gave orders for everyone to rest as they would not be breaking camp that day. He walked around the huge trunked trees, until he came upon the clearing.

Sophy was leaning against the log, lost in thought, but she looked up when she heard his approach. Promptly she jumped up and looked around for somewhere to run. That made his heart clench.

"Sophy?" he called in his best soft voice. She did not dart away, yet she averted her face.

Oakheart felt a wave of pity. Lillia was right—Sophy had been treated badly in Argenterra, by him most of all. Information that would have eased her mind, he could have easily provided and unfortunately he had not. Despite this, time and time again she had shown her worthiness through her deeds. This outlander may be closed to him, but she was no Rufus. The Lake of Reflections had shown him that.

Sophy did not speak and would not look at him. He stepped in front of her, reached out and gently brought her face to his. She tried to pull back, and gave up. Even then she cast down her gaze so that she was looking at his chest instead. Not to be outdone by those tactics, he eased her chin up.

"We need to talk," he said softly. His tone made her glance up. She coloured when their eyes met, although she did not drop her gaze or turn away.

"About last night..." he began.

"There is no need. Please forget it. I apologise," she blurted out in a rush and tried to pull away from him. He picked her up, sat her on the log and held her there, his knees either side of her legs.

"There is a need. Sophy, look at me. I will not dally with you, nor you with me. No wait...hear me out. I do not know your ways, yet I suspect a kiss does not have much meaning for you."

"I...I..." She could only shake her head in denial.

"For you to kiss me is nothing. Nothing more than changing your gown. I will not have it so."

"You don't understand. I wasn't dallying."

His eyebrow lifted in response. "If you were not playing games with me, what were you doing?"

Sophy's cheeks were burning, and she lifted her hands to her cheeks in an effort to cool them. "I I...not..." she garbled.

"Mmm. That does not tell me a lot," he relaxed his grip on her chin.

"Are you angry with me, or not?" she asked.

He shook his head and smiled at her. "No. I have no anger at you for that."

"Then I do not understand why you..."

"I will not allow you to trifle with me. If you truly—"

"It wasn't only the wine," she blurted out. "I really wanted to—" Her limbs trembled. If only he could 'see' her, then he could know for certain. He closed his eyes for a moment and relaxed. "You wanted to...what?"

"I...er...wanted to be close to you. I wanted your friendship..." She was struggling. "I am... Darn it. I don't know."

With a sudden lunge, she unsuccessfully tried escape from his embrace. Settling back into position, she gave a quick flick of her eyelids and met his gaze. He was smiling at her. For however inarticulate she had been, he was sure that his choice was the right one and that he acted for the best. "I will have your oath here and now," he said seriously.

Her eyes rounded with disbelief. "Oath? What oath? You want me to promise what? Not to kiss you again?" A wash of anger stained her cheeks.

"No," he said quietly. All around them the forest became hushed. He could see the pulse beating in her neck and she trembled again.

"I want an oath from you before you kiss me again."

She gaped at him as if she had never seen him before. "You want me to kiss you? But..."

With one hand he moved his fingers through her dark hair, which flowed straight down her back. "I want you to kiss me... but not from wine... because you wish to...with a clear head, and from your heart."

Sophy's smile was wide and her dark eyes glittered as she searched his face. He rubbed the back of her neck, and she leaned into his hand.

"I have a clear head," she said breathlessly.

His thumb stroked her cheek and her eyes closed. "Then say after me...I swear to you, Oakheart, and let the *given* bear witness, that I will share my kiss, my heart and my body with you only while I live in this land."

SOPHY WAS TRAPPED WITHIN THE FRAME OF OAKHEART'S LEGS AND arms, while his thumb traced along her jaw, making her skin tingle and her heart thud. He had asked her for an oath before she could kiss him again. His lips were so close to hers. His touch was affecting her though it did not frighten her as Hanal's presence had. It was rather a strange oath, she thought, yet, she felt she could promise it. They could be friends again and things would be like they were before—and so she repeated the words.

Oakheart repeated the oath. The serious manner with which he spoke made her think there might be more to this oath than she first thought. Before she could make sense of it, he leaned forward and, cupping her chin in his hand, kissed her. Her thoughts went wild. A strange fluttering rose from her stomach up through her chest. Ramifications, what are they? she thought. Oaths, promises, no problems. Her mind went haywire as his lips stayed on hers. The kiss was warm and soft and then he deepened it.

Sophy had never been kissed like this. She moaned into his mouth, desperate for more. His hands crept up to her hair and took hold. She surrendered as he invaded her mouth with his tongue and stroked her own. Her body began to throb while heated shafts of desire laced her skin.

The kiss became more aggressive. Pliant and eager as her restraint broke free, she kissed him back. Her heart beat like a hammer in her chest. The kiss went on and on.

Oakheart broke contact at last, holding her against his chest as he breathed roughly against her ear. Her hormones were running rampant. That was some kiss, she thought, as she tried to calm her pounding heart. That was not a friendship kiss, by any sense of the word. Their relationship had taken an unexpected turn. Through the fabric of his jerkin she could feel Oakheart's powerful heart beat and knew he was as moved as she was.

While her blood ran unbridled in her veins and split her thoughts in divergent directions, he began to nibble on her ear and to softly nuzzle against her neck. She gasped. Electric shocks travelled up and down her neck, she grew hot. She didn't pull away, since the sensations he was creating were addictive. His hands stroked her, rubbed her back, her arms and her thighs. She returned his stroking. His body was firm and smooth. The deep vee-necked jerkin left his arms bare and she ran her hands up and his muscles twitched with her touch.

Feelings she never knew she had buffeted her as desire rose bidden from deep within by Oakheart's caresses. He kissed her deeply and thoroughly, she kissed him back in the same way. He broke contact at last and she looked into his eyes. There was passion in his gaze; his green eyes glowed with it.

He lifted her unresisting body from the log and carried her beneath the tree with the low-lying branches. Within the screen of leaves, they were hidden from view and she lay back on a bed of sweet smelling leaves. Words were out of place so she reached out and kissed him again. This time they caressed freely, openly wondering at the joys of exploration. His skin was smooth and firm and she pulled at his jerkin so she could run her hands over his chest. His medallion looked over-large on his naked chest.

He undid her clothes, exposing her flesh. Suddenly a realisation of where their petting was heading hit her. "Oakheart?" Her breath was coming fast. "Maybe we should slow down."

"There is no shame,'" he whispered, while nuzzled behind her ear. His hand was inside her clothes gently caressing her breast. "We have an oath."

Sophy frowned, a bit distracted by Oakheart was doing. "An oath? I...er yes...but..." She moaned again, when his caress and kisses became more demanding. When he released her mouth, she panted out. "I'm frightened."

"Me too," he said with a grin and continued to undo her clothes and kiss the exposed parts of her flesh. Something was out of her control, and it was her. Oakheart created amazing sensations. She could no longer think straight. The remainder of her clothes were removed without further protest. And then Oakheart's heated flesh pressed against hers. She pulled his hair free of its tie and his white blond mane fanned out against his shoulders. She ran her fingers through it and pulled on it, pulling him down for another kiss. Naked and trembling, they embraced, cocooned in the branches of the tree. Oakheart placed himself so that he could slide inside her. "Are you sure about this?" she asked hesitantly.

"Sophy?" he held himself still. Those passion-filled green eyes fixed on her face. Sophy moved suddenly and Oakheart's groan filled the air.

"What is it? Are you okay?" she asked through her hazy mind. They were in a very difficult position. He certainly had restraint.

"Yes...but...you...Sophy?" he said and although his voice sounded strained. Then she relaxed and he could move. She never expected lovemaking to be like this. Her stomach burned, her legs flamed and she squirmed out of control. Her nails dug into his skin. He had handfuls of her hair as he dredged kiss after kiss from her mouth. He touched her and she undulated. She kissed, licked and bit softly at his flesh wherever her lips found purchase. He moaned in response, and she took that for encouragement and exhilarated in his surrender. Her movements became uncontrolled then settled to match his powerful rhythm. Out of nowhere she had a strange sensation as she felt herself unwind. "Oakheart?" she cried fearfully, uncertain what was happening to her.

"Go with the *given*, Sophy. I will meet you there." And he did.

After, they lay entwined, nestled in the leaves and dozed until Oakheart brought her to wakefulness with his hands taking excursions along her naked flesh. He began anew. She was a little tender, yet she couldn't stop herself, didn't want to stop. Her body responded to him.

Afterwards they slept. A cool breeze on her naked skin woke her. Looking down at Oakheart, she stroked back the blonde hair from his sleeping face. A sudden and hectic recollection of what they had done galvanised her. What had she been thinking? This was terrible. What would everyone say? Gathering up her discarded clothing, she dressed quickly before she slunk back to camp, hiding behind trees and tents. Hoping all the while that no one would realise what she had been doing. She didn't need to deal with that embarrassment.

❦

OAKHEART WOKE. HE SAT UP AND LOOKED AROUND FOR SOPHY. HE could not halt the smile that spread across his face when he thought of their lovemaking. It was well that he could not 'see' her, for if he had sensed that tempest of desire within her before, he would have lost himself long ago, cursed looks or no. He sighed, noting that she had run off. He looked about for his clothes and a patch of red caught his eye. He picked up a small oak leaf that was red with blood: Sophy's blood.

He rummaged about looking for his small knife. He pricked his finger and mixed his blood with hers. He twirled the leaf in his fingers and then opened his medallion and placed it inside. Then he took his time dressing, before ambling back to camp with a simple melody on his lips. Once inside his tent, he moved his gear around, rearranging the space. He was interrupted by Fern, who burst through his tent flaps not five minutes later.

"What have you done?" Fern asked, barely concealing his anger.

Oakheart continued to arrange things, giving the impression that he was deep in thought. He knew what Fern was asking, but he was not beholden to anyone, least of all his friend. "Fern, good to see you," he said in mock surprise. "I have an errand for you."

Fern drew himself up to his full height but he still did not reach Oakheart's stature. "Do not change the subject. Everyone knows. What do you think you were doing?"

Oakheart put down a pile of clothes and turned towards Fern. "You have no say in what I do. And you can say nothing to Lady Sophy. She is oath-bound."

"Oath-bound?" Fern paled and fell back a step. "Y...you cannot be serious. You must break the oath. Straight away, before it is too late."

"I cannot. The oath is sealed in blood. Even if I could, I would not." Oakheart undid his medallion and held up the blood red leaf and then placed it back inside.

Fern sat heavily on Oakheart's bunk. "Your father will be livid. The high king will be furious that you have mangled his plans. Why, even now he has probably contracted some glorious maiden for your betrothed."

Oakheart nodded. "That is why you must return quickly and tell him to cancel any contract and cease negotiations. I am oath-bound and you must tell him the details."

Fern stared blank-faced for a few minutes. "Does she know the full extent of her commitment and what it means?"

Oakheart shrugged away guilt. "I think not. She will learn in time. Soon, in fact. You must leave straight away, your errand is most important."

Fern stood and straightened his jerkin. "I would rather stay. How can I face Leda with this news?"

Oakheart looked up in surprise. "What has Leda to do with it? You do not mean that she wanted to wed me?"

"Yes, of course. Why do you think I treated Lady Sophy so badly? To befriend her, to encourage her, was betrayal to my dear sister. I thought our friendship would lead you to consider Leda. Although, I must admit half the maidens in the kingdom and the wider expanse wanted to wed you from what I could see. Yet it is that plain, ignorant and ungiven girl that wins you. I do not understand what you see in her."

Oakheart stood stock still, eyes widening. "What did you say? Ungiven? Yes—Ungiven as in Vorn's final visions. Why did I not see it before?"

Fern threw up his hands. "What are you talking about? She cannot use the *given* is what I meant.'

"Yes, I know what you meant. Go now, please."

Fern made to argue more, but something in Oakheart's angry stare made him hold off.

"Very well. I will be ready to depart within the hour."

After Oakheart saw Fern on his way, he went to speak to his men before there were any more slights on Sophy's honour. He could not face Lillia. Not yet.

When he returned to his tent, Lillia was waiting for him. It was with trepidation that he commenced this interview. He had flouted the forest maiden's chaperonage.

"It was for the best," he said, before Lillia could open her mouth.

"The best? If so, why did you not share this motivation with me? You have made a mockery of me and my duty."

"I know I have injured you with my actions."

"And what about the girl? Her feelings? Her tender heart?"

"It seemed the only way to keep her safe, by allowing her to be close to me."

"So you bedded this young girl to protect her?" Lillia swore under her breath. "That is ridiculous."

"We are oath-bound. There is no shame in that—"

"Hah...shame? What is that compared to honesty and truth?"

"I do not understand you."

Lillia stalked to the front of the tent and then paused. Turning back to him, she said, "Do you love her? Can you live with a loveless oath? Does she know your heart?"

Oakheart looked down at the floor of the tent. He knew he had bound himself, but love? Could he love anyone, particularly someone he could not 'see'? "Regardless of my feelings, Sophy's care has passed to me."

"I have never been so sorry to lose a burden. I hope it turns out well. I have been your friend for a long time. I care for her, Oakheart. Do not break her heart. Do not wound your own."

With that last word she was gone and the tent flap hung limp.

❧ 41 ❧

WITH EYES OPENED

SOPHY MANAGED to avoid Oakheart for the rest of the day, but eventually hunger drew her to return for the meal. It was quiet repast. No one spoke much. Sophy avoided looking at Oakheart. After finishing her food, Lillia slipped quietly away and went to their shared tent after giving Sophy a long, expectant stare. She could only shrug, not quite understanding what Lillia was silently asking of her. Did she guess what she had done? She hoped not.

When she opened her eyes again, Oakheart was looking at her steadily and his scrutiny made it difficult for her to eat. Her chewing slowed until she lost her appetite altogether. The way he looked at her brought vivid memories of their time under the tree. She tried humming to herself and looking around the clearing to take her mind off what she was thinking. Already, she was feeling rather warm.

One by one, his men retired. While she watched some of them head for their blankets, Oakheart stood and walked over to her. He squatted next to her.

"Will you join me in my tent, Sophy?" he whispered to her sweetly, placing a loose tendril of her hair behind her ear. He smiled, eyes sparkling with reflected firelight.

She slapped his hand away. "I will not. You're joking, surely?"

He laughed at her response. "No, I am in earnest."

Sophy put her hands to her cheeks as they were burning with embarrassment. Again, he laughed as he watched her reaction. Before he finished laughing, she hastily climbed to her feet and stormed off. She grabbed a pot of hot water and went into the tent she shared with Lillia. A single firestick burnt in its holder. Lillia was awake in her bed staring at the roof of the tent.

"Are you all right?" Sophy asked as she stripped off to bathe.

Lillia took her eyes of the roof of the tent and glanced at her. "I am well, Sophy. And you?"

"Oh, I'm okay." Sophy lathered herself and tipped the warm water over her body. After a quick dry off with the towel, she put on her nightgown and slid into her bed. She couldn't bring herself to look at her friend. As she huddled into the blankets, and Lillia quenched the light, Sophy could almost hear the forest whispering about what she had been doing with Oakheart that day.

She didn't wake until first light, when she was being kissed and then caressed in her very private places. It was like she was dreaming about that wonderful time with Oakheart all over again. She smiled and groaned luxuriously, until she gasped with surprise. Her eyes flew open, and she realised that Oakheart was indeed kissing her and that she was in his tent. He stopped and moved his head back to gaze at her.

"Good morn, Sophy. You slept well…Are you well?"

"Oakheart?" she said, pulling out of his embrace with a blanket drawn up to her chin. Then she glared at him. "What in hell's name have you done? You cannot bring me into your tent. Everyone will start talking?"

He caressed her face tenderly and whispered sweetly, "They already know."

Bolting upright, she yelled, "What? How?"

"I told them, of course," he replied, reaching for her to draw her back up against his bare chest.

"What?" she yelped in surprise and tried to beat his hands off her.

"We are oath-bound," he said matter-of-factly, as if she would understand the significance of the statement. "You have done nothing of which to be ashamed."

"Oath-bound?" she repeated. "What does that signify? Although already I think I'm not liking the sound of it."

"Well," he began, as he lay back casually and put his arms behind his head. She noted belatedly that he was naked. So was she. "'Tis sort of like being wed."

She choked.

His greens eyes rested on her. "We will need to formalise the arrangement when we can and seek permission from Dellbright," he said in all seriousness. Then he smiled at her incredulous look and continued. "But the oath is binding and recognised." He put his arms around her again, sliding his hands softly up her arms.

"Bloody oath, it's not. It can't be." She bounded out of his arms, carefully avoiding his huge hands. Snatching at her discarded nightdress, she tried to put it on, but she couldn't seem to distinguish which end was which.

Oakheart lay on his side, blanket draped over his hips. He hadn't moved but he tracked her movements.

She threw the tangled clothing on the floor, trying to fight back the panic. "You don't mean I'm married to you, do you? I mean, you are playing a trick on me."

His blanket slid off as he came over to her. She received a rather healthy look at what she failed to the day before. She was in no mood to be impressed. She was shaking as he tugged her by the hand and led her back to his bed. "In a sense you could say that we are married," he said as proceeded to nibble at her neck.

Distracted, she turned to him. "In what sense?"

"In every sense. We exchanged a vow, a promise, called upon the *given* to witness it and then it was confirmed by deed...and blood."

"So it's true. I am married. But...I'm too young to be married," she wailed and tried to push him away, but he was too big to budge. "Couldn't we have...you know...lay together...without the oath bit?"

"Yes, 'tis done on occasion. Without an oath, the joining is not binding. But I would not dishonour you so."

"This can't be happening to me," she breathed. "Surely you...I mean…I don't understand. You don't love me, do you?" Her voice was quiet but the question floated in the air clear and bold.

"I have more faith in oaths than I do in love."

"That's no answer. Why would you bind yourself to someone you didn't love?"

His eyelashes shaded his eyes. "I have seen the effect of fickle love on others. But the oath in this land is true. Like high king Vorn, I have bided my time and I have made a choice."

"Vorn? The big guy in the tapestry? What has he got to do with you being oath-bound with me?"

"Vorn was wise and through his wisdom he was happy."

"And?"

"I try to follow his example." He was smiling that smile again.

Gooseflesh rose on her arms and a tingle grew at the base of her spine. The mention of Vorn unnerved her. "And did he love his wife?" She pushed a lump of tangled hair out of her eyes.

"I have no idea. How can I know that? It was so long ago?"

"You brought it up. Don't play cute with me."

"I do not play 'cute', at least, I think I do not. You have challenged me, riled me and withstood my punishments. I care for you, Sophy. Our joining will be fruitful and…"

"Fruitful? You mean children? But I'm only eighteen, I think." She had lost track of how long she had been there.

"Of course, I mean children Sophy. 'Tis the natural consequence of…of….mating. You need not worry about your age, I have enough years for the both of us."

Alarm bells were going off. How did this happen to her? It was a kiss. Her eyes narrowed. "How old are you?"

"I have passed thirty summers," he said, assessing her, ready to leap in case she made for the tent flaps.

"You don't look thirty. You can't be that old."

He frowned at her. "I am what I am. I cannot change it. 'Tis said at the retreat that the *given* lengthens our lives."

"How old is Dellbright then?"

"My cousin is a year younger."

Sophy was startled. "But he looks no more than a teenager." There really was a lot about this place that she didn't know or understand.

"Sophy, come here. You are avoiding the task at hand." Before she could dodge out of range, he tugged her forward, flipped her gently on her back and he began attacking her by gently nibbling away at her defences.

"Oh God, this really shouldn't be happening." Her eyes rolled up as she revelled in the sensations snaking through her. When he touched her nipples with his arm as he went to embrace her, she moaned.

"But it is, little jewel," he replied.

Leaning down, he began a breath-stealing kiss. How did this happen? She wanted to be drawn in. He felt so good. His skin on her skin, firm against soft. All of her arguments dropped away as she joined Oakheart's sensuous rhythm. The more she responded, the more urgent his caresses became.

Tears bathed her cheeks as she experienced that moment again, when all the tension peaked then undid itself.

"Come to me, Sophy. Share the *given* with me," he whispered urgently in her ear. "Look at me."

Opening her eyes, she saw his burned with fire. The crystal leaf in her chest throbbed. She thought she had experienced ecstasy before through him, but now he took her elsewhere. Where each breath seemed to take an age, where each heartbeat lay suspended, where each ripple of pleasure eddied and flowed along the pleasure senses as if suspended in thought.

UNITED FOR A TIME

THE FOREST FOLK arrived before nightfall, and Lillia's explosive yelp of surprise made Sophy look up. She had left Oakheart's tent for a moment of privacy when she spied a dark-haired man stepping out of the forest to embrace her friend.

Slight movement around the edges of the clearing caught her attention. The forest seemed to come alive with people. Short of stature and dressed in tones of brown, green and grey, they emerged from among the trees carrying various items, including freshly killed game and various other food items.

From the reception she was receiving, it appeared that Lillia was well liked and had been missed. There were hoots and happy shouts as Lillia was thoroughly kissed by a man, who Sophy presumed to be her husband. He had a touch of grey above his temples. While occupied in greeting each other, their clan members tousled them with slaps and shoves.

Once Lillia and her husband stopped to draw breath, Lillia wiped silent tears of happiness from her cheek. Sophy smiled tentatively. It had been many months since Lillia had been among her people and she was surprised, now that she witnessed the reunion, how well Lillia had borne the separation.

Lillia caught her eye and waved her over. "Come, my lady. Please meet my husband, Mellowbark."

Feeling shy, Sophy greeted Mellowbark in the way Lillia had taught her, arms crossed, hands touching her shoulders and bowed to the waist. A presence at her shoulder and she guessed Oakheart had come to greet the new arrivals.

"Greetings and well met, Mellow. You have met Lady Sophy," Oakheart looked sideways at her. Sophy could do nothing but blush when she realised that this was the first time she had shown her face outside since spending the night in Oakheart's tent.

"We are recently oath-bound." Oakheart draped a weighty arm over her shoulder.

Lillia's expression indicated that they would be discussing the thwarting of her chaperonage sometime soon.

"Congratulations, Oakheart, and not well before time. Among the forest kin you would already be a grandfather by now."

"I am not that old."

Mellow burst into laughter and Sophy guessed that it was a standing joke between them. When he calmed himself, he said, "Time and reason to celebrate, I think." He gave Lillia a hug before moving a step aside.

Oakheart lifted his arm from Sophy's shoulder, tweaked her ear, and then gestured for Mellow to go ahead of him. There was an almighty thwack as Oakheart hit Mellow on the back and said, "So how are you, old man?"

Off they went, leaving Sophy with Lillia. Sophy's face still hot, and she tried to look everywhere, except at Lillia. However, her friend broke into her reverie. "Come, my lady, we must prepare ourselves. I think the dark blue with silver trim is most appropriate for you. As for me, I think I will wear that dark green leafed dress from Silverdale, for none like it is to be found here in Gilton Forest. If this is to be where I have my reunion with my husband then I must make it a special occasion." Her eyes twinkled mischievously as she took Sophy's arm. "I remember that you complimented me on how well it looked on me."

Sophy found her voice. "Yes."

Lillia held the tent flaps open to allow her to pass inside, and then drew the dress out of one of the chests. "My lady, who would have thought that you wearing Oakheart's colours would lead to your oath-bonding." She chuckled to herself.

Sophy's colour rose. "I...oh, Lillia, it's not what it seems. I didn't realise...that we...that...um..." When she couldn't get her sentence out she gave up in frustration. "Oh bother."

Lillia only laughed more heartily. Then seeing Sophy's discomfort she said, "It is natural to feel a little strange. I remember my oath-bonding to Mel... But enough of my tales. We must prepare for this special night."

She clucked as she helped Sophy to dress and then, in turn, let Sophy assist her to put on the green gown. The smell of roasting meat wafted into their tent and Sophy's stomach growled in a very unladylike way. She tried to quell it by holding her abdomen.

"My, Sophy, what have you been doing to get so hungry?"

Sophy's eyes widened. "Lillia, please."

The sounds of laughter joined the delicious odours. "Come, Lillia," Mellow called. There was a sound of a person being shoved.

"Stay, Lillia, and send Sophy out." Oakheart's laugh was accompanied by other laughs and cat calls.

"Buck up, Sophy. I think the festivities have already commenced." Arm in arm, Sophy and Lillia walked out regally to join the festivities.

"Well, well," Mellow said bowing like a courtier. "What noble treasures have we here in this majestic kingdom?" He threw his arms wide indicating the forest around them. He smiled at Sophy, but his eyes burned with desire when they rested on Lillia.

Oakheart beckoned to her and Sophy joined him, letting his powerful arm encircle her waist.

It was quiet. The light was fading and the shadows exhaled. The forest darkened and green leaves turned to black. The occasional bird chirped and then quieted. The rhythmic twitter of an animal or insect punctuated the night.

Sophy was uneasy. She was oath-bound, and she had no idea what that meant for her or the future. She opened her mouth to speak but Oakheart swallowed her words with a kiss that rivalled Mellow's welcome. She struggled, conscious of the onlookers, but he only deepened the kiss, sending his tongue to tease hers. Soon there were calls of encouragement and cheers from the onlookers. When he finally released her, she could barely stand and had to lean against him. He raised her face with his hand beneath her chin and angled it left and right.

"What is it? Do I have dirt on my face?" she asked dreamily.

"No. Just checking to see that I had the desired effect." He turned her round and led her to the feast.

"Which was?"

"To replace your embarrassment with desire."

"I never thought you could be so shameless!" She couldn't hold back her aghast expression. "You, who always lectured me about being a lady and behaving properly."

"Mmmm...you are right. But you were not mine then, and the forest folk are more open and free in expressing themselves. Let us enjoy it while we still can. Silverdale and Valley Keep will be different."

☙❧

SOPHY HAD NO OPTION AFTER THE FESTIVITIES, BUT TO GO TO Oakheart's tent. It was not only that Oakheart had a good hold of her, in case she took herself off to the forest to hide, but Mellow was with Lillia and they had retired early, like a couple of honeymooners.

Oakheart carried Sophy to his tent and, while she was in his arms, she looked at him closely. She could still only see the bland face, yet his presence warmed her, it was there in the eyes, something that could not be hidden or masked. He laid her on his bed and kissed her around the neckline of the dress, as she squirmed.

"Stop, stop. What are you doing?"

"Kissing you."

"I can see that, but shouldn't we be doing something else?"

"No."

"What do you mean, no?"

"Do you remember the week after Princess Aria's wedding?'

"Yes"

"Well...?"

"Well what? It was so boring. I couldn't understand what they could possibly be doing for all that time?"

He nuzzled her softly at the juncture of her neck. She moaned in response. "You are about to find out."

"Please, Oakheart, be serious."

He nuzzled some more.

"No, I don't mean that. I still don't understand what Aria has to do with you kissing me."

He stopped nuzzling and lifted himself up on his elbows so he could see her face. "This is our wedding week."

She glanced around the tent. "We don't have time for that."

"Do not concern yourself. Lillia is having a reunion with Mellow so everybody will work around it. After our week is finished then we will move on to Queen's town."

"Do you mean to tell me that we are to stay in your tent for a week and do nothing but..." She saw his smile and understood his answer. "I will not be able to walk at the end of it."

"That is how it should be," he said and proceeded to extract her from her gown.

⚜

THE NEXT MORNING, THE TENT FLAP OPENED, DRAWING SOPHY TO weary wakefulness. Two of Oakheart's men carried in a small tub. Others followed and emptied scented hot water into it. The sound of the water swishing brought her fully to wakefulness. Oakheart thanked his men and turned towards her, rubbing his hands.

"Now, my little lady, I will bathe you."

"You will?" She couldn't repress her laugh. "I'm sorry, but I cannot picture you as a ladies' maid."

"You jest at a time like this? Come," he drew closer and dragged her from the covers. His chest was bare and he obviously didn't mind getting his breeches wet as he eased her gently into the tub.

"There, 'tis not so bad. A ladies' maid...I must admit the occupation does appeal to me."

"Stop," she protested as he grabbed a cloth and attempted to rub her down. "No one has bathed me since I was a child."

He held her hand and continued to probe with the cloth. "You tell an untruth. I myself have bathed you on a few occasions."

"You are teasing me. Of course you haven't. Lillia would not have let you do such a…thing."

His left eyebrow rose. "You are mistaken. Lillia needed help to care for you in your illness. I bathed you…among other things. Now do not take to the blush. Your maiden honour was not tainted. And believe me, my thoughts did not stray to interesting things. Now sit back and let me wash your hair. I have not had the pleasure."

Holding his gaze for a short moment, she nodded and lay back. Strong fingers caressed her scalp as he lathered spicy soap into her hair. With a pitcher of warm water, he rinsed it clean. Feeling relaxed, she lay back. "What did you think when you saw Aria and me come out of the forest with Dellbright?" she asked.

"Nothing but surprise I assure you. 'Twas the most unexpected thing." His hands traced circles on the skin of her abdomen.

"Yet you didn't show any surprise."

He rubbed her skin until it was pink and glowing and then lifted her from the water. As he spread her out on the bed, he patted her dry with a linen towel, taking his time as he examined every part of her. "It was strange. But what could we do? There were two of you and that was that."

"And what did you think of me back then?"

Oakheart chewed the inside of his cheek for a minute before answering. A diplomatic profession had its advantages, she thought to herself as she watched him battle it out.

"You seemed to be very….self-centred, spoilt, impossible, vain, aggressive, childish, intelligent and lost."

Sophy burst out laughing. "That about summed me up back then. I was seriously not coping with Argenterra."

Kisses rained down on her face. "'Twas hard for you. I could see it even though I did not know you well then. I was fascinated with you, too. Who would not be? You came from beyond the Crystal Tree Woods, from another world. I held back though, for the reasons we have discussed before. I could 'see' Aria but not you. It unnerved me. Aria's natural beauty and elegance overshadowed you in Dellbright's eyes but I am sure I have the best of the bargain."

"I don't think so. Aria is everything you say she is. It is why she is such a good friend. We are different but we understand each other. I miss her terribly. It was such a blow when she married Dellbright. I hope she is happy."

"So you think she may not be happy in her choice?"

"No. She loves him...and I think he loves her. But you know him better."

"He loves her, yes. Never have I seen him so smitten. But I fear Dellbright is needy."

"Needy?"

"Yes, he needs her love."

"Is that bad to need someone's love?"

Oakheart frowned, his mouth pouted. "Not usually, but sometimes the need can be too great and its source unrelated to the object of that love."

"I don't understand...I wouldn't like to love you without you loving me back."

"But that is not the case, is it? Do you love me?"

She closed her eyes. Her emotions were in a whirl. "I don't know if I love you yet. I care for you as a friend, as a companion." He bit her neck gently. "I desire you...but I..."

He cut her off with a kiss. "I care for you, too. And for a long time now I have felt an attraction to you, one I could not understand or tame."

"Really? You hid it well, then. You have spent weeks ignoring me."

"I was not ignoring you, really." Oakheart kissed her again, and she forgot about the past and thought only of the moment. She managed in the dark of night to tell him of Hanal's visit to her rooms. Oakheart's anger had her worried. "How did he get into your room?" he near yelled.

"I told you, he came while Lillia had her audience with the high king." She rubbed her hand over his forehead lightly, hoping to distract him.

"He did not touch you or..."

"Not really...he threatened to take me with him though. For some reason he thought I was important...but I convinced him that I was nothing."

Oakheart sighed. "I apologise for not being there to protect you. I should have been."

"What could you have done? You were sent away." She snuggled into his shoulder and luxuriated in his warm arms.

"Yes...I know."

DARK TENDRILS' TOUCH

OAKHEART STIRRED IN HIS SLEEP. Sophy moaned and struggled. Raising himself up on his elbow, he peeled the blanket back to wake her. He stopped. Embedded in her chest, the glowing crystal leaf threw light into the shadowy recesses of the tent. He had to blink a few times before he could make out the outline. It had grown. The glow encompassed her legs and arms until she was all but radiance. She cried out. "Aria...Aria!"

"Sophy, wake up," he said gently. She thrashed about, her hand whacking him in the side of the head. He blinked and shook his head slightly. There was something not right about her dream. Why was the leaf glowing with power?

He lay his head down on her chest and closed his eyes. The *given* surged through him from the leaf. As he slowed his breathing, he began to catch fragments of her dream. It was strong, powerful and sharp with malice.

Rufus in his white form, adorned in feathered wings, danced with Aria. He held her strangely and then with glowing red eyes thrust Aria in front of him with his clawed hands clasping her stomach. Aria's eyes shone with pain and love.

His talons tightened painfully and blood began to drip down Aria's gown. Roughly, he shoved her, dragging her skirts up. Then as she screamed, he mounted and rode her while reverting to his true feral shape. Aria's screams rent the air while Rufus's eyes shone brighter and his form grew more muscled. Aria's skin faded to grey, her eyes became dull. With a final thrust, he dropped the hollow shell of her body on the floor and smiled. Then Rufus's face took on the semblance of Oakheart's own face, distorting it with evil.

Oakheart drew upon the *given* to wrench himself free, seeking Sophy within the maelstrom of colours as the vision began to reassemble to replay from the beginning. His breathing was hoarse as he sat up. Sophy still thrashed as she fought the vision. He slapped her, pleaded with her to wake. At last, her eyes flew open, dark pools of fear.

"God, Aria. Aria? I have to help her."

He drew her to him, holding her tight. "Quiet now. Aria is with Dellbright, and he will protect her. Rufus is not in Valley Keep."

She cried with reaction, wiping the tears from her face. "Another dream of the dark?" she asked.

"Not quite." Oakheart furrowed his brow, uncertain what to tell his new, oath-bound wife.

Sophy sat up, rubbing her eyes with the back of her hands. Her hair was standing on end in tangled clumps. That was more to do with Oakheart's lovemaking than anything else.

"What do you mean? You experienced it somehow?"

Oakheart nodded warily. "Yes, I saw. But it was a sending. Rufus is close. Seeking you, perhaps. But it was too directed and too strong to be a dream of the dark. Have you experienced others like that?"

"Some. That was the strongest and the scariest. Why would he send me visions of Aria? Why would he defile her image?"

He looked into her troubled, dark eyes. "I know not, but I feel there is no good in it. It leaves me with a sense of foreboding. There is danger for you, that much I already knew, but I did not connect Aria with it. You are bound in friendship, and he could use that to manipulate you. Together, you would have been stronger. I now regret your separation."

"Then you also think Aria is in danger?"

"Not at this moment, but Rufus surely has her in his sights. He understands your bond with her."

"We must warn her! Can you use the talkstone?"

She rushed over to get the stone but before she laid her hand on it, he said, "No."

"Why? It uses the *given*."

"Yes I know, but it is tuned to her. Adage altered the crystal while he was at the keep so it would work for her alone. They are rare things and only the very skilled adepts can focus them. It is beyond my skill to get it to respond to my command."

"I didn't realise you arranged for Aria to have it."

He flushed with embarrassment. "Yes. It was mine. A gift from the retreat."

"That was so good of you. But if we cannot call her, how can we warn her?"

"We cannot warn her immediately. For that we can only trust in the *given*. I will send a messenger, of course. But I know not how long it will take in this weather to reach her. We must hope she calls to us beforehand. Come, rest. I would dispel that creature's touch from your mind."

"Rest? I've been resting"

"Yes, I know," he said, folding her into the cradle of his arms. He ran his hand down her smooth white skin, feeling the curve of her hips. He smiled when she sighed in response. It was amazing to him that his touch could evoke such a response that she felt the call of his blood. Outside, the dawn was nearly breaking. His oath-bound wife melted like butter as he kneaded her breasts and stroked her neck with his tongue. Her movements became urgent and uncontrolled and he knew he had dispelled all thoughts of the 'sending' when she tugged his hair and kissed him deeply, stealing his breath.

He entered her warmness with his ears filled with her cries. As he moved within her, he heard footsteps. He slowed, smothering Sophy's cries with his hand. Her eyes flew open. Nothing. Only the tension of expectation filled the air. She bit his hand and he lunged again. Her cry was loud.

"Oakheart?" said a voice from outside the tent.

"Mel?" Oakheart was alert.

"Yes. May I enter?"

The tent flap moved. Oakheart disengaged from Sophy quickly and slid to her side. Sophy tugged the blanket around her, too shocked by the interruption to blush.

Mel stood inside the tent opening, his voice tense and tight. "Illart brings word. Screavers have been detected in the outreaches. They are on their way here."

Oakheart sat up quickly and tied his hair back. "Wait for me outside the tent. I will join you shortly."

Mel retreated, dropping the tent flap behind him.

Oakheart reached for his breeches, pulled them on and then struggled into his shirt. While he searched for his long-sleeved doublet, he glanced at Sophy. "Stay here for the moment. I will send you word."

He rushed out, bracing himself against the sudden chill.

⁂

SOPHY SCRAMBLED ABOUT ON HANDS AND KNEES, SEARCHING FOR her clothes. The whole tent was in disarray, which was expected, she supposed, considering how her time had been engaged. The tent flap flew open sending a cool breeze against her skin.

"Lillia?"

The forest maiden entered with a bowl of steaming liquid. "I bring you this. You will need it, I think. We have some little time until we depart." Lillia walked over to a chest, cleared the clothing and goblets off the top with a sweep of one hand and lay down her basin.

Sophy watched the proceedings, a tad embarrassed by the mess. She hadn't been expecting visitors. "We're leaving? But I can't ride a horse...er like this...I can barely walk."

"Sit in this."

"But what is it?"

"Do not argue. I have anticipated your need. I myself have been thus afflicted."

"Oh," she replied and with her blanket draped over her, she did indeed sit in the basin.

"More herbs?"

"Yes. They will soothe the tenderness."

While Sophy was thus submerged in the herbal concoction, Lillia swept through the tent with swift efficiency. She folded clothes and tossed dirty plates and goblets to Oakheart's aide outside the tent.

During the last exchange, she returned with a suit of forest folk clothing. Leather leggings, a green and brown jerkin, flax woven shirt and soft boots with fine climbing hairs on the soles made up the pile.

"We have no more time. You must dress in these."

Sophy lifted herself from the basin and dried herself as she walked tentatively to the pile of clothes. She did feel better. She could walk without pain.

"Thank you. I feel better already. And thank you for the clothes, they're...very practical."

"They are suitable for travelling through the forest. A pretty gown will get you killed, but these will help to camouflage you."

"Killed? I thought we were safe here."

"I thought so, too, but things have changed. Screavers stalk the outer rim. We must hasten to Queen's Town. Only there will the power of the Heart Tree protect us."

"Screavers?"

"I forgot you have not heard of them. Here let me help you tie those up. Screavers are cousins to warren beasts, though they are larger, faster and more vicious. We do not get them often in these parts or in such numbers. If enough attack, they could kill many of us. There, it is done. Come."

When they left the tent, Oakheart's aide and a few of his men ran in to stow the gear and bring down the tent.

Forest folk and Oakheart's men worked together to screen the horses with branches in their pen. Larger items of luggage were hidden in hollowed out trees, usually used for storage. The rest of the gear was divided up and handed around so that all could share the carriage of it.

Oakheart's voice travelled across the clearing as he talked with Mellowbark. Occasionally, he would shout an order or instruction and always called for haste. Approaching him with Lillia at her side, Sophy's tension increased. Their wedding week was at an end, cut short by fear and the march of death. His expression was severe, and his frown grew as he listened to Mellow's urgent re-counting. With a wave of his hand, he motioned Mellow to silence and tried to smile as she neared.

"You look very becoming," Oakheart said. "You fill out the forest garb readily."

"How can you talk like that? Lillia told me we're in danger. How do we possibly ride through these trees?"

Mellow answered. "We cannot. My men have secured the horses. They will be safe. We must take the forest road and head to the heart."

"On foot?"

"Yes," Oakheart said. He glanced at Lillia. "Is she hale?"

"Yes, excellency."

Sophy's face heated. Was nothing private with these people?

◌◌◌

SOPHY FOLLOWED OAKHEART ON THE FOREST PATH. HE ASSISTED her over the difficult parts, sometimes nearly throwing her to another limb or into the waiting arms of the forest folk. The way was dark and damp, as if the sun's rays never ventured this far into the forest. Large red-capped mushrooms decorated the base of the trees and the smell of damp mould permeated the air. It rained, and the sound of the drops beating against the branches and dripping off trees echoed and reverberated. The hugeness of the forest made her feel small and alone even though she was among a group of travellers.

Lillia bounded from limb to limb and tree to tree as if she was born with that talent. Oakheart led Sophy along an easier path, knowing that they couldn't travel the way of the tree people. She had a hard time imagining Oakheart doing so. If anything, he was too big. He was twice as wide and nearly twice as tall, as the tallest of the tree people she had seen.

They stopped to rest and the rain receded to a light drizzle, sufficient to remind everyone that it was still damp. Dried meat and stale bread served for a meal. The group clustered in small numbers at the base of the enormous trees. Mellow smiled as he approached with a large round of bread for Oakheart. He and Sophy were leaning against a fallen tree trunk, so huge Sophy couldn't even see over the top of it. She was just estimating how tall it was when Lillia dropped onto the top of it. In her fright she nearly dropped her portion of bread.

Oakheart stood behind her and rubbed her back with his free hand to soothe her. Mellow threw Oakheart the loaf of bread, which he caught and theatrically bit into it. Sophy did her best not to laugh as Oakheart demolished the bread. His appetite was a well-known trait and often joked about.

After scrabbling down, Lillia spoke quickly and tersely and the tone of her voice foreshadowed trouble. "We must move faster. A herd of screavers are near. They have picked up our scent. We must cross the Fell Falls quickly, before they come upon us."

"I cannot believe screavers dare to venture this deep into Gilton Forest," Oakheart said.

Lillia drew closer. "Screavers have seldom passed beyond the out rim of the forest before. I had never even heard of them in such numbers until last summer. Then they started attacking the smaller outlying clans, those of us that have joined with the overlanders and live beyond the forest's protection. Since I have travelled with you, they have grown bold. My clan tells me only the land between Fell Falls and Queen's Town is immune to the beasts. It is well my mission to bring you here was successful. My clan fought a horde of them a few moons past, so they thought their numbers had lessened, but Illart has scouted them a day behind us, which is why they have our scent."

Oakheart offered his hand. "We must travel as the tree people do, Sophy. Do you think you can manage it?"

"Yes, but why are they coming? Is it Rufus again?"

"I fear so." He frowned as he heaved her up to Mellow's waiting hands on the top of the log. Oakheart leapt up unaided and then unfurled a rope that Mellow gave him. He wrapped it around her waist and tied it with a knot.

"Now, little jewel," he kissed the tip of her nose. "You will not fall. Come."

He grabbed her hand and followed the fleet-footed forest folk. His men followed in the same way; being frequent travellers they knew the way of these people. Sophy slipped and panted, as she did her best to follow along. She looked down to the darkness below and felt faint. Leaves brushed against her, leaving oily green smears to stain her clothes; soon she had dark patches all over her. She leapt along with Oakheart between two huge limbs. The dark bottomless gaping maw below her loomed up and her heart leapt into her throat. Her hand slipped from Oakheart's. She cried out in fear as she fell. The rope on her waist tightened. Arm over arm, Oakheart pulled her back onto the tree limb. Then when Oakheart secured her in his hand again, they continued. With no time to be comforted, she continued on.

The sound of the beasts approaching made her skin crawl. They sounded like bears and cats mewling and growling. The trees seemed to shiver around them as the screavers ripped and shredded their way through the living forest.

The sound of the falls grew closer "Faster," Lillia yelled, and they increased the pace. Sophy was propelled along by the speed of Oakheart's gait. Suddenly he stopped, and she ploughed into the back of him. They were at the falls. At first, she had no idea how they were to cross. Edging around Oakheart on the limb, she saw what passed for a rope bridge with a wheel on it. Then she happened to see the chasm opening up underneath it and was suddenly queasy.

Half the group had already started across. Dismayed, she realised they were the last —probably because of her slowness. The screavers sounded close, very close. She could hear their ragged breathing. Oakheart moved her in front of him, and they edged nearer to the bridge. Some of the forest people managed to swing across on hidden ropes. They appeared so graceful, as they swung with the rising mist from the falls wafting off their feet. The forest was being crushed around them. There were a few screams, Oakheart's men or forest folk, Sophy didn't know. Oakheart turned back. She glanced quickly behind her and saw that his feet were planted firmly on the wide tree limb and he held his sword out in readiness.

"Come, Sophy," Lillia said, as she tugged her towards the wheel. "Do not be afraid, hang on."

Sophy put her hands on the wheel. "Don't worry about me, I've done this before. What about Oakheart?'"

Too late, Lillia gave her a huge shove, and it was all she could do to keep her hands on the wheel. She kept her eyes towards the other side, with the noise of the screavers intensifying as she fled. She was afraid for Lillia, Mellow and Oakheart. She saw one of the forest people with his hands outstretched to catch her. She let go and landed heavily. He grabbed the wheel and flung it back. Sophy edged over to peer across the divide. They appeared to be arguing on the other side. Lillia and Mellow grabbed the wheel together, leaving Oakheart alone. Then she heard a scream. It was hers.

A huge ugly beast leapt at Oakheart. Nothing could be done. Lillia and Mellow could not halt the wheel. They landed and then Mellow cut the rope.

"No!" Sophy yelled as she watched the rope and wheel drop into the crevasse. She couldn't repress her heart wrenching cry: "Oakheart!" He had no means to escape. She whirled on the forest folk. "What have you done?" she screamed at Mellow and Lillia. "You've killed him."

Another beast, then another, leapt at Oakheart, already blood stained his clothes. "It is for the best. There was nothing else we could do. They would cross otherwise and more than Oakheart would fall."

"Listen to Mellow. It was what Oakheart wished." Lillia was visibly distressed and wrung her hands together.

Sophy's gaze was riveted to the other side of the chasm, where Oakheart seemed to be holding his own, as he edged the lip. He seemed to be looking for a rope.

"Come, we must leave." Lillia pulled on Sophy's hand and dragged her along. Sophy yanked her arm back, but could not fight Lillia's vice-like grip.

"Come, my lady, we must flee. They may try and cross." Lillia's voice was tight.

"No!" Sophy said and something in her tone made Lillia loosen her hold. "You go. Lend me your bow. Perhaps I can hit some from here."

Lillia looked at her, then across the chasm at Oakheart. She slid her bow off her back, strung it, and handed it to Sophy with an arrow. She whistled once, shrill and loud—a signal.

Sophy edged to the verge, trying to get a clean shot. A beast was about to leap on Oakheart's back. She aimed, held her breath and let it out. The arrow held true and strong, thwacking against the screaver beast. Then, as if her arrow had been a sign, countless other arrows rained down on the beasts, killing them where they stood. The horde kept coming, but the lull caused by the onslaught of arrows allowed Oakheart to find purchase on a rope and to swing across. His first pass was not long enough so he pushed off again and leapt. Sophy tried to get around to where she thought he had landed, but was held back by Mellow.

"No, my lady. You must wait. Lillia will tend to him. Come," he said as he grabbed her by the arm.

"No," she said jerking her arm out of his grip.

"Oh yes, you will."

At his tone, Sophy's head jerked in his direction, suffocating anger near overwhelming her. He latched onto her forearm and forcibly dragged her along. "Let. Me. Go." She aimed a kick at his heels. He turned, glared at her and kicked her back. She punched him in the thigh. In retaliation, he grabbed her fists and squeezed.

"Cowards... Betrayers..." she hissed at him.

His punch came from nowhere. She fell backwards as yellow stars flew in a halo around her head.

❧ 44 ❧

INTO THE HEART

Sophy had no idea how long after Mellow had hit her that she awoke in a dark room smelling of damp leaves and mould. Crawling along the floor, she groped around until she encountered a wall, and then felt along it until her fingers touched the edge of a door. Finding the handle, she pulled on it and when the door didn't budge, she beat on it. The injury to her jaw left her weak and light-headed. Worry for Oakheart made her persist in screaming for help—but no one came.

She slumped there feeling morose and dazed. Finally, the door opened. Lillia poked her head through the opening, light haloing her hair. "My lady? Are you well?" she asked, as if Sophy was a strange creature she had never seen before.

Bounding to her feet, Sophy faced the woman, fist clenched and smarting from betrayal. "Let me out of here." Her voice sounded like a caged animal.

Lillia stepped through the door, leant against it and surveyed her with her agile gaze. "And where would you go, my lady?" Her voice was constrained and wary. Sophy was puzzled by her behaviour.

"To find Oakheart."

Letting out a sigh, Lillia then nodded like a salute. "Come, I will take you to him. He is injured, but well." As Sophy passed out through the door, Lillia put her hand on Sophy's forearm. "Forgive Mellow's roughness. We feared for your safety and thought it best to bring you in here. Yet we feared also for the welfare of our friend Oakheart and all our kin. Mellow said you were difficult."

Sophy rubbed her chin where Mellow's fist had connected. "I was... with reason though."

Lillia frowned. "Your behaviour endangered everyone. My clan does not know you as I do. They are naturally suspicious. Yet they are friend to Oakheart and would protect him."

"You think I'm a danger to Oakheart? You left him to defend himself. I'm his oath-bound wife, doesn't that mean anything?" Sophy clenched her fists. Lillia's kin distrusted her, just when she thought all that was behind her.

Lillia clenched her jaw and after a moment of assessing Sophy's face, her tense expression eased. "I am pleased to hear you say it. Yes, it means a lot, Sophy. At this moment, Oakheart needs you to be strong. His injuries are severe. I have done what I can but—"

A slice of ice slid through her gut. "What? Tell me."

"Some of his men were lost. He will not take that well and right now he needs be encouraged. The price of repelling the screavers was high."

Sophy eyed her friend suspiciously as they walked. "Are you accusing me of something? I'm beyond making Oakheart's life difficult. I...care...for him. I...love...him," Sophy said, realising it for the first time.

Lillia drew her close and hugged her. "I am glad to hear it. Come, I will take you to him."

Night had fallen, and she could see the lights peeping out from small windows. The tree branches intertwined to make large walkways where people could walk at least six abreast. Walkways sloped between and joining the separate tiers. They took a ramp to the next level and stopped outside a bole. Lillia motioned her to enter and then turned and left.

Sophy gingerly moved her head around the door. A small lamp flickered in the corner. She could just make out a large form reclining on a bed.

"Oakheart?" she said softly.

There was no answer and no stirring under the blankets. She edged in and eased the door shut. Oakheart's hair spilled over the pillow, glowing yellow in the lamplight. His scratched face appeared puffy and a bandage was plastered to the left side of his neck. She stepped forward slowly, drinking in the detail. His chest rose and fell and her breathing fell into sync with his. One arm lay on top of the covers, scratched and rent along the forearm. His upper arm was swathed tightly in bandages.

The smell of herbs grew stronger as she neared. She blinked when he suddenly jerked and then winced in his sleep. There were other hurts, she surmised. She peeled back the blanket carefully. He was naked underneath, except for bandages. Dark blue bruises covered half of his ribs. His hip was grazed, perhaps from where he had hit the rock face as he fled. Just near his groin a bandage began and fanned out down his thigh. Blood seeped through the fabric and it looked as if he nearly lost a good part of his groin in the attack. She leant in close and smelled the scent of him and herbs and blood. She saw the gooseflesh rise on his skin, but before she replaced the covers, she stripped off her clothes and squeezed in next to him.

He breathed in and out, strong and clear. Tentatively, she put her hand on his chest and detected his strong and powerful heart beating. As she lay next to him, there was something else she sensed, a thread of awareness that pulsed with life. Oakheart's hand moved to her hair, and he stroked it once or twice. His eyes didn't open, but Sophy smiled and sniffed away her tears. He knew she was there and suspected that he drew comfort from her presence.

They slept. Sophy dreamed. Red eyes followed her as she ran. Oakheart called to her for help. The red surrounded her. She looked at her hands, and they were dripping blood. She looked up and Oakheart stood there, blood pouring from his wounds. His eyes were empty sockets, and when she looked into their black depths, she screamed. Oakheart screamed in her dream, and he screamed next to her. They were joined in the nightmare and were not released until Sophy was shaken and slapped.

She put up her hands. "What?" Sophy yelled as she struggled awake, dragging in heaving breaths.

Lillia loomed over her. "You were dark dreaming. I thought it best to wake you."

Sophy rubbed her chin. These forest folk had it in for her, she was sure. She eased her jaw. "Thanks, I think." Lillia's eyes left her and flicked to Oakheart.

"Sophy?" Oakheart said weakly.

She eased herself around and let her hand touch the undamaged parts of his face.

"I'm here," she answered and squeezed his hand. He closed his eyes and was back asleep in seconds.

"Let him rest. You need to rest, too. I will prepare a special herbal brew for you."

"I am letting him rest. What else do you think I'm doing? I want to be near him...you know how injured he is."

Lillia looked up from her preparations. "Yes, I know, I tended his wounds. Nearly the same spot as the warren beasts' attack. Whoever is behind this attack wishes to unman him."

Sophy's eyes widened, surprised by Lillia's matter-of-factness. "Really? But why would they want to do that? Why not kill him?"

"I know not. Perhaps the maiming of a person can give more satisfaction to those with evil intent. Death is a sleep, a resting place. A life maimed is long-suffering, a torment without end. Oakheart is an only son and it is his duty to sire an heir. What better way is there to make him fail than to take away the means to fulfil his duty?"

"I never thought of it like that." Her face began to heat as Lillia regarded her. Oakheart enjoyed making children, too, as she had discovered. He wasn't half bad at it, either. Lillia still regarded her, waiting.

"I'm too young to have children. I'm only eighteen or nearly nineteen."

"Nonsense," Lillia spluttered as she crushed herbs into her small cauldron, which was issuing steam. "I was wed to Mellow right after my first blooding. I had three children before I was your age."

Sophy's eyes bulged and she swallowed. "Three by my age? Then how many do you have now?"

"I've have fifteen children living. Hopefully that will be the last of it."

"So many...and you left them to go on a mission?"

"Yes, but most are old enough, and we share the raising of children here. I have tended many that were not my own, though kin they all are."

Sophy laid her head back down and closed her eyes for a moment. She tried to picture Lillia so young and with so many offspring, but she couldn't. By the look on Lillia's face her friend was on the verge of asking her something.

"What do you want to ask me?"

While she stirred her herbal brew, Lillia stared into space. "I wish to know how you managed to become Oakheart's oath-bound wife. One moment you were at war with each other, casting verbal missiles and smiting glances, and the next you were in his bed. How was such a thing accomplished?"

Sophy gazed at Lillia as she laid her face on her hand. "I...don't know where to start. I wanted to be friends with Oakheart. It pained me that we couldn't be friends. Everything I did seemed to end in disaster. After the Lake of Reflections, when I saw his true face and he mine, I thought there was some understanding between us, an attraction even. Yet, the path of friendship was a rocky as it always had been. In fact, it became worse."

"That I saw to my dismay, daily." Lillia rolled up her eyes.

"I guess I felt rejected by everything. The lake showed that I am who I am, though my true face is hidden. It also revealed that much of Oakheart was hidden from me. I don't understand magic, the *given*, so I can't even comprehend the how or the why. Oakheart was just as surprised. And still we could not shake free of our armour against each other that we had carefully built since we had met."

"Or?" the forest maiden prompted

"Or what? I see by your look you mean to accuse me. Yes, I was difficult and childish and spiteful to him. He only ever tried to help me."

"I am glad that you see it...finally. So what happened next?"

"The night we arrived in the Oaks Glade I was so down about everything. I was in a hole and I couldn't climb out. I wanted to get drunk and lose myself in oblivion. Yet, before I tasted too many drops of wine, I was alone with Oakheart. I can't say what made me do it. Some impulse, some feeling of the moment, the moonlight...I'm not sure. I kissed him."

"Was it then that you bound yourselves in oaths?"

"No," Sophy said. "He rejected my advances. I was hurt, wretched, confused. I went to bed dreading the next day, believing all chance of friendship was at an end. It was almost impossible to bear. I knew it wasn't the wine that made me do it, though it may have bolstered my courage."

"And then what? You were gone from the tent before I woke. That was surprising, to say the least."

"I went to a clearing nearby, a smaller ring of trees, to be alone to think."

"And what did this thinking bring you?"

"Not much comfort, I assure you, and then Oakheart turned up. I wanted to run away and hide rather than face his rejection again."

Lillia handed her a cup filled with brew. "But you did not run away."

Sophy shook her head. "It was puzzling. Oakheart was not angry with me. Nor did he want to reject me. He said I had to make an oath before I kissed him again. I did think it strange at the time. It was only a kiss, after all. But, when I repeated the words, he kissed me. Oh god, what a kiss! I swear to you that I had no idea where that kiss would lead. Oakheart had always been so...rigid about appearances, about doing what was right—prudish even. The next morning when I woke in his tent he told me I was his oath-bound wife and what that meant. I nearly died of fright."

Lillia frowned as she stroked the hair from Sophy's brow. "So he tricked you. You did not...seek to lure him?"

Sophy frowned. "Is that what you think? That I would do such a thing? I didn't know those words would make me his wife. I thought they meant that I had to be faithful to him and not sleep around with other men…which is sort of a big commitment for a kiss, now that I think about it. I was otherwise occupied at the time with him being so near to me, touching my hair, my neck…"

"It is hard to know what to think. I never thought Oakheart would trick you into an oath-bonding, yet he did. And he has his reasons, which he does not share. You knew not the consequences of what you did. You lay with Oakheart and told me not of it. I admit to being offended by the omission. But not by the act. For a long time now, I have known you two should be together. Both of you ignorant of your feelings."

"But Oakheart doesn't love me. He cares for me. He cares more for oaths than love, he told me so."

"Yes, that I can understand in him. He was abandoned for love, abandoned by love. It is no wonder he does not trust it. But you have love in your heart for him. I have seen it in you, for a long time now. Your deeds have proven it."

"Tell me more of this abandonment."

"Another time, perhaps. However, it is Oakheart's tale. Now, drink up and you can rest some more."

Dutifully, Sophy swallowed the evil tasting concoction. Lillia took the cup from her willing hand as already the brew made her drowsy. She heard Lillia's light tread as she departed, but she couldn't remember hearing the door close.

Oakheart was awake when next she woke. She eased out of the bed and tended him. He didn't like her fussing over him, especially when he could not leave the bed to relieve himself. Initially, she didn't know how to react. She was tempted to fetch Lillia but squelched that thought. She put on her best impersonation of the forest maiden and stood firm.

"Pee into the thing, Oakheart. I'm not expecting great prowess, just accuracy."

Oakheart raised an eyebrow at her comment. She could tell it hurt him to move any muscle on his face. His speech was even affected.

"Sophy…" he mumbled with a hint of anger. "Go awaysth."

"No. I want to be with you. Didn't you tend me when I was ill?"

"Yesth," he mumbled again. "But you were unconsciousth."

"Well, that's worse. How did I know you didn't take advantage of me? I'll go and make you some herbal tea while you work on your aim. Okay."

Sophy turned around leaving Oakheart in bed with the strange contraption to relieve himself in. She whistled and hummed as she worked, wondering all the while whether he could eat something solid. Food would definitely improve his mood.

With occasional assistance from Lillia, she tended him and, after a few days, he was stronger and less tender. At least he could limp about the bole room to relieve himself. His mood wasn't good. He snapped at her many times when his leg pained him. He was angry when she absented herself and angry when she returned with food.

Eating mollified him, so she thought, and visits from Lillia and Mellow certainly helped. Oakheart wanted to see his men and, reluctantly, Lillia agreed that he was well enough to do this the next day.

Oakheart woke early and struggled into his borrowed clothes, as his had been cut away when his wounds had been tended. The new ones were not quite big enough for him. The men assembled and three were missing. Oakheart noticed straight away. He greeted them all one by one, thanked them for their valour, though she could tell the way his hand trembled slightly that he was hurting on the inside.

Sophy was surprised by her own insight into his moods and thoughts. The realisation came suddenly that he was no longer bland. Their relationship had somehow eaten away at whatever enchantment prevented her from seeing the true Oakheart. There was a bond there between them; she could almost see it, touch it, a feather-light thread of ether.

The men left, and Oakheart gingerly lowered himself down on the stool by the fire. Yellow and blue flames licked the heat stones, and he seemed to lose himself in thought. Sophy stood in the dark shadows watching silently. When she thought he had enough time to come to terms with everything, she stepped quietly up behind him and rubbed his tense shoulders. He didn't speak, but his muscles relaxed.

He put his hand on hers, lifted her hand to his mouth and kissed it. Urging her in front of him, he drew her close and hugged her. Sophy stood and hugged him back carefully, aware of all his various hurts. Then he kissed her deeply, his kiss hot and urgent and burned with loss. Sophy longed to surrender to it. Somewhere, a little voice told her to back off, that he was not ready and was still too hurt, but his touch was louder. Her clothes were shucked in an instant, and Oakheart's soon after. Their lovemaking was heated and urgent as if death itself was panting against the door. Something wild and demanding had wrenched free from within her. She gave herself with honesty, and when she took from him it was with desire and love. The more demanding she was the more ardent he became and, even injured, he drove her on with his desire. When their passion retreated, they stared at each other in wonder, almost glimpsing each other's true faces.

"Sophy?" Oakheart murmured, his eyebrows framing the question.

"Yes?" she replied dreamily, closing her eyes to savour that moment.

"I am at a loss for words...you took me to the *given*. I feel our bond...I almost see you. No...at that moment of surrender I did see the real you."

Her eyes fluttered open. She gazed into his serious and somewhat shocked face.

"I love you," she whispered. "That is all that matters to me."

He gaped at her in open wonder.

❦

ANOTHER WEEK AND OAKHEART WAS WALKING ALONG THE RAMPS between the tiers and taking in the dappled sunlight. Soon he was fit enough to do what he had been sent to do. Together, they dressed with care in borrowed clothes and went to join those gathering by the Heart. The crowd of forest folk parted, revealing a slightly plump, middle-aged woman with brilliant green eyes like a cat and a predatory smile. Waving to Sophy, the woman stepped closer. "Lady Sophy, how pleased I am to meet you finally," the Queen of Gilton Forest said. "My cousin, Lillia, has told me much about you. Surely you have the heart of a forest maiden with such bravery and valour as you have shown."

Sophy half curtsied, not sure of the protocol. "Your majesty, I haven't done anything to earn such praise. Though I must thank Lillia for her compliments."

The queen moved her unnerving gaze from Sophy and turned to Oakheart. "My good friend, Oakheart," she said sweetly, hands held out to grasp his. "Is it true what I hear that you are oath-bound to this valiant lady?"

"Yes, your majesty. 'Tis so," he replied, smiling lightly and releasing her hands.

"Well that leaves me heartbroken. All the time I thought it was me that you wished to wed," she said with a laugh. The queen inclined her head and turned to talk with the some other forest folk.

Sophy thought a thousand thoughts at once. Confused, she looked at Oakheart and when he saw her look, he laughed heartily. She punched his good arm for taking advantage of her. The forest folk had a strange sense of humour. The queen was already wed. In fact, she had three husbands, one from each of the major clans. The arrangement seemed to work well. Sophy couldn't help thinking that the queen had been serious, the way her eyes seemed to devour him, as they ranged over his well-proportioned frame.

Oakheart had told her the night before why Lillia had come to Silverdale. The adept that served the queen and the rest of the forest people had fled, leaving them with no one to renew the connection of the heart tree to the *given*. To keep the branch of the Crystal Tree grafted to the heart tree an adept must perform a rite of some kind.

More of the story was revealed when Sophy caught up with Lillia. Lillia said that that act of the adept running way was strange, as he was one of the forest folk himself and was bonded to their Heart Tree. However, the gossip was that he had run off with a young forest maiden.

"I must admit to some share of embarrassment," Lillia confided. 'It was one of my daughters that ran off with him. She had tried everything to put him from her mind and heart, but when he confessed his love for her it was too much."

"Are you angry with her?"

"No...she really did try to overcome it. But she had been keen on him since she was a child."

"So adepts do not marry normally?" Sophy asked still confused.

"Of course they do...sometimes, although usually to other adepts. It is their way of life and the hours of study that usually preclude them from finding a mate."

"Then I don't understand why they ran away. If he could marry and you have no objection..."

"We did not say that," Mellow said, voice sounding harsh. Sophy stepped back, not having realised he was there. Mellow had been curt to her since he'd knocked her out. Sophy wasn't about to apologise so they tried to ignore each other.

Lillia explained, "Sophy, Adept Lione was Mellow's brother..."

"Half-brother," Mellow almost grunted.

"But that would make him her...oh I see,' Sophy replied. "Then it wouldn't be acceptable for them to..."

Lillia nodded. Mellow looked fierce, as if she had insulted him.

"Mel," Lillia said warningly, seeing her husband's expression. She smiled at Sophy. "Not really acceptable, no. But now his disappearance has put us in great need. Without the renewal of the Heart Tree the forest will lose its ability to fend off the screavers, for one thing."

Mellow almost smiled. "I hope the Retreat will send our son back to us now there is a vacancy."

Sophy blurted out. "You have a son who is an adept?"

Lillia looked startled. "Of course. Why should we not?"

Realising how her outburst had sounded, Sophy tried to cover it up. "No reason. It's not Adage is it?" She shivered at the thought.

Mellowbark looked frozen in time and then he guffawed and slapped his thigh.

"Adage? The Adage? He is older than time itself. It is said that he is the grandson of Vorn, preserved through time because of an ill-worded oath."

"I didn't know. He looks so very young, except for the eyes."

"'Tis true," Oakheart said as he joined them. "Adage is the grandson of Vorn, and the founder of the Retreat. His oath to a dying Vorn bound him in youth."

Sophy's face crinkled. "An oath?"

"In the early days, oaths were not well understood." Oakheart said, then leaning closer to her, he whispered, "We can be bonded officially here, Sophy. But I would have to officiate."

She looked askance at him. "But I thought you must seek Dellbright's consent to make it official."

"We could make our bonding official. There would be some diplomatic difficulties if we did so without Dellbright's consent, as he technically has wardship over you. However, I am sure he would not withhold it. I mean would be hard to do so seeing that we have—"

"Yes, a little bit. Not that I like this wardship stuff. Dellbright is not in charge of me."

"'Tis not so straightforward. However, if you prefer we could wait until we gain Glassy Mountain Retreat. There Adage can perform the rite, a great honour that would be too, and then he could attempt to solve the riddle of your leaf."

"What about in Valley Keep? Shouldn't we go there before the Retreat?"

"Yes, of course, you wish to have Aria with you."

She smiled as she gazed into his eyes.

"Then we will wait."

She turned around. "So, what do you have to do here?"

Oakheart pointed to the large tree in the centre of the clearing. "I am sufficiently skilled to invoke the Crystal Tree. This is enough for the Heart Tree ceremony. 'Tis called the 'Reunion of Hearts and Souls'."

"Do you start now?"

"Soon," Oakheart replied, and kissed her cheek.

As a full Walker moon rose, all were gathered around the Heart Tree. Silently, Sophy looked on with the others as Oakheart sang a deep rhythmic song. The crowd chanted a chorus that lifted up to the tips of the trees and hung above their heads as if the sound itself had its own magic. The hairs on her arms pricked up, and she swallowed the lump forming in her throat.

Stepping forward, Oakheart wrapped his arms around the trunk of the Heart Tree. His muscles strained as if he was trying to squeeze the life out of it, or as if he was trying to merge himself with it. As he squeezed a cleft began to appear, splitting up and down like a dark and angry wound. When Oakheart removed his arms, the cleft gaped as if it had always existed. As the chorus began a new song, he eased himself into the Heart Tree. Fear clenched Sophy's stomach as the cleft closed up around him. She tried to rush forward, but Mellow held her in place.

"Keep your peace. Do not give into fear."

At that moment, she supressed the urge to punch him in the jaw, but Lillia's solemn look made her flush. The forest maiden seeming to know her thinking. The chanting continued and, as the sounds moved and flowed over one another, her stomach punched and heaved. The *given* emanated from the tree and flowed over them. Her head ached, her teeth were twisting in her gums. Worry for Oakheart overrode her discomfort. She waited and still the tree remained sealed. Her eyes darted in all directions, trying to assess from the assembled people's expressions to determine if there was cause for alarm. However, their faces were sombre and calm.

Snowflakes fluttered down from the sky. She kept watch, blinking the snowflakes from her lashes. Then the chanting grew faster and louder, rising to a crescendo. The queen moved forward, singing in counter-point to the chorus. Her song wove through the air. It was hard to breathe. The crystal leaf within her chest swelled and throbbed. Her knees began to buckle. Just as the queen touched the tree, the cleft spilt with a resounding tear. Oakheart stepped out. There was an expression of awe on his face. He sang to the tree again and stroked it. After convulsing once, the tree sealed itself.

Sophy's mouth hung open in wonder. There definitely was more to Oakheart than she had ever guessed. He could wield power. But he hid it. Why?

A gong sounded, breaking the mood. The males of the forest folk began to dance. At first, their capering seemed humorous. Petals fell along with snowflakes and soon the purpose of the dancing revealed itself as the movements became more earthy and sensual. Mellow flew past, and she was surprised by the look of heat in his eyes as they fell upon Lillia. Lillia's eyes darkened as she followed his dance.

A pair of arms encircled her. Oakheart lifted her in huge bear hug and swung her around.

"Stop, stop," she said, caught up in the revelry and giddy with love for him. He put her down, but kept his arm over her shoulders.

"Come we must celebrate. I have never done the Heart Tree ritual on my own. I cannot even begin to describe the experience." He drew her along and she followed willingly. When she noticed that they weren't going in the direction of the feast, she tried to pull back.

"Hang on. Where are you taking me? The food is over there." She indicated the large array of food.

"Do not worry. You will eat later. I will even feed you myself."

When he bent down and picked her up, she was still lost for words. While he carried her off in the direction of their bole room, she did manage a few feeble protests. He kicked the door open, flopped her down on their bed and fell on top of her.

"Now," he said, busy with the laces of her leather garments. "What were you saying about food?"

45

THE REALNESS OF DREAMS

It was midnight and dark shadows perched in the corners of the bedroom. Aria stumbled to the cradle to feed young Gillcress. Dellbright stirred, but to her relief he did not wake. While he slept, there was little sign of the anger and the need in him.

Fatigue weighed Aria down as she reached into the cradle to bring the small babe to her breast. She tried to relax and let her milk flow. The rhythm of the baby's suckling wooed her into a daze. She couldn't allow herself to dream, and that meant staying awake. After his feed, Gillcress fell asleep, a bubble of milk on his pink lips. Placing him back in his cradle, she ran a finger down his chubby cheek, knowing that she had to protect him. His life was in danger.

Aria was reluctant to go back to bed. The visions of blood were with her all the time now, sleep allowed them to run rampant. She knew Dellbright was worried. She heard his whispers to his mother and knew, of course, that it couldn't go on. Eventually, she had to sleep, yet she could not allow Gillcress to leave her side. Her dreams foretold danger for him, of a room filled with blood and his soul-wrenching baby cries.

The lamp made the shadows dance and she looked around

anxiously. Her eyes fell again to Dellbright's sleeping form. Her dreams had created a barrier between them. He could not understand them, and that left Aria alone and afraid. She dared not think of Sophy for then she would weep, and that would make Dellbright angry.

Fatigue won out and she sat down in her armchair, letting her eyes slowly close. The image of her bedroom altered into one filled with blood. Red blood poured from her mouth and her milk was blood and, the final insult, her eyes glowed red. Her own soul-curdling scream startled her into wakefulness. Dellbright was standing over her, fear reflected in his eyes. Gillcress cried and wriggled in his arms.

"Aria! By the tree, what is the matter with you? Will we get no peace?" Dellbright had dark smudges under his eyes and his skin was pale. The sound of feet on the flagstones echoed outside the door. Aria looked up as Aurore stepped in with Master Willow following close behind.

Gillcress now lay quiet in his father's arms. Aria could not stop the tears that slowly tracked down her cheek.

"Daughter?" Aurore said. "Let me take the child for the night. You must rest."

"No," Aria gasped. She turned a pleading look to Dellbright. "Please. I cannot sleep without the dreams coming to torment me. I'm sorry, truly. But I must have Gilly with me. I must protect him."

"Aria," Dellbright said with a touch of anger in his voice. "Gilly is well protected in this keep. No harm will come to him here. Let mother take him."

The false dawn lightened the darkness at the windows and with that Aria drew some hope.

"I thank you for the offer," she said in her best princess voice. "It is nearly dawn. I'm sorry I woke you all. You see, Gilly is fine, and nurse will come soon to help. I will be able to rest then."

Dellbright gazed at her searchingly, then nodded to his mother and Master Willow. He placed Gillcress back in his cradle and ushered the others out. He lingered in the hall. Aria could hear their whispers and knew that it would not be long. Soon something would happen: they would take Gillcress and the terrible thing would happen.

After sunrise, Aria sat at her dressing table. The reflection in the mirror showed a stranger's face. Her skin hung loosely from her cheek bones, and she could see no beauty in her face. Black shadows curtained her eyes and the whites were shot through with blood. It was as if she existed alone in the bottom of a deep, dark well.

Dela knocked on the door and brought her some tea. Aria shook her head to refuse it.

"Please your highness. It will soothe away your woes."

After placing the tea in front of her, Dela began to draw a brush through Aria's hair.

"You will feel better soon. See how nice it is to have your hair brushed?"

While Dela applied rhythmic strokes, Aria sipped the tea and the lull of sleep gradually overcame her. Dellbright entered, suddenly and noisily, and Aria's eyes snapped open at the sound. She sighed, glad that he had interrupted her journey to sleep.

"Aria..." he began. Dela moved away and Dellbright stroked her hair tenderly. "At mother's urging I have sent for an adept. He will be here soon. I think he must advise us. You are not well."

Aria looked away, unable to look upon his betrayal. He knelt by her and brought her face to his. "Please. I do not know what to do. I cannot bear to see you like this, unable to rest, unable to smile..."

Aria couldn't speak, didn't want to. She reached for the tea and drank it all down. Dellbright's glance followed the cup—and then she knew. The something had happened. The brew worked quickly. One minute she was looking at her reflection and the next she was slouched over her dresser, unable to move and fighting for consciousness. Dellbright carried her over to the bed and watched over her. The drug was quick and powerful. She couldn't fight it. She was locked tight in the terror that assailed her, unable to scream and unable to wake.

Later towards evening, when the drug had worn off, she saw in the mirror that her eyes reflected the horror of her dreams. The intensity of her fear left her unable to speak of it.

A wet nurse had been brought into feed Gillcress during the day but they let him come to feed to ease her milk-filled breasts. At least she could look upon Gilly's beautiful face. Dellbright sat heavily on the bed and took her hand. She knew that look. He was going to lecture her, order her, take away her will. She drew in a breath in preparation.

"Aria, you must eat," he began and Dela brought her a bowl of soup and a piece of bread. Aria took the bread, but eyed the soup suspiciously.

"My mother will care for Gilly this night," he said and then paused. She said nothing and only looked out at him through her saddened eyes without blinking. "You must sleep this night and on the morrow you will be well." He finished by squeezing her hand.

"No," she said quietly almost to herself. For her, it was a terrible act of defiance to speak against his decision, to say 'no' to him. She had never crossed him so directly. Her gaze flicked up quickly to his. "No, I won't be all right. It won't be all right." Her voice was dry like a desert. "I beg you not to do it. Giving him to your mother will only bring him danger. I must protect Gilly."

He stood up quickly, his face tight with anger. "Nonsense! You are weak, Aria. Weak. You must get stronger. I need you to be strong." His words fell like hammer blows and he walked out.

❧

ARIA'S SHRILL VOICE WOKE THE KEEP AGAIN THAT NIGHT. WHEN SHE woke, her cheek stung from Dellbright's slap and his hands were fisted in her nightclothes as he shook her. Fighting him off, she managed to say, "We must save him! We must stop him before it is too late."

The lamp was lit. Dellbright tried to shake her off. "Are you crazed? Stop... please...stop," Dellbright pleaded, his voice breaking. He rose up and pinned her against the bed by her hands.

Aria threw her head from side to side. "I'm not crazed," she growled out, sounding feral. "You must believe me. Something terrible has happened."

Dellbright hissed in her ear, "Nothing is amiss. 'Tis only in your mind."

His face loomed above hers, wretched with dark hollows around his eyes.

Aria softened her tone, pleaded. "No. Please believe me. Let me see

Gillcress and...and if all is well...I will sleep—I promise—I will speak no more of it."

He nodded once, eased off her and quickly thrust his arms into a robe. Aria waited by the door, still in her nightdress, afraid to go out on her own.

Dellbright jerked the door open, and grabbed Aria's hand. He led the way down the corridor to Aurore's room. It was deathly quiet. Aria was barefoot. Dellbright wore his slippers, so their steps didn't echo. Dellbright quietly pushed the door ajar to peek in, and Aria edged inside. It was pitch black. No lamp lighted the shadows. Aria took another step right into the room. The stench of death hit her—blood and gore. A damp stickiness slicked the soles of her feet. A terrible wail stole out of her throat. Dellbright jumped, startled by the sudden sound. He darted out the door, yelling for assistance and returned with a lighted firestick from further down the hall. It cast his shadow from the doorway. Aria had not moved, was not able to move. This was her dream—the dreaded blood filled vision.

Footsteps sounded on the flagstones, signalling the arrival of aid. Dellbright stepped next to her, his breathing ragged. No sound had answered Aria's scream.

More light revealed dark stains flung up the walls, blood, lots of blood. Willow's hushed exclamations reverberated as he held firesticks high. The floor itself was dark with blood. Tentatively, Dellbright edged in and brought Aria with him by the hand. His hands were slick with sweat. They angled around the bed. On the far wall were Aurore and the wet nurse, spread-eagled with their life and insides ripped from them.

Aria could not speak; small whimpers escaped her throat. She shivered. The cradle stood by the window and overcame her fear she raced towards it. Reaching in, slimy, liquid gore met her fingertips. Her hands came out dripping blood. The cradle was full of blood. There was no Gillcress. She screamed—a never-ending scream. Then she heard the laughter, saw the red eyes, and knew the name.

ARIA DID NOT WAKE FOR THREE DAYS. THE NIGHTMARES HAD stopped, and they were replaced by a reality she could not accept. Sleep helped her body to heal, but it could not deaden the pain. Dellbright nudged her awake and when her eyes fluttered open, she saw her pain mirrored in his face. His mother had been killed, and Aria's dreams had come true. His son and heir was gone.

"You must drink," he said, handing her a goblet of mulled wine. As she drank, she realised that he had not slept for days. His face was drawn and his earthy skin-tone was dull.

"We must call for help," Aria said.

Dellbright's lips quivered. "Of course. I have already called for help."

Aria sat up and grabbed his hand. "We must call Sophy."

Dellbright pulled his hand out of her grasp, stood up and ran his hand through his hair.

"How could your friend help us? You are out of your senses..."

Aria threw off her covers, reached for her robe and struggled into it. Her head spun so she sat back down. "No, I'm not out of my mind. He wants her. That is why he took our son. Gilly is the ransom for Sophy. Only she can save him."

Dellbright's brow furrowed as he rubbed his red and sore eyes. He sighed loudly, not bothering to disguise his impatience. "How do you know that?" His voice sounded fragile and used.

"It's hard to explain...I just know that I'm right," she said sadly, reaching out her hand to brush lightly against his. She could not bring herself to embrace him; she was too far away emotionally for that.

He withdrew his hand and turned away. "I will fetch the talkstone." Facing her once again, he spoke in a hard, callous voice. "If she is the cause of all that has befallen us, I would wring the life out of her with my own hands."

He headed for the door, and Aria called out to him. "No, don't say that. She's not the cause. She's a victim, like us."

The face he turned toward her was haggard with pain. "My mother was murdered. A deed that breaks the oath. For the first time this keep has been invaded by an enemy. Blood has leeched into the very fabric of the keep. I will have my revenge. She is the cause. I know it."

The door slammed shut after his exit. Aria tried to tell herself that it was his grief talking, that he wouldn't actually harm Sophy. Then her thoughts turned to those times when her husband lost control with her. Perhaps he was capable. Nothing that he had ever done before had prepared him for this. Then again, nothing had prepared her either.

46
OATHS

SOPHY SLEPT DEEPLY and peacefully while entwined in Oakheart's spacious embrace. Her dreams were full of light and happiness, and she knew she was smiling. Aria's voice called to her, piercing her dream with its sense of urgency. Sophy sat up in a rush and could barely draw breath as a surge of fear hit her. Looking around, she saw that it was still dark outside, and the embers of the fire filled the room with warmth and an orange glow. She blinked away sleep, unaware of why she was suddenly awake. In the quiet of the night, she heard Aria's voice again, coming from the small cupboard where Sophy kept her things.

"Sophy? Please Sophy answer me. Wake up."

"The talkstone," Sophy said, her voice husky from sleep. Unravelling herself from Oakheart's embrace, she quickly and quietly crawled over to take out the talkstone and then tipped it onto the table. Aria's image floated in the crystal, looking strange, eerie and frail.

Sophy drew her legs under her and knelt. "Aria? I'm here. What is it?"

Aria's eyes met hers through the stone. "Sophy...oh Sophy..." Aria cried, wiped her tears and then started to sob.

Sophy's breath caught, not sure how to proceed. Perhaps, Dellbright and Aria had had a quarrel. "Come on, Aria. It will be all right. Whatever it is."

"Oh no...Gillcress is missing...Aurore murdered?"

"What?" Sophy inadvertently yelled. "How? Why?"

Aria leaned in closer to the talkstone so that her eyes, reddened with weeping, loomed large. "I have been dreaming these awful dreams. No one believed me, but they came true. I kept seeing red eyes. And I know...oh...how I know that he wants you. He took Gilly to get at you and only you can save him."

Sophy nearly fell backwards. "Me?"

"Promise me you will save him. Promise!"

"Of course, I'll do whatever I can but..."

Aria's brows furrowed. "You must make me an oath. You will be the one to save him. Only you can save him."

"I swear—"

"Sophy, do not say it," Oakheart suddenly commanded. He tumbled out of bed and grabbed her, covering her mouth with his hand. "Have you not learned that you must be careful of the oaths you speak? Argenterra binds them with the *given*, and they cannot be broken. Understand?" Sophy nodded and gently Oakheart removed his hand and stroked her face. "Something dire has happened at Valley Keep?"

Sophy nodded, bereft of speech. She moved closer to the talkstone. Aria's image looked hollow and wild. This was not the friend she remembered.

"Princess? All is not well, I hear. How may we help you? How can Lady Sophy assist you where others cannot?"

Aria's eyes widened. "Oh Oakheart...I..." Her persistent crying dissolved the next of her words. Dellbright's face appeared in the crystal's depths.

"Oakheart, praise the tree that you are near. My mother...is murdered. My son and heir taken. Through these dark dreams of Aria's she foresaw it all and now she insists that whoever took Gilly wants Sophy."

"Sophy, too, has had dreams of the dark and even sendings. I fear it is Rufus..."

"Rufus of the Lower Warrens? That fell beast you told me about?" Dellbright asked, his voice strangely detached. "Why would he suddenly turn his malice towards Valley Keep?" His eyes bored into Sophy's.

"That I do not know..."

"Oh Aria..." Sophy moaned, praying that Dellbright's angry and accusing gaze would be replaced by the image of her friend. What must Aria be feeling? Why did she not warn her that she was suffering? Sophy would have ridden to Valley Keep alone to protect her.

"Do not make excuses for the outlander, Oakheart. You cannot tell me she is not involved with this."

Oakheart lowered the tone of his voice. "It does not bode well that he wants Sophy. He has already shown too keen an interest in her."

Dellbright's expression soured further. "I was right. She is the culprit. Did you send him to us on purpose, Sophy? Does it give you joy to see us suffer? My mother, who was kind to you, had her throat and innards ripped out."

Oakheart placed himself in front of Sophy to protect her from Dellbright's view, nearly flattening her in the process.

"You speak from grief so I will forgive your words. Sophy is innocent of malice. She is Rufus's intended prey."

In the talkstone, Aria inserted herself in front of Dellbright. "Yes. That is it. He wants her."

Sophy was shaking from fear. Oakheart put his arm around her. Dellbright's anger scared her to the bone. If she had been within his reach, she was sure he would have killed her with his bare hands. He had suffered, she understood that, but to be the focus of so much hatred was too much. She needed to speak with Aria, so she had to brave Dellbright's spite. She patted Oakheart on the shoulder to let him know she was okay. He made way for her so she could speak into the talkstone again. "Don't worry. I will go and get Gilly back from Rufus, even if it is my life I must trade to do it. I swear it."

Oakheart let out an expletive but was too late to silence her. What did he expect? She had no choice but to try to save the child. It was because of her he was taken.

Dellbright's expression softened, so much so that there was a hint of the Dellbright she'd met in Crystal Tree Woods. "If you return my son to me, I would forgive you anything."

Aria's face once again filled the talkstone. "Hurry, I don't think I can live without my son. He is so little! Dearest Oakheart, can you help her?"

Oakheart swallowed heavily and said, voice was full of emotion. "Princess...How I wish that you had asked me first. I would have sworn an oath to return your son. Now all that is left to me is to protect Sophy."

Aria sighed. "As much as I care for you as a friend, Oakheart, I would prefer that it had been you. But I know that creature wants Sophy. It is in my mind until I'm driven near crazy with it. If they had let me keep Gilly near...If things had been different, I'm sure he could not have taken him. That's why he waited until I was asleep."

Oakheart frowned. "I think I understand. Rest easy. We will do our utmost to return your son to you."

Aria turned to Dellbright and sobbed. The images in the talkstone faded. In two heartbeats, Sophy began darting around the room to search for her things. Straight away, she shoved clothes and other odd items into a bag. After a few minutes, she noticed that Oakheart was not moving and that he stood there, hands on hips, glaring at her.

"Why are you standing around? We have to hurry?"

Oakheart lunged and grabbed her by the shoulders to pull her toward him. In his embrace, she could feel him trembling. "Why did you utter those words? Did I not warn you? If the *given* holds true in you Sophy, then you will be compelled to fulfil it. You should have let me do the talking. Dellbright is my cousin. 'Tis my duty to save the child."

"Let me go," she said, struggling out of his grasp. He released her and they glared at each other, as much as odds as they had been before they had bonded. "Aria says it is because of me that Gilly was taken."

"I know what she said. I am not deaf. You are not listening to me. I wanted to go in your stead." Oakheart was near to yelling at her.

Sophy realised that she was hollering back. "And because I swore I would go, you cannot stop me? Is that what you are saying?"

"Yes, by the tree, Sophy. You have no choice. Your oath will compel you to the very end."

"Do you think I want to face Rufus?" She paced out of his reach. "Do you think I will succumb to Rufus...that I desire him..."

Oakheart stared at his feet. "No...that is not what I think. You cannot break your oath to me, either."

Sophy sunk down to the stool by the fire and shrugged. "What then? I must go. There is no way around it."

Oakheart pulled another stool out, drew it close to hers, and enfolded her hands in his. "I do not wish you to go into danger."

Sophy held his gaze. "A little baby boy is at risk because of me. If what you suspect about Rufus is true, then the attacks on you and on me are related. Do you know why he wants to harm me or capture me?"

Oakheart's expression was haunted. "No. In all honesty, I do not know. The only thing that I can think of is that you are the real Gift of Crystal Tree Woods and your inability to feel or touch the *given* is somehow linked. I was hoping we could get to the Retreat and that Adage would have discovered the mystery surrounding you before...before anything happened."

"I don't know if this oath thing is compelling me or not. But deep inside, I know I have to go. I want to save him for her. She is my friend."

"I am coming with you."

Sophy nodded. "I was counting on that. However, I want you to promise me something. If the child comes into your hands, you will return him to his mother straight away."

Oakheart appeared to mull this over as if there was an unpredictable twist to the wording. "I swear that I will return the child to its mother if the child comes into my hands, may the *given* witness my vow."

Sophy smiled at him, despite the grief and the fear reflected in his expression. Next thing she knew Oakheart had enveloped her in his arms. When she lifted her face, his mouth sought hers. He caressed her and kissed her thoroughly, dispelling dire thoughts of Rufus, murder and kidnap for a time.

Finally, when the morning light was creeping into the room, he released her. As they packed, she thought she saw tears in his eyes. He loved her, too, she thought, although she could draw no comfort from the realisation. The future loomed ahead, unknown, terrifying and real.

❧ 47 ☙

HOLLOW QUEST

OAKHEART HAD CALLED MUSTER. His orders flew around the Oaks Glade. Forest folk dropped sacks of food and supplies from the treetops. A watch had been set for the screavers, who had disappeared after being repelled on the perimeter of Queen's Town. Even though their numbers had been decimated the forest folk, Oakheart had not relaxed his guard. Oakheart had said to her that while he suspected that Rufus wouldn't prevent Sophy from coming to him, anyone accompanying her was fair game. The scars on Oakheart's body attested to that.

In the clearing, Lillia stood a little apart with Mellow, keen eyes on the preparations. Wearing her armour, Sophy stepped over to the couple. Mellow nodded and stalked away, making her wonder if she had done something else to upset him.

Lillia had not taken the news of Gilly's kidnapping well. The theft of a child was something she found hard to comprehend. "I am not sure you are fit for this journey, Sophy."

"Why?" Sophy grabbed a lock of her dark hair and re-braided it.

Lillia drew closer and whispered. "You have not come to me for cloths. Your blooding time has long passed."

Sophy dropped her unfinished braid. "Has it? But isn't yours is before mine?"

Lillia looked grave. "Aye, it is true. I wondered as I fed young Ivyn why my breasts were tender. I fear that my reunion with Mel will have lasting consequences."

Sophy's did her best to check her reaction. "Do you mean you're..." She blinked, she supposed Lillia wasn't that old. Another thought occurred to her. "You were breastfeeding Ivyn? But I thought he was Liandra's child?"

"He is. But he was hungry, and I was near. I see from your expression that this is strange to you. We feed and look after each other's children. It is natural. Most women, once they have milk, never lose it. Even if a child has no need of the breast then her mate will have a use for it. Breast milk is a curative, too, and used to treat illness."

Sophy's stomach clenched. "You didn't put it in those brews you fed me, did you?"

Lillia laughed, wincing as she nudged her breast. "I told you I would not reveal my recipes."

Mellow had stalked back toward them. Ignoring Sophy, he said directly to Lillia, "I am not happy about this."

Lillia lifted her chin. "I do not ask that you be happy...I am leaving with Oakheart." Lillia's shoulders bunched as she turned away to regard the goings on, ignoring her mate.

Mellow touched Sophy's hand. "Speak to her, my lady," he said. "She must stay here...we need her."

Sophy was stunned at Mellow's request for her help. "I'll try."

She stepped in front of Lillia and squared her shoulders, careful to avoid the woman's eye though. "Lillia...ah...um you should stay..."

All trace of humour left Lillia's face. "I will not. No one can tell what my duty is. He least of all. The queen has sanctioned my journey...that is enough for me."

Mellow's glare silenced any offerings of commiserations. Without a backward glance, he raced off into the woods.

With a tight-lipped expression, Lillia watched him go.

Sophy kicked some leaves, sending them floating. "You haven't told him, have you?"

Lillia didn't smile. "It is not his business...he would use it against me, and I would not have it so."

Sophy noticed Oakheart walking through the trees. He waved and changed direction to join them. She smiled as she watched him walk up, a sense of contentment settling around her as he neared. Without warning, a force punched into her gut. She grasped her stomach as she doubled over. An unbidden howl rose out of her throat. She staggered and fell to her knees. Hot blood leaked down her legs.

"Sophy?" Oakheart's voice sounded distant.

Lillia's face hovered over hers. Turning her head to the side, Sophy vomited into the leaf mulch. Shivers took over as cold snaked through her body. It hurt everywhere, and she cried out as Lillia tugged her armour free so that she could examine her.

"What is it? What is wrong?" Oakheart asked, his voice urgent and tinged with worry. Sophy felt his hands in her hair, stroking softly. Tears leaked out of her eyes, she couldn't hide from the pain. Another tremor rippled through her. Her insides acted as though they were being clawed from her body.

Lillia's worried face loomed over her again. "I have never seen anything like this. Get someone to make a litter and we will carry her to a tent. We cannot leave until it passes."

Sophy's moan echoed around the clearing. Mercifully, she must have passed out because when awareness came next she was settled in a tent and Lillia was trying to get her to drink from a cup.

"Come, my lady, take this for the pain. After this you will drink broth to replace the blood you have lost."

"What happened to me...?" Sophy sniffed, numb from shock. Her body throbbed as if someone had put it through a mangle.

Lillia pursed her lips. "I fear that you were with child. A young pregnancy, but it is gone from your body now. The bleeding has slowed. I think you will be well soon."

"A baby?"

Lillia stroked her hair. "I am not sure if it was a boy or girl...it was too small to tell. Yet the manner of it has me puzzled. Had you no warning? Pains? Spotting? Illness?"

Sophy moved her head dully, not quite a shake of her head. "No, it was like someone ripped it out of me."

Lillia took her hand and squeezed. "Sleep now."

Sophy closed her eyes, numbed by pain and loss. She and Oakheart had made a child in such a short time and now the possibility of its life was gone. No. It was taken.

When next she woke, Oakheart was sitting next to her, playing with her hair as he stared into space. "Thirsty," she said, as she eased a sore spot on her back. His eyes flew to hers. He kissed her brow and went to the pitcher to pour water. He held her up while she sipped.

"Thank you," she said, groggily.

Oakheart eased her gently down and then sat beside her again. "Lillia told me what happened. I am sorry for your pain."

Sophy tried to smile, but sniffed instead. "You didn't cause it. And you are a great comfort to me."

He edged closer and resting his forehead against hers. "How do you feel now?"

"Better. I would like to leave in the morning."

Oakheart's eyebrows rose. "But 'tis already morning. You have slept nearly a full day."

Sophy tried to push him away. "It can't be. What about Gilly? I can't waste time lying about here."

Oakheart held her on the bed. "Yet if you wish to go, we must delay. If you can sit up tonight, we will leave tomorrow."

With a nod, she lay back down on the bed. She had to admit that she was tired—very tired.

❦

POWDERY SNOW LITTERED THE GROUND IN PATCHES. NOW AND again clumps of it slid from branches to thump against the forest floor. As the party assembled, Sophy noted a few additional forest folk appeared to be joining them—Illart, his mate, Raven and one other.

Sophy spied Mellow and went over to Lillia. "Why is Mellow here? He's not coming with us, is he?"

Lillia's eyes glittered. "He has sought and gained the queen's permission to accompany us. He is not happy to be leaving the forest, but being with me is some consolation."

Sophy studied Mellow's short, sharp movements. "He doesn't look very happy."

Lillia chuckled but kept her eyes on her husband, her mouth curving upwards. "He will adjust...in time. It will be his first excursion out of the shelter of the forest."

❧

A WEEK LATER, THE FOREST FELL AWAY AS THEY HEADED ACROSS A barren plain with the Lower Warrens in their sights. The forest folk had warned them that the plain was almost devoid of the *given* and that even water was hard to coax to the surface. They would have to carry what they needed because the scrubby plants that littered the plain were resistant to the *given* and yielded only sour berries anyway. Hard and bitter winds pummelled them from the north, flinging snow and sleet. In one of their layovers, Lillia had suggested they ride two per horse. Mostly it was for the warmth, but for her it was more concern for her husband, who was no horseman. After much discussion, Oakheart had agreed, provided they stopped often to rotate the mounts. The conditions were so bad anyway that Oakheart called halts frequently to check hooves for ice and to rearrange the packs.

Mellow was not alone among the forest folk for lack of horsemanship. Illart and Raven huddled under their cloaks and let their mount trail after the others. Even though Sophy was cocooned in a cloak as well, as Oakheart's large arms, she thought she'd never been so cold. Every piece of exposed skin was numbed. Their pace was pitifully slow as the horses staggered through snowdrifts, wafting misty breath from their muzzles.

"This storm is getting worse. We must head for those hills. There will be some shelter at the base," Oakheart said, his breath warming

403

her neck. "We will not last much longer in this and neither will the horses.'

"How long until we reach the warrens?" Sophy asked, squinting against the icy breeze to where Oakheart pointed. She did her best to disguise her frustration. Always in the back of her mind was the fear that Gilly was dead. Would a creature like Rufus know how to care for a child? When she voiced her concerns to Oakheart, he had comforted her with the dire reminder that Rufus was after her and that he would need the baby alive to achieve his aim.

"Another two to three days at this rate...if the screavers do not attack. Let us eat in the saddle and make shelter before the sun goes down."

Sophy snuggled deeper into his embrace, casting her gaze over the others. Mellow, she guessed, had never ridden a horse before this expedition. The expression on his face as he clung to Lillia clearly showed his terror. At Oakheart's instruction everyone delved into their packs to bring out something to eat. The sky was so grey that sunset was upon them while they were setting up camp amongst fallen boulders that littered the base of the hills. Sophy's feet were so cold that she didn't notice the temperature drop. She stood around stamping her feet while Oakheart organised the horses and the supplies and the forest folk helped make a shelter. Lillia called to her from across camp, so Sophy went to help cook a meal.

That night, there were no stars due to the cloud cover and, thankfully, in the shelter the wind was less. Except for the sentries Oakheart had set, the group huddled around the fire. Every available blanket was draped over huddled forms. A distant howl sent the horses nickering and prancing. Oakheart was up on his feet, flinging off his blanket and letting in a cold slap of air. While Sophy closed the blanket, Oakheart went to the edge of camp and called out. "Illart?"

Illart and Raven came into view. Both were walking stiffly, a legacy of riding horses

"Scout around. See if there are signs any fell beasts near."

Illart grimaced. "On horse or on foot?"

"On foot, 'tis quieter. And be careful."

With a curt nod, Illart slipped away from the camp. A few curses sounded as he stretched his limbs, and then bounded off with a lopsided gait.

Raven stayed behind and joined them under the blankets. Small portions of broth and hard stale bread made the meal. Sophy could taste none of it. She chewed automatically and swallowed. When she finished eating, she sipped from the mug that Raven handed to her. While she choked, Lillia soothed her by rubbing her back. The liquid burnt her throat and filled her stomach with fire.

"Newin's brew. Always does the trick. Soon your blood will be hot."

With a short laugh Raven spoke. "The way she and Oakheart look at each other their blood needs no warming."

Lillia laughed along with Raven. Sophy was still trying to a draw breath that didn't freeze her throat. By then she was used to the forest folks' teasing way. The drink did make her feel warm. She wished Oakheart was next to her but he was checking on sentries. She dozed for a while. Next she knew she could hear the sound of rapid footsteps as they cracked snow crust.

"'Tis Illart," the sentry called.

Panting, the forest man ran up to them, just as Oakheart returned from reviewing his sentries. Bent over double, he managed to say, "Three screavers on our trail. They bring another creature. A snow bear, I fear."

Oakheart's gaze ranged out. A black wall of night greeted him. Walker moon had not yet risen and clouds obscured the stars. "How long before they reach us? Can we outrun them?"

Illart panted some more. "Fifteen minutes...no less. Best we prepare for an attack rather than get picked off on the road. Here we can defend ourselves."

Oakheart nodded once, his mouth in a grim line. He hissed orders to his men and brought his sentries in and handed out weapons. As precaution Sophy ended up with a short sword and bow with a quiver of arrows, and a kiss.

While they waited the sound of scrabbling over rocks and snow grew louder. Sophy's heart thudded. The hiss of breath and the rub of fur drew closer. Then it grew quiet. The whistle of the wind disguised any further sound. The attack was sudden: screavers darted forward from behind the camp, and while the men engaged with them, a lumbering snow bear lurched into their midst from the front.

Sophy was the first to see it. "Oakheart!"

Thankfully, from beside her, Lillia thwacked arrows into the bear. Sophy's gaze darted around. A screaver had escaped Oakheart's blade and began to stalk Lillia's back. While the bear did not like the arrows, it had not slowed much. Galvanised, Sophy threw a handful of snow at the screaver. The beast turned slowly towards her. Sophy had her sword held low, a bad move. She tried to adjust her footing and bring the blade up, only to stumble on a rock. The screaver leapt. Her scream was cut off when the heavy mass of fur smothered her. The beast grunted and rolled. Tangy blood had sprayed over her clothes. Not quite realising that she had escaped death she lay there looking at her sword sticking out of the belly of the beast. The sound of battle continued and then quieted. Too scared to get up, too scared to see if her friends were dead, she lay there unmoving. Oakheart's cry startled her. Next thing she knew he was there, leaning over as he knelt by her side.

"Sophy?"

She reached for him and he scooped her up. Smothered in his embrace, Sophy murmured, "I'm okay. Are they gone? Is everyone..."

"For a moment I thought..." Oakheart looked dazed.

Lillia strode up with Mellow at her side, blood-smeared but grinning. "If that is the lot of them we should sleep soundly tonight," Mellow said, wiping blood from his sword. He had a satisfied look as if he had worked off some of his anger.

Oakheart drew some windswept hair out of his eyes. "Yes, we must rest. Mellow, please set the sentries." Gathering Sophy up close, he whispered, "Come, little one. We have shelter."

Once on her feet Sophy took a step, wobbly at first, and followed Oakheart to the sleeping place he had selected. He urged his horse down to the ground. Then when he was satisfied with the horse's position, he talked to it, soothing it. Next, he pulled her down with him and snuggled into his horse. As some light snow fell, he tugged a horse blanket over them.

"The horse smells earthy," Sophy whispered as she snuggled close.

"So do you," Oakheart murmured, nuzzling her ear.

THE FOLLOWING MORNING, BEFORE THE SUN HAD FULLY RISEN, THE sentries reported in. One was missing. Oakheart sent Illart and Mellow to search for signs of him.

On his return, Mellow said, his voice flat and hard, "There were only blood stains left. The sentry went to relieve himself. There was no indication of what had taken him, but it was not a screaver or a snow bear. There were no tracks."

Oakheart frowned and slapped his thigh with a loud thwacking sound. "I have no idea what stalks us, for I have never heard tell of a beast that leaves no sign, no flesh, no piece of cloth." Sophy saw that his face looked haunted.

The party skirted the hills, keeping within its sheltering effects. The way was rocky, but the snow was not so thick. At their next campsite, Oakheart set the sentries again, including himself this time.

Sophy couldn't sleep without him beside her. Worry, as well as the cold, kept her awake. She sat by the fire, staring at the flames and thinking of Aria's pain. Her leaving Aria had made her vulnerable to attack. She tried to analyse all of her exchanges through the talkstone. Something had not been right from the start. A sound of a twig snapping off to the right caught her attention. Fellman, one of Oakheart's men, was stationed there.

"Fell?" she called. Edging closer to the perimeter, she called again. "Fell, are you all right?" That sound came again, with a scent, like overripe fruit. There was another noise, a grinding. She waited, her breath misting in front of her. Unexpectedly, a few drops of hot liquid flew in her face. Hands raised protectively, she staggered backward. She spat blood. "Ahhhh!" she screamed throatily.

Footsteps pounded towards her. "My lady?" It was Lillia, freshly woken from sleep. Sophy pointed shakily to where the sentry was stationed. "A...a...thing. It was black like the night. It...it ate Fell in one...in one...in one..."

Oakheart arrived, sword drawn. He took in the scene: blood over Sophy and on the ground and no sentry. "Tell me."

Lillia put up her hand to quiet his questions. "Later, Oakheart," she dragged Sophy back to the fire. "She is in a state."

Lillia poured some liquid into a pot and heated it over the fire. Numb, Sophy watched closely, noticing that Lillia's hand shook. Although she hated to see the forest maiden rattled, it did give her some comfort that her reaction was proportionate to what she had witnessed.

After two mugs of Newin's brew Sophy thought no more about the Nightstalker, the name *given* to the phenomenon she'd witnessed. Giddy with the brew, she almost sang as Oakheart carried her to their blankets.

The next day her head ached painfully. Newin's brew carried quite a punch. No *given* was used in its making so her hangover could only be attributed to overindulgence. She should stick to Argenterran wine as only a few drops had the same effect.

"'Tis a beast of stealth, quiet and cunning," Oakheart announced, after another of his men had disappeared at their next encampment. He looked as if he was living a nightmare. No matter how much he tried, thought Sophy, he couldn't fight this creature that picked them off one by one. Yet being Oakheart, he would try.

Camped south-east of Crystal Tree Woods, in a rudimentary campsite surrounded with tethered canvas to provide shelter, the group shared a meal. The weather leached away Sophy's strength. Memories of other journeys through Argenterra came to mind. The warm fires, cosy blankets, heated baths scented with rose petals were reminiscences sent to torment her with bitter regret. As she looked around she saw that her companions seemed as depressed as she felt.

"This is the most disgusting thing I have ever eaten," Sophy complained, getting ready to chuck the offending dried sausage on the ground.

"Do not," Oakheart growled and plucked it from her grasp. It disappeared down his throat with one swallow. "Food is scarce," he said around a mouthful. "It does not ask that you like it, only that you eat it."

Sophy slapped grease from her hands. "It has probably gone off, you know, rotten, and you will end up with pains in your belly."

Oakheart managed a light smile. The first she'd seen in days. "No, 'tis the flavour of the meat that makes it taste thus. Tree bark is used to smoke it."

They continued to eat bread and cold sausage. Sophy didn't dare comment further and swallowed the food silently. Drinking water from a goblet that Oakheart offered her, she gulped the last of the foul tasting food.

"Where did Rufus come from?"

Oakheart looked at her sharply. He'd been thinking about dark things, Sophy thought. "I do not know for certain."

Sophy edged closer, more for warmth than from the need to touch him. "But you have an idea?"

"Yes..." he made to turn away, but Sophy put her arm on his. She noticed that Lillia and Mellow were listening in.

Sophy blinked rapidly. "And...?"

Oakheart would not look at her. "Adage's theory is that he comes from Yulandir. The world from whence Vorn and his kin fled. He believes that he is an agent of Unesta, the ancient evil that pursued Vorn."

"Unesta?" Lillia echoed in a hollow voice. "She has reached her hand into Argenterra?"

Oakheart was avoiding eye contact with her, yet he answered Lillia. "Not directly. Rufus is an agent only."

Sophy's anger simmered. Oakheart was hiding something. "How did he get here? Tell me that."

Oakheart hesitated. Lillia took Mellow further away to give them privacy. "He came through the Crystal Gate, which is nestled within the Glassy Mountain range. 'Tis a gateway to other worlds."

"People can enter this world from this gate?" Cold sliced through her. The knowledge that Oakheart had not been honest with her stung. People could come and go from this place? Aria and she could have gone home—yet they were not offered that choice.

"Yes, one has. That is Rufus."

Sophy frowned as she thought it through. "And can people leave as well? Has that happened?"

"I do not—" He turned away, his face reddening.

Sophy scooted around so that he had to face her. "You're not telling me everything. People have left, haven't they?"

His green eyes looked saddened. "Yes," he said quietly. "Do you remember your oath to me?"

"Yes, of course I do. What has that have to do with the Crystal Gate?"

"Oaths in Argenterra cannot be broken. You cannot be with another as you have with me while you live in this land."

"I think I realise that," Sophy whispered. She couldn't break her oath if she wanted to. She was bound emotionally to Oakheart and he to her.

"Have you not wondered about the high queen and Dellbright's father? Surely you have heard the tale," he asked, while studying her face.

She sucked on her upper lip and nodded. "I assumed they were dead or...well I never really thought about it. Why?"

Oakheart shook his head. "They are not dead. Well, I am not sure if they are or not, they have been gone for so long now. The high queen fell in love with the Prince of Valley Keep. They could not break their oath to their spouses so they escaped through the Crystal Gate. Once free of the confines of Argenterra I assume they were free to be... together. That is why I did not tell you about the gate. I thought perhaps you would wish to leave..."

The gate led to other worlds. The possibilities were endless. She frowned. She was fairly sure that Rufus didn't come from her world, from Earth. But where had he come from? As she looked into Oakheart's tortured gaze, she realised he was afraid of abandonment. She remembered Lillia's words, yet she couldn't ask him about his history now. She reached out to him, and caressed his face that looked plain to her eyes. "Oakheart, I would not willingly leave you. If I ever chose to leave this land, I would take you with me. You have my love and that is stronger than any oath. Don't think about Rufus and gates any more. Come, let's go to bed."

Sophy stared into the darkening sky and watched the first of the moons rise. The pale light made everything look flat. She looked over to where Oakheart readied their blankets and sighed. Stretching lazily, she ambled over to wiggle into the bedclothes with him. She was halfway in when she noticed that Oakheart was naked. She struggled back out and peeled her leather clothes off. Her nose wrinkled in distaste when she caught a whiff of her own body odour. With a shrug, she realised that Oakheart, too, had not washed for a few days so he couldn't complain about her smell. Ice knives pressed against her skin, sending her shivering into the bedclothes and into Oakheart's waiting embrace.

Oakheart covered her completely with his body, and then captured her mouth before she could utter a sound. Whatever she had wanted to say was forgotten, as they writhed beneath the blankets hidden from the moonlight and protected from the fierce cold.

THE SCREAVERS ATTACKED BEFORE DAWN. THE GUARD THAT Oakheart had posted was either a deep sleeper—or dead. Oakheart bounded from the bedclothes and freed his blade from his clothes. Naked, he stood above Sophy, who was still fighting her way out of the bedclothes t. Lillia and Mellow were already shooting arrows with swift, sharp shots that left blood and gore in their wake. Oakheart hacked and thrust, kicking the corpses when they stuck on his blade. Illart was weaving in and out, using a hooked blade that mangled flesh when he thrust it in and out. By that time, the rest of Oakheart's guard were fighting with them. When the sun burst full over the horizon, the screavers retreated, as swiftly as they had attacked.

Sophy scrambled up the mound of earth and bushes that sheltered them, to see where they had gone. The ugly beasts had melted into the landscape. "Why is he doing this? He must know I'm coming."

Oakheart was bloody. He turned away from the others to sluice off the blood with ice-melt. "He wants you alone and vulnerable. Without protection, he could do what he wanted with you."

Sophy slid back down from the mound and helped him wipe down, inspecting him for injuries as she worked. "That makes sense. I'm glad I have you with me."

Her blanket slipped a few times, exposing her cold hardened nipple before she wrenched it back. Oakheart had a wound on his back, a triple scratch as long as Sophy's forearm. She cleaned the gashes, until the blood ran freely and then slowed. She had been so intent on Oakheart that she hadn't looked to the others.

The sound of Lillia's weeping reached her. Sophy and Oakheart swung round to see the forest maiden bowed over Mellow. Sophy cursed loudly. Oakheart began to dress while she raced over to Lillia. Mellow was alive, but bleeding profusely from a wound in his leg. Lillia, too, was bleeding from various shallow wounds.

"Here, let me help you," Sophy said. "I will press on it to stop the bleeding while you get something to bind the wound." Lillia didn't respond. "Hurry up. Do you want him to die of blood loss?"

Lillia looked ready to shout back at Sophy. Then, as if she had been slapped into action, she crawled away to rummage for bandages and healing salves. Oakheart was now dressed and he circled their shrinking number, tallied up their losses. No one, save the guard he had set last night, was dead. Wincing, Sophy inspected Mellow's wound: it looked bad. If he did live, he would slow them, and if he was returned to Gilton Forest, it would reduce their numbers.

Oakheart knelt down and grasped Mellow's hand. He was fading fast. The bleeding was slowing, but Sophy thought it was because he had no more blood left. She looked up at Oakheart, and he nodded. He pulled out some healing bark and squeezed the juice into Mellow's wound. Sophy held the wound together and watched while it began to seal up.

Lillia dropped to her knees beside her. "Praise the tree! You have some healing bark. Thank you," she cried, her tears falling unashamedly down her face.

"It was the last of it. I was saving it for an emergency," he looked at Sophy when he spoke and she realised that he had saved it for her, in case she...

Lillia took over tending her husband.

"I'm sorry, you have to worry about me."

"You have nothing to be sorry for," Oakheart said as he grabbed her hand and pulled her upright. "You have caused me not one day of misery. Difficulties, yes." He stroked her hair and tried to straighten out the disarray of her tangled tresses. "I am your oath-bound husband. I chose to bind myself to you. I did it willingly. I would do it again, and again, until you understand."

❧

It was hard to rally after the attack. Even with the healing bark, Mellow was weakened through loss of blood. Lillia exhausted her supply of herbs stuffing him with brews that she spent every hour making. Snow fell heavily, causing them to huddle together for warmth and protection. The remainder of the group tried to draw strength from each other. There was nothing Sophy could do about the delay, except hope that Gilly was all right and that Aria could bear the separation a little longer.

Two days later Mellow was sufficiently recovered to be moved. He was to accompany them and nothing anyone could say would sway Lillia. Oakheart gave the horses a quick brush, but Sophy knew he was regretting the ordeal the mounts were being put through. They were thin. On the horizon, Sophy could see the foothills that marked the boundaries of the Lower Warrens. The lower plateau rose up, a wedge marking the edge where the land had fallen away sometime in the past.

"You see it?" Oakheart asked.

Sophy nodded.

"'Tis said the place is riddled with tunnels, hence the name warrens."

"Will we get there tomorrow?"

Oakheart shrugged. "Perhaps. It depends on what else Rufus throws at us. I will not let you go in there without an escort."

"I appreciate that...I wish—"

Oakheart kissed her forehead. "I wish the same."

As they rode along, Sophy was absorbed by her thoughts, mostly the ones where she had no plan. The bleak, brown landscape spread out around them. Patches of snow lingered. The wind, however, was unceasing. With the plateau looming above them, they lit a fire, using the remainder of their heat rocks and the kindling scrounged on their journey.

"We will keep the firesticks for the warrens. I doubt Rufus will light our way." Oakheart counted them twice, before returning them to storage.

It was obvious from all the attacks that Rufus knew where they were, knew their numbers and knew their weaknesses. Sophy felt like a lamb heading meekly to the slaughter. No one spoke about what would happen the next day—the day when she would present herself to Rufus in exchange for the child. Fear held Sophy's stomach in its cold clutches. She twisted her hair, until Oakheart stilled her hand.

"If you insist on this twisting and tugging, you will have no hair left. Tell me what is worrying you." Oakheart smiled at her tenderly.

Sophy sighed and let herself be caressed. "I don't know what is going to happen tomorrow. I haven't planned an approach or anything."

"I have a plan. You must not do anything rash."

"A plan? You promised that if Gilly comes into your hands you will go straight away to Aria. No matter what."

"Yes, but if I killed the creature first then we could achieve both aims—saving you and the child."

"Could you kill Rufus? Doesn't that go against what you believe in, against the binding oath?"

"To save you and the child, I could. You forget the oath pertains to people of this land, not to him."

"So I am outside this oath too. I am as foreign as he is."

"I care not. I will be there to protect you, and you will listen to me." Oakheart ran his hand down her back.

"I will try." With that, she nestled next to him, while he rubbed her back until she went to sleep.

Red eyes invaded Sophy's dreams. She could hear Rufus calling her, his voice strong and bending her to his will. His angel form uncloaked in her mind and then shifted to his true form. Her heart beat frantically; she wanted to struggle yet he mesmerised her, held her like a butterfly pinned to a display board. Her clothes fell away with a touch of his claw. Sweat started to bead on her forehead and then to drip off her body. A claw extended and Rufus traced it from her neck to her navel. She trembled. His tongue snaked out and licked her along the line he had made. He was filling her mind with terrible images.

"Help," she called out. Suddenly she was awake, her face stinging from Oakheart's slap. The images Rufus had put in her mind had to be expunged. Sophy lunged at Oakheart, kissing him savagely, biting him on the lip until she tasted blood. She caressed him. Oakheart tried to stop her, as they shared their blankets with all the others but she persisted, biting his skin along his arms and chest. Oakheart lifted the covers, grabbed a blanket and dragged her to the far side of the clearing.

"I do not know what has taken hold of you this night, and I will not ask." Oakheart smothered her moans with his mouth. The sounds of their lovemaking wove through the camp. Sophy couldn't care less about any potential embarrassment. She wanted Oakheart's presence to fill her mind.

Next morning, Oakheart rubbed his lower back as he helped ready the camp for their departure. When she closed her eyes, the image of Oakheart filled her mind and her skin tingled from his touch. When she thought of a kiss it was Oakheart's and yet those red eyes were still there, watching her, calling to her.

❧ 48 ❧

TRAPPED

THE ROCKS WERE GREY, so was the sky and the mud that clung like dung to Sophy's boots. The opening to the warrens was like a black maw ready to devour her as she followed the others inside. It was quiet. Only the sound of squelching boots echoed, mingled with the rasps of anxious breaths.

Sophy had dressed in her blue and silver dress. It wasn't practical, but she needed the ego boost. The chill damp air served to keep her awake. Her night of passion may have driven the memory of Rufus's shadowy touch from her body and mind, but it left her fatigued. The cold would maintain her focus.

A faint drip-drip of water on rocks sounded ahead and the tunnel began to darken. Lillia passed around her firesticks. Sophy couldn't hold one because of the *given* so she walked closely behind Oakheart. He held a long, vicious-looking dagger in one hand and the firestick in the other. His face shifted with the play of shadows when he turned to look at her. "Stay close to me."

"As if I need reminding," she said, and grabbed the waist of his breeches to make sure.

The floor of the warren was uneven. The sound of scratching and scuttling came from a side passage. They kept going along the central tunnel; a few of the party gave the side tunnel a nervous glance and quickened their pace. Mellow, Illart and Raven had stayed outside the warrens to guard against attack from the rear and to assist as a reserve in case they were attacked within. Apparently, Lillia's shrill whistle could reach Mellow and his friends, even from deep within the warrens.

Sophy's legs grew tired. Lillia handed around a tankard with something in it that tasted of mud. Expecting Newin's brew, she almost gagged when the taste hit her tongue. The forest maiden took back the tankard and handed it around.

"I thought you were out of herbs," Sophy hissed into the dimness.

"I was. I ground up the last of the healing bark. Although most of its powers have been used there may be some residual benefits."

Sophy's stomach lurched precariously. Something of the *given* was inside her, and the thought made her light-headed. More sounds assaulted her ears. A deep hum vibrated the ground beneath her feet, and Oakheart complained about his teeth paining him. They turned the corner and all of the firesticks went out in unison. An amber glow up ahead lit their way. Distorted shadows moved and shifted against the walls. They edged slowly to the opening of a huge cavern and the sound of a goat bleating heralded their arrival.

"That sounds like a goat..." Sophy whispered.

"What is a goat?" Oakheart asked.

Sophy peered at him through the darkness taken aback by his question. "It's an animal common on my world. Its milk is suitable for babies."

"Gilly," he breathed.

"Yes. But how did he get it?" Sophy didn't have time to puzzle it out.

"I know not. Yet, he cares enough for the babe to feed it."

Oakheart stuck his head out to get a look at the large circular chamber and pulled back quickly. "There are many warren beasts and screavers gathering hereabouts. We must ..."

Hoots and growls from the darkness behind interrupted him. They were discovered. With little choice in the matter, they backed into the cavern. Oakheart swung around, holding Sophy closely as he walked out in plain sight. His dagger had been replaced by his sword. He kept his weapon in front of him and directed it at the beasts that retreated as he advanced. The beasts parted and gathered around the edges, surrounding them in a ragged semi-circle.

Under a lit bowl of burning oil, Rufus sat on a rudely carved throne. Bones and filth littered the ground and the crevices. A baby's wail sounded from the base of the dais. Sophy's gazed zeroed in on the tip of a little, pink foot waving above the side of a makeshift cradle.

"Greetings, my lovely. So happy you could come to me at last," Rufus said in a sibilant voice. He glared at Oakheart, hissing, "You will leave. She has come to me willingly. You have no power over her."

Oakheart anchored himself to her side. "I will not leave without her."

"I didn't come here willingly," Sophy shouted.

Rufus smiled. "Oh, but you did. You want me...desire me...I can taste your desire for me." He stepped down from the dais of roughly hewn stone. His spindly legs bent backwards at the knees like a misbegotten flamingo. His arms, too, were thin. He stroked the baby as he passed, and it wailed in fright.

"I have come for Gilly. You will give him to me."

Rufus paused. "You want the child. What will you give me for it?"

That claw tapped on his bony chin, click, click, clicking. The sound distracted her. She didn't know how to answer. Then she saw a strange thing: a large gold band, like a wedding ring, though as tall as she was, embedded into the wall a few paces below the dais. It drew her by some invisible force.

Rufus smiled, showing blackened gums and rotted stumps for teeth. "Oh yes, my lovely. That is for you. You will go into it, and then I will give you the child."

With difficulty, Sophy managed to pull her gaze from the alluring ring of gold. "No," she said. "You will give me the child first, then I will go into it. Willingly."

She heard Oakheart's hastily indrawn breath and willed him to be quiet. His protests were the last thing she needed at that moment.

Rufus's wings flapped. "You will go in there first, before I do anything."

Sophy averted her eyes from the ring, although that didn't lessen the lure of it. Hiding it the best she could, she raised her chin. "I have no faith in your word. The child is nothing to you, so give him up. You want me. I am here. Stop playing games."

Oakheart sent her a warning hiss.

Rufus punched the air with a fist. "Look at the ring." Rufus' voice wove around her, the spell of his words caressing her ears, making her want to step that way. Sophy had to fight against its pull, had to shut her eyes so that she wouldn't look at the ring and be subsumed by the power of it. Had to fight stepping into the trap. "You are in my power. You will do as I say."

Sophy's resolve didn't break, even though the effort cost her dearly. Resisting the spell or the power of the ring hurt in so many ways. "If you will not hand over the child I am leaving." She turned away and took a step, pushing with all her might against the compulsion in his voice. She couldn't give in to it, not until she knew Gilly was safe.

"No!" Rufus's denial sent a ripple of alarm though his beasts. They started to close in, and more poured in from the side tunnels. "You will die before you leave."

Her heart thumped but she tried to hold onto her composure. "If I die you will have nothing." She turned back at him. "I'm no use to you dead, am I? This Unesta you work for wants me unharmed, doesn't she?"

Rufus stopped mid-screech, mouth falling open to gape at her. Then he changed his tone. "How do I know that you will stay when I release the child to you?"

Sophy thought hard. "Give the child to him," she pointed to Oakheart. "I will enter that ring at the same time you pass Gilly over."

"Sophy, no!" Oakheart said, his jaw clenched and betrayal in the flash of his eyes.

"Oakheart, take Gilly home to his mother. Tell Aria I love her. Take my heart with you." She turned towards Rufus and the ring.

Rufus moved back towards the cradle, reaching in to grab Gilly.

Sophy saw the faint red curls on the baby's head, and Dellbright's crest on the now grimy jacket. Rufus slowly edged towards Oakheart, never taking his red-tinged eyes from her.

Oakheart handed his sword to Lillia and he stepped a little closer to Rufus. Gilly wriggled as Sophy took another step. The ring of gold filled her sight. It seemed to pulse as it drew her towards it, tendrils of curling gold mist beckoned. She stopped her ascent to the ring and waited, fighting the desire to step into Rufus's circle of power. Already she felt less than she was, as if filaments of her were snaking into the ring.

Rufus moved closer. Oakheart was a step away, reaching for the baby. She took another step. She could almost touch the golden band with her fingers; another step and she would be within. Her teeth tingled and itched as the ring's power throbbed.

There was a cry from Oakheart, and she turned towards the sound. He held the baby high and then tucked him within his jerkin. He pulled a breastplate from his back, tying it in place over the child. He retrieved his sword from Lillia and took a step towards Rufus.

Sophy cried out, "Go, Oakheart. Take Gilly and leave—remember your oath."

Oakheart gave her a dreadful look, as if with those words she had betrayed him. He didn't move. Lillia and his guard closed ranks behind him.

The ring sung a disharmonious chord, jangling her teeth. Her fingers and toes began grew numb. She took the last step, and Rufus scrambled up to his throne. She could hear him giggling with glee. "She is mine. All mine. The power will be mine."

The binding of the ring was like a strange surge of fire. Cold, azure flames leapt up, enveloping her in a blue haze. The crystal leaf so long entombed within her swirled and twined around her. A cold shaft of pain stilled her, even as she heard Oakheart's shout of despair. The cold seeped into her bones as she stiffened. Her vision warped to prisms as her breath cooled to ice. As her awareness winked out, the last thing she saw was Rufus' glowing red eyes smiling in triumph.

Oakheart's shout echoed in the chaos. Warren beasts were pouring in from all sides. He looked to where Sophy had stood. Her beauty had been revealed in the last instant before she succumbed to the ring. The flames had died away and in their wake was a gem, a dark blue jewel. It pulsed in a heartbeat rhythm. He knew that she existed within it. Anger and regret surged out of him as he battled the desire to crush Rufus with his bare hands. He had pledged his oath to take the child home and it cut him like a knife to leave Sophy. Yet, even then his oath compelled him, pushing him to get out of the cave and into the light.

That foul beast was caressing the jewel that was Sophy as if it was a well-favoured maiden. Sophy, as a gem, was faceted, cut to reflect the light. Oakheart did not understand the strange power at work. He was sure Adage could explain it—he was the grandson of Vorn, over five hundred years old. He had pledged his life to stop Unesta placing her hand in Argenterra. Now that hand, through Rufus, had snared Sophy, his oath-bound wife.

Rufus peered into the gem, practically drooling on it. He appeared oblivious to Oakheart and his followers.

"Go quickly," Oakheart shouted above the chaos.

He yanked on Lillia's hair because the forest maiden still gaped stupidly at the ring where Sophy was now entombed.

Lillia flung around, her face filled with horror.

"Flee," he yelled.

Lillia shook herself and as one they retreated, backing into a cave with the least amount of beasts. While Rufus caressed the jewel, his mind was elsewhere, and his beasts were directionless. Oakheart knew that would not last long.

They made it to the central tunnel and headed towards the exit. Oakheart slashed and kicked beasts from his blade. Lillia cut throats and leapt on backs as she laboured along the tunnel at his side. He could see that she was weeping. The child struggled within his jerkin and he prayed that it was well.

Illart, Mellow and Raven closed in from the entrance, felling beasts with well-placed arrows. Oakheart could see daylight ahead as it peered to the mouth of the tunnel.

RUFUS STROKED THE JEWEL. "MINE," HE SAID. "SHE WILL NOT HAVE it yet. No...I am the master here. She cannot come here. Vorn has barred her way." He strode around, then he sent his awareness into the depths of blue, searching for Sophy's life essence. As he gazed with his other sight, he saw it, a thread of something within the jewel. His scream sent his creatures into a mindless rage.

"This cannot be! It is flawed!" he screamed. "Flawed, flawed, flawed." He stamped his feet and beat his spindly arms in the air. Then he peered closer and traced the line of flaw in the jewel. "How can this be? I took every precaution." Pacing, he ran through the possibilities. Again and again, he went back the jewel and sent his other sight into the thread, pondering, examining, twisting.

With a scream of utmost outrage, his taloned finger punched the air. "Oakheart! She is bound to him. I will rip his heart out for this. With his death, I will master her. Her power will be mine."

He motioned to his beasts and yelled shrilly, "Go quickly. Kill him. Kill Oakheart. Bring his beating heart to me. You can eat the rest."

He returned to the jewel, which glowed brightly at his touch. "Oooh, you do desire my touch, do you not, my lovely? Shame you are tainted by an oath to that brute...but never mind, you will be free of it soon enough and then you will surrender to me. Nothing will stand in my way. Strange, that I did not know of this oath's existence. You are very sly, my sweet. I like that in you."

The flickering light within the jewel increased frequency and became erratic.

"Do not fret, pretty one...soon you will be full of power, soon you will suck this land dry of the *given* and will only need me to wield you. Come, let me look at you. I want to know by what arts Oakheart has taken my place. I was to be the one to taste your nectar. I was to be the one to part your flesh...to drink your blood."

He poured his essence into the crystal, trying to wrench the secret of the oath from the jewel's depths. He rubbed himself up and down against the glowing Sophy, mimicking the love-making act as he probed deeper and deeper. From each side he attacked the threaded flaw within the jewel. He sampled it, tasted it with his mind. He pounded on the jewel with his claws clenched in fists when its secret was not easily revealed.

At length, he drew back, staggered by what he found. "She loves that hulking idiot. I do not believe it, yet she tells me that she loves him. Her love is stronger than an oath. But I hid him from her and her from all eyes. How could they find one another with everything stacked against them?" He stormed across the cave, kicking the cradle to pieces. "There was no sign of it at the ball....I should have killed him then when I had the chance." He let out a guttural screech of rage and expanded his wings to beat them in the air.

"She desires me. Has she not succumbed to me in her dreams? He must be an enchanter himself to counter the spells I have woven."

❧

FOUR OF HIS MEN WERE DOWN. THE SNARLS OF PURSUING BEASTS swelled around them. The air was full of their maddened cries. Oakheart heard them above the cuts and drags of his blade. "We have to keep moving. He means to kill us all now that he has Sophy."

Oakheart reached his mount. Grabbing Lillia up by the forearm, he swung her up on hers. Mellow scrambled up behind her. The others clambered onto their horses.

"Oakheart," Lillia panted. "I do not understand what happened. What has become of the Lady Sophy? Where did she go?"

"I have no time to explain now. She lives, and I will return to free her. But first I must fulfil my oath. I must return Gilly to his home. We must flee."

"She lives? You are still bound?"

Oakheart kicked a beast away from his mount and slashed at another. "She lives and we are bound. I can feel our oathbond."

❧

THEY RODE HARD. OAKHEART CHANTED AN ODE TO THE *GIVEN*,

urging life into their already weary mounts. It seemed to work. They could not stop until it was safe, yet they would never be safe while Rufus lived. This much he knew. The increase in beasts pursuing them told him that Rufus would never rest until he was dead and Sophy thus unfettered.

The warrens fell away, though not quickly enough to prevent pursuit. Oakheart reined in, choosing a place to turn and fight. In the ensuing fracas, Oakheart lost two more men, and Gilde received a heavy wound. Mellow, already weakened, barely kept his seat as Lillia's mount trampled warren beasts, with legs dripping blood from myriad wounds.

Between them they thinned the beasts for long enough to take shelter in a ring of boulders. Oakheart did his best to bolster the small party's mood, even though his own thoughts were morbid. The child cried, startling him.

"Give the child to me," Lillia said. "I will ward him and feed him."

Lillia helped him ease off his blood-smeared breastplate so she could tug the infant out and cuddle it with tender care.

"Oh, my little love. What a ride you have had," she cooed. She held Gilly close, soothing his red down with an unsteady hand. "Come and drink, little one." She loosened her jerkin to free a breast. Gilly sucked hard, drawing the nipple down his throat. Lillia closed her eyes, though her mouth moved as it in prayer. Having the child in the open made Oakheart nervous. Screavers were gathering, so many he could not count. More than they could possible kill.

Mellow shouted. "Hail!" He stood and waved frantically.

"Get down, Mellow. What are you doing?" he yelled.

Mellow grinned. "Aid! The high king's men approach."

Oakheart nearly leapt from his spot. He thought he spied Fern at the lead. Dellbright must have requested aid. Arrows cut through the air and hit with startling accuracy around the ring of boulders. The dying cries of screavers wove a spell around the circle. With tense eyes and clenched mouths they waited. Oakheart peered over the rim. Some of the rescuers had fallen as Fern led the horses to trample the beasts too bold to flee. Though Oakheart's heart was heavy, he smiled.

Fern led at least fifty men. They would be safe. The remaining screevers and warren beasts fled. Oakheart looked around and spied Gilde on the ground with Raven kneeling next to him. His man was not faring well.

"Hold on," Raven said, holding his hand. "Help is near." Gilde smiled at her words and then died. Raven wept as she covered him. Oakheart turned away and said another death lament under his breath while he walked to meet Fern.

Fern swung down from his mount, bellowing a greeting. "You are well?"

"What is left of us, yes," Oakheart replied, gathering Fern into a bear hug.

The child cried lustily as Lillia changed breasts. Shoving his chubby fist into his mouth, he sucked hungrily until it was replaced with a nipple.

"You retrieved the child. Sophy?" Fern asked as he looked around.

Oakheart shook his head. "She is lost."

"Lost...not dead?"

"She lives but she has been transformed into or encased in a jewel of some kind.

Fern frowned. "A jewel?"

"I do not have time to explain it to you. That is for the Adepts' Retreat to do. I must deliver the child to his mother and return here to free Sophy."

"Let me take the child and Lillia. I will aid you now to wrest your oath-bound back."

Oakheart shook his head. Fern's words brought comfort and pain. If only Fern had arrived sooner. "I cannot. Sophy urged me to swear an oath to return the child to his mother. I am bound to fulfil it. Before I can free Sophy, I must seek advice from Adage. 'Tis no simple thing to undo what has been wrought this day."

Lillia stood and handed Gilly to him. He brought the babe to the crook of his arm and mounted one of the fresh horses that Fern had brought with him.

Lillia and the forest folk climbed onto fresh horses, too. Oakheart nodded, grateful for their support.

"To Valley Keep," he called into the wind and tucked the child within his jerkin, securing the ties.

Fern and his troop mounted up behind him. "To Valley Keep," their voices chorused.

EPILOGUE

Sophy floated dreamlike in a blue haze. Awareness grew. There was a thread of something that anchored her. Something warm and fluid existed at the other end of it. Green eyes and white blond hair framed a beautiful face. That was he...the one she loved. A name...what name did he have? It was hard to think, everything was so hard, so unmoving, so cold.

A dark presence threatened. Anger, fear, lust like the tines of a fork dug into her. She resisted.

Red, like blood, trickled over her, tried to sink into her. But her skin was hard, like rock, and the blood fell away. She sought sanctuary in the blueness. She hung there, pulsating in concordance with an ever-present thrum.

A shaft of red-tinged thought rocked her. She fought it. Then she recognised Rufus as he thrust his awareness into her and played with her. He conjured up horrible visions of love-tangled and lust dripping scenes. He invaded her. He tried to possess her.

And failed.

Please note:
British/Australian spelling conventions are used in this book.

For example, words like color are spelled colour, recognize are recognise, traveling are traveling and so on.

430

DID YOU ENJOY ARGENTERRA? CARE TO LEAVE A REVIEW SO OTHERS can enjoy it too?

Keep up to date with my publishing by joining my newsletter Wing Dust.

PREVIEW OF OATHBOUND: BOOK TWO OF THE SILVERLANDS SERIES

To the valley

The sound of baby Gillcress's hungry wail pierced the haze of Oakheart's dream, bringing him to wakefulness. He heard Lillia stir as she went to tend the child, whispering soft words that calmed his shrilling demands for food. Oakheart breathed deeply, trying to ignore how Gilly's cries sounded like heartbreak and abandonment, the very feelings that churned within him as he lay there, hoping for a moment of oblivious sleep. Horror ebbed from his mind as the tendrils of the dream receded like the fading aftertaste of too much wine.

Camped in a wooded hollow as they fled from the warrens back towards Valley Keep, they huddled against the cold and the threat of pursuit. Sentries periodically whistled an 'all is well'. Oakheart counted the signals and relaxed the tension in his neck and arms. Wearily, he opened his eyes, and groaned as the recollection of events came flooding in with uncalled-for clarity. They had saved Aria's and Dellbright's son, Gillcress, but he had lost Sophy, his oathbound bride, to Rufus and his dark enchantment. He grimaced at how he had let Sophy spring the trap set by Rufus—baby Gilly in exchange for herself.

Oakheart tried to understand what the being Rufus had done to Sophy. The leaf from the Crystal Tree had been growing within her, that much he had witnessed. But a total transformation? How had Rufus bound her in that crystal shape? What effect did it have on her —and on Argenterra? While he did not know the full of it, deep in his gut he knew it portended ill. Something was very wrong, not only with Sophy but also with Argenterra.

Knuckling sleep from his eyes, he squinted at the sky, still dark with night's cloak. Lifting his head, he saw faint wisps of dawn creeping up the horizon. Still an hour or so short of daylight, not enough time to go back to sleep before they had to pack up and leave again.

A yawn seized him and he stretched out his aching limbs. By the given, he was tired. Even after many nights, he was not accustomed to the repeated nocturnal waking of the babe. Lillia was constantly feeding him and the little boy's body was now well-rounded and his cheeks chubby and pink. That the child was safe and thriving was all the comfort he had for the moment. Again, his mind was brought back to the scene in Rufus's cave, the churning noise of the warren beasts as they clawed the stone floor and ground their teeth together in anticipation of blood. His blood.

Within that memory was Sophy, tall and proud, willing herself forwards into the trap prepared for her. Oakheart had detected the power of the golden ring as it twisted and bound Sophy. Her metamorphosis dragged at his senses. Being oathbound allowed him to feel her edges hardening as she was wrenched and bent into that unnatural state. Even now, they were tethered by their oathbond that remained alive and strong between them, fixed in blood and deed. He sighed. It kept him going, knowing that she lived still within that gem.

"That child has a lusty appetite," Fern commented, his words muffled by his blankets. Oakheart heard his friend shuffle and turn on his side. In the dim starlight, Fern was a dark mound. "Are you sure he is not your close kin for he eats as much as you do?"

Oakheart chuckled quietly, glad that Fern's light banter helped dispel his morose thoughts. His cousin, Fern, was a fine warrior and natural commander and had saved them from certain death, arriving with help just in time as they were surrounded by Rufus's screavers and beasts. Now that Rufus had Sophy, he wanted Oakheart dead.

"No, not so close in blood as his appetite would lead you to believe. I wonder how Lillia bears it," Oakheart said, and then placed his hands behind his head to stare at the deep, purple sky and watch the stars fade.

"Oh, but she does not bear it well. She nearly knifed me yesterday when I commented on how well she looked."

Oakheart smiled in the dark and shook his head. Fern would never change. His mouth caused angst wherever he went, unless of course there was a pretty maid to be lured away for a cuddle or a kiss.

A frown of annoyance marred his features when he remembered how Fern's acid tongue had flayed poor Sophy, for days, even weeks, on end. In fact, Fern pointing out all of Sophy's faults had only led Oakheart to think well of her and to focus on her good points.

A sound of scratching interrupted his musing. Oakheart's hand closed upon his dagger, and he listened intently. The scrabbling noise grew louder and a man-shaped shadow rose up and then hunkered next to him. Oakheart tensed.

"Oakheart?" Mellow whispered urgently.

Oakheart tried to slow his heart rate; it was only Lillia's mate. "What it is it? The child?" Oakheart hissed, flinging off his blanket and fearing some threat to his charge.

Mellow's shadow rose, a dark shape blocking out the stars. "No, fear not. The child is hale. It is of Lillia I come to speak."

"Lillia?" Oakheart braced himself and repressed a groan. He had been expecting Mellow's entreaty for some time.

Mellow leant in closer and lowered his voice. "Yes. She has served you well, excellency..." As he hesitated, Oakheart could hear Mellow breathing. "Is it not time to free her from her duty when the child is returned to the valley?"

Oakheart closed his eyes for a second, opened them and tried to look Lillia's husband in the eye. It was difficult. Mellow's eyes appeared like dark holes in his head. Daylight spread thin fingers into the sky but the forest man was cloaked in grey gloom. Oakheart softened his voice. "Mellow, good friend, your mate has served me well. But she does not do my bidding. I cannot influence her where you cannot."

Mellow's breath grated in his throat. "But she is with child..."

Oakheart let the air sigh out of him. He knew about the pregnancy because Sophy had whispered it to him as he held her in the night. The memory of his oathbound came tantalising and pure. Her soft flesh pressed against his and the burning warmth of her love. "And..."

Mellow edged closer and spoke urgently in Oakheart's ear, keeping his voice low so he could not be overhead. "She cannot continue to feed the babe and fight off attacks and keep her...our...unborn child. Surely you see it. Daily she weakens."

Oakheart reached for Mellow's hand, now grasped tight to Oakheart's blanket, and squeezed it companionably. "My heart goes out to you both. Soon we will be in the valley. The task of feeding Gilly will pass from her. There you must decide what path you will take. Lillia would be affronted if I tried to dictate her duty. She would not even listen to Sophy..."

He thought he heard Mellow sniff and then noticed him wipe his arm across his face. "I cannot shake her from this path. Never has she been so stubborn. She will not even speak about the matter with me."

Fern chose that moment to speak from his bed. "Best you disarm her before you try..."

Oakheart rolled his eyes as Mellow swung round, still crouched. "Be still..." Mellow hissed. "I will knife you myself if you speak against her. She is the mother of my children, a warrior in her heart, the love of my life since we were children. We drank from the same breasts. We climbed our first tree together. We dived from Fell Falls to the pools below, our first feat of daring. Our breath and our life are in the Gilton Forest."

Pausing to draw in a breath, Mellow faced Oakheart again. "How do I get her to return? What sway does your oathbound wife have on her?" Mellow's voice was plaintive.

Oakheart did sympathise, but there was nothing he could do. He had tried on many occasions to dissuade Lillia, to send her home. Making an enemy of the forest maiden was not wise, and nor did he want to for she was dear to him. She would become a bitter foe if he persisted or stood between her and her desire to serve. He could not help but be glad of her aid.

He ran his hand through his hair. "I cannot answer for her, my friend. You must bare your heart to Lillia...only she can tell you what you wish to know. Lillia is a forest maiden, a warrior; that much you have always understood. I know Sophy touched her heart somehow... since they first met she warmed to her."

Mellow's inarticulate expression of defeat sounded in the quiet of the night.

"Very well...I will make the attempt at Valley Keep, even though every day I am away from Gilton Forest I feel less of a man and more like a ghost. I do not feel whole without the spirit of the trees, or the smell of the damp earth, or my tree home surrounding me. I miss the sounds of the children...I miss her."

Oakheart sighed. "Aye...I understand your need. Your help on this quest has been valuable. If it is any comfort to you, your presence has made Lillia happier."

Mellow slunk away, disturbing the loose soil and rocks with his feet as he headed back to his blankets. Oakheart did not think his words had comforted the man. Biting his lip, he realised that he understood Mellow's situation all too well. Sophy, too, was headstrong and independent.

❧

Next morning, after cresting a slight hill, Oakheart pulled his mount to a halt next to Fern. His friend had sent scouts out and was peering into the distance, his face creased with concern.

"What is it?" Oakheart asked.

The wood was open, thinning to haphazard groupings of trees. A few hillocks in the distance could hide an ambush. He recalled that there were a few farmsteads in the area, though they were isolated from each other and the main road linking Silverdale and the valley. If they rode hard, they could reach Valley Keep by moonrise. An uneasiness crawled up his spine. Something did not seem right. Mist lay in shallow depressions in the fields, clinging to trees and floating above a small pond.

Ahead, the exposed grassland appeared white with frost. Unease, like a knife's edge, dug into his gut. Oakheart's breath curled in the air as he exhaled. Steam rose from the flanks of Fern's horse. His disquiet grew in the still morning atmosphere. Oakheart's eyes slid sideways as the guards nocked arrows. Expectation filled the air.

The sound of distant hoof beats thumping the ground alerted him to the lone scout riding hard towards them. Clods of damp earth flew up behind the rider, churned by the horse's hooves. His men bristled with tension as they waited for the rider to draw closer. A few horses shook their heads, jingling bridles and bits. Fern signalled for four men to angle around to the right and another four to the left. His gaze never left the approaching scout.

Without looking behind him Fern spoke. "Lillia, take the child to the rocky outcrop behind us. Make your position defensible." Fern spared Oakheart a quick glance. "You best stay by me for the present. But be ready."

"Of course." Oakheart watched as Lillia slid from her saddle and scurried to where there was a cleft between two boulders. She crouched and backed into the gap with Gilly fast asleep in her arms. Mellow took the horse behind the outcrop and returned with an armful of branches. After disguising the horse's hoof prints, he also backed into the cleft, sheltering Lillia and the child with his body and holding the branches in front of him to disguise their presence. His dark and angry gaze peered out, knife at the ready. The other forest folk, Illart and Raven, crouched in the shadows on either side of the outcrop, ready to provide protection.

Oakheart could not believe danger lurked so close to the valley. For many years he had travelled along these trails free from harm. Dellbright talked of the occasional skirmish with Puri raiders, but they were not fraught with danger and evil. Surely whatever surrounded them was sourced in Rufus and his hate.

The scout rode up, his red face clenched with worry and fright. He was young and his brown hair flew about, loose from its tie. "I found a farmstead burnt-out. There were no signs of inhabitants, dead or alive.

Something stalks these parts, though. I heard it, saw traces. I came to give warning as soon as I could."

Fern chewed his lip as his grey eyes surveyed the ground ahead. Another scout hove into view, galloping from the opposite direction. Behind him followed a riderless horse with what looked to be a body draped over the saddle. Another look and Oakheart saw the leading rein. A whispering spread through the men. Oakheart waited, his heart beating a rapid time while the scout drew nearer.

When the scout rode up on his foam-flecked mount, Fern leapt from his horse and rushed to him. Oakheart eased himself out of the saddle, all his senses on alert. Fern grasped the rein of the second horse. By the clothes, the body appeared to be a dead farmer. The scout held the reins while Fern jerked the body free of the ties binding it to the horse and eased it to the ground.

Oakheart's gaze roamed about the countryside warily. He eyed the mist, which seemed to move and shape by itself. It distracted him.

"Oakheart, look at this," Fern called from beside the body.

Shaking off his disquiet, Oakheart strode to where Fern was leaning over the body. Oakheart crouched and took in the farmer's blood-stained clothes and the face stretched by death. The stench of wrong emanating from the body almost knocked him over. Murder; another death taken in hate and anger. Oakheart kept his expression bland but knew he had failed. His jaw clenched. He did not like what he was seeing or feeling. All these happenings spoke of dire portents, he thought as his heart iced over.

"There is a dagger." Fern pulled it out, with the sound of a squelch, and held it up to the light. He stared at the handle, rotating it slowly in his bloody fingers. "Look, 'tis a Puri blade."

Oakheart's attention flew to the hilt. The dark handle was etched with silver swirls. It was a familiar pattern and definitely of Puri manufacture. "Yes," he said, taking it into his own hand. He examined the pattern closely. "Nasheen's markings." He stared at it, not believing the evidence of his own eyes. Nasheen was a Puri troublemaker, leader of a relatively small tribe. Oakheart knew him from his travels through the wastelands. He thought he understood Nasheen and his ways. This knife seemed out of place, not only in Argenterra but also in the back of some innocent farmer.

Fern stared at him expectantly and Oakheart met his unspoken query.

"Puri do not kill like this, nor would they leave a dagger behind. It is too precious an item. They steal goods and people. 'Tis not their way to...take life like this. They are bound by the binding oath as are we. I have met Nasheen many times...trickery, theft, maybe, but I cannot believe him capable of cold-blooded murder."

Oakheart near spat the word—murder. It was a word to scare children, an unknown bogey man that lurked in the legends of old, the time before Vorn brought them to this land. A time of war and death and suffering. A time of the Ancient Evil.

To take a life was to break the binding oath. Oakheart's heart sank at the thought of it. He did not want to accept that the time Vorn feared was nigh upon them. He did not want Argenterra to lose the given. It was part of them, part of who they were. This had to be Rufus's doing. Did that evil, alien creature's deeds undo the oath? That was Oakheart's single vestige of hope. That Rufus was not oathbound and therefore his actions did not harm the relationship with the land.

The sparkle in Fern's eyes died quickly. "Yes, but they do say the Puri know how to bend an oath." Fern glowered at the body, shaking his head. "Mostly to do with taking wives though."

"Perhaps. But there is no reason to harm in this way, risking the oath and all that means. I cannot credit it." Oakheart inspected the body closely, searching for evidence that would reveal the truth as to why this poor farmer had been killed. The man was not that long dead. A sense of alarm troubled Oakheart. Convinced that he saw movement out of the corner of his eye, he leapt up. Alert and tense, he moved to a fighting crouch. Surely that slight alteration in the shadows signalled movement.

Fern also bolted upright. Wiping his hands on his breeches, his head swivelled left and right. "The mist moves stealthily. Strange..."

The mist! Oakheart understood—the mist had crept furtively, oozing from branch to branch while their attention was on the remains of the farmer. Fear jabbed into his belly. There was purpose in its stealth.

Movement and a grunt beside him surprised Oakheart and the knife was ripped from his hand. He looked down at the crouching corpse, waving the knife like a serpent's head. Fern's throaty yell brought the others, who circled warily. The dead thing lunged for Oakheart. He kept his gaze riveted on the hand that clenched the deadly blade, circling out and away. The eyes flashed red in the dead farmer's face. Wrong rippled from the walking corpse like rotting effluent. Rufus!

His men were hesitant, uncertain. Oakheart caught a glimpse of the fear and revulsion in their faces. Such an unnatural act was beyond their ken. Perhaps it was better, no one underfoot to hamper his defence.

Oakheart backed away, all his senses riveted to the animated corpse. The blade thrust forwards again. He sucked in his breath, and stomach, away from the tip of the blade. Too close! Sweat dripped into his eyes. His breath was short and painful in his throat. Fear. He was afraid of this thing, afraid of death and all that it meant. Afraid of failing Sophy. If only he had an extra second or two to pull his own knife free. How did one kill something that was already dead?

The eyes hungered for him, for his death. To look at them for any length of time was to lose one's soul. Another cut severed the air to his right as he bounded left. The farmer's face grimaced in a sickly parody of a smile. Rufus's control was not complete. The automaton was clumsy and it had lost the element of surprise. Oakheart sensed there was a chance to evade it, maybe destroy it.

A yell from behind distracted him. Oakheart rotated to see the guard, Duen, smothered by mist. "Ware, Fern. The mist is..." He saw Fern move to assist Duen as he turned his attention back to the corpse.

The knife swished close to his thigh. He winced as the blade found flesh. Oakheart darted backwards, his cut spraying blood onto the dirt. The corpse did not follow. Finally, enough distance to retrieve his own dagger from his boot. Grasping it, he circled the corpse, all the while his mind raging: How do you fight the dead? The thought that Rufus inhabited this body, that it danced to his tune, made Oakheart shiver. The binding oath must truly be broken for a travesty like this to assail him. Or Rufus was more powerful than any of them, including the most learned of the adepts, had ever estimated.

Oakheart circled. When the corpse lunged, Oakheart kicked the dagger free from its grip. Unperturbed, the corpse advanced with bare hands outstretched, fingers clawed ready to grasp him. Oakheart threw his knife and caught the body in the chest. It faltered for a heartbeat, only to step more purposefully towards him.

Out of the corner of his eye, he saw Lillia approach. He began to think of the child she protected when he saw she held his sword. He angled towards her, hand held ready for the toss. The corpse hissed and threw itself forwards. The sword flew in the air, arcing towards him. Oakheart stepped back and reached up. In one movement, he caught the hilt, which settled like an old friend into his palm, and swung the blade, still full of momentum, to sever the head from the corpse. The head landed with a wet thunk and rolled, mouth stretched in a feral grin and the eyes smoking holes. The headless body took a few faltering steps and fell jerkily to the ground. Oakheart, filled with revulsion and what he hoped was not hate, staggered over and thrust the sword through the corpse's back into its heart, anchoring it to the ground.

The mist dissolved with a drawn-out sibilant hiss. Rufus's presence fled, but the sense of unease and defilement remained. The stench of the corpse mired their resting place. Oakheart pulled a kerchief from his pocket and held it to his nose. His eyes met Lillia's. The forest maiden staggered from the stench, her hand clasped tightly over her face. He nodded his thanks to her.

Fern stepped up and kicked the corpse, spilling more gore. His face was pale. "We should bury it," he said, his grey eyes now storm-dark. "If it will not defile the soil of Argenterra."

Oakheart nodded, too weary to disagree and too ready to weep. "Yes, bury it. 'Tis not the farmer's fault that his body was thus corrupted. But hurry, I do not think I can bear to remain here any longer." Gilly cried and squirmed in Mellow's embrace. "'Tis not good for the babe to be so exposed to Rufus's influence."

Mellow succeeded in soothing the child, a sight that seemed contrary to the man's general air of anger and command. Yet, that was the way of the forest folk. Fern signalled to three guards and, after standing stunned for a few moments, they grabbed small shovels from their packs and began to dig a grave. Soon they had dug a sizeable hole. In their eagerness and relief, they worked hard. They too did not wish to linger.

The corpse fascinated Oakheart. He backed away, his heart still beating wildly with the realisation of how close the encounter had been. The next time he might not be so fortunate. He shared a look with Lillia and nodded to Mellow. His heart was heavy as he walked away to distance himself from the stench, from the memory of that unnatural thing.

Lillia found somewhere to sit and began to suckle the babe with Mellow standing over her, eyes alert to any threat. Sunlight bathed them clean and pure, transforming the clearing, making it superficially look like Argenterra again. As he watched, Oakheart could see normalcy returning. The men joked. Duen, the guard that had nearly been smothered by the mist, looked pale but there was a smile there. Oakheart sighed. He wondered if it was resilience in the face of adversity or just blindness to the situation. It seemed so strange to experience what they had and then to move on with things as if it had never happened.

Leaning on a rock, he bound his leg would and watched the burial proceedings only to turn his mind again to what he feared most. That the time of prophecy was at hand and if that were so, worse was yet to come—Vorn's dark vision and a future so desolate that he could not bear to dwell upon it.

Get your copy of Oathbound now.

ACKNOWLEDGMENTS

It's been a long journey with this book. Argenterra is the second book I ever tried to write back in 2001. I found fantasy difficult. I had to delve original ideas to give my favourite genre something special. It was a story that I cut my writing teeth on. It's been chopped and changed many times. The beginning the most difficult I have ever come across. Knowing what to say and how much to say has been excruciating to say the least. I've been tempted to forget Argenterra, to toss it and then after lots of work and encouragement finish it. It's been to acquisitions in traditional publishing houses twice and not been taken up for publication.

Argenterra owes much to Envision, the manuscript development program that ran back in 2003, where I workshopped this story with Louise Cusack. Many thanks to the other tutors there, Kim Wilkins, Rowena Cory Daniels and Marianne De Pierres and to Fantastic Queensland for running it.

For many years, Argenterra sat on my hard drive not doing anything much in particular. Occasionally, I would get it out and tinker with it, often I would just get drawn into the story. There's a certain point in the book where I just can't stop. I am secretly or no so secretly in love with Oakheart and Sophy always warms the cockles of my heart.

Many thanks, too to my editor, Kaaren Sutcliffe, who provided a good eye over the text and sharpened up my dialogue. Other thanks go to Stephanie Smith, who was very positive about the story and Nicole Murphy for moral support. Keri Arthur is owed many thanks too for prodding me to publish this trilogy. Pronto!

Donna Maree Hanson

ABOUT THE AUTHOR

Donna Maree Hanson is a Canberra-based writer of fantasy, science fiction, horror, and under the pseudonym, Dani Kristoff, paranormal romance. She has been writing creatively since November 2000 and has been a member of the Canberra Speculative Fiction Guild (CSFG) since 2001. She has had about 20 short stories published in various small press and ezines. In January 2013, her first longer work, Rayessa & the Space Pirates, was published with Harlequin's digital imprint, Escape. This was followed by Rae and Essa's Space Adventures in 2015. In September 2014, the first book in the Dragon Wine series, Shatterwing was published Momentum Books (Pan Macmillan Australia's Digital Imprint). The second book, Skywatcher, was published in October 2014. After Momentum closed down, Donna regained the publishing rights to the Dragon Wine Series. The series is now complete with six books in the series.

In 2015, she was awarded the A. Bertram Chandler Award for services to science fiction in Australia.

Donna is currently a PhD candidate researching popular romance fiction.

Her new epic fantasy, Argenterra: Silverlands Book 1, is out in 2016. *Oathbound*: Silverlands Book 2 and *The Ungiven Land* will be out in 2017.

You can find out more about Donna on her website. Sign up to her newsletter Wing Dust for special deals, freebies and author news. http://donnamareehanson.com

On Twitter @DonnaMHanson
On Facebook https://www.facebook.com/DonnaMareeHanson/

9 780975 721735